ELEGY

Gray sky.

Black earth.
Dead white flesh.

Red blood.

Pale ash hangs
in the air, coats the tongue.

Odors of sweat and death
clog the nostrils.

Buzzing flies.

Arguing murders of crows.

Wind whispers to charred corpses.

A battlefield elegy.

Beneath a body, a fading tracery of blue
in the black depths
of a gem-born battle-axe.

Elegy
The Black Diamond

First Slipaway Trail Publishing Publication December 2012

Martha Gilstrap
www.MarthaGilstrap.com

Slipaway Trail Publishing

Author's Note:

As with any major undertaking, writing a book cannot be done alone, although it's largely a solitary endeavor. When it's the work of our heart, as it always must be, we rely on other people for a multitude of things that make it the best book it can be.

Numerous people read part or all of *Elegy* and gave me feedback and stories of their own that became part of Shay Bladen's story:

- The Summit Scribes, a group of talented and helpful writers in Lee's Summit, Missour
- The volunteer judges of the Pikes Peak Writers, who liked *Elegy* enough to make it a finalist in the Paul Gillette writing contest.
- My good friend, Rhonda Roth Glazier, who showed me how Shay could view the world through the prism of the stones.
- The members of Write Stuff Novels, who read *Elegy* a chapter at a time and gave me feedback: Carol, Shirley, Emily, Mary, Jen, and Marisha.
- Shirley and Carol, in particular, are my subject matter experts for anything about horses.
- Specific thanks to Shirley Guldenschuh for sharing a real-life incident that became Silence's amazing turn-around at a dead end above 500 feet of air.
- My daughter, Oleha Verlander Larson, for sharing personal information that helped me develop one of my key characters.
- My sister, Sherrie Randall, for sharing the moments of her husband's death, which I used for Shay's experience when Cinny dies.

- My brother, Paul Gilstrap, for sharing his enthusiasm for stones of all kinds.
- My editor, Karen L. Syed of Sassy Gal Enterprises, whose input strengthened the book and got it ready for publication.

And a very special acknowledgment of Carol Roth Englehaupt, who writes as C. L. Roth. She's my sister-friend of a lifetime, and I don't even know how to say what she means to me, how much I depend on her wisdom. She has supported and encouraged me every step of this journey and made her own journey alongside mine (always a step ahead). She's an inspiration to me, and a solid rock in my life–a diamond, or perhaps a deep blue skystone (sapphire).

1. GODTEARS

Stones endure. People die, parents abandon children, friends become enemies. But stones are eternal, the solid bedrock that supports the world.

He needed the stones.

Master gemsman Shay Bladen ran a finger lightly across a smooth silverstone. Its warmth skittered through him like hot blood through a vein. Warriors had been known to rub their bodies with this stone to protect them in battle–but then, warriors were a strange lot. Who would willingly choose to live a violent life? He shuddered, more aware than usual of the scars he bore–the normal nicks and burns from working the stones, but especially the thin, jagged line across his belly that had spread wider as he grew up. Similar scars and a few puckered dots covered his back, legs, and arms. None came from working with tools, metals, or sharp gem material. Life had given him these scars–a life now behind him that he preferred to ignore. He had a different life now. A better one. A perfect life.

Shay selected several stones with care and spaced them out on the counter of his gem shop: golden beryl, silverstone, opal, amber, lazh, torquis. Six would be enough for now. Their beauty soared through his soul.

Content-even happy-as a man like him could never have expected, he sat on a tall stool before the counter and balanced his four-year-old son on his knee, fighting the urge to hug him. Instead, he held the boy loosely, just enough to keep him from falling.

"Are you ready for the stones?" Even his voice smiled at this bright, happy child! "Here, feel this one first. It's your stone, also named beryl. What luster do you feel?"

The child looked at Shay earnestly, his jade eyes like

his mother's. "Like glass?"

"That's right. Its luster is '*vitreous*,' but that word is bigger than you are. 'Like glass' is fine for now." His son's hair matched the dark gold of the polished beryl–a stone that always made him think of his son.

"There you are!" Cinnabar stood in the doorway between home and shop, hands on the hips that heated Shay's blood. "Let him down, my love. He has other lessons to learn, too."

Shay did as she asked, as always. Well, almost always. He turned toward his seven-year-old daughter and winked at her. "You, too, Piper." He pretended sternness until she glanced back over her shoulder and giggled. The tilt of her chin looked so like Cinny's, and she had almost the same red hair, although she'd inherited Shay's ordinary brown eyes.

Piper fingered an elaborate work of rubies and diamonds sitting behind the polished wooden counter, out of the sight of clients. "This is a beautiful necklace, Father. Why isn't it displayed for sale?"

"First of all, it's commissioned, which means created for a specific client. And second, I found a tiny flaw I need to fix."

"Where? I don't see it."

He crossed the room to her. "It's right here. See the–"

"Shay!" Cinny laughed, but she meant business. "Let both my children go!"

"*Our* children." He quirked a peaked eyebrow in her direction.

Still smiling, she shooed Piper and Beryl back into the home behind the shop.

At the end of the day, Shay surveyed his displays, pride swelling. This began his day's-end ritual of renewal. He used a long match to ignite the surface of the fire dish, which held an odorless liquid with no wick. Expensive and rare like all magic, he'd have paid twice as much. In two years, none of the liquid had been consumed. The flame spread across the liquid, igniting deep red glints from the newly-cut rubies nearby–by tradition the gem of passion and love. For him, Cinny's gem.

Finally, Shay picked up his finest piece and turned it to catch the light: a horse figurine, six inches tall, carved of golden tauz with hooves of gold, eyes of skystone. The tauz felt alive, a faint tickle on the ends of his fingers when he stroked it. He had crafted the mane and tail of thin filaments the color of raindrops–rainsilk, the costliest material in the world. Too bad it was commissioned; it would have been a fine birthday gift for the king.

His soul filled by the stones, he closed the shop for the night. All gems and precious metals he locked into boxes stored underneath the counter or in the workshop, out of sight. He removed all gemworks on display or covered them. He doused the fire dish and pulled the curtains across the large glass window Cinny kept so clean and bright. Last, he removed the loose smock he wore over gray wool trousers and linen shirt when he worked and hung it from a peg in the back room with his equipment. He locked his shop, leaving all danger and fear outside.

With one last look to be sure everything had been done properly, he left his business and stepped through the door into his home, careful to secure that door as well, locking happiness inside his home so it could never leave.

The front room, or parlor as Cinny called it, glowed with flickering yellow light from the fireplace. The scent of oak logs, accented by smoke, wafted through the house and the soft crackle of the flames welcomed him. Even better was the smell of dinner and fresh-washed children, who threw themselves into his arms and covered him with wet kisses and soft hugs. A perfect life, indeed!

That night Shay and Cinny tucked their giggling children into bed, then shared their day while she trimmed his silver-sprinkled dark hair and beard.

"I know you want the children to learn about gems, Shay–and so do I, so they can join my family's wagon trains as traders or learn to work the stones as you do. But they need to learn other things, too. They must also learn the chores of everyday living–cooking, cleaning, caring for the horse, tending the herb garden . . . not to mention reading and numbers and a score of other studies."

"I've never had a family before, Cinny. I need our most wondrous creations to be where I am. Just looking at them, touching them–and you–fills this great hole . . ."

She set down her scissors and brushed the fallen hair from his shoulders and face, fingers lingering on his skin. "And leaves them untrained and unused to work. Besides, children playing in the shop will not impress a nobleman come to purchase a gift for his mistress."

This old argument would never be resolved. Shay ended it–for the night–by folding Cinny in his arms and kissing her.

It worked.

When they finally slipped into their own bed, Shay snuggled in warmth, Cinny in his arms. Heart swollen with the joy of his perfect life, he slept without dreaming.

Spinel licked dry lips, shifting his weight yet again as he watched the building across the street from his corner. It stood apart at the edge of the spreading city, mirroring similar buildings nearby–small, wooden, well cared for–except for the fresh coat of pale golden paint. His sister's idea, to help customers find it easily.

He'd hardly drunk anything tonight, just enough to

muffle the fear without making him clumsy. Yet he jumped at movement out of the corner of his eye–a stray dog.

Behind him, two men chuckled.

"Nervous?" asked the grizzled one with the long scar across his cheek.

What *was* the man's name? Had Tarver even said?

He'd never done anything like this before. Why did Tarver insist he be here, instead of just sending his thugs? They smelled; even from three feet away, one reeked of unwashed flesh and sex, the other of onions and ale. Spinel tried to avoid touching their grimy clothes.

"Night watchman," announced the one that smelled like onions. "You got the money?" He held out a hand.

Spinel dropped a small leather bag into his palm without speaking.

"*Onions*" slipped away, surprisingly silent for such a large, coarse man. He returned a few moments later.

"Done," he said. "Give 'im time to finish his rounds and disappear."

Spinel rubbed sweaty palms on soft, expensive woolen britches, careful not to touch his fine silk shirt. "One of you get the lamps."

The second thug cursed casually as he walked into the street, vile words spoken like pleasantries. Candle-lit lampposts on every block provided more light than Tarver considered safe, but soon the ruffian returned, the area now as black as night should be.

Spinel took a deep breath and put all the confidence he could into his voice. "Don't hurt the woman or the children. They're my family. Do what you like with the gemsman." In his mind, the eyes of his sister's husband carried derision, contempt for a gem merchant who knew nothing about how gems were created. But it wasn't his fault. Father hadn't spent the time with him that he'd spent teaching Shay, the

11

street urchin.

His greatest fear tonight was that these ruffians would leave nothing safe. He worried about his sister getting hurt, or the beautiful children he loved as much as she did. Cinnabar, not Mother, had kissed his tiny hurts, wiped away tears, enfolded him in hugs. Her children liked and accepted him without judgment–a gift children gave that adults could not.

"Sure, Spinel. We'll watch for the wife and kids," said "*Scar*" with a grin.

"It's time," said the one smelling of onions.

A loud crack ripped across the night. Shay bolted out of bed, alarm lacing his head and arms. The outer shop door hit the wall and heavy feet thundered into the shop. Shay scrambled for britches and a shirt.

Cinnabar struggled into a housecoat, eyes wide with fear.

"Go to the children," he whispered.

The thieves would grab the ruby necklace and the horse– they were as good as gone–but maybe they wouldn't find the locked chests of gems and precious metals. They likely wouldn't bother with the home at all. Still, Shay's hands shook as he pulled up a hidden trapdoor and lifted a heavy battle-axe from the cubbyhole. Maybe its gleaming blackness would intimidate them; his fighting skills wouldn't. He removed the leather hood from the axe head. The double-bitted axe, made from a single black diamond, had been in Cinny's family for generations. A magnificent heirloom, its mystery called to him when he touched it–and sometimes in his dreams.

A terrifying weapon.

And yet . . . and yet . . . Shay's hands caressed the naked haft, cool and smooth. This above all other gems

12

seduced and excited him. It almost seemed to hum with energy and power. Swallowing, he turned for the door, hands clenched around the leather-bound grip.

With a crash, the door between shop and home shattered. The intruders hadn't even paused in the shop. Shay ran for the parlor while Cinny darted into the children's room.

In the low, flickering light of the banked fireplace, he blocked the thieves' passage, the axe barricading him and his family. "Hold," he yelled. His voice squeaked.

He faced three men, two larger in front of the slender third.

"There it is! There's the axe!" The third man pushed forward, blurred by shadow, leaving only his distinct voice. He pointed as his cohorts paused.

"Spinel?" Cinny's surprised voice came from the children's doorway.

Shay glanced back to where she clutched the children against her skirt. Cinny's *brother* was a part of this?

"What are you doing, Spinel?" Fury shocked through him, burying his fear.

The two brutes separated, Shay between them and Spinel alone in a wider space.

They wanted the axe! Spinel had betrayed his sister. How else could they know it existed?

Spinel stepped forward into the lighter area, redder hair than Cinny's glinting in the banked firelight. Drunk. Of course.

Spinel sneered. "Give me the axe, Shay! You know it should have been mine!" He stepped forward, reaching toward the axe.

"No. It's *not* yours. It was gifted to us."

"Shay!" Cinny's cry spun him toward her.

A large, smelly man held a knife to Cinny's throat. The

13

terror in her eyes shocked through Shay. Tears and snot streaked the faces of the children clinging to her. Their frightened whimpers filled his ears.

Behind him, Spinel spoke again. "Lay the axe on the floor and step away from it. Your family won't be hurt."

Such confidence, for a drunkard.

Well, they could have the axe. He wouldn't risk his family. But his fingers tightened on the haft that fit his hand so perfectly. He couldn't make his knees bend to put the axe down. He stood like a post, frantic to surrender the weapon, unable to move, his skin prickling in horror.

"Shay! Put it down!" Cinny's voice shrilled in fear. "It's only an axe!"

The power of the axe hummed through him. Knives, swords, human flesh, could not stand against this axe. With it, he could destroy any of them. All of them! How dare they invade his home and threaten his family!

"Shay!" A scream, not a plea.

He blinked, as if returning from a far place. Slowly, he squatted and laid the axe on the wooden floor. His fingers lingered until he forced himself to his feet.

"Back away," the thug snarled.

Free of the axe, he stepped back. One foot. The other. It was an object! Priceless and beautiful, but still only a gem! What was the matter with him?

Spinel darted in to snatch up the axe. The heavy axe head dropped with a clunk, gouging a large splinter from Cinny's carefully polished floor.

The second bully shoved him aside, lifting the axe from Spinel's soft, long-fingered hands.

Beyond that man, a sharp knife sliced through Cinny's throat. Shay heard a long, screaming roar of pain, bewilderment, horror. His own voice. He leaped forward as Cinny thumped to the floor, eyes as wide as her throat.

14

The thief grabbed the screaming, blood-spattered children.

Shay's horrified bellow intensified as their throats split open in macabre smiles.

With a similar cry, Spinel stared at his sister and her children.

The man holding the axe shoved Spinel away from him and faced Shay.

Ignoring him, Shay ran for his wife, her killer backing out of his way with a low laugh.

He dropped to his knees beside Cinny. From the corner of his eye he saw Spinel slip on the bloody floor as he fled.

Blood still surged from Cinny's open throat. Frantically, futilely, Shay scooped blood from the floor and tried to pour it back in, tried to pinch the flesh closed, to hold the blood inside.

She blinked.

"Oh, Cinny," he cried.

He'd meant to say, "I love you."

Her eyes dulled as her soul departed its ruined shell. Bodiless, she would drift here for a few hours before leaving the earthly plane.

Desperately, he threw himself toward the children. A black and orange haze–flame and ash, black jat and orange jagounce–filmed his sight. But the knife had nearly beheaded such small ones, and they had left before their mother.

Fury expanded his veins. The pain could not be contained within one body. With a roar of anguish and rage, he flung himself at the thug with his axe.

The man's laughter subsided to a sneer as he swung the axe at Shay.

Shay stopped abruptly, sucked in his stomach. The bit cut through his shirt, but not his flesh. Momentum carried

15

him forward, behind the swing. One hand clamped on the brute's wrist, the other around the haft of the axe.

Wrist trapped, the brute couldn't swing the axe. Shay moved his hand, grasped the axe between the man's hands, and twisted with both arms. Rage fueled his strength as he poured his weight into the twist.

Surprise widened the man's eyes as Shay tore the axe from him.

But he couldn't hold on. The axe went flying, skidded across the floor. Shay threw himself atop it, got his hands on it.

Hard, hairy fingers dug into his shoulder and yanked him up from the floor. He stumbled, gained balance, backed away as he adjusted his grip.

The brute came after him, reaching.

Shay swung.

The man jerked his hands away from the blade's arc.

The other murderer closed in from the side.

Shay shifted, put his opponent between himself and the other thug. Then he charged.

The axe whooshed as he swung, forehand and back.

The thug danced away, colliding with his partner. The tip of the axe blade sliced across his stomach. The foreswing nearly spun Shay around, but he stepped in with the backswing. The second bit split flesh and entrails. He gagged on the smell of blood and loose bowels spilling to the clean floor. Bile thrust into his mouth.

Shay spun toward the second man, and his giant overhead swing split the murderer's skull. The axe pulled out of his grip, stuck in bone, as the man dropped.

He let the axe go, heaving in huge gulps of air, trying to return to the normal world, to leave the fury behind.

Silence dropped over the room as he struggled, a tight cocoon of cotton buffering him from his rage. As the world tilted back into place, reality settled like a heavy blanket over his shoulders. The weight of it forced him to his knees.

His world hazed in pale green light, a sickly echo of godtears, named for the frozen tears of somebody else's god, a gem he would forever after associate with the murder of his family.

He collapsed in tears, rolled into a tight ball of grief and pain.

Shay couldn't breathe around the huge crack splitting his heart. He laid Cinny's body in their bed, the children on either side of her, tucked gently to her side. He folded their hands across their bellies, kissed the white, bloodless faces. Hot tears dripped onto his dead.

His knees buckled under the enormity of his loss. Here lay the only people in the world who had ever loved him.

Spinel would be back, or send more toughs for the axe. Maybe more than two next time.

With no other friends or family, Shay dared trust no one. He'd never trusted until he'd met Cinny, and without her he fell easily back into old habits. Loneliness wrapped him like an ancient cloak, tattered and familiar.

He filled a pack with essentials, added two fistfuls of his finest gems. Another handful went into the pockets of his lone pair of leather pants. He reached into the hole in the closet where the axe had been stored and withdrew a small, flat pouch. Swallowing, he withdrew an ancient parchment, careful not to tear the sharp, brittle creases as he unfolded it. Keep it or leave it? It had always accompanied the axe, but if it wasn't necessary . . .

He scanned the elaborate script, then read it more carefully. Keep it. He returned it to the pouch and slipped it inside his shirt, next to his heart.

Then he retrieved a rat's nest of straps and buckles

from the cubbyhole.

Shay saddled the brown horse, tied the pack behind the saddle, then turned to the axe's harness. He untangled the straps and buckles and fumbled with them until the axe rode head-down behind his back, safely hooded. Twice he levered the axe over his shoulder and into his waiting hands, to make sure he knew how to retrieve it at need.

No neighbors appeared. No watchmen had been summoned. The buildings weren't far apart; perhaps his neighbors slept heavily. Or simply huddled in fear.

It must be well past midnight by now. The Dark ruled, although its Eye, the moon, remained hidden. Shay couldn't allow that malevolent god to claim Cinny and the children. In the dark shop he groped for the magic fire dish. He carefully poured its unique oil onto the bodies of the ones he loved.

The bodies, and then the house, went up in a roar and crackle of flame that filled it with Light, protecting his family's souls.

Then he prayed as the building burned.

The blaze brought the neighbors, and one sent his son running for the watchman. He asked them to let it burn, knowing it an odd request in this city of a religion different from his.

The flames thundered up toward the heavens. He watched them hungrily, desperate for one last glimpse of his family, his life. There. Beryl's tiny face in the flame, going first. Piper's face already looked upward; she didn't see him watching. But Cinny did. Her spirit rose in the most beautiful colors and undulations of flame he'd ever seen, her fire eyes locked on his.

His soul called to hers. *I will always love you. Take care of our children, in the Light.*

The flame smiled, and "*I love you*," echoed in his head.

18

Then only flame remained. A small measure of peace enfolded him. Their ascension into the Light freed him to move on, too.

Shay Bladen turned his back on his home, his city, his perfect life. They would never return. And neither would he. He climbed onto his horse and rode away without looking back.

2. Conspirators

"They killed my sister! They killed the *children*!" Spinel leaned forward, arms waving in agitation. He gasped for the air he'd lost running all the way from the tavern to Tarver's columned home in the wealthy section of Porphyr. "*They* weren't supposed to die!"

"Calm, Spinel, calm." Tarver's deep voice soothed, his thick-fingered hands patting the air before him. Gold silks accented tawny eyes in a broad face, and gold gleamed on every finger. He smiled between the deep frown crevices in his face. "Come in, where we can talk."

Tarver led the way down a hallway that shrank as his height filled it. They entered a room created to impress wealthy friends, a room where Spinel felt even smaller than usual.

On one wall hung a gold ceremonial sword in a scabbard crusted with opals. A delicate blue vase occupied a niche to one side, its impossible sweeps of glass and deep, rich color unequaled anywhere in the world. Its maker had filled it with glass flowers of pink, yellow, and green so true Spinel almost expected to smell them. An ancient illuminated map adorned the back wall, and fine silks billowed from the ceiling in a flow of colors. As a merchant, he recognized the exorbitant expense of each object. Some were beyond any price.

His host turned to face him. "Did my men get the axe?" A sharp glint in his eyes disappeared as quickly as it came.

"If so, I'd have it with me." Spinel paced. "Your men are dead. He killed them with the damned axe." He didn't know that, but if they weren't already here with the axe, it seemed likely.

This was all Tarver's fault.

Tarver flicked a finger to his right. A slender young woman stepped from the shadows with a tray, her full lips parted slightly, ice-blue eyes turned on her master. Spinel stared at her gauzy garments and half-naked breasts, wondering if he dared request her services.

"What a dreadful night you've endured!" Tarver's voice dripped false sympathy. "You could use something to drink."

Spinel knew when he was being mocked, but he could already taste the Malice on the tray. "Yes, I could use a drink. Or two." One bottle of the exotic liquor cost more than his finest horse, but oh, the flavor of fire! He licked his lips.

"I will not be stinting on this night, my friend."

The woman poured thick, silver liquid into a tiny cup of delicate blown glass and held out the tray.

He snatched the glass and gulped down the contents in one huge swallow, barely tasting it. That should be enough to get him drunk. He held it out for more. Sweet flame burned through him, expanding his veins and tickling his brain. He drained the second one and held out the glass again, then tossed that one down, too. The images in his head wouldn't go away. He still saw Cinny's eyes, the look of surprise and betrayal as she died. Head spinning, he held the glass out yet again, trembling.

This time, the woman took the glass from him to refill it.

Unsteady on his feet, Spinel sought a heavy, cushioned chair. He lifted the bottle of Malice from the tray in passing.

Tarver dismissed the servant with a nod and sat nearby in a soft, stuffed chair laced with gold thread. Spinel's chair was almost as fine, without the gold.

"Did you see my tauz horse there? Perhaps bring it with you when you fled?" Tarver's tone held a touch of impatience, maybe a thread of underlying threat.

Spinel blinked, took a moment to let the words sink in. "You only asked for the axe."

"A horse, carved of tauz, with rainsilk mane and tail?"

"Sorry. You can send someone to pick it up."

Tarver pushed back to his feet, a big man but not as soft as he looked. "You imbecile! There's nowhere to pick it up *from*! The house and shop burned to the ground!"

Spinel blinked. "Burned? I didn't see any fire."

"After you . . . departed. Bladen burned the building and the bodies inside, and rode off. Nothing is left!"

"Did he take the axe?" Spinel left his tongue unguarded. Tarver was his friend, and Malice loosened his voice, anyway. "What about the document?"

Tarver sat slowly. He hadn't even tasted the Malice sitting by his elbow. "Spinel." He stroked his short beard with ringed fingers.

Spinel, lost in his cup, didn't look up.

"Spinel! What document?"

"The one with the axe. The one that mentions the mysteries."

Tarver glowered. "What mysteries? What are you talking about?"

Spinel sniggered. He knew things Tarver didn't. "It only hints at secrets and where to find answers." The room swayed like Spinel's words. Oblivion beckoned. He tipped the bottle to his lips and drank. Surely he'd drunk enough for some sleep. Without nightmares.

"Put that down! I need you to talk to me!"

The bottle slipped from Spinel's numb fingers and bounced on the thick carpet, slinging silvery drops through the air. He landed on the bottle and the puddle of liquid fire as he slid off his chair, out cold.

Spinel awoke in a room wrapped in darkness, where he always slept off his binges when visiting Tarver. Thick blinds smothered any stray light from outside, except one streak of brightness that had worked its way through the bambu slats and seared into his brain. It pulled his gaze back whenever he tried to look away. He groaned and sat up.

Cinny was dead, her children with her. The memory flooded in, with no Malice to soften the blow. He leaned over the side of the bed and threw up, then yelled for a servant to come clean it up. Older memories of his sister, from their childhood, clamored for his attention, but he couldn't bear it. Or the smell of vomit in the room. He staggered out.

Light struck him in the face like a mallet. He groaned again, covered his eyes with his hands, and reeled half-blind down the hall.

"There you are!" Tarver's cheerful voice didn't match such an awful day. "Come sit with me while I break my fast. We have things to discuss."

"No, not food. I couldn't bear it."

"I can. I'm hungry, and you owe me after last night's debacle. Come."

Tarver drew him to a sitting room, where breakfast had been laid out for him on a large table of dark, massive wood, its finish satin-smooth and its edges elaborately carved. It stood on a rich carpet of deep blue, figured with red and gold.

No place had been set for Spinel; the staff knew his habits.

Tucking a pristine white napkin into his collar, Tarver launched into an enormous omelet. The odor of its meats, onions, and costly spices made Spinel nauseous.

23

"Spinel, we have work to do. Don't talk, just listen unless I ask a question," Tarver said between bites. "First, I sent some men to sift through the debris from last night. They recovered a chest half full of gems, mostly uncut. Second, Bladen took my axe with him."

"*My* axe," Spinel interrupted. "My inheritance."

"No, *my* axe. After all, five people died last night–everyone but you and the gemsman, and no one knows where he is. I lost two men, the axe, the document, and the horse figurine. Now that a chest of gems is also missing from the shop, it could look very bad for you, should your name reach the City Guard.

"I will protect you from this fiasco, point the authorities toward Shay Bladen, but the axe is my price." Tarver lifted his chin and eyebrows at Spinel and took another bite of omelet.

Getting the axe was the whole purpose of the venture, to right an old wrong! It should be his. Dread and loss wormed through heart and stomach. He had no choice but to give up the family heirloom. He could hardly fight Tarver for it!

"I require your assistance to retrieve the axe and the document. Have you read it yourself?" Tarver lifted a small bowl of fruit and spooned some into his mouth. "That was a question, Spinel. You may speak to answer it."

Resentment squirmed, but he obeyed. "I skimmed it once, years ago. At the time, I expected to inherit it, so I paid little attention to details."

"What do you *remember*?"

Spinel hesitated, but he had no choice, really. He owed Tarver a very large number of gold pieces; Mother had cut off his funds last year. Then there were Tarver's extortion threats. "It referred to the Crystal Mountains, I think. The secrets are there, perhaps more black diamonds."

"What secrets?"

"Some kind of mystery, is all I remember."

Tarver patted his lips with his napkin and set it aside. "Here's what we'll do. The chest of gems we found will pay your debt to me, and we'll be partners in pursuit of the axe."

"Partners? What do I get out of it, if you get the axe and the document?" Spinel's resentment wormed its way up his spine, but he fought not to show it. His friend could be scary.

"I share your risks by protecting you. Anything above those two items will be yours. I've already sent trackers after Bladen, and I'll send more until the axe and document are secured. Since he's likely headed for the Crystal Mountains, I can implement a two-prong approach.

"Take a few men and ride directly there with all speed, to get ahead of him and cut him off. You're to take the axe, then use the document to find the source of the black diamonds.

"Kill Bladen. This isn't optional. You may assign the deathblow to one of your men, but his death is your responsibility. Think of it as a chance to punish him for your sister's death."

Spinel drummed his fingers on the arm of his chair. "So, according to our agreement, if we find the source, all the other black diamond material is mine."

"Of course!" Tarver arced a hand through the air to emphasize. "I have little interest in the material, only in the worked gems–and I'm willing to purchase finished gemworks from you."

Spinel hid his reaction. His brother-by-law could have created beautiful gemworks for him, but he'd lost that option. Hiring someone else would be exorbitantly expensive. Tarver's kind offer was no kind of offer at all.

Tarver stretched a cold smile. "With men behind and

before him, our success should be a simple matter. Bring me the axe and its secrets at all costs." Tarver leaned forward, eyes suddenly dangerous. "Upon pain of death."

That little crotch-grout! Almost useless now. Why had he ever gotten mixed up with this . . . this idiot? Too weak, too sensitive, too stupid.

No, not stupid. Cowardly. And always drunk.

Tarver settled into his favorite cushioned chair and smoothed his yellow and blue silks with one hand, careful not to touch it with the bloody length of cotton rope in the other. He stared out the window at the line of exotic mimusi trees he'd imported from somewhere across the land bridge. Their feathery leaves and wispy pink flowers drew admiration from all who saw them, further enhancing Tarver's image as a collector.

Like the beauty who'd graced his bed last night. Too bad about her injuries, but the doctors could probably patch her up enough to work in someone's kitchen. He had other women.

Folding the cotton rope, he grasped its ends with either hand and yanked his hands apart, snapping the rope loudly. Still-fresh blood droplets arced through the air. He could think better when using his hands. He snapped it again.

He already had what he wanted from Spinel: the introductions into polite society, with its wealthy wagon train owners, patrons of the theater, and serious collectors. He'd met all of Spinel's remaining family and knew their names, going back several generations, although he hadn't bothered connecting them to individual people. Opal. Ruby. Jade. Granata. Jat. Labra. Bastar. Carnelian. Tauz. Spinel, his key to the family's inner circle of friends, had invited him to events and introduced him to whomever he wished to meet. Generous gifts and compliments had cemented these friendships and provided access to many of the treasures he coveted. His current wealth and breathtaking treasures brought him the admiration and respect his former life as an assassin never could.

He didn't really need Spinel anymore–except for the black diamond battle-axe.

It was an impossible object. Diamonds could only be shaped by careful cutting along the planes of cleavage–the very planes that made them easy to shatter, and therefore useless as a weapon. But the battle-axe wasn't faceted at all, according to Spinel, and Bladen had sunk one blade into a man's skull without damaging the axe. And the size? What diamond could be so huge that a full-size axe could be formed from it? And what gods-forsaken idiot would make a bladed weapon out of a diamond, anyway? If it truly was a diamond, not something mundane.

As for the source of the black diamonds, that would belong to him, too. Spinel could enjoy "owning" it until Tarver could be rid of the little sot.

He stopped snapping his rope. He needed to burn it, to be rid of the telltale bloodstains. The woman had been a high-quality servant, as uppity as the snottiest merchant. Servants at that level would never work for him if they knew what he'd done to her. Discovery could jeopardize everything he'd worked for–his wealth, his place in society, his reputation.

Better to avoid the mess than have to clean it up.

Which brought him back to the mess named Spinel. The little runt could be replaced, but he still had a wealthy mother and many wealthy friends. And he knew more about the magic battle-axe than he had yet shared.

The battle-axe tugged at Tarver–a powerful, magical weapon of destruction and terror, made of one of the rarest, most valuable gems in the world. He could almost feel the smooth, hard haft in his hands. Magic. Value beyond price. Powerful. Unique. Deadly. All the things he most prized. He wanted the battle-axe so badly he salivated.

He needed Spinel crotch-deep in this venture. His family's wealth and connections could be helpful if the authorities caused trouble. As long as Spinel could help him get what he wanted, fine. But if he proved useless–again– during this errand. . . well, a long journey was dangerous.

Tarver tossed the bloodstained rope into the fire, listening to the chatter and crackle as the flame ate it. Then he called for a trusted servant, the kind never seen by his visitors.

The stringy-muscled man appeared silently and bowed, his eighteen thin black braids nearly sweeping the floor.
"Prepare the pit, and set out all my usual weapons." Fury burned through Tarver, but unleashing it against men was foolish and unnecessary. "Six dogs, as fierce and as large as you have. I'll take them all at once." He lifted a sword from the wall.

3. The Dainty Slipper

Driving rain pricked Shay Bladen's skin and he wished for the oiled cloak lost yesterday in a wild ride to escape pursuit. Shoulders sagging under water-weighted clothes, he endured fat raindrops pounding on his bowed head and dripping into his eyes from flattened hair. The battle-axe lay across his saddle in front of him, cold comfort today. Raindrops the color of silverstone slid down the lustrous haft while lightning lit the world. Thunder cracked like boulders splitting.

Two weeks out of Porphyr. Two weeks of tears and anger.

The first week he awoke every morning expecting to find Cinny next to him, their giggling children piling on top of them. The world instead held its breath, as if marking time. As if nothing could move forward ever again.

In the second week, as he began to accept he would never see them again, guilt hammered him. If he'd lost his family, it was his own Dark-damned fault. He'd been too slow to set down the axe. Why had he held onto it so long? If he'd only been quicker, they'd still be alive.

Alone in the world again, as in childhood, he wept. When the rain began, at first he thought his own tears dampened his cheeks. As if guided by Shay's heart, the rain came faster and harder throughout that day and the next.

The first two weeks also brought constant flight. He'd killed the first two pursuers from ambush with a landslide of rocks. The next two died in a face-to-face fight so grisly he'd thrown up. The dirty tricks learned in childhood became a mainstay of his life.

His small wounds had never been tended, but dried blood had at least rubbed off against his shirt. The Light grant that he receive none larger.

He'd learned to carry the axe across his saddle, not across his back.

Thunder crackled again, like ice breaking across a pond. His horse splashed and slipped through deep mud, laboring under him. He feared its wind was broken, feared he might ride it to death on this black night.

There should be a small town on this road, if he could just find it.

Lightning sheeted across the sky, revealing the town already around him. Window lights became visible through the cataract only in the lightning's lurid purple. That looked like a tavern, with a barn for his horse, but he couldn't read the sign through the downpour until he was almost under it–a painting of a woman's delicate shoe covered with jade and pearls below the words *The Dainty Slipper* in not-yet-faded lettering. He dismounted inside the barn, wiped his horse down, and forked it some hay when no attendant appeared.

Weary in heart and bone, he walked into the tavern and dripped. A floor cloth just inside the door absorbed his runoff as he examined the room. Just like any other tavern– wooden walls and floors, heavy beams holding up the roof, a warm, comfortable fire–except for the murals. Broad strokes of black paint outlined loud splashes of color. He'd never seen tavern walls with such gaudy pictures. He decided they depicted townspeople, though with little detail.

He liked the look of the place, well scrubbed, bright, and clean. Like Cinny's house. He made a note of the kitchen, where he'd find a back door if he needed one.

Water saturated the cloth under his feet and started runnels across the boards, but he didn't move. His beloved Cinnabar had trained him well not to make her job harder, and apparently the woman bringing more cloth his way was of the same ilk.

At first he thought her skin had been charred. Then his heart leaped. Could there be a connection between black skin and black diamonds? Could he be so close to his goal already? The woman looked like anyone else in the room, except for the brown-black skin. Neat and tidy, elegant of movement, she appeared to be nearing middle age, a few years younger than he. Perhaps the color was a disease? Or a face paint for some fashion or ritual? When she spread more cloth on the floor, he saw that her hands were black, too, with dusky pink palms.

"Welcome to my place." The woman's deep voice felt as smooth and rich as dairy cream, with a lilt Shay didn't recognize. She laid another cloth in front of his feet. "Please step onto this cloth." She handed him a thick, rough towel. "Use this one to wipe your hair, hands, and face. You will feel more comfortable. I am Bibi. If you need anything, please let me know."

Shay scrubbed excess water from himself as directed while Bibi collected the towel he'd stood on. "Can you provide a room for the night?"

"I can, indeed. Most of my rooms remain empty tonight."

A bed. Longing filled him. Even a straw mattress would feel wonderful after so long sleeping on the ground. Could he afford such luxury? He hadn't seen his pursuers for two or three days, but if an entire town could be hidden by rain, so could they.

He hesitated. "A bed sounds wonderful. After ale and food, if you have them."

As Bibi led him to the fireplace, he said, "Interesting murals. They're different from anything I've seen."

"The style is typical of my birthplace. I painted these

31

myself." She smiled with pleasure, then shooed locals away from their table to give him space closest to the warmth.

Shay sank onto the hard wooden chair with a relieved sigh. It felt good to sit on something that wasn't moving. He laid his fighting axe on the table within easy reach. Its black leather hood and grip would require some work after this soaking, but at least the axe itself was impervious to the wet. Raindrops rolled down the haft and dripped off the knob onto the table and floor.

His fingers itched to remove the hood and admire the sleek axe fully, but he resisted. Already, men at nearby tables cast surreptitious glances at the weapon. He couldn't blame them. The glass-smooth black handle glowed with reflected firelight, sparking the bits of inner color peculiar to diamonds.

Bibi brought him a tankard of ale, followed by a plate of bacon and eggs wrapped in a large, thin pancake that melted on his tongue. He welcomed the warmth spreading through him.

As she delivered his second ale, a muscular farmer at a nearby table spoke to him. "Unusual axe. Never seen one like it."

Shay mumbled unintelligible words in a polite response intended to discourage.

Undeterred, the man asked, "What's it made of?"

Ears pricked up at nearby tables as talk fell away. Shay cursed silently. "Wood and steel, like any axe."

"Never seen black wood before."

"Ebony, polished to a high gloss. I spend a lot of hours maintaining it."

"I'll bet you've had some fine adventures with that axe. Ever use it in battle?"

Shay wanted out of this conversation, but couldn't think of any polite way to shut it off. "It's just a showpiece."

He closed his mouth before he could give away the lies. Lying came hard to him, unusual for someone who sold things for a living.

He caught Bibi's eye. "I could use that bed now."

"Come. I'll show you to your room." Black eyes tilted up at the corners. The spark in them acknowledged his need to escape the questions.

Shay stood, picked up his axe, and started toward the stairs at the back of the room. A puff of cool air touched the back of his neck. He twisted to look behind him.

The tavern door cracked against the inner wall. Three men boiled in from the street with rain and wind, bellowing and swinging weapons.

The locals froze, staring, but Shay bolted for the back door.

Behind him a man's scream cut off to a wet gurgle. Chairs screeched and broke. Shay glanced back. One local dead from a sword slice across the throat. The second intruder's sword stabbed at another victim's belly, but the farmer caught his wrist with implacable strength. People scattered away from the attackers as the first one swung a huge sword at another farmer. Blood sprayed across the room with the man's scream. The third man swung a spike-and-chain flail in front of him. It whistled louder than the men's terrified shrieks.

The big man with the spiked flail charged Shay, wicked weapon swinging.

Shay darted through the kitchen doorway just ahead of Bibi, who stopped in front of it to face the attacker. She carried a bullwhip too heavy for a woman and with inadequate space for it.

Shay's hair rose in horror and he broke back in her direction.

Bibi swung the bullwhip around her head. She sent its

33

tip singing through the air. The tip tangled with the chain.

"*Spike*" grabbed the tangle of chain, trapping the whip. With a powerful jerk, he yanked Bibi toward him. She released the whip and backed up fast as the man lunged at her.

Shay tore the hood off his axe as he threw himself forward to intercept. He swung with the full weight and momentum of his arms. The axe caught Spike just below the armpit, sheared through flesh and bone and organs. The man's fall ripped the axe from Shay's hand. Precious seconds dripped away as he struggled to pull it from the corpse.

The farmer stepped in, grabbed the haft from him, and jerked it easily from the body. "Run," he yelled.

"Give me my axe!" Shay tore it from the surprised farmer's grip and pushed Bibi through the doorway ahead of him, leaving behind the farmers and merchants, the dying and the dead. "Go!" Ahead of him, Bibi tripped on the hem of her skirt and Shay caught her elbow. Then they were out the door, into the black downpour, the growl of thunder, and the splinters of lightning. They dashed for the stable.

The scents of warm, moist hay and horses rolled into his face. Shay pushed Bibi into the stable's shadows ahead of him. He looked for something to ride besides his own exhausted horse. "Hide in here until they're gone," he said. "And be careful returning to the tavern. They'll follow me, so it won't be for long."

Bibi grabbed his arm with steel fingers, arresting his long strides. "I will go with you, for now. Your presence has destroyed my life here." The words matched the stone of her face.

"I don't have time to argue. The tavern can be fixed, and you still have friends here."

"There is blood on my floor, soaked into the boards,

34

and evil spirits fill its air with death. It is no longer safe for human beings. I will ride with you to another place and start over."

"Then get a horse." Shay jerked out of her grip, threw his saddle onto the first horse he came to, a flea-bit gray, and threw himself into the saddle.

"Bibi?" Shay didn't see her. Fear trickled down his back. Every second of delay could bring death. Or loss of everything.

That sounded like cloth ripping. Twice. Yells pelted into the rain with his pursuers.

"Bibi?" Shay's voice rose as the gray danced under him, picking up his tension.

She rode out of the shadows astride a tall, elegant mare that embodied the tauz horse destroyed in the funeral fire. Blue eyes like skystone and a golden coat reflected the lightning that flashed from a high window.

The sides of Bibi's skirt had been ripped from mid-thigh to ankle for riding. "I am here. Try to stay with me." She charged toward the door at a run, directly toward the oncoming thugs.

Caught off-guard, Shay booted his horse after her, lifting the heavy axe by its throat with one hand.

Bibi screamed, a sound of fury and the echo of death. One hand brandished a steel sword, threatening mayhem. At the last second, the two attackers flung themselves aside, leaving a clear path for Shay to ride through. He pounded out of town after the tavern keeper without slowing.

When they approached a Y in the road, Bibi took the narrower right-hand path. Shay, about to follow the main road, reined in. He yelled at her over the storm noise.

She didn't slow, had apparently not heard him. She knew the area. He did not, so he followed. For now, escape trumped destination.

He pointed the gray at Bibi's distant back and urged the horse to a gallop.

By early morning, the storm eased to a downpour and he could see individual raindrops sliding down his saddle like tears. Ah, Cinny, he thought, how did I ever come to be *here*? His longing intensified–for his own home and hearth, filled with joy and the most wonderful wife . . . He swallowed, lest his tears swell the rivulets of rain on his cheeks. Gone from the world was the passionate ruby of Cinny's presence, leaving a hole so huge he could fall through it forever without touching the sides.

Something else. Think of something else. Not his children, or his shop, or his finest gems, or the axe, or the document. Frantically, he cast about for a distraction.

Ahead, Bibi's golden mare slowed to turn off the road. He followed, forcing curiosity.

The sound of rain muted under the thick trees. Pungent wetness filled the space. He almost gagged on the thick air. Here, most of the cold drops sliding down Shay's neck dripped from trees, not clouds. For the first time since leaving the Dainty Slipper, he could hear something besides wind and rain.

Bibi dismounted. "We can rest here a while, for the horses' sake and our own. Have you any food with you?" She unsaddled and slipped the mare's bit as she spoke.

Exhaustion dragged Shay from his dripping saddle. Their breaks had been few and short, and he was grateful for a real rest. "A little." He unsaddled as well, took the saddle pouches with him as he stumbled toward Bibi. "It won't go far." The weight of the axe had become unbearable. He wanted to shuck it for a while, but he feared to let it out of his hands right now.

"I would like to know with whom I ride, as well as

where we go, and why." Bibi turned obsis eyes, black and bright, on Shay.

"I travel alone, not wanting my ill luck to befall others," he said. "The less you know of me, the safer you'll be."

"Pah! No woman in this world is ever safe. But I am a warrior of the Sheethe. Wherever the road takes us, I will be safer than you. Death has followed me all my life. But I cannot live and work where evil spirits dwell, nor should anyone, and so I must make a new start. I will ride with you until I find a new place." She waited expectantly.

Make up a name? Shay's new companion would be safer, but would he remember it? Part of him wanted human companionship, someone to share troubles and divide work. Another part of him dreaded human complications. He opened his mouth, interested to hear what would come out of it. "I'm Shay Bladen, a gemsman enroute to the Crystal Mountains to find what stones I may for my work."

"Who chases you?" asked Bibi.

"Ruffians hired by someone who means me ill. I don't know who." More lies.

"You are an artisan, not a warrior, and you carry an axe such as I have not seen, although you do not know how to fight with it. I would guess the value of your axe exceeds the lives of ourselves, our horses, and everything else we have with us." Bibi pursed her lips, thinking. "It appears you have acquired some luck, a companion who can perhaps keep you alive on this journey. If such a thing is possible."

4. Axe Training

Shay fell into a deep, black hole filled with sleep, for once, free of dreams and restlessness. He seemed to close his eyes one moment and open them the next, instantly alert.

Darkness still enclosed the area beneath the trees, but just outside the foliage, he heard the sounds that had awakened him. Hoofbeats. Drumming in place. He snatched at the axe he kept near his right hand as he slept.

It wasn't there.

Panic bounced off ribcage and brain as he groped. He scrambled to his feet, glancing around wildly.

Voices. Including Bibi's smooth chocolate voice. She was stealing his axe!

He flung himself toward the road, furious with himself for trusting her.

A horse neighed and a man's voice answered Bibi's just as he burst through to the road.

The horse shied. The rider tilted. Bibi reached out of the shadows and pulled him off the horse before he could rebalance. The dim shape of the axe sliced through the air and into the downed man's throat. Blood spurted.

Shay's hand closed on Bibi's elbow, which slammed into his face before he even got a grip. He fell. Someone yelled. Hoofbeats pounded away.

Shay sat up, holding his forehead with both hands.

Bibi's elegant voice spoke inelegant words at some length before she turned to him.

"One dead, but the other takes word back to his owner." She offered him a hand up.

He almost refused it in his fury, but dizziness changed his mind.

"It is never wise," she said, "to touch a warrior without warning."

He barely heard. "What are you doing with my axe?"

"Saving both our lives." She held out the battle-axe to him, her tone as cool as a shaded stream. "I apparently rolled away from my sword in my sleep."

He snatched the axe from her, the sudden weight dropping the axe head almost to the ground, next to his foot, and fear exploded in his chest. "Don't touch it! Don't ever touch it!" Shaking, he forced calm, as the axe had been neither stolen nor harmed.

She appeared not to notice his anger. "I understand now your awkwardness with this weapon. It is too heavy for either of us to handle well."

"No one touches this axe but me!" He couldn't explain, even to himself, why it mattered so much.

Not just the axe itself. Losing it would be almost like losing Cinny again. It was all he had left of her, a connection that nothing else he owned could provide. Such a horrible connection! And yet . . . the awe and joy on her face when her father had gifted it to them, the welcome her family offered him with the gift . . . those moments were irreplaceable. The time they had later spent stroking and examining the axe–and each other . . . He took a deep, shaky breath.

"Then you are lucky to be alive still," said Bibi. Her calm, matter-of-fact manner was disconcerting, even icy.

So different from Cinnabar. His sudden need for his wife's sparkling eyes and ready laughter landed on his heart like a boulder.

My fault. My fault. Why didn't I think? The axe wasn't important. Not like Cinny. Not like Piper and Beryl. Why didn't I just let it go? He dropped his chin to his chest for a moment, hiding the weakness of grief and guilt.

As dawn hinted at the new day, they saddled up without breaking their fast and led their horses out from under the thick-leaved trees. Mud squished under Shay's feet and a few cold water drops landed on his head and face. He found a patch of grass to wipe off the worst of the mud before mounting.

Despite the disturbance, Shay's perpetual exhaustion had ebbed a little. She could have killed him as he slept, could have just ridden away with his axe. She hadn't. His sleep had been short, but deep, after too many nights of light sleep on hard ground. Someone keeping watch for him would be a luxury, and he wouldn't mind taking his turn in exchange.

Maybe traveling with Bibi wouldn't be so bad. If he could trust her.

The Eye of the Light came out from the clouds. Cool, fresh-smelling air felt too damp to be comfortable, but Shay didn't care. Yesterday's flat land rolled up into low green hills as they rode. How odd to see the earth, instead of the sky, reflect the seasons. He had rarely been out of the city, and never far. Here, the height and deep emrel color of the grasses and their seed heads, the new leaves on trees, the smell and touch of the breeze, all announced spring's arrival. The world was being reborn while death shadowed Shay's life.

The contrast heightened his melancholy.

The hard-packed road was slick on top from the rain, another new experience for Shay. The second time the flea-bit gray slipped, Bibi moved them off to the grass verge to ride, something Shay wouldn't have thought of.

He hated today already, and not only because of the mud. The fight at the Dainty Slipper had unlocked memories he'd tried hard to imprison during his flight from

Porphyr.

The first time he'd killed someone, he'd been ten–a knife in the heart of a sleeping older boy who took pleasure in tormenting and hurting him. He associated the second memory with both black jat and lurid jagounce, the colors of the smoke and fire that killed his parents.

He hadn't killed again until the night he lost his wife and children. That memory was too close, too painful, but he didn't push it away–not even the death wounds of his innocent children.

Children! How could anyone do that? And Cinny's throat gaping, the hot blood pumping out . . . Grief twisted his insides. It never left, but sometimes it lay in wait to catch him unawares. He didn't want to live through it again, but memory insisted. The images had blurred, but not enough. Never enough.

Why? Yes, Spinel was a little greedy–but enough to take part in his sister's murder? To hire toughs to do the dirty work? Rage fought with grief until he thought he'd die of it. He almost wished he would. He had to keep the axe from Spinel's–or Tarver's–hired killers, had to find the bloodstone pillars before they caught him.

The remainder of his killings had been pursuers bent on taking the axe. He couldn't submerge the sickening thud of axe striking flesh. He hated blood and gore, but it seemed the Dark had removed his choice.

"So, traveler, who do you flee? And why?"

Bibi's voice jarred him back to the present. He needed a moment to collect himself. She'd asked before, must not have believed him. "I'm riding to the Crystal Mountains to look for gemstones. I don't know these men."

She smiled, professionally friendly. "No coins or loose gems to pay your way?"

He stared at her, taken off-guard. "Why do you want to

41

know?" Then he cursed himself for a fool. He'd as good as told her he did.

"We will need supplies. I carry a small emergency stash at all times, but I hope you also carry coins or gems. Our destination, the Crystal Mountains, is a goodly distance from here, unless we can catch the Slipaway Trail."

Shay blinked, diverted at last from his pain. For the moment. "The what?"

"The Slipaway Trail. It goes everywhere." She studied his face. "Everyone knows of the Slipaway Trail, though few use it."

"I've never heard of it." Shay kept his voice flat, unfriendly.

Bibi arched an eyebrow. "The Slipaway Trail is magic and short, usually about four hours from one end to the other. When you get to the end, you may be hundreds of miles from where you started. Only one path exists; you cannot leave the trail except at one end or the other."

"So how does it know where to take you?"

"The trail neither knows nor cares. Like most magic, you can neither control nor predict it. It may open anywhere in the world, and the opening may remain for several hours or only for a moment. We ride until we recognize something that seems closer to our destination, which will be boring and irritating. Nevertheless, we can sometimes cut our journey by days or even weeks."

Shay thought about it. "So, unless my pursuers are right behind us, the trail would take them to a different end than it did us, and we'd be free of them. It sounds unreliable to me."

"Indeed. We must rely on ourselves, always. The trail does not change that. Nothing changes that. Whether you lose them depends on timing you cannot control."

"How do we find this trail?"

42

"It will appear suddenly, and it may not stay long, so be watchful. Look for a path flanked by two tall trees, wound with vines bearing flowers."

But though Shay craned his neck, swiveling in his saddle, the trail did not appear.

That evening, as they ate a frugal supper, Bibi studied Shay's face for a long moment. "Would you learn to handle your axe?"

"I'm no warrior." Even he heard the uncertainty in his voice. Warrior or no, he longed for better skills. His strength lay in hands and fingers, not in shoulders and back.

"If you would like, I can teach you axe fighting."

"Why would you do that for me?"

"I need sword work every day, now that we are safely away. And your skills may benefit me, as mine do you. You are clumsy with the axe, wasting motion and strength."

"I do all right. I've survived so far, haven't I?"

"You can learn to fight better, with less effort."

Shay shrugged. Why not? Then he wondered why he resisted, instead of embracing the opportunity. Trust, again. In his childhood, no one offered help of any kind unless they wanted something in return–usually something not mentioned until later.

"Then come." Bibi picked up a stout branch about three feet long. "Bring your axe."

"Now?" Exhaustion tugged at all of Shay's limbs. "Why not in the morning, when we're fresh? And fed?"

"We do not choose when we may need to fight. If you would train, it will begin now. And every evening, for an hour or more."

Shay's stomach tightened in dread, but he needed to do this. He resigned himself to looking the fool.

They found a level, if wet, area in the grass and Bibi stood facing him. For a long moment, she only looked at him, as if deciding where to start. Her eyes lost their beauty, now obsis-hard and focused, and something in her posture bespoke the strength and attitude of a warrior, rather than the welcoming warmth of the tavern owner.

I've never seen anyone stand so still, Shay noted, stroking the haft of his axe. Already he thought of her differently–even a little fearfully.

"A lighter weapon is easier for the beginner," she said, "but you will grow into the axe."

He floundered for an adequate reply, wondering what she meant. The axe was what he had, so he must learn to use it. How hard could it be, to swing something heavy at someone mean? He'd already done so, many times now.

"The task I will set before you," said Bibi, "is a difficult one. It may seem boring, you may seem to make no progress; it may sometimes seem painful or frightening. If it does not, you are doing something wrong. I will teach you as I was taught, although I have no affinity for the axe. For our purposes, what I can teach you will be more than adequate.

"Always after training we will examine our weapons for dents, nicks, chips, and other damage. I do not know what your axe is made of, so you must determine for yourself how such wounds must be treated. The condition of any weapon is crucial in battle."

"My axe won't be damaged by training or battle."

"Your axe is not made of ebony despite what you told my customer. Stone, perhaps. You owe me no explanations. I have my own story to shelter and will not ask for yours."

Relief poured through Shay. She couldn't know the gift she'd just given him.

"Now"" said Bibi. "We will approach your training as would a formal school of the Sheethe. That means proper respect and form. We will speak later of rules and respect,

44

but the light wanes. Let us make use of what remains to begin our exercise. Make no mistake; these first nights are exercise only, not fighting techniques. We begin by building your strength and shaping your muscles for fighting."

She then drove him without mercy until Shay could barely see her in evening's gloom.

At first, he resented her calm, casual handling of the heavy branch, without tiring. Then he forgot such pettiness as he squatted on the balls of his feet and held the axe in front of him, across his palms, at shoulder height. His arms could not hold the axe so high, to Bibi's apparent disgust, but he did the best he could. His ankles ached immediately, and then the arches of his feet. When his balance wavered and he dropped to a flat-footed squat, Bibi barked him back to the more precarious position. When he lowered his arms just for a moment, she glared at him, her own stability rock-hard.

"What is this supposed to accomplish?" he asked through gritted teeth.

"What do *you* think?"

"I have no idea! Why else would I ask?"

"You must learn to work things out for yourself."

"I think my feet are about to break. I didn't even know I had muscles in my feet. Or my ankles." He thought about that, gritting his teeth. "That means we're working to strengthen those particular muscles."

"And why," asked Bibi, "do we work on those particular muscles?"

Silence, as Shay struggled again. When the answer came, he knew it was right. "To develop balance."

Bibi nodded. "And discipline. Rise and shake out your feet, walk around a moment."

Repeating the exercise hurt just as much.

Then she showed him how to stand for solidity and safety. And for the next exercise, she had him swing his axe overhead and down, trying to stop it at waist level.

"Exactly at waist level." She demonstrated. "Your strikes need not be hard, but they must be controlled. Shay, be certain your axe head is covered and will not slip."

At last, something easy. He checked the cover with a glance. Then he pictured Spinel's face and swung his axe up, hard. It slipped from his grip and sailed into the brush behind him. Embarrassed, he retrieved it, not looking at Bibi.

When he finally looked up, Bibi regarded him thoughtfully.

"Your grip will improve as your strength does," she said.

Shay tried again, pushing Spinel from his thoughts to concentrate on his grip. It became easier as he worked, but despite Bibi's exhortations, he could not bring the heavy axe head to a steady stop in the right place, without wavering.

"For the next strike," Bibi told him, "do not stretch your arms above your head. Hold your elbows in, not spread out, to guard your head. Use your wrists, not your arms, to drop the axe behind your head and to draw it forward into a strike."

It made sense when she showed him and explained, but his wrists didn't have the strength to do it right.

Bibi made it look easy. A woman!

"When we strike, why must we stop the axe without the end moving?" she asked. "Once we hit the attacker, it will not matter, so why work to learn it?"

The ache in Shay's arms gave him the answer. "We use different muscles to stop the axe than to begin the blow. So in each strike, we strengthen two muscles and improve our control."

Bibi almost smiled, her eyes alight. "Very good. Now, when you have reached waist level, take your axe up hard, as you did before, but stop it hard, without wavering."

When at last Bibi called a halt, he discovered muscles in his arms, chest, and shoulders he'd never been aware of. The aches kept him awake, offsetting the good sleep of the night before, and in the morning he could barely move.

Bibi made him remove his shirt, then coated his neck, shoulders, and arms with a spicy-smelling ointment and rubbed it in. It burned, but it did help.

Her firm, brisk touch felt good, like Cinny's only because her hands were a woman's hands. But with calluses.

He hoped the training would at least make the pain worthwhile, but at least it had distracted him from the constant ache of loss. That alone made it valuable.

5. Crookback Trail

Bibi's rules were simple: she ruled; Shay obeyed. Respect meant formality, alacrity, and proper attitude. And doing most of the work. The Sheethe warrior must be addressed as "senesa," meaning "the one who goes before."

He scrubbed out the last pan from supper, grumbling to himself silently, having learned to dread the wrath of Senesa Bibi. Last night, he had moved a pile of rocks, each the size of his head, from one side of camp to the other. After supper, she'd required him to move them back.

Still, Shay didn't complain aloud, having been taught by Cinny the proper respect for women. He winced, still embarrassed and shamed by the lesson.

"Supper isn't ready yet?" His voice became the bucket for all the day's frustrations and weariness. Demanding customers, never satisfied, had tried to bargain down his prices, already set ridiculously low to build his clientele. And that fat Lady with her nose in the air, muttering something about "their betters" had soured everything. Maybe Shay wasn't as talented as he'd thought. Maybe no one would want his work–or too few, at least. He tried to think of another occupation for which he might be qualified. How could he support a wife, with their first child due to arrive soon? Cinny's father's seed money for the shop had been spent, and he would not go begging to him for help.

Cinny turned from the fireplace, perspiration sliding down her cheek beneath a sweat-born curl of red hair. Her belly protruded so far she had trouble bending and stooping these days. Looking at the enormous child-bump had once warmed Shay, but now his fingers chilled every time it entered his line of sight. The burden of responsibility threatened to overwhelm him.

"No. It's not." Apparently she'd had a bad day, too. Her eyes blazed.

How could a woman have a bad day, especially with a child on the way? She had a cozy home, she glowed with pregnancy–most of the time–she was fed and loved and cared for and pampered. All she did was putter around the house while he worked and worried, and she couldn't even have supper ready for him. Women had easy lives compared to men, who carried the burden of providing everything for both of them.

When her chin lifted, he realized he'd spoken some of that aloud.

The bitterest argument they'd ever had followed, and Shay had thankfully forgotten the words. He would never forget the anger billowing throughout the house, though, or Cinny bursting into tears without warning.

"You try it," she shouted through her tears. "I work hard keeping a home for you, as clean and cheerful as I can make it–especially *carrying all this extra weight! All you do is dabble with beautiful things, argue with customers, and make my life hell with your moaning and groaning!"*

He gaped at her, stunned.

Cinny's eyes widened in shock. Her fingers covered her lips. "I didn't mean it."

Shay's legs wobbled, as if he stood on pegs instead of solid feet. He stumbled to a chair and sat, light-headed, head in hands. She had never spoken so to him. On top of the rest of the day, it was too much. He needed a few minutes to regain his composure. When he finally looked up, she hadn't moved, her beautiful fingers still covering her lips. The look on her face would always be imbedded in memory.

They talked then, and he found out the difficulty of a

woman's life.

The next morning, she pushed him out of bed and turned over. Mumbling, he stoked the fire and made breakfast for them both, a much harder task with the small cask of nails strapped to his belly under his clothes. He hadn't slept well with it, either.

Cinny went to the shop in his place, and he heard laughter as she sold the objects he'd been about to take apart as unsalable.

Shay's back soon ached from the ungainly weight strapped to him, but he gritted his teeth and did the chores and the cleaning she'd planned for the day, and all the cooking. Supper ran a little late, to his chagrin.

She'd done better at his job than he had at hers, but they shared stories and laughed, then kissed and made up. Especially made up.

The lessons Cinny had taught him made it easier to surrender to Bibi's–Senesa Bibi's–will during axe training. Even when she required him to stand on one foot for five minutes. If the other foot touched earth, the time started over.

And that followed a full day in the saddle.

Shay sighed. Bibi had spent much of her emergency stash on supplies, including food for both of them. Shay should have chipped in, too, but he still couldn't bring himself to reveal the gems he carried. They were all he had left, and they bore enormous value. He didn't trust Bibi enough to show what he had. Nor did he trust his own instincts about her honesty.

After losing all that was bright in this world, he might never trust again.

He'd like to convert one or two gems to coin, but he needed a town large enough for a good gemsman. Even then, the amount would have to be small, for so many superior gems would draw too much attention.

Shay pulled out the special ingredients Bibi had purchased.

"Ready?" she asked.

"Yes, ma'am." He hoped that term of address passed in place of "senesa." It came more readily to his tongue.

She didn't correct him, so it must be all right. She seated herself across from him.

The idea of a woman wearing britches still made Shay uncomfortable, but the new ones were more decent than the skirt she'd slashed for riding; he'd just have to get used to the idea. He concentrated on looking at her face.

"Now," she said, "did the battle balm help your sore muscles last night?"

"Yes, Senesa."

"And did you pay careful attention when I showed you how it is made?"

"Yes, Senesa."

"Good. You may begin."

He stared at her in surprise.

"You did watch closely, did you not?"

He swallowed. "I don't know that watching once qualifies me to make it."

"It does not. Nor does making it once. But practice will achieve competence. I will watch tonight, to assure the battle balm is made properly. Let me see the ingredients you have set out."

He indicated small vials, twists of fabric, and oiled paper packets, naming the contents of each: "Camphor, beeswax, sanxle essence, oil . . . uh . . . another essence with a long name."

"Emberest essence," Bibi supplied. "Which are you missing?"

"Am I missing one?" He glanced around for another

packet.

"The secret ingredient," she reminded him. "Klovais." Finding the packet, Shay carefully measured pebbles of klovais into the mortar and pestled them to powder. He added the other ingredients under Bibi's stern eye, paying particular attention to proportions. The sharp aroma of the herbs and spices nearly smothered him. He stifled a sneeze.

"Senesa, why make such a small amount?" Shay asked. "Wouldn't it be easier to make a large batch all at once? It would last much longer."

"Ah, but fresh is best, and the cost of the ingredients is too dear to risk losing or spilling the leftover portions."

Fresh suited him just fine, and this task would go quickly, once he became used to it.

When the mixture had reduced and cooled, Shay rubbed it into sore muscles. His legs could use it, too, but even being shirtless embarrassed him. Bibi seemed not to notice, urging him to rub the battle balm in thoroughly, not just spread it around.

The burn began slowly as the balm heated with body warmth and friction, until it became almost painful as it loosened the tightness and eased soreness. Shay sighed in relief, even knowing he would smell of klovais all day.

"Tomorrow," he said, "we need to make better time, with a sharper eye. More men will be coming, and they could catch up any time."

"If we do not soon encounter the Slipaway Trail," Bibi said, "there is a more hidden, more difficult trail we can take, one they are unlikely to know–the Crookback Trail. If they do not see us take it, they will not know it is there."

The magic trail remained elusive, and in the afternoon, Bibi slowed to a fast walk along the left edge of the road.

Shay glanced across the broken, rocky hills they had

entered, and when he looked back, she had disappeared.

"Shay! Here!"

Following her voice, he looked over his left shoulder. She rode in a narrow rocky crevice, angled steeply up and back. This must be the Crookback Trail. He'd have missed it if she hadn't called. He turned his gray to follow her golden mare.

Then they turned again, up an even steeper crevice. The gray lunged up the rocks, misstepped once, but caught its balance. Shay's throat closed in fear. He tried to give it support with the reins, but succeeded only in throwing its head to one side. It flailed, neighing, and slid backwards on its feet.

Shay stopped to allow his horse to catch its breath and settle, then drove it up the crevice again. He leaned forward to give its hindquarters more freedom of movement. The gray surged up the slope, hooves clattering. It slipped again on loose rocks, teetering dangerously. Shay smelled his own oily sweat, tasted the bite of acid in his throat. The horse regained its balance and climbed onto a level area where Bibi waited. Shay's mouth dried up and his heart battered his ribcage. That could have been a nasty fall. Next time he'd lead his horse.

The faint trail continued upward through thick oaks and cottonwoods, steep but smoother. They wound in a circuitous route until Shay swore they'd circled the small mountain three times before they reached a plateau scattered with boulders. Here they rested and ate, giving the horses a chance to graze and drink from a stream.

Shay studied Bibi's elegant mare, who had taken the trail nimbly and without any trouble whatsoever–a remarkable horse. The next tauz horse he created would have a shorter back, slimmer legs, and that beautiful arch at the crest. And rainsilk feathers, as well as mane and tail.

And paler skystones for the eyes.

Bibi watched him studying her mare and pride filled her voice. "She is one-quarter Curzon and has the heart and intelligence of that breed. And the feathers. Her name is Silence. What is your horse's name?"

"I have no idea."

"Then you can name him what you like."

"Why would I? It's just a horse. It gets me where I'm going. So far."

"Flea," said Bibi. "Call him Flea, for his coat."

Shay managed not to roll his eyes.

Bibi stood, brushing crumbs from her hands. "We have far to go yet, and we must get through the next canyon before dark."

The descent from plateau to canyon proved as steep and difficult as the initial climb. The trail switched back and forth, and Shay soon dismounted and led his horse.

He stopped at the edge of a three-foot drop down onto a steep slope.

Below and well ahead, Bibi glanced back, then rode Silence to one side to wait. She must also fear his horse would fall.

Shay froze. He didn't trust Flea's surefootedness on this leap. Even walking alongside, he couldn't decide on a safe path to get the horse down.

He couldn't find a good way for himself, either, and finally sat down and scooted off the edge, reins clenched in his fist. He flailed to keep his footing on the loose rocks, sliding and running a few steps for balance. His grip on the reins pulled his agitated horse off the ledge. Suddenly, a thousand pounds of horse went down on loose gravel and slid. Dust billowed, engulfing and hiding the animal.

Shay had nowhere to go. He heard Bibi's distant voice but it was only sound.

Cinny, I'm coming! He closed his eyes.

Flea screamed as he slid over a shelf of rock bulging from the path.

And finally Shay could move. He ran at a tree and two steps up the thick trunk, just enough to grasp the lowest limb.

The horse slid by beneath him while he strained to hold on.

His fingers slipped, scraping painfully across rough bark as he dropped. He hit hard and fell backward, his head snapping against the ground.

Bibi reached him, then. "Are you hurt?" she asked as he struggled to sit up.

He shook his head, unable to breathe enough to speak.

"You have had the wind knocked out of you." She slid an arm behind his shoulders. "Allow me to help you sit up."

When he finally made it, he rested forearms on knees, still fighting to get air down his closed windpipe.

"Relax. It will come in a moment." She left him, and he heard her speaking gently to the gray horse. Leather creaked.

Air started to work its way in and he looked over his shoulder at her. She ran her hands down the horse's legs and checked under the saddle for bruising.

Shay worked his way to his feet and joined her. His dust-covered horse looked fine to him. Except for the wild look in the eye. Flea sidled, still upset.

"Lead him for a while," Bibi instructed. "It will be safer for you until he calms."

Not that he wanted to ride this unreliable beast. He took the reins she handed him and followed her back to Silence.

Still shaky from the fall, he took his time; he gradually worked up to normal walking speed. His soul felt as bruised as his body, but within the hour, he walked normally again, except for a vague limp to mollify a painful bruise in his lower back.

By the time the trail seemed to peter out, Shay's legs no longer trembled. The late afternoon Eye of the Light reflected from the rocky land, forcing him to squint much of the time, and his face ached with it. The trail didn't seem to affect Bibi at all.

Maybe Senesa would call a halt for the day, find them a level, shady place to recuperate. Maybe Silence's feathers would fly her above the clouds, too.

Bibi stopped and waited for him to catch up. "It is time for you to ride once more. The easy part of the Crookback Trail is behind us. Now it takes us through Mangler Canyon. We must complete our journey through this canyon before dark. Avoid shadows. Danger hides within. Stay close, and keep a hand to your axe." She turned Silence and once again led the way.

6. Mangler Canyon

The Crookback Trail had been brutal, and now Senesa Bibi would allow no rest at all?

Shay drooped, exhausted from the day's ordeal. Bibi set Silence to a flowing trot and Flea followed, his trot short and choppy.

The horses picked their way through rocks to find the flattest surfaces on the pathless route through Mangler Canyon. The red walls continued to rise on either side until they blocked most of the sky. Sandstone mostly, a place where few gems would be found—perhaps querk varieties, or labra. Ahead of them, the walls narrowed the passage alongside a small river.

The farther they rode, the smaller the sky became. Black caves of various sizes and shapes pocked the canyon walls. Some looked large enough to sleep in tonight, if necessary. Whatever danger Bibi feared, an attack could only reach them from one direction in that haven. Shay almost suggested it.

As the canyon walls drew in, lengthening shadows blocked the sun's heat from much of the floor. Darkness already lurked too deep within the shadows to see what they hid. Shay shivered, dread prickling his skin like spider legs.

Bibi, of course, appeared as relaxed as ever, if more alert than before. She carried her branch across her saddle, above her sword and a large knife in a worn scabbard on her belt.

What could be out here to put Bibi on alert? The horses sensed something, too. Both mounts tossed their heads and Flea bounced on tippy-toes under him, working up a sweat. What did they smell?

57

Bibi rode back. "Shay, your axe should be in your hand, without the hood. Stay alert, and stay out of shadows. There is something you need to see."

Shay fumbled for the axe strapped across his back and rode forward with her, tucking the axe's hood inside his shirt.

Nothing prepared him for what she'd found. Something red lay in a heap, piquing his curiosity. Then he rode close enough to see, fighting his horse to advance.

Horror shrieked through him and lifted his hair. His stomach clenched, and the first thing out of his mouth wasn't words. Bibi should have warned him, so he wouldn't vomit down the side of his horse.

She offered her waterskin. He reached for it with cold, shaking hands, cleaned himself and Flea. He took more time than necessary, delaying as long as he could. When he finally looked up, his stomach roiled again.

Blood. No wonder the horses sidled, trying to avoid the heap.

Worse than blood. A human corpse, with no face. Only a scarlet hole showed where the face had been, and the rest of the head looked little better. All the corpse's bones had been broken, lying at awkward angles, or loose on the ground. The remainder was worse. Shay averted his gaze as quickly as he could, but the smell of rotting flesh nauseated him.

"What did this?" Shay's voice came out as a hoarse squeak, and not just from the acid bile lingering in his throat.

"Manglers." Bibi's grim voice matched her eyes. "No one who has seen a mangler has lived to speak of it. They are believed to dwell in the caves along this canyon, and they keep to darkness and shadow. The canyon is safe by daylight but impossible by night. Even evening's long shadows are dangerous."

So much for sleeping safe in the caves tonight.

"How many are there? Is this the work of one beast?" asked Shay.

"Judging from tracks left at scenes like this, perhaps dozens or hundreds. The tracks are . . . strange. Some believe them to be birds; others think them furred predators. No one has explained the holes . . ." Her voice faded.

"We have to go back, find another way," said Shay. "We can't get clear through the canyon by dark. Look at how long the shadows are already!" Even he heard the near-panic in his voice, and it shamed him. *Oh, Cinny, I need you. You were always the strength I relied on.* Somehow, he had been braver, stronger, more competent with her in his life. He straightened his spine. *If only I could be in truth the man you always thought me.* He set his jaw, determined to get through this. No choice. He reminded himself of the Dark-damned axe, and of the mysteries awaiting him in the Crystal Mountains.

"It is farther back than forward,"" Bibi said. "I know the horses are weary, but we must ride as fast as possible until we are free of this place. Come." Without another glance at the corpse, she aimed Silence at the far end of the canyon and turned her loose. With a last, sickened look at the corpse, Shay followed her.

They ran. While they had footing, while energy remained, they ran, racing the advance of looming shadows.

Flea shied twice, nearly unseating Shay each time, and even Silence flicked her ears constantly. The rocks soon forced the pace slower, until Shay wanted to dismount and run on his own feet, just to feel he was making progress. The air thickened, curling sinuously down Shay's throat as he sucked in each breath. Imagination again. Nothing wrong with the air.

Something stirred the grass and bushes near Flea's hooves. The gray shied again, and Shay held on. He did not see what set the bush in motion, but kicked the horse even faster. He ducked at a twitter above his head, heart thudding. Flea shied again as a sparrow sped past.

Shadows draped the canyon floor. A piece of shadow detached.

Flea's hindquarters dropped suddenly, his head nearly striking Shay's face. As the screaming horse collapsed under him, Shay kicked his feet out of the stirrups and tucked his shoulder. He hit the ground and rolled to his feet, axe quivering in his hand. The world around him dulled and slowed as his mind tried to decipher what was happening.

He saw the mangler's sharp beak jab into the horse's rump, its gripping talons already drenched in blood. A pony-sized vulture with a big, ugly head–wrinkled, red and naked. But the shape was wrong, the beak straight and sharp, not hooked. And the wings . . .

Leathery, ribbed wings carried spurs on the joints, and dim canyon light filtered through the thin, translucent membrane. Not a bird at all. He staggered back, horrified and repulsed, as a second mangler landed on the horse's head, jabbing a vicious beak at the eyes.

Shay ducked away, unable to watch, and ran for his life. More manglers attacked Bibi, who clubbed them away as hard and fast as she could.

His axe. Shay had forgotten he held it. Adjusting his grip, he started for Bibi.

A mangler slammed into his back, knocking him down. He landed atop his axe. The smell of blood and rotten meat gagged him. The shock of the heavy blow held him in place. He screamed when the long beak stabbed into his shoulder, and again when stinging talons dug into his back. He rolled to throw the creature off and swung the axe upward. A thin wing bone crackled lightly as it snapped. He got to his knees, swung again. The wounded mangler leaped toward him, chittering madly. Its head flew off in a spray of blood and it staggered in circles, waiting to die.

Battle energy poured through him as he leaped to his feet and raced for Bibi. Half a dozen manglers swooped at her, clicking and chupping. She swung ceaselessly, but he saw bobbing red heads stab at her again and again.

That shrieking in his ears . . . his own voice? He felt his throat scraping with the force of his scream. With little control, he swung at the creatures, injuring two, which turned on him.

Still ahorse, Bibi cracked another mangler out of the air. Silence reared, attacking the creatures with teeth and hooves. Bibi was free. For the moment.

Seeing Shay on foot, she raised her gaze to where his horse lay under a mound of black and red. "Up!" She reached for his hand, and he landed behind her, somehow managing not to hit Silence with the axe.

Shay couldn't swing in such close quarters, but when Bibi crushed two more mangler skulls, he snatched her knife from her hip scabbard and stabbed upward at every creature that came within reach.

The last two veered and glided away.

They ran again, stumbling over stones and sliding on blood-slicked grass. Movement pulled Shay's attention as more manglers floated off a high ledge. The Eye touched the canyon rim, threatening death by shadows.

"We'll never make it," Shay gasped. He didn't know he'd spoken aloud, until Bibi's fierce voice answered.

"Yes. We will. I will not die here."

The thunder of hooves drowned out the strange, thick purring noise made by the pursuing manglers–a blessing to Shay. It allowed him to believe they had enough head start

61

to escape, to survive nightmare.

When the walls of the canyon turned, they rode into fading sunlight. The manglers circled and turned back into darkness. Truly, these were creatures of the Dark.

A moment later, the walls turned again, back into shadows. The canyon widened past the turn, but the lone mangler they saw floated far from them.

At last, as bloody streaks across the sky announced the demise of day, they rode out of the canyon onto a wide, flat plain. Relief flooded through Shay, washing away tension. It was over.

The wounds on his back began to burn.

Under a broad, black sky littered with stars, Shay lay face down on a blanket. Bibi cleaned his wounds while a small fire nearby heated water.

Barely aware, Shay moaned, struggled to turn onto his back, tried to thrash. Hands held him down, but their owner didn't understand. Every drop of water into the lower wounds seethed in agony. The shoulder wounds just hurt. Surely smoke arose from the grooves made by talons, the flicker of flames devouring flesh. He heard the crackle of their feeding, smelled the roasting of his skin, felt the acid bite of the water.

He screamed again and again, echoed by the nearby screaming of a woman, until he floated somewhere else. A ghostly figure danced like red flames, sharp talons extended. He watched the slow drip of pain, shrank back from its anticipated touch, screamed when it landed.

Red. A thousand shades of red flickered or wafted or waved languidly, hissing over his body. The figure cursed him, welcoming him to the Dark.

Pain shot through him, clenching at his body, consuming his soul. He burned, but with no Light-embracing fire. As his whole life had burned–and now his eternal death.

His screams died away with no energy left to sustain them. Lightning knives slashed the wounds deeper. He whimpered. Not much longer.

He faded at last into sleep, Cinny's soft hand stroking the hair back from his face. If he could have moved, he'd have turned his head to kiss the palm she laid on his cheek.

"Rest," she whispered. "All will be well. Sleep."

He obeyed, and time disappeared, returning only when he woke again an eternity later. He blinked, sense returning slowly. Pale gray light streaked the horizon, slowly drawing dawn after it. Safety. He inhaled a long, ragged breath, emerging at last from red nightmares. As he oriented himself to the world, he recognized them as delirium.

Groans of pain caught his attention and he turned his head the other way. Bibi lay curled in a ball, soaked in sweat, shivering. Surely victim to the same madness.

Shay had to try twice to turn over onto his back. When he succeeded, the pressure of the earth against the wounds made them ache, but at least they no longer burned. He sat up slowly, light-headed, and waited for the world to stop spinning.

Shay crawled over to see. Deep round holes on Bibi's upper back and left biceps closed his throat. He swallowed. Twice. Her scalp bled from where talons had tangled in her hair, piercing the flesh.

She seemed to sense him near. "Water . . ."

"No," he said. "No water." His voice felt scratched and raw. "I think the talons carry venom, and adding water makes it burn like hell. It should be okay for your shoulders, though."

She moaned, her voice hoarse. She dwelt in the delirium of her own hell.

So she'd know she wasn't alone, Shay spoke his thoughts aloud. "The round holes appear to be from their beaks, and the shredded wounds from talons. I think."

He wiped his face with one hand, hating his helplessness, filled with despair. "Is there anything in your kit to fight the poison?" Expecting and receiving no answer, he pawed through Bibi's pouch and found two small vials.

He examined the labels and shook his head. "I don't even recognize the language."

One by one he removed the wax seals and sniffed the contents, tipped a dot onto his finger, tasted. "I think this is pungis. I don't know the other one."

How to use it? Poultices, to draw the poison out, perhaps. How did the healers make a poultice, anyway? Aching with worry–and wounds–Shay applied the pink pungis directly to Bibi's shredded flesh. There wasn't enough to treat the beak holes, too, so he cleaned them with heated water, trying not to look at the older scars on her shoulders and back–wretched, ugly things. He didn't want to know how she'd gotten them.

If she died, he would be in desperate circumstances. He didn't know where he was, or how to find civilization. Little food, no knowledge of how to live off the land or how to find his way. A lifetime in the city hadn't prepared him for this. Bibi had to survive!

He sat back to watch over her and wait.

As dawn's bloody fingers stretched across the sky, she moaned.

Shay hovered, despairing.

She moaned again. Her eyes opened.

"Senesa? Are you with me? Wake up."

Slowly, awareness returned to dark eyes turned inward in pain. "I remember screaming," she said, her low voice a step above inaudible. "I remember both of us screaming."

She quieted for a moment, as if gathering the strength for more speech. "I screamed while I cleansed your wounds and could not stop."

"Shh. You don't have to talk right now." Shay wiped sweat from her brow. "Water makes the poison worse. I used pungis for your talon wounds, water only for the holes made by beaks."

But she didn't hear. She'd slipped back into sleep.

He hoped she slept.

Again, he watched and waited.

When she awoke a few hours later, Bibi stayed awake. She sat up slowly, drank the mug of tea with honey Shay handed her, and sat without moving, her eyes dull with pain.

Shay closed his eyes, exhaling long and slow, feeling the sharp twist and pull of his own wounds. They'd survived.

Now they could treat each other's wounds–and Silence's–until they could travel. He'd tended the mare's wounds as best he could, but she seemed to blame him for them, flattening her ears if he spread the pungis with too-heavy fingers.

They'd lost Shay's pack with his horse. The supplies and his stones would be missed, but at least he carried his best gems in his pockets.

The next day they went on. Part of the time Shay walked alongside the mare, sometimes Bibi did. Gradually, they recovered from the manglers, except for bad dreams.

Shay hated sleep, hated adding these new, awful images to the dreams of the woman and children he missed so badly. Sometimes mangler and murder dreams mingled. He awoke in a cold sweat, teeth chattering.

He was not alone with nightmares, though. He saw Bibi's restless sleep, heard her call out and wave an arm as if knocking a mangler from the air.

Even days later, Shay still kept a close eye on shadows, even though manglers didn't exist outside of their canyon.

7. Recovery

"Why are those men after you?"

Shay looked up at Bibi. "Does it matter?" He turned back to the task of oiling Silence's bridle, keeping his movements small to avoid pulling at his wounds.

"We have struggled together against hardship and death as comrades in arms. A struggle for survival is always paramount; under such duress, explanations become unimportant. But no danger threatens now. By this time, you trust me or you do not."

Memories flooded in. Shay fought them off, trying to hide from her the vast pain that shrank his heart. His tears caught in his throat. Unable to speak, he rose and walked away, stopping with his back to her. His face flushed, sudden sweat sliding down through his beard.

If he didn't trust Bibi by now, he never would. Shay took a deep, slow breath, blew it out in a rush. He spoke without turning. "It's the axe."

Silence behind him. He understood that she waited, letting him choose. He turned slowly, hating to face her, knowing he must. She deserved to know something of it. "They want my axe. It's unique and priceless."

He studied Bibi's calm face before returning to his seat again.

Staring at the small campfire, he spoke slowly, deciding as he went what could be shared and what mustn't. "I'm from Porphyr, Palernia's capital city, where I own–owned–a gem shop. My wife, Cinnabar . . ." His throat closed in grief, and he waited for it to open again. ". . . is from a wealthy family of gem merchants, from whom I purchased stones for my creations. She was her parents' eldest. I had nothing, except my talent and hard work.

67

When we married, her father underwrote my shop, believing I would soon make a name for myself, and sent his friends to me for their gemworks. As a wedding gift, he presented us with a family heirloom–the axe." He still didn't mention the ancient document next to his heart.

Bibi handed him a waterskin without speaking. He accepted it gratefully, allowing water to force open his tight throat. He handed it back.

"I realize now that, as the son, my wife's brother believed he would inherit it. But it's hard to believe he hated us so much he'd betray its existence to someone else. I know who it was–Tarver, a wealthy man who collects rare and unique objects, and Spinel's friend. It has to be.

"One night, not long ago . . ." Shay found he couldn't continue. His interlocked hands whitened as he stared at the ground between his feet until he regained his voice. "Spinel came in the night with two others, who murdered Cinny and our children before my eyes. I killed both of the thugs with the axe and fled. Since then, I've run." He didn't expect the sob that came with the words. "I would gladly have given them the axe to save my family."

No more. He couldn't do more. He couldn't speak. His head swung from side to side as if seeking escape. He couldn't cleanse his mind of the images, of his beautiful Cinny's throat opening, and the children, the blood, the screams . . .

The Dark-damned godtears moments, filled with sickly green. And tears.

Shay fled the campfire, walking as fast as he could. He didn't know where he was going and didn't care. The breeze of his passing couldn't dry his tears fast enough, and his tortured breathing sounded more like sobs. Twice, he tripped over rocks, once stepped into a depression that jarred him. He splashed through a stream, only realizing halfway across that he was wet.

When at last he stopped, drained physically and emotionally, he stood atop a rocky hill he didn't remember climbing. Below him lay a barren, rocky landscape, as jagged as the knife that had. . . He forced the thought away and sat on a smooth surface. Unheeding, he stared out over the shattered earth–not thinking, just sitting.

He sat there a long time, empty.

Shay discovered a benefit to baring his soul. He no longer worried about keeping things from Bibi. The remaining secrets weren't on display and could be kept easily. Her casual acceptance of his tale, with concern but no sympathy, helped.

Her questions the next morning didn't surprise him, as they touched on what he'd intended to tell the night before. She seated herself across from him while he rubbed oil into the axe head's cover, but he only waited, without looking up.

"You spoke yesterday of the axe, of how it is unique and priceless."

"I'll answer your questions willingly, but first I'd like a solemn and binding oath that what I tell you will go no further."

"Hold out your hand, Shay." Bibi drew her knife.

Suddenly uncertain, Shay did as she asked.

She brought out the packet of klovais and crushed a few pebbles with mortar and pestle. Then, quickly and lightly, she cut a diamond shape in his left palm.

He yelped in spite of himself, then took the knife and cut the same sign in her left palm.

Bibi rubbed klovais thoroughly into both wounds. "Do not wash the wound until it has healed. The scent will disappear soon, and the color will remain.

69

"Now swear."

Bibi swore an oath by the gods of the Sheethe. Shay swore by the Light, feeling an unseen precipice before his feet. And a strange sense of certainty.

"Will that suffice?" Bibi quirked an eyebrow in his direction.

"Yes, and more. Thank you." Shay lifted the axe across his palms for her inspection and took a deep breath. "The axe is made of black diamond."

Bibi looked it over. "I see no seams where the head and haft were joined."

"There are none. It was shaped from a single diamond of unheard-of size."

"One diamond?" Bibi asked. "It has no facets. How could it be shaped thus?"

"That's a mystery I'd like to solve," Shay said. "Cinny's family owned it for several generations, but they didn't have answers, either."

"How can an axe of diamond be used as a weapon without shattering?"

"Another secret I hope to discover. The axe is indestructible, and its fire isn't as brilliant as other diamonds, perhaps because of the darker color. Magic has to be involved."

"This is connected with your goal of reaching the Crystal Mountains, is it not?" Bibi ran a strong hand the length of the haft, tested the sharpness of one bit with her thumb, then sucked at the thin line of red that appeared.

Shay hesitated, mentally shrugged. "I suspect more black diamonds exist there, with a few samples I can study to learn how to shape them without facets. They would make exquisite gemworks, and perhaps unlock ancient secrets lost even to Cinny's family." He replaced the hood over the head. "You understand, now, why I'm so protective

70

of it."

Besides it being his only remaining physical tie to his family.

By midmorning they continued their journey, in no hurry now. Shay rode behind Bibi on Silence, whose wounds seemed no longer bothersome.

She twisted to speak to him. "You need a horse, and we need supplies. I have spent what I had. Do you have funds to assist with such purchases?"

She had asked before, but this time they had sworn an oath for the keeping of secrets. "I have a gem, Senesa, but I need a reputable gemsman to exchange it. It should buy a fine horse and provisions, with a little cash left for later." Oath or no, she didn't need to know the extent of the wealth in his pockets.

"So much for a single diamond?" Bibi's eyebrows lifted.

"Seastone, in this case. Value depends on the quality and size of the gem," Shay said.

Bibi looked impressed, but he couldn't be sure, with her. She was very good at locking her thoughts away from her face.

For the next few days, they bartered labor for food at widely scattered farms in the area. When they found no farms, they lived off the land. As usual, Bibi provided the expertise and Shay did the grunt work.

"It is the only reliable way to learn," she told him, when he became careless with his irritation.

They trained every evening. Shay learned to strike from any angle and any direction, switching his hands on the fly. She began showing him how to use her knife for fighting, too.

And always, they watched for the elusive Slipaway Trail.

71

At first, Shay welcomed the blending of rocky terrain into grasslands. Gradually the rocks disappeared, except for an occasional upthrust of blond and gray stone. He watched for signs of querk or agate among them.

As they rode, his discomfort grew. He wasn't used to such wide exposure to the brilliant Eye of the Light, so different from the casual glance of the Eye in the city. He felt it focus on him, examining him inside and out, picking at his soul.

His burned face and hands looked like rubies when he glimpsed himself in a stream—a searing sign that the Light had found him wanting.

He longed for the refuge of the city of Sarinta, which Bibi insisted lay in this direction, and at last he saw signs of it. A dusty crossroads intersected their way, and then they found the main road to Sarinta. Feeder roads joined this one with increasing frequency, and other travelers began to appear. Here a shabbily dressed man ambled with a tall, crooked staff and an ugly black dog. A shepherd looked askance at the black dog so near his small flock. There, a couple pushed a handcart laden with produce. Two fashionable young men in silks rode by on sleek horses, laughing and ignoring everyone else. A family with eight children and bare, dusty feet trudged drearily toward the distant gates. As Shay and Bibi progressed, the road increased in crowding and noise.

At last, colorful pennons on tall towers fluttered above the trees. Thick walls protected the city, their blond stone now near-black with dirt and smoke.

The gates of the city stood open—permanently, from the look of them. Excitement clutched at Shay and his energy pulsed with the city as they rode in.

"The fine artisans are down the street three blocks and left half a mile," Bibi said. "I will look for a place to stay, then come find you there."

He dropped off Silence's rump, and started in that direction.

He walked without looking past booths and open-air shops, slowing only as he reached more permanent establishments. Crowds thinned until most of the ragtag people had disappeared. Wealthier clientele strolled these streets, often with servants to carry their purchases. The farther he went, the finer the merchants themselves dressed. He stopped to examine the wares from time to time under the watchful gaze of the proprietors.

When he encountered edifices with professional guards stationed inside the doors, he slowed further, examining the wares in more detail.

Shay wandered past shops selling enamelware, beautiful glazed tiles for decoration, flooring, and mosaics. A juggler performed before a shop of superb fabrics and he stopped to watch for a moment. A plain-dressed man with a blocky jaw stared at him. A cutpurse, perhaps? Shay turned away, toward a trio of dancers who pulled colorful scarves through the air behind them. Proprietors hired such performers to draw custom to their shops, an idea Shay tucked into the back of his mind.

He saw tapestries, musical instruments, pottery, elegant iron scrollwork, blown glass goblets and vases, and leathers of many colors, soft as a fine lady's cheek. The shop selling screens of interwoven black and red bambu drew the eye with colorful whirligigs that spun in the lightest breeze. Two rough-looking men seemed lost in their conversation, but as he brushed past them, they watched him from the corners of their eyes.

He passed shoes and sandals begemmed and costly, scented perfumes and soaps that tickled his nose, combs of tortoiseshell or the eggshells of robins and meadowlarks,

73

fine swords, knives, and tableware, and a wide variety of wares Shay didn't even recognize.

Forgetting his rumpled, sunburned appearance, he entered the second of three gem shops, accompanied by a wary guard. He fingered his superb seastone without showing it, speaking with the proprietor at some length. It seemed to whisper to him, but he knew the slender thread of sound was only his imagination. A few minutes later, he exchanged his seastone for three generous bags of coin and a promise to offer future work for sale here, should he produce any.

He found Bibi in a different section of the enormous market and helped her with provisions: Rope, wires for snares, a few simple tools, two needles and thick thread, two waterskins, blankets . . . Shay stopped paying attention. Until they went to a local stable to replace Flea.

Shay immediately noticed a docile brown gelding. The horse looked at him, flicking a fly off his rump with his tail, before ambling toward a water trough.

"That brown one will do," Shay told Bibi. Such a complacent horse wouldn't challenge his meager riding skills and would undoubtedly cost less than the more energetic beasts in the pen.

Bibi looked at him. "No."

"Why not? He looks fine to me."

"You know nothing of horses. That one is old, half-crippled, and underfed. The stabler hasn't been able to sell it, so he cuts the horse's' feed to reduce the expense of keeping him."

"How can you know that by looking?"

"Experience." Bibi craned her neck, looking across the pen. Without explanation she climbed between the rails and approached several of the horses, running her hands down legs, checking eyes and teeth.

74

Why teeth, of all things? To see if they could bite, like he'd heard war horses would?

With a sigh Shay turned to watch the passersby, bored. This should be a lot simpler than Bibi was making it.

"I have your horse, Shay. Pay the stabler."

He jumped, so caught up in a child's whining he hadn't heard her.

By the Light! She thought *this* horse was right?

Much younger than the brown one, this one had a flamboyant red coat, not horse-red but spinel-red. Even softened by a blond mane and tail, he drew the eye.

Bibi patted the muscular neck and the horse tossed his head. "He is swift and strong, more compact than small, and he's willing. He's even-tempered, intelligent, and obedient. And surefooted. He will make a fine mount for you, better than any other horse here."

How could she know all that? He feared to ask, lest she actually tell him.

She also purchased a pack mule, to Shay's relief. He named it Bray.

Bibi named his horse Spark.

When they rode out of the city the next morning, three men stared after him. The same men he'd seen in the merchants' sector.

Under a rayed sky of pink and yellow, Shay squinted at a pair of tall trees standing alone in an field half a mile away. He grinned. "Is that the Slipaway Trail?"

For answer, Silence leaped into a run. Spark leaped after her as Shay leaned forward and, to his surprise, kept up with no trouble. He grinned in delight—a good horse to escape on! And then clenched his hands in apprehension that Spark might be too much horse for him.

Spark snorted and shook his head without a break in

stride. Shay relaxed his grip.

Two tall sentinel trees guarded the entrance to the trail. Vines wound up the trunks, covered with numerous small, colorful flowers like strands of faceted gems. Bibi led him onto the trail beneath thick overarching branches in full summer leaf. Tangled bushes filled all the space between and beyond the trees on either side, disappearing into impenetrable mist.

"What's beyond the brush?" Shay asked when they slowed to a more normal pace.

"No one knows," replied Bibi. "No one can get through it."

"Does that mist ever clear up, so we can at least see sky?"

"Not to the best of my knowledge. I've heard that the world ends beyond the brush. Just. . .gone. But we can see blue sky overhead, at least."

"How will we know where to leave the trail?"

Bibi rolled her eyes. "When we reach the end in a few hours, we will see what there is to see and decide if it might be close to our destination. If not, we turn about and come to this end and decide again. Or wait until it closes there and reopens elsewhere. I prefer riding to waiting. We do this until we find an opening that looks likely."

"So it could take longer than regular roads."

"Yes. Sometimes it does. Even so, any pursuers have lost us."

"Unless we meet them riding the other way." Shay's stomach gnarled. The trail had little room for a fight.

"I have never met anyone else on the Slipaway Trail. Nor seen signs of others' passage."

Shay glanced behind him. "I see our hoofprints just fine."

"You will not, when we ride the other way."

They rode in silence for a while before Bibi spoke again. "I do not mean to speak of things you would rather not, but I have a curiosity. You told me you left Porphyr within hours of your family's deaths. Did you have other family there to arrange their funeral rites? It seems strange to me that you would not be there for those rites."

How dare she! To ask a question so personal, so . . . intrusive!

Even he heard the stiffness of his reply. "I had no time to linger because others would come for the axe. Nevertheless, I did burn their bodies and prayed as they ascended to the Light, and that's the most important part of any funeral." His throat clogged with unshed tears and he struggled to push down the freshet of grief.

Bibi's hands clenched on Silence's reins; the mare pranced. The shock on her face didn't give Shay enough warning.

"You burned their bodies? Why would you desecrate them so hideously? How can they make their way to the blessed sphere without feet to take them there? How can they drink the sweet rose nectar of Paradise without tongues to taste it? Burning bodies dishonors the dead. Sheethe would not do that even to their enemies!"

"It is our way, those of us who worship the Light and spurn the Dark." Shay bit off the words to keep his anger from spilling onto Bibi. His jaw ached from clenching.

Eyes flashing, Bibi pulled ahead of him and rode alone, without looking back.

The first time they reached the far end of the Slipaway Trail, it opened onto sand dunes dotted with pale grasses. Shay even wandered among the dunes for a few minutes, surprised at his own boldness, since the trail could move at any time. Bibi seemed to think they'd have warning.

The trail opened next in the midst of lush forests, but

77

with no mountains in sight.

And as their old companionship slowly returned, Shay ventured a question of his own.

"How did you come to be a Sheethe warrior, Senesa?" he asked.

"My mother was a Sheethe, and her mother before her. The girl children of Sheethe warriors are raised as Sheethe warriors," she said.

"Are there no men in your society? Or are they all warriors of a different type than Sheethe? I've never heard of a single-gender society before."

Her beautiful smile displayed even white teeth. "The Sheethe are a society of their own, unlike any other. We fill all functions ourselves, with no men. And no women who are not Sheethe. We do not marry, but we sleep where we will. We cross-train with male troops in the area because, as a rule, men are larger and stronger. We need experience fighting them, learning to use our strengths and their weaknesses against them."

"What if a Sheethe warrior bears a son instead of a daughter? What happens to him?"

"Mostly they are given to their fathers. Men generally crave sons and welcome them. Where a father cannot take a son, or when the father is not known, the Sheethe may find a family willing to take him, or find a place for him in a religious order. After that, our sons are no longer a part of our lives."

Shay couldn't think of anything to say for a long moment. Then his horror spilled. "How could you? What mother could willingly give up a *child*, as if he were some trinket?"

"Do not judge me because your ways are not ours." Bibi's tone could have snapped his fingers with frostbite. Her eyes glittered like shards of black glass. Any closer to

78

her, he could not have met her gaze.

They rode in silence for a long while before Shay dared another question. "How did you end up at the Dainty Slipper, a businesswoman instead of a warrior?"

"Not instead of. In addition to. Being Sheethe is not a thing of choice, of coming and going. We are born Sheethe, we die Sheethe." She seemed to consider for a long moment, then explained, "I fell in love. I followed my lover here. It did not bother me he had a wife. Many men have lovers as well as wives. But he turned away from me, as if I were only a substitute for his bed when his wife was not there. As if I meant nothing to him."

That didn't sound like the sensible Bibi Shay knew. How much had that rejection changed her?

Shay listened to the mule grumble, trying to imagine Bibi in love.

"So I killed him." Bibi didn't look at him. Given the look on her face, he was glad of it.

8. The Crystal Mountains

Once again axe training occupied the evenings. In one session, Bibi showed him how to fall or drop with the axe, how to disarm an opponent with it, and how to use it from the ground.

Another evening, she told him, "*Every* surface of your weapon can be used, not just the sharp ones." She drilled him in using the haft to block, the head to thrust, the knob to butt an opponent ahead or behind.

She worked him hard to develop strength. "A normal axe does not weigh eight pounds," she told him, "only three or four at the most. Yet you must be as quick as a lighter weapon, or you will die. A lighter weapon will defeat a heavier weapon, not because it delivers a mightier blow, but because it delivers its blow first."

She showed him how to hook ankle, knee, or neck and yank the axe to himself.

Shay tried not to think too much about what happened to the enemy.

One morning, the trail opened atop a high, broad arch overlooking water far below. Travelers on foot, on horseback, in wagons followed its length like any other road, with a few still putting out their morning campfires before resuming their journey. One edge of the arch was just visible from within the confines of the trail.

"This is the land bridge," said Bibi. "I have crossed it three times, once almost swept from it into the sea by high winds."

Shay shuddered. "It's a bridge? I can't see the other side of it."

"I believe it is about a half mile across, so broad that the traveler seems to be on a normal road if they stay in the center. And it is several miles from one end to the other."

Wonder filled Shay. How could such a thing exist? He'd seen amazing landscapes from the trail, from burning mountains to burning sands. Things he'd never dreamed of. Things his life in Porphyr had never hinted at. What a place the world was turning out to be!

The next time, the trail opened to thick bambu gardens that obscured a white marble wall, and after that it opened on a busy city street, where people saw their sudden appearance and screamed.

Two days later, they saw a range of rocky, jagged mountains in the distance, sparkling in the sun.

"The Crystal Mountains, I believe," said Bibi, leading them out of the shady tunnel. "We will be there in a few days."

Shay stared at a light beaming from the mountains below a deep skystone firmament, where the Eye of the Light struck something shiny. Excitement sizzled through him. His destination, within reach at last! "Cinny," he breathed, so low Bibi couldn't hear, "I'm almost there. We'll have our answers soon." He felt her presence, as if she'd joined him for the climax of his journey.

He'd heard of the Crystal Mountains, of course, but nothing had prepared him for their stately beauty. They felt familiar, an exultant thrusting toward the Light. He hadn't even arrived, but already it felt like home.

The peaks drew him as a feast draws a starving man. He watched them as he rode, allowing Spark to follow Silence without interference. Sometimes a sharp crag glowed as the Eye struck light from its surface. Sometimes a mountainside reflected a bright spark of blue, pink, or yellow. Once, a fleeting flash of red almost blinded him.

His heart swelled with joy. Here lay an adventure for one like him! Excitement thrummed through him, as he imagined what might await him there. Especially the black diamonds–the gems that fevered his brain. So much to discover!

If only Cinny could see this! He wanted her by his side, discovering all of this with him. He wanted to point out the colors to his children. His joy dropped as suddenly as it had come. Loneliness swept through him, sharp enough to cut.

As they entered the foothills, Shay and Bibi began to see villages where uncut gems lay out on blankets along the streets. They encountered the most wretched dwellings first, still far from the peaks, but as they rose higher, so did the prosperity of the villages. Hopeful owners sat beside their wares, hawking the quality of their finds. In every one of the villages, after a single glance, Shay rode without slowing, disappointed. Perhaps they would find better in larger towns or cities, closer to the mountains themselves.

They encountered a village with a faded, weathered sign at the entrance: Hope. Someone had scribbled the word *Lost* at the top.

Moments later, he passed a worn woman, surely younger than she looked, with two small children, a boy and a girl. The woman gave him a tentative smile, hopeful and half-fearful. Something in the shape of the woman's face, the line of her jaw, reminded him of Cinny. Grief clutched at him. He stopped, sat a moment to get control of himself, then rode back and dismounted.

Bibi stopped to wait for him.

Fear flitted across the woman's face when she saw the axe, but her shoulders straightened and she looked him in the eye. Her meager collection lay on a worn, faded blanket. He glimpsed the frayed edges of a hole, just visible at one edge of the stone pile.

"Good morning, mistress," he greeted her as he

squatted at the edge of the blanket.

"You don't want hers," yelled someone across the road. "She got no man to gather for her, and her boy don't know nothing. Mine are the best, gathered with the knowledge of generations of gem merchants."

Shay didn't even look up, though he was pleased when Bibi turned Silence in the man's direction. With her neighbor scaring off her customers, no wonder this woman displayed such poor offerings. And no wonder she and her children appeared more ragged than most. "Please show me your best, mistress." He kept his voice low and gentle, to put her at ease if he could.

While she hurriedly sorted through the pile, Shay looked up at her children. Not so different in age from Piper and Beryl. His throat closed and he could barely breathe. He swallowed. "How old are you, boy?"

"Eight." The child stared at him wide-eyed. "But I know how to find the best gems. I go places the men don't fit." Despite a pinched, hungry face, the boy's bright eyes and yellow hair reminded Shay of his own son.

It hurt. He tried to ignore it.

Catching the alarm in the mother's eyes, Shay turned his attention back to her and the three stones she held. "What do you fear, mistress? I won't harm you or your children."

Her furtive glance across the road confirmed Shay's instinct. "Please, sir. My children are hungry. The men bully my son, chase him from the best hunting. So he hunts in perilous places, and they sometimes steal his stones from him before he gets home. These are my best. I'll sell them to you for whatever you'll pay." She held out the stones.

A woman without a man to take care of her led a hard life in any circumstances. This one's courage and determination to care for her children reminded him of

83

Cinny, too. Shay took the small stones and examined them. Their quality, when cut and polished, should be above average, if well below what he usually worked with. If these represented the everyday findings of the foothills he could expect some very fine stones higher in the mountains.

He looked up at the boy. "Which one do you like best?"

The boy looked at his mother, waiting for her reluctant nod. "None of those," he said, filled with a child's confidence. "I like this one best." He reached into his pocket. "No one else has seen it, so they can't steal it from us."

Shay shifted his feet to relieve some of the ache of squatting and held out his hand.

"It's still raw. We sell all our gems raw." The boy's tone parroted someone else. Likely he didn't understand what a "raw gem" was.

Then the boy dropped a chunk of gleaming stone into Shay's palm. Shay stared at the dark golden, translucent chunk–the color of his son's hair. As if punched in the heart, he fell over to sit straddle-legged in the dirt. "Beryl," he croaked. Emotion flooded him, trickling sweat from every pore.

"Is that what it is? I don't know the names of things. Do you like it?"

His son's namesake and color. "Do you have any others like this?" He didn't look up.

"Only what's here," the mother said. "We don't know the names of many of them. My husband died, and no one else will teach us."

Oh, my son. What if you were in this child's place? Shay looked at the meager pile of stones on the blanket. "I'll take them all," he said. "Mind, boy, you must work harder than ever to replenish your supply of stones, so that you

84

may serve other customers as well as you have me." He stood, closing his hand about the beryl, feeling–or imagining–its warmth. The color and warmth of the sun, of the Light. He chose to take the stone as an omen.

He paid the woman twice the stones' value and packed them with care into Bray's packs. Except the golden beryl, already dubbed his "son stone," which he carried in a pocket.

Bibi turned away from the rude man across the road and led Silence over to him, looking vaguely pleased. "I enjoy bullying a bully," she said, eyes dancing.

The little girl stared at her, round-eyed. Well, a woman warrior would surprise anyone.

"Did you find what you needed, Shay?" Bibi asked.

"I found a treasure." Shay made sure the boy could hear. He watched pride glow in the child's eyes–and his mother's.

Bibi winked at the boy's sister, who watched solemnly, finger in her mouth and dirt on both cheeks. Then the Sheethe warrior sprang lightly to Silence's back. The mare reared high, front hooves pawing the air, mane and feathers flying.

Without prompting, Spark joined in the prancing and head tossing, though he had no feathers to show off. Shay fought to calm his horse enough to mount, but the children's delighted laughter was worth the effort.

He reined over toward the boy. "If I can, when I finish my business, I'll come back through and teach you the names of the stones." With a smile and a wave, he rode after Bibi, hoping he'd made life easier for the family, for a little while.

A mile down the road, he realized he hadn't even asked the boy's name.

9. Ledge

Shay rode with one hand in his pocket, clutching the golden beryl, rubbing it with his thumb. Its feel brought a pang to his heart, but it brought a smidgen of comfort, too.

As they drew closer to the mountains, he noticed an occasional worker searching for crystals along streambeds and slopes. Many others surely hunted back in the foothills, in hidden places. These villages appeared more prosperous, and he saw an occasional gem worth more than a small coin or two. He purchased none of them.

The hills rose more steeply along a road so rutted and worn it could barely claim the name. Jutting granite shelves and gray rounded boulders glinting with mica outlined the road and spread into fields of grasses and wildflowers.

Bibi dropped back to ride next to him. "The same three men have been behind us since noon yesterday. No, do not look back."

Shay arrested his head's movement.

"They disappear from the road when we stop, then reappear wearing different clothes."

"Are you sure it's the same men? If they look different, perhaps they are different." Shay's thumb rubbed the beryl harder.

Bibi shook her head. "The horses are the same."

She led the way into a stand of rocks and scrubby trees, dismounting inside a cluster of tall granite boulders. "This time we marred the pattern. We will see if they bypass us."

"And if they follow us in here?" asked Shay, dismounting beside her.

"If they are not normal travelers, we should see them searching for us as they ride. We can watch through the gaps between rocks without their knowing."

Shay leaned against the shielding rocks, peering through a likely view hole. "They're coming, about half a mile away and in no hurry."

"So they could be normal travelers." Bibi spoke slowly, as if thinking aloud. "What does your gut tell you, Shay?"

"I think my enemies have found us again."

"From here forward, I do not know the way better than you, but I do know mountains. With your permission, I will continue to pick the path. If you cannot keep up, whistle."

Shay's gut tightened. He'd better keep up then, because he doubted she'd hear his whistle more than twenty feet away.

Bibi rode Silence to the back of the rock jumble, turned to her left, and disappeared, a hoof at a time. The sound of hoof against stone rose up the slope behind the rocks.

Spark pranced, ready to go, and Shay followed, aware that Bibi's slow progress meant difficult footing. He dreaded the next few hours.

The Crystal Mountains loomed. Shay tipped his head far back to see the tops of the nearest peaks, watching for bright sparks as the Eye touched color, wondering what gem each represented. This range was fabled for the richness and diversity of its gems, and he salivated at the thought of finding them.

Then he stopped watching the sparks and attended the path—or rather, the lack of one.

Bibi attacked the most difficult trails possible on a mare who flew up the rocks with ease, but Shay's breath caught in his throat as he envisioned Silence slipping and falling back into him. He stayed well back, but not even a

87

dozen lengths would help if the mare fell.

Soon perspiration salted his lips and the smells of warm horse and leather clogged his nostrils as they climbed. Hooves striking stone couldn't be softened or disguised, but the grunting and snorting of the hard-working animals would rise, as sound does. Maybe those below wouldn't hear them.

Bibi turned right to ride around the tall hill, rather than up. He followed her onto a broad ledge, staying as far as possible from the precipitous drop to his right.

A few minutes later, they dismounted to give the horses a breather.

Without the noise of their movement, the world seemed preternaturally quiet. Shay blocked out the sounds of the horses' breathing and listened to the pristine silence below a sky the color of darkest skystone, shading to lazh directly overhead. He began to calm inside to a peace rarely available in the city.

As his breathing slowed, he heard the hooves far below.

Bibi curled her toes over the edge and stared down the perpendicular hillside. She cursed.

Calm shattered, Shay looked down where she pointed, careful to stand well back from the edge. Three riders, tiny with distance, crept up the hill.

They remounted and renewed their ascent.

Bibi disappeared.

Off the easy path again, to hide their progress and slow their pursuers. Shay followed her up a steep, rocky cleft, not looking down. She must be insane! Fear dried his mouth.

They made it to leveler ground, still tilted upward. Shay slowly released a long, deep breath and followed Bibi along the narrow ledge.

He'd hardly settled onto the new surface when Bibi stopped.

"Back up! Back up!" She glanced behind her–at the trail, not at him–and all around.

"Back up where?" His dry mouth made his voice raspy. He couldn't go back down that chute. Up had been all he could handle.

"There is nowhere to go forward and no room to turn up here. Go back!"

Shay dismounted, legs trembling. The wall of boulders to his left provided no extra room, and on the right a sheer drop-off dizzied him until his stomach rolled. A horse couldn't back up here, either; he'd have to turn around. But he had too little ledge for it.

Hands shaking, he dropped Spark's reins to the ground. He walked back to the mule, took his time turning it in place, and led it back past the slot they'd come up. He found a place to anchor the lead rope and returned to his horse.

Trying to project confidence to Spark, Shay turned his horse around in the too-small area while fear sweat nearly blinded him. Spark didn't like it, either, shuffling his hooves constantly to make the turn.

Shay's foot landed half off the edge. His balance tipped outward. He teetered over emptiness. Far below, jutting boulders and steep slopes of loose rock punctuated the drop. Death awaited him here. He closed his eyes. *I'm coming, Cinny.* But his head spun and his eyes popped open again. Spark threw up his head and pulled back on the reins, haunches down and eyes rolling. It was enough to tip Shay's balance back to solid ground. His legs couldn't hold him up and he fell to his knees. He knelt there until he could breathe again, before leading Spark to the anchored mule.

Then he turned toward Bibi, trapped at the top. Dread filled the pit of his stomach and perspiration his palms as he watched, unable to look away.

Bibi's mouth set and eyes widened into a fearsome, determined aspect.

Silence rose on her hind legs. She spun in place, golden forelegs and feathers pawing the air. Bibi clung to her back like a tick above the sheer drop. Then the mare's front feet landed safely on the ledge.

As nonchalant as if this happened every day, horse and rider returned to Shay.

As Bibi started to lead the way up another slope, Shay called, "Wait!"

He walked up the ledge Bibi had just left. Here he pulled a thread from his shirt and caught it in a crack in the rock. A little farther, he scraped a noticeable scar on another. He walked almost to where Bibi had been trapped before leaving a few bright horse hairs.

When he returned and mounted without speaking, the approval in Bibi's eyes warmed him, though she didn't speak. Then she found another way up, still steep and difficult, but somehow less harrowing than it would have felt an hour earlier.

When they stopped higher up to catch the horses' breaths, Shay saw the ledge again, now far below. Their pursuers were making their slow way along it. They found the clues Shay had left and followed the ledge to its end.

Their voices drifted up the mountainside as they argued, trying to find a way forward. The second and third riders managed to turn their horses, although one nearly stepped off the ledge.

The leader was trapped where Bibi had been. His horse, however, wasn't Silence and didn't make the turnaround. Shay wrapped his arms around his head and ducked away from the screams of man and beast, like the shattering of diamonds amid the clatter of falling rock.

Nothing had prepared him for the horror of that sound, or his sudden sympathy for his pursuers.

Bibi murmured to Silence as they listened. He didn't know the language she spoke, but the tone described her appreciation to the extraordinary horse.

Extraordinary rider, too, Shay thought, sick to his stomach.

They did not see their pursuers again, although Bibi checked their back trail often. Still, she continued up steep, dangerous trails, some apparently carved out by mountain goats. Several times they had to lead their horses through the shattered terrain.

When at last they paused in a broad meadow, Shay leaned his head against Spark, grateful for the horse's surefootedness, convinced that had he ridden Flea, he'd be dead now.

Shay and Bibi rode into a broad canyon with a young river dashing madly through it, flinging white water against the rocks in its path.

An interesting jumble of stones by the river caught his eye. They had most likely washed up over time, perhaps hidden entirely during high water.

"Let's break near those rocks," he said. "I just saw an interesting flash of color there."

Bibi shrugged. "It is as good a place as any. And who knows what we may find?"

Shay soon lost himself in the possibilities of stone. A number of querk specimens lay scattered throughout the jumble, as expected, giving some hope of amyth or other colored stones. He pulled aside several rocks to reach for a dark, squarish one mostly hidden underneath.

"Watch out for snakes."

Shay jumped, snatching his hand back. He'd been

concentrating so hard, he hadn't heard Bibi join him. "Snakes?"

"They like hidden places, and they do not like being disturbed."

He stared at her for a long moment. "How should I proceed?"

"Reach in with this first, instead of your hand." She held out a stick.

He accepted it and poked around the nearest rocks before moving them.

Bibi craned her neck, watching. "What do you expect to find?"

"Whatever's here. There's a lot of querk, which opens the possibility of amyth, citrine, agate, and so on. Or I might find something unrelated and unexpected."

"Such as?"

Shay only half heard. He stared into the shadows at that angular piece . . . Remembering, he poked his stick around before reaching in and closing his fist about it. Excitement bounced his heart against his ribs.

Larger than his fist, the stone seemed to explode into sparks. Its surface exhibited the deep, true blue of midnight, accented with specks of golden color. A sound soft as a butterfly wing touched him and his lips turned up in amusement at his own imagination.

Next to him, Bibi's breath stopped. "Are those gold flecks?"

"Fool's gold," Shay said. "Lazh, and a very fine example, indeed. A top quality lazh is more costly than skystone." He picked up a smaller piece, apparently broken off from the one he held, and slipped it into his pocket. He wrapped the larger piece carefully and stowed it on the mule–lazh material was too soft to carry unprotected–after Bibi had admired it at length.

Shay's find stimulated enthusiasm in his companion. Bibi combed the rocks with as much energy as he did. "Shouldn't we find more lazh near the first one?" she asked after a few minutes spent pawing rocks aside.

"Not necessarily. If this one was deposited by the river, there could be more in the area somewhere, but we may have to dig for it." Shay picked up a knobby globe. "I wonder . . . this could contain amyth, citrine, or agate, but I don't have saws to cut it open."

"Should we attempt to break it open" asked Bibi, glancing around for a hammer stone.

Shay shuddered, picturing a thousand tiny gems scattered across the ground. "I'd rather open it properly, to maximize the value, if any."

That night, he kept his axe covered as Senesa drilled him on broader tactics for axe fighting. He had difficulty concentrating, with the lazh on his mind—and the black diamonds. How close was he to those gems? Where, in all these mountains, did he look?

"Repeat to me what I have just said." Senesa Bibi glared at him.

He stammered, trying to make something out of nothing, but he had no idea and could only stare, wide-eyed and stupid.

"A warrior," she said, "focuses *always* on the important. She—he—blocks out the unimportant, refuses to admit the unimportant until the battle ends. Even training is dangerous. I once watched a woman cut her own toe off when her thoughts strayed. With that cut, she became ordinary, no longer Sheethe." Bibi's voice dripped contempt. "Discipline is required—discipline over your mind which controls your body. If you cannot control your thoughts, you cannot control your weapon—or your enemy."

Shay withered under her lecture. If he'd had Spark's

ears, they'd have drooped. Taking a deep breath, he focused harder. But his thoughts soon drifted back to the gems waiting to be found. He thanked the Light for the hood when the axe bounced off his shin, leaving a bright bruise.

Bibi gave up with a disgusted snort. "In the morning. Before breakfast. Before even thinking about the stones. While your mind is still fresh and clean. At that time, we will combine today's training with tomorrow's. I will wake you at first light."

And she did.

"Dead?" Tarver's eyes narrowed, his jaw thrust forward. "What do you mean, dead?" His voice lowered, gravelly and menacing. "That was one of my best trackers." His fingers turned white on the arms of his favorite chair.

Spinel stiffened. "Tracking wasn't the problem, Tarver. They got close enough to see Shay Bladen's party above them. Several hundred feet straight up. Your tracker followed them right to the end of the trail before he fell off the mountain."

He didn't like this room, especially standing while Tarver sat behind the desk. This room was plain, unornamented, with polished dark woodwork and a neutral-colored, if expensive, carpet. It held no warmth or friendliness. In this room, Tarver meant business.

"Fell off the mountain." Tarver's voice flattened.

"That's what his men told me."

"How did Bladen manage and he didn't?"

"Shay wasn't in front, where the trail ran out. Your tracker was." Spinel winced at the string of oaths–the ugliest, most vile he'd ever heard.

"Who does ride in front? Who does he follow?"

"Some muscly black-skinned woman. Looks like a man, rides like a man, and fights like a man. I don't know who she is."

"Tell me the rest."

"May I sit?" He had ridden long and hard to get here, without even stopping at home to bathe and make himself presentable. Tarver should have invited him to sit and offered at least a drink, if not food, as well. Tarver was born common; it showed in his lack of courtesy.

"No, you may not sit!" Tarver roared, eyes bulging. He leaped up from the seat behind his desk and leaned on his fists. "You can sit when you're on your horse, going back to the mountains. Why did *you* come, instead of sending someone?"

Spinel ran a hand through his stubby hair and licked dry lips. "I can ride better, I have a faster horse, and I wanted you to have accurate information as swiftly as possible. Your men foundered their horses to reach me quickly, as this is a matter of some urgency."

"Or a matter of some stupidity." Tarver leaned closer, took a long, slow breath through his nose, nostrils expanding. The volume of his voice dropped. "You weren't in too much hurry to stop at a tavern or two, were you?"

Spinel could never tell how Tarver's voice would sound when he opened his mouth. It made him jumpy. He shivered, his throat closing. Tarver's my friend, he reminded himself. He can be very dangerous, but he won't hurt *me*. "I filled a waterskin with wine and another with ale. I drank those as I rode, rather than water." Tarver had no way to disprove it. After all, Spinel had done it before.

Tarver stood straight, his eyes calculating. For a long time he didn't speak, only glared.

Spinel shifted his feet, tried to find something else to look at.

Tarver's disbelieving snort jerked Spinel's gaze back up to meet his.

"How many men have died pursuing Bladen?" He sat and leaned back, fingers steepled.

"Six? Eight?" Spinel relaxed. His friend had calmed down–not that this made him any less dangerous, of course. "Somewhere in there."

"Two in his house the night you ran away–without the axe. Two more who chased him from Porphyr, two more to replace them, and then three men! One more in that damned tavern, found with the bodies of some locals. One more down the road from there." Tarver ticked off his fingers, his gaze pinning Spinel's. "And now one more. How many is that, Spinel?"

"Twelve."

"What would you recommend we do?"

Spinel could feel the trap settling into place but couldn't see it or how to avoid it. "Lie in wait for him, rather than pursue, perhaps?"

"Excellent idea. If we know where he's going. What assignment did I give you?"

The trap had just sprung. Spinel swallowed, licked his lips again. His voice croaked. "To go directly to the Crystal Mountains, get ahead of him, and wait. To anticipate and cut him off."

Tarver heaved himself to his feet and came around his desk, toward Spinel. "Now, see?" he boomed happily, his arms opening wide. "That wasn't so hard, was it? And here, you've been acting like you're afraid of me."

The grin disappeared as one beefy palm cracked loudly against Spinel's cheek.

His head spun, pulling his body with it. He staggered into the wall with a crash, staying on his feet only by pushing his back against it hard.

Tarver wrapped his hand in the expensive silk of Spinel's shirt and twisted so hard the smaller man could barely breathe.

"You should be terrified of me." Tarver's mouth twisted. Thick brows met in the middle, above his nose. "So far, you've bungled every task. You're as drunk as you are stupid, and apparently both conditions are permanent."

Tarver leaned in. Spinel felt warm breath on his cheek. Once again he had complied with Tarver's will: He *was* terrified, afraid to move, to open his eyes, to breathe, to twitch. His jaw hurt like hell. Maybe Tarver had broken it.

"What do you think your men are doing, while you're here?" Tarver whispered. "Do you think they're where you left them two weeks ago, watching for Bladen?" His voice rose to cannon-level, spittle peppering Spinel's face. "Will you even *know* where they are and what they're doing while you're gone?"

Spinel winced, from the spray and the voice.

Tarver released him and turned away. "You disgust me. Leave. Now."

Spinel already had his hand on the door when Tarver stopped him. "Oh, Spinel. Put together fifteen or twenty armed men and leave *immediately* to complete your task. Added to the men awaiting your return, you should have more than enough men. And lay off the drink. If I catch you drinking before the axe is mine, you'll beg for an easy death."

Spinel yanked the door open and ducked out of it, dignity forgotten, hands trembling as much as his legs. He stumbled away from Tarver's fine house, eyes searching desperately.

His mouth felt like paper. He needed a drink.

Fortunately, the only place to find toughs was a tavern. Tarver would get over his anger. He always did.

Smug at outsmarting his good friend, Spinel gathered over a dozen men from the nearest drinking house, a ramshackle wooden building with old bloodstains soaked into the wood near the door. By the time he'd buddied up to a number of men, bought drinks for all of them, and selected the ones he wanted, his head buzzed pleasantly. He wobbled out to his horse, then needed three tries to get his foot into the stirrup, cheerfully joining in the general laughter at his own expense. That's how these friendships were cemented, so it didn't bother him at all.

Spinel didn't care that dawn broke well before they left the city. He was a man. He could decide for himself the urgency of his errand. Tarver was his friend, not his employer.

"Hey, Spinel," one of his hired men called as they started down the road. "There's a shorter way to get there."

"Which way is that?" Spinel allowed his morning-after surliness to show.

"There's a little town about halfway there, and just beyond that, if you know the back ways, there's a long canyon . . ."

Spinel drew himself up. "Yes, I know of it. It's shorter, but Mangler Canyon is deadly."

The man laughed. "Are you afraid of it? Nobody's ever reported seeing a mangler. It's just an old story."

Spinel had sobered up–somewhat–as they rode, and their laughter angered him. But every one of these men was bigger and meaner, and he prided himself on knowing his limits. "It's only shorter if you survive," he said. "We go the long way."

His men looked at each other, and Spinel thought he saw one of them nod ever so slightly. *He* was giving these men permission to follow Spinel's orders? They must be old friends, even brothers. Now, that made sense. The bigger, stupider one who laughed took his cues from his older brother. When he thought of it that way, Spinel felt pretty good. He had someone to enforce his orders, underscore his leadership. He named the man his official second-in-command; the cunning eyes and weasel chin made him look dangerous enough the men would obey him.

Now he just needed to listen closely, to find out the man's name. Obviously, he couldn't remember from introductions inside a noisy tavern. Come to think of it, he should probably learn all their names and use them liberally—the mark of a good leader.

He took a swig from a skin containing a violent liquor from the Kingdom of the Snows, the traditional enemy of Palernia. The barbarians sure knew how to distill liquor. Imagine, a whole nation of sots, drinking this stuff from their mothers' tits. He'd heard that this "joos" was what made them such hard, violent men. Spinel's throat burned, and for a moment he couldn't breathe past the liquor fumes.

At least this stuff was cheap. And it would get him drunk quickly.

10. Tauz Pillars

Shay swung his axe hard and stopped it exactly right, the head quivering without dipping. His axe work was improving quickly, thanks to the plethora of gems to be found. Bibi insisted on equal time: for every hour spent searching for gems, they spent an hour in training.

Gem hunting usually came first because they needed daylight to comb through rocks and sift through dirt, gravel, or sand. Training could be done by firelight. Bibi had harvested a handful of gems–emrel, citrine, beryl, godtears, amyth, and others. Shay, more particular, had six fine specimens, all too large for his pockets.

He frowned as he swung the axe again. Where were his pursuers? Spinel and Tarver would never abandon the chase without the axe. He knew it with a fear that simmered down his nerve endings.

This evening they worked on something Bibi called a "form," a specific pattern of movements that incorporated a variety of weapon strikes and techniques. He didn't know the form well enough for her to explain the meaning of its moves yet, but he remained hopeful. His footwork felt sloppy, but at least he forgot none of it.

"Shay, your mind is not on what you are doing. You cannot divert your attention, even for a moment, when working with a weapon. I have spoken of this before. Heed me.

"Remember, everything you have goes into the form. Every time. If you hold back the tiniest bit of yourself, you have not done it correctly."

She ended the session and Shay, drenched in perspiration, headed to a nearby stream for a bath. The shallow water made bathing more of a chore than usual, but also gave him an unexpectedly clear view of his own body. Startled, he examined it. Soft gemsman muscle had hardened. He didn't have a warrior's rock-hard, well-defined muscle, but he'd become leaner and more solid. He ran his hands down the soft, flat hair on his chest, to his belly's new, faint ridges.

Longing struck him. Cinny would have such fun with this. They both would. He missed her more than ever this morning, missed making love to her, sharing and joining their bodies. He allowed himself to become lost in sensual memories, his hands moving as hers would have, seeking release.

Later, hair still damp as he relaxed by the campfire, he reached into his shirt, next to his heart. The parchment packet blew out of his hands when he withdrew it, but he snatched it out of the breeze before it got away from him, pleased at his quick reflexes. He spread out the note to read yet again. By now he knew every word by heart, but he still searched for any clues or insights he might have missed.

Nothing.

He found himself looking at Bibi in a new way, though. When she caught him examining her stringy curves from across the campfire, he hastily looked away, pretending to examine the note again. But his attention remained on Bibi and the smug line of her mouth.

He was careful not to do that again.

If I were to settle in the Crystal Mountains, I could do much worse than this valley, Shay decided as they rode. Heavy with long grasses and colorful wildflowers, the valley sat peacefully in the bottom of a bowl formed by old, worn peaks and a blue-sky lid. A wide, bustling mountain stream flung itself over rocks near the small town of Echo, which nestled in one lush corner of the valley. The town appeared large enough to be self-sufficient. Rows of wheat and corn combed the floor of the bowl near Echo, with other crops he didn't recognize.

He and Bibi rode down a dusty but well-kept street. Neat shops and houses lined the main street, and gardens brightened some of the homes. All the buildings were stone, some whitewashed, most with wooden roofs trimmed in blue or yellow or green and slanted to one side to shed rain. A well-kept place, he thought, where the residents took pride in their town.

"If we can find a tavern," said Bibi, "we can obtain information."

"I don't see any, do you?"

She shook her head. "Just one half a mile back, well out of town. It is dilapidated, perhaps even abandoned. What a pity, for such a lovely town."

"How about the dry goods store up ahead, then?" He led the way there.

The proprietor replenished their supplies and, when Shay asked, gave directions to the bloodstone pillars, only a dozen miles away at the foot of Blue Mountain. Shaking his head, he warned them the way passed through a canyon filled with tauz. "It's a strange sort of place, and people don't like to go there much. Some who do never come out."

Shay barely heard the warning. Excitement trickled through him. The long journey had an end, and everything he sought hovered just beyond the horizon.

Everything he sought, but not everything he wanted. What he wanted most was lost forever. He looked around at the elegant, carved-out landscape. Cinnabar would have loved it here. His children would have run and played, skinned their knees and elbows, made friends with the other children in this town, and joined him in the search for gems. Eventually, Beryl would have handled all the searching and

102

much of the cutting, and someday taken over the shop. Shay tried to picture his son as a young man. That led to images of Piper as a young woman, and Cinny as an old and gray grandmother. That one he couldn't manage. To him, his wife would be eternally young and beautiful.

While Bibi spoke with the proprietor, Shay walked out into the valley a little ways, into the area that looked to be a favorite playground for children. Scruffy little boys and big-eyed little girls ran, jumped, and turned somersaults and cartwheels under the supervision of older children who were barely more circumspect in their joyous behavior. Two of the children ran circles around each other, yelling just to hear their voices echo off the mountains.

The wildflowers nodded at him as he waded through them. He saw red, purple, three different yellow flowers, an orange one, some blue, and a wide variety of white flowers. Even speckled flowers farther out. Their scents mingled gently, sweet and dusty and sharp. He drew in a long, slow breath through his nostrils, eyes almost closed to concentrate on them.

Shay smiled, his heart lightening for the first time since . . .

A brief pang tugged briefly on his heart and let it go.

In his head, laughing jade eyes danced under red hair. Cinny had always loved the flowers he brought her, whether from one of Porphyr's twelve public gardens or the side of the road. He swallowed, missing her so much it hurt. Not grief, not like it had been, but just . . . missing her. And the children. He forced down the pain while trying to leave the memories clear and bright.

And after I find the black diamonds? After I learn the axe's secrets? What then? Build another shop, return to my old life? Without my family?

In this town, in these mountains, it might be possible.

If he could bear to rebuild. Memories would not be kind to him here. No man could recover the past, and every day in that shop would remind him of all he'd lost.

So cold a future, but the best he could hope for. Life no longer appeared as black as the Dark, but gray felt almost as bleak.

Too soon for such thoughts. He'd lost Cinny, Piper, and Beryl only two months ago and his heart's wounds remained raw. This decision could not–should not–be made now. Perhaps after he knew the axe's mysteries would be the time. If ever.

Life held too many ifs.

He stroked the golden beryl, his "sonstone," burying himself in the comfort it brought. Especially the memory of his son's laughing face.

"Do you know," said Bibi thoughtfully as she joined him, "these people could use a good tavern. When we finish your quest, I may return here to explore possibilities."

Shay felt a sharp constriction in his chest. So soon? He'd always known they traveled together only for a while, but this felt too sudden. He'd grown used to her being there. He should have been more prepared, guarded himself better from another abandonment. His parents. Every so-called friend of his childhood. Cinny and the children. Now Bibi.

"Stay if you like," he said, too abruptly. "I don't need a nursemaid." So cold, that voice. Yet he couldn't find the words to apologize–even seeing the quickly-lidded surprise in her eyes.

Her face turned hard, but he didn't remember seeing it change. Maybe it hadn't. Maybe he'd only imagined her reaction.

He turned away and mounted for the final leg of his journey, already hurting from being alone again. As if she left him, when he was the one riding away. He refused to look back, mortified by his reaction.

A quarter mile down the road, he heard running hoofbeats, and Silence caught up.

She put the mare across Spark's path, forcing him to stop. "You have the right to put me aside without cause, though it is poor courtesy for one who has endured hardship alongside you. But I would know your reasons."

He wanted to be angry, the only way he'd be able to look her in the eye. Instead, he felt small and mean-spirited. Why was he acting like this? He ran a hand through his hair, scrambling for a way to repair the damage.

He shrugged. "You're the one who wanted to stay." That wasn't what she'd said, but he couldn't find different words.

He rode around her at a walk, then stopped. Idiot, to let it end like this. He looked back. "I suppose you want to see what's at the end of the trail, too. If you insist, then come on."

She turned Silence to ride next to him. "Why are you angry with me?"

Shay glanced at her. "I'm not," he said. "No longer, at least. Please forget I spoke."

To his surprise, the hardness drained away and she nodded at him once, briefly. As if she understood him, when he did not.

Only hours later, they rode into a broad canyon that couldn't exist.

Tauz. Everywhere, bared to an Eye that struck blindingly bright bursts of gold from the surface. The crystals filled the canyon, like a gigantic geode split open to expose its belly.

Boulders crusted in tauz, fields strewn with it, translucent prisms of pale yellow, as if the gems absorbed

105

sunlight's warmth and color.

Then Shay and Bibi curved around an arm of crystal and found a wilderness of pillars–pale yellow, yellow-orange, and true gold.

Tall, blazing in the Eye of the Light, resonating with the earth, some pillars reached perhaps twenty feet high. Shay dismounted and wandered among the obelisks and pillars, the earth singing under his feet. Did he feel or hear it? He wasn't sure. Then he scoffed at his agile imagination.

He laid a hand against the sleek, glassy side of the largest tauz pillar in sight, glowing with a pure gold color never matched in Shay's experience. He dubbed it the grandfather pillar. Gazing at the noon sun through the tauz showed him a gold purer than the findings and chains in his old workshop. His heartbeat sped up.

Then his hand began to sink into the stone. With a yelp he snatched it back, staring at the stone in horror.

"Magic," breathed Bibi in awe. She placed her own hand against the smooth face and watched it sink in, up to the wrist.

"I don't think that's wise," Shay told her.

"It feels good, cool and snug."

Uneasy, Shay looked the pillar over carefully. "Look down. This pillar eats living things."

Near the base lay the bones of animals. A few more stuck straight out of the solid gem. Kneeling, Shay saw the faint outline of more bones inside the stone, just beneath the surface.

"Get out of there, Bibi," he yelled.

Bibi yanked her hand. It didn't move. She tried again, a slow, gradual pull. Again, nothing.

"Trapped," said Shay needlessly. "Now what?"

"I can feel it pulling at me." Bibi's voice remained impossibly calm.

Hands shaking with fear of the crystal's strange magic, he grasped her arm and added his strength to hers in a firm, steady pressure.

"Do not break my arm!"

Under his feet, the earth still sang a light, frolicsome melody, but the pillar's hum changed, dropping to a low, eager note, as hungry as if it had not feasted for centuries. "We have to get you out now!" He saw the distorted image of her arm inside the tauz, now halfway to the elbow.

Frantic, he redoubled his efforts, but still nothing happened. Bibi appeared calm, but fear enlarged her eyes. He wondered if anyone had ever seen fear there before—one of those stray thoughts he didn't need right now.

"Turn your face away from the stone," he told her. The cover came off the axe head.

She twisted her face away and squeezed her eyes shut.

Shay raised the axe and swung it into the golden surface. The shock ran up his arms, and he felt the scream of the pillar, screeching across his nerve endings. Shards flew like chips of sunlight, one imbedding itself in his forearm. He swung again, and again, with all his might.

The pillar shattered, tumbling with a roar into a pile of rubble, exposing the bones of half a human hand near the top of the pile.

Bibi snatched her hand back and jumped away from the tauz as it fell. She cradled the hand against her chest as she staggered back. Small red gashes peppered her skin, and her hand was a deep, bruised purple with a long gash reaching from her thumb past her wrist.

The beautiful melody of crystals in sunlight had changed. Shay dropped the axe and fell to his knees, covering his ears. The earth rumbled, its voice deepening in pain. The tauz still screamed, the agony sliding through Shay's bones as if carried by the shard in his arm. He yanked it out, gritted his teeth, and curled into a ball.

"Shay, what is it?" Bibi shook his shoulder hard.

He watched her lips, unable to hear her over the scream burning inside his head.

She dragged him away from the pillar's rubble. She knelt before him and grabbed his wrists. Her mouth and body screamed at him, but he heard only the crystal's agony, reflected a thousand times by all the crystals in the canyon. He thought he might be screaming, too, but he heard only the tauz. All of it.

She hauled him to his feet and pushed him onto Spark's back. The horse pranced.

The song's volume dropped. The buzzing in his bones eased. He opened his eyes, saw Bibi's determined face at his knee.

The screaming disappeared. The earth's hum dropped to the background, and instead of the pillar's voice, he heard many tinier voices, a chorus of the tumbled parts of the grandfather.

Bibi clutched her bloody hand to her chest. "Are you all right?" she screamed at him.

He winced, spoke in a normal voice. "I'm fine now. The falling crystal hurt my ears. They must be more sensitive today than usual."

She challenged his honesty with a hard stare. Then she released whatever disbelief she held, shedding tension with it. "Thank you. I feared that pillar would devour me."

"How badly are you hurt?" Shay leaned over for a closer look.

She held up her arm for his inspection. "The wound is mostly superficial. I will clean it, smear it with pungis, and wrap it. I will be fine, and I have earned some new scars."

"Earned?" He glanced at the traceries of pale scars against the charred color of her skin. They weren't as bad as

108

the ones he'd seen when he tended her mangler wounds. No woman should ever carry such scars.

Although these scars seemed far too few and too minor for a warrior. He had more than she did already!

"Scars are medals of valor, Shay. They are *earned*, by surviving whatever comes. Fear not, you will earn your own in time, besides the scars gifted you by the manglers."

Shay stared at the ruins of the grandfather pillar, remembering its songs of earth and death. That he could hear the crystals at all worried him. Was he going insane? Was it his imagination, born of his love of gems? Did he have some special affinity for tauz?

If he asked Bibi, she would think him daft. Cinny would have understood.

11. Destruction

As soon as possible, they left the tauz behind. They camped for the night a few miles away, on a slope covered in granite and grass. Normal dirt felt good under his feet for the first time he could remember.

That evening he read his document aloud to Bibi, as they sat by a small campfire next to a granite shelf.

"'If you are one with the axe,'" he read, "'come to me to learn its mysteries. Meet me among the bloodstone pillars in the Crystal Mountains. I will know when you arrive.'"

Shay glanced up at Bibi. "It's signed 'Robayne.'"

"Who is Robayne?" Bibi asked.

"I have no idea." Shay shook his head. "He's long dead. The document came to Cinny's family with the axe, generations ago."

"*Her* family? On her death, would not her inheritance stay in her family?" Bibi's direct gaze made him uncomfortable.

"It wasn't her inheritance. Her father presented it to us as a wedding gift. Never fear. It's legally mine."

Bibi swallowed the remainder of her breakfast tea. "No wonder the son believed it to be his by right."

"Yes, but the real impetus came from his friend, Tarver. Spinel is too timid to do this on his own." He scratched his head absently. "The real question now is how to interpret the note."

Bibi's next words came slowly, as she thought out loud. "'One with the diamond,' from a warrior's perspective, would indicate a skill level in which the diamond weapon becomes a part of you, like your arm. You are comfortable with it and you use it without conscious thought, for the knowledge of its techniques and quirks is stored in body as well as brain. The Sheethe refer to this as being 'blood sisters' to the weapon."

"So I can find what I seek only when I reach that skill level? That may be years, if ever."

"Or perhaps it means ownership, a way of saying, 'if you are the rightful owner.'"

"The document has existed for many, many years, but he wrote it as if he would still be here," said Shay. "Maybe it was a message to a specific individual, for a specific occasion. That's why Robayne would keep an eye out for his arrival."

"Ah. Not a message for the ages at all. That makes sense."

"If that's the proper interpretation, there's no longer anything for me to find. It's a wasted journey." He shriveled inside.

"Except for the black diamonds." Bibi's expression softened slightly. "Then again, none of our guesses may be close. We will not know until we reach the bloodstone pillars. Do not allow wild speculation to discourage you."

Shay received the advice with gratitude. The loss of those mysteries would crush him. He had so little left in his life now.

"It is time for some serious training." Bibi rose to her feet, ending the discussion.

Shay groaned. That meant a minimum of two hours, and he'd barely be able to stand afterward. He reached for his battle-axe.

Blood sister? he wondered. Do weapons have a gender, as ships do? Presumably, I would be blood *brother* to the axe . . .

Then he forgot such silliness as he concentrated on the new pattern Bibi showed him.

❖   ❖   ❖

111

Spinel rode hard, leading a band of over a dozen men. Or at least he rode at the front of them. He didn't like the pounding head he rode with now, but drinking with other men was the best way to obtain information; he couldn't help it if he enjoyed his work. He winced at a spike of sunlight through the tree branches. The foothills of the Crystal Mountains rose ahead.

Jonus drew abreast of him. "The horses need a breather. If we keep going at this pace, we'll kill them."

"They'll be fine," Spinel shouted back above the rumble of hooves. "We need to make up time." He hated Jonus, wished he'd never hired him. All the men now looked for his reactions before obeying Spinel's orders.

He put heels to his horse. If he could get a little farther ahead, he could pretend Jonus wasn't there at all, that he hadn't taken over the gang.

Abruptly, Jonus no longer rode alongside, and the pounding of hooves faded. Spinel looked back over his shoulder. The men were slowing to a trot, then to a walk. Spinel jerked his own horse around, felt it stagger under him. He trotted back.

"What are you doing?" he snarled. "I said we don't have time for a break."

"Will you buy us all new horses as these die?" Jonus stared at him, gray eyes hard and jaw thrust forward. "My next one will be a Curzon cross. Can you afford that?"

Spinel stared at him. He hadn't thought that far ahead, but he couldn't let on. "See the mountain out there that doesn't match any of the others? That's from the gems scattered all across it. Enough to make us all rich. We're close to our goal. We'll stop at the next village, only two or three miles from here." Lies slid so easily from his tongue now that he didn't even think of them as lies. He knew of no village, and he didn't care.

112

"You'll ruin the horses before we get there." The speaker, a man with granite eyes and lean, chiseled features, had been a horse trader in another life–before he earned the large horseshoe-shaped brand on his right cheek. The one identifying him as a horse thief.

Facing open rebellion, Spinel had no choice but to give in. His mood soured further when he lost a large, if imperfect, diamond in a dice game as they rested. Jonus had cheated. He had to have. At that moment, Spinel hated everyone, even his friend, Tarver.

When they rode on again at a more reasonable pace, Spinel's blood still simmered. He pictured his fist breaking Jonus's nose, took pride in the imaginary spray of blood and subsequent humble obedience of the man.

Then he realized the proper target for his anger was Shay Bladen, and his blood seethed near boiling. If Shay hadn't been so damn set on keeping the axe, Spinel's sister and her children would still be alive. By rights, that axe belonged to him! He was the son, not Cinny.

The face crumpling under his imaginary fist was no longer that of Jonus.

They did find a village, to Spinel's surprise, although they rode twice as far as he'd told the men. That would show Jonus!

No matter that the village was small and poor. The main street's ruts forced them to ride slower, and the shabby wooden buildings, gray with age, hurt his eyes with their ugliness. Even in so small a place, a dozen people sold gems and fine stones gathered from the surrounding foothills. The better-off sold from rickety tables in front of shop or home, but most spread their wares on a blanket on the hard ground.

One woman, worn and rough-skinned, caught his eye–

not for herself, but for her two ragged, dirty children. The girl looked about four. Her older brother . . . Spinel caught his breath. About the same age as Piper, this boy had Beryl's blond hair and green eyes.

Momentarily, an unreasoning hatred consumed Spinel–hatred of the thugs who had killed his sister and her children. Not hatred of his friend, Tarver. That wouldn't be safe. Besides, Tarver could be hard, but he'd never condone the murder of children. Onions and Scar had acted on their own. Spinel *knew* it.

Jonus rode up as Spinel reined away from the children. "Why are we lingering? There's nothing here, no tavern to drown yourself in."

"The blond boy. He reminds me of my nephew, that's all." Spinel immediately wished he hadn't mentioned the boy.

Jonus leaned forward, elbows on the pommel. "The one Bladen got killed?"

The skin on Spinel's face tightened in anger. "The same."

"Do you think Bladen came this way?" Jonus leaned to one side and spat.

Disgusting. Why did so many common men do that? Spitting called attention to an uncouth, impolite upbringing, a far cry from Spinel's peers.

"He may have. Have the men question these people to see if he did, and if they can tell us where he went from here."

Jonus pursed his lips with a slight tilt of his head, as if pleasantly surprised. "Good idea." He rode away, calling to Spinel's riders.

Feeling at last like a true leader of men, Spinel sat his horse in the center of the street and watched his riders spread out to talk to the villagers. *This* was how it felt to be

114

a captain, the one to whom all men deferred, to whom they listened attentively.

He began to talk to the men along the street himself, asking about the bloodstone pillars. He hadn't mentioned the pillars to Jonus; he didn't need to know about them yet.

"At the foot of Blue Mountain," one man told him. "It's blue because of the torquis imbedded in the slopes of the mountain, a very distinctive color. You'll know it when you see it."

Spinel had already seen the distant mountain but hid his impatience. "How far? How long to reach it?"

The man mused for a moment, rubbing his chin. "Oh, I'd say about four, maybe five days. Just follow this road out of town. Third village or so you come to, ask. They can point it out to you, if you haven't caught sight of it by then. And they can tell you the fastest way to get there."

At last! A chance to get ahead of Shay, to fulfill Tarver's orders and prove himself. Spinel thanked the man politely.

The smack of flesh against flesh pulled his attention toward the center of town.

One of his riders had dismounted and grabbed a local man's shirtfront, pulling him nose to nose. He slapped him again, rocking his head, and snarled harsh words into his face–words Spinel couldn't make out from here, though the sneer on the rider's face defined their intent.

He could interfere, insist on gentler questioning, but he rode with hard men. These men could as easily turn on him, treat him like that. Torn by indecision, he didn't move.

Nearby, the former horse thief described a muscular woman with black skin and an older man with a black axe to a dignified elder behind a small table of gems. When the elder shook his head, the horse thief grinned, pocketed all the gems on the table, and walked away.

The elder's eyes widened and his nostrils flared. He leaped at the horse thief, demanding the return of his stones. The thief backhanded him. He fell, and his tormenter kicked him. And kept kicking, while the man yelled.

Spinel turned in every direction, seeking Jonus to help him put a stop to this.

Jonus was speaking to a man across the street from the woman and her children. As Spinel trotted up, he heard the man say, "Yeah, they came through here. The woman thought she could bully me. I tried to warn her friend he was buying the poorest gems in town, over across the street, but she must have had it in for him, trying to cut off my warning. He bought the entire inventory! If he'd known anything about gems . . ."

Jonus interrupted. "Do you know where they're going? Which direction they went?"

Spinel waited politely until the conversation ended, pleased that his hunch had been right. As his henchman finally gave him his attention, he opened his mouth to speak.

But Jonus stared past him down the street, his face curled in on itself in anger. "You bloody fool!" He threw himself onto his horse.

Spinel, mouth still open, turned his horse in confusion. Did Jonus mean him? Or the tormentor?

And when did all this mayhem start?

Screams and yelling filled the street, yellow fire filled the buildings. Three dead bodies–no, four–no, five!–lay heaped in the center of the village. One was a woman. As he watched, three more went down under fist, knife, and sword. Someone dragged a woman behind a building and emerged a few minutes later, blood on his mouth and still tying his britches.

116

Frozen in shock, Spinel couldn't even see Jonus now. Wobbly tables fell as two of his riders fought each other for a young woman and a handful of gems. The winner ripped the woman's clothing from her on the spot, never noticing the bloody welts she scratched on his face.

Spinel averted his gaze, unable to watch the rape, only to see a tough swinging a child by his ankles.

He fled. Spurs to horse, he raced for the edge of town.

Two bodies lay in front of him in the street, the woman and her small daughter, both raped and killed. And next to them, the blond boy struggled with one of Spinel's riders. The boy who reminded him of Beryl.

Spinel yanked his reins. "Stop!"

The man glared at him through narrow, lust-glazed eyes. "Mind your own business."

"We need him alive!" *I can't believe I'm doing this, I can't believe I'm doing this.*

"Why?"

The child kicked the thug's knee and tore loose. Cursing, the bandit caught him in two steps and slapped him.

"Because we need him. Because we can use him." *I can't do this, I can't . . .*

"Why, Spinel?" asked Jonus, suddenly at his shoulder. "I gave the men permission to have a little fun; we've been riding hard for days. Couldn't have stopped them, anyway."

Spinel jumped, steadied himself. "Because this is the boy who reminds me of my nephew. We can use him to draw Shay to us." It was all he could think of to help the boy.

Jonus held up a hand toward the man clutching the boy's shirt.

The man stopped, watching Jonus for instructions.

"Keep him reasonably healthy," Jonus told him. He

117

turned back to Spinel. "You know, that's not a bad idea. I can see possibilities. And I'll be sure to tell Tarver how helpful you are."

Pride flashed through Spinel, followed by horror at himself for it.

Jonus glanced around casually at the destruction of people and property, his eyes lighting up. "Join us, if you wish. Or just stay out of the way." He strode back the way he'd come, into the heart of the devastation.

Cringing and sickened, Spinel cast about for a place of refuge but saw none. He spurred his horse for the edge of the village. Half a mile out of town, he found a place behind a tall boulder, beside a lazy creek, where he drank every drop of liquor he had. Even from here, he heard the sounds of destruction. He choked on thick smoke that tasted like charred meat.

He sat with head stacked on elbows on knees and bawled like an infant, unable to push the images out of his head.

Spinel rode resolutely at the front of his riders, convinced that Jonus humored him by allowing it. How did he get himself into this? He only wanted what was rightfully his–the diamond axe.

Without liquor to sustain him, he hurt all over. His head pounded. His hands shook uncontrollably, so that handling his reins became difficult for him, confusing for his horse. But he depended on the horse, because walking was a shaky, disorienting experience.

In fact, his whole body trembled. With his vision affected, confusion pooled behind his eyes. He hated feeling constantly off balance.

Worst of all, he could think too clearly. Tarver didn't send him to lead this group; Jonus had met him at the tavern door and offered himself and his friends to help find the axe. Hindsight–especially sober hindsight–appalled him.

Spinel was there to lend legitimacy to the enterprise. Officially, he was in charge–which meant the one to blame. Officially, the rightful owner sought his property, which he had promised to gift to his friend.

Oh, he heard the talk, the sniggering behind his back. The men made jokes at his expense, as if he wouldn't recognize them as insults.

And he hadn't. Nor had he wanted to. Easier to pretend he was one of them, sharing in their rude sense of humor.

Until he became accidentally sober.

The campsite Jonus chose consisted of more damnable rocks and trees. They sickened him, closed him in, and seemed to stare accusations at him. He huddled at the campfire, wishing to be back in the city. Maybe he could find an excuse . . .

An innocuous looking man, round of face and eye, cut an eye-corner look at him, a sneer on his face. "Can this really be our leader?" he asked loudly, for the benefit of the camp one evening. "*Spineless* don't know what to do with hisself, sober."

He'd overheard the offensive name often, but never had anyone deliberately intended him to hear it. If he hadn't been so miserable, he might have thought twice. Permanent nausea fought with a constant fluctuation between burning with sweat and chilling to the bone. Knowing he'd regret it later, he shot back, "Better than being known as Moonface, complete with pockmarks." Spinel laughed aloud at his own joke; all men did when they exchanged such insults.

He didn't see the man move, but the sudden touch of cold steel at his throat cut off his laughter. Death threatened from the eyes only two inches from his own.

"Moon." Jonus's voice was barely audible over the

laughter. He didn't move from his place by the fire, or even look up at the man.

Slowly, eyes still glaring into Spinel's, the man straightened up. He flipped his knife around two or three times, a showy exercise meant to intimidate. Spinel cringed. Smirking, Moon returned to his seat by the fire and ignored Spinel the rest of the evening.

With no liquor to dull the fear, he'd wet himself. More humiliation. More laughter.

He hated all of these men! Spinel ground his teeth in anger and shame. He needed a drink.

He hated liquor. He needed liquor. He especially needed to be drunk.

For the second time, he paid a fine gem for a rider's skin of ale. It didn't last long, though he nursed it carefully. And it did get him through one night of the boy's screams when his abductor dragged him out of camp into woods or rocks. Spinel didn't want to know what was happening, or even to know that the boy was in the clutches of evil men.

So was he! And he had to take care of himself, didn't he?

Spinel didn't handle violence well. That's why the men scorned him. But he didn't know how to toughen up, to make himself like them, to become one of them.

Oh, he needed to be drunk!

12. Meilin

From this distance, Shay couldn't be sure what gem created Blue Mountain's distinctive color. He'd watched it rise above other peaks all day, but the distance didn't show much detail. He studied the mountain for hours as they rode, comparing its color to his mental catalog of gems and minerals, and finally concluded it had to be torquis. He had seen that in a variety of blue and green shades, but never this pure a blue.

He needed to reach the mountain and examine it closely, to be sure. Bluestone was the only other possibility.

Bibi stirred up a pot of vegetables for an early supper, adding a little oil and salt, and black grains of something he didn't recognize–she called it "pepper"–humming quietly as she worked.

Shay heard no words and no tune in her humming. The notes didn't go together in the ways he expected, almost as if she didn't use the same musical scale he was used to. "What's that song you're humming, Bibi? I don't recognize it, and I'm not sure if it's because I don't know the song or because you can't sing it." He smiled.

Bibi lifted one disdainful eyebrow. "I sing very well for a warrior. Perhaps you do not know how to listen to the songs of the spirit world."

Shay accepted a plate from her. "It's a religious song?"

"Yes. Many of ours are, although we also have lullabies and bawdy drinking songs." Her eyes twinkled.

Shay laughed. It was good, if rare, to see Bibi in such fine humor.

When they rode on, Shay pushed forward to lead. He didn't feel like a tender-toes anymore, but a man capable of taking care of himself. He grinned, enjoying the discretion to choose easier paths than Bibi would. They tended to be more circuitous, but if she minded, she didn't say so.

Besides, he liked the view better than staring at Silence's hindquarters. And the mule would follow Silence as easily as Spark. They rarely put a lead on him anymore.

Ahead of him, something in the rocks moved, probably a stray tuft of summer-soaked grass in the light breeze. Then a human figure stepped out, and Shay jerked Spark to an abrupt stop. The horse protested with a grunt, and Bibi cursed softly behind him. Shay threw up a hand to stop her from coming forward.

He stared at fear personified. Jackrab eyes flicked in every direction, frightened and haunted. Dirty, ragged clothes barely covered a stick-thin frame. Bruises and scratches covered dirt-streaked arms and face. Trembling hands and shaking legs signaled a readiness to flee, and perhaps exhaustion.

The boy. The one who had sold him the sonstone. Shay's heart flipped. He slid off his horse. He took one step toward the boy, who scrambled backward, diving back toward the rocks.

"Whoa! Wait," Shay called to him. He forced his voice to calmness as best he could, reaching toward the child without moving forward. "I won't hurt you!"

The boy paused halfway between two boulders, gaze flitting between Shay and Bibi. The tip of his teeth appeared, chewing at his lower lip, but he held.

"I remember you." Shay reached slowly into his pocket and showed him the golden beryl. "You're the one who found this. But I never learned your name, and I wish I had." He waited.

"Meilin." The soft voice wavered, hesitant, maybe hopeful. Or too afraid to hope.

Behind him, Bibi dismounted and slipped into the

woods and rocks to search for danger. Shay, too, wondered if the boy could be a distraction or lure; his presence here seemed improbable.

"Meilin. A fine name for a fine lad. I remember how well you took care of your family. You're a long ways from home. Are you here alone? Where are your mother and sister?" A tiny widening of Meilin's eyes drove him to ask, "What's happened?"

Meilin burst into tears.

Shay wouldn't have hesitated to gather his own son into his arms, but he barely knew Meilin. He eased closer, as he might approach a skittish horse. Well, as Bibi might; Shay would avoid such a horse. He smiled at the thought.

Hope flickered in the boy's eyes at the smile.

Shay intended to put a fatherly hand on Meilin's shoulder, but by habit opened his arms.

Meilin threw himself into Shay, almost knocking him over, and clamped his arms tightly around his middle. Great, heaving sobs, muffled by and soaking into his shirt, made Shay's own throat ache with unshed tears. For the moment, this child could be his child—and that released his grief to twist his heart again. He folded his arms quietly about the child and let him cry.

Why would a young boy be so high into the mountains, apparently alone and on foot? A search for stones to sell couldn't possibly take him so far. How did he get here? How could he be ahead of Shay, if he'd walked?

He couldn't. He had to have ridden, although Shay saw no sign of a horse. His grief seeped away as he worked through the thought. In his gut, he knew it had something to do with his pursuers, but he saw no connection between a fatherless boy and bastard murderers.

Perhaps Meilin had pursuers of his own, for reasons Shay couldn't begin to comprehend.

123

As Meilin's sobs eased, Shay gave him a squeeze and released him, keeping a hand on his shoulder. Tears and snot streaked the boy's face, and shame bloomed there. *He's been the man of the family so long, he's forgotten he's only a boy, who can still cry without losing honor.*

"Can you ride?" he asked. "With one of us, I mean?"

Meilin nodded, eyes filled with hope and fear.

"You're safe now. I'll make sure of it." Shay set his jaw. He hadn't protected his own boy, but he would, by the Light, protect this one.

A sudden shout startled them both. A cacophony erupted from the trees, the sounds of fighting. Bibi's blood-curdling battle cry echoed off the rocks, and the screaming began.

Meilin whimpered.

Shay tightened his grip on the boy's shoulder to reassure him. "Go back into the rocks, Meilin, but stay close. I'll call you when it's safe."

"There's lots of them. They'll kill you. We have to run!"

"Not yet." He shook his head. "Hide, Meilin. Be safe, but stay close. I won't let them near you." Axe in hand, he waited while Meilin glanced at it, eyes wide, and ducked into the rocks.

Then he ran.

Shay had no trouble finding the battle in the rocky terrain's wispy forest, where Bibi wielded her sword with sharp precision. Three men lay in heaps on the ground. Two more groaned and bled. One, still standing, stared at the stump of his arm, screaming as blood spewed.

Bibi faced two opponents as Shay sped toward her. The swordsmen split, tried to circle her from opposite directions. Agile footwork left the larger blocking the smaller one's access to her. She engaged the one in front.

Shay had no time for admiration. He joined the fight with a roar. Battle energy bloomed. The first swing of his axe sliced open a man's stomach.

He spun as something crashed into him from behind. A body, not a weapon, thanks to Bibi. She thrust his attacker's knife into her belt.

More careful to notice those around him, Shay blocked a sword with the haft, slammed the knob into someone behind him. He bungled a grappling move but managed to hook the man's leg. His opponent dropped, shrieking amidst the spray of blood.

The attackers fell back toward a line of rocks and trees.

Battle energy still raging, Shay looked around. Bibi chased two of the fleeing attackers, but let them go to remain in sight. Strewn across the slope lay a dozen bodies, most still moving and groaning. The man who'd lost his hand lay dead.

The smell of hard perspiration, blood, and voided bowels roiled Shay's stomach. The taste of blood hanging invisibly in the air only made it worse. How many of those men had he killed or maimed?

"Get to the horses," Bibi ordered. "They will regroup and return."

Shay ran, Bibi retreating under more control, keeping an eye out behind them.

She leaped to Silence's prancing back, ready to flee.

"Meilin?" called Shay, ignoring her. "Meilin, it's safe. Come on out. We've got to go!"

No response.

"Meilin?" Shay set his axe against a rock, heel up for easy grabbing. He walked toward the rocks where he'd last seen the boy.

A rustle of movement, just beyond the rocks, and a

125

pair of terrified emrel eyes appeared in the brush.

"Meilin, it's all right. They're gone, at least for now. We've got to ride, stay ahead of them." He held out a hand, winced at a gobbet of flesh clinging to the sleeve. He waited with all the patience he could muster while the boy slowly emerged.

As soon as he saw Meilin's face, he understood. "You watched the fight, didn't you?"

Meilin nodded, coming no closer. Poised to run.

Shay blew out a long breath, releasing the battle energy, the tension. "We won't hurt you, Meilin. Neither of us will. We did what we had to, for all of us to stay alive."

Meilin didn't take the extended hand, but he did come forward, and Shay led him back to where Bibi waited.

"He will ride with me, at least for now." She looked at Meilin with eyes still alight from battle.

Shay lifted the child into place in front of Bibi, where his lack of riding skills wouldn't be an issue.

Meilin gripped his forearms, refusing to let go.

"You will be safe." Bibi's voice gentled. "I will not hurt you." Gentle for Bibi, anyway.

Hesitantly, Meilin released his grip.

Axe across his saddle, Shay followed Bibi up the mountain, knowing the mule would stay with them. He glanced back often, expecting the enemy to leap from the rocks at any moment.

Bibi drove them hard toward Blue Mountain, flying up the steepest, most difficult paths she could find. As if Meilin weren't already frightened enough. Shay groaned every time she rode without hesitation up a cleft filled with tumbled rocks, or straight up a terrifying incline.

When they finally stopped to rest, he sighed with relief. Safe ground again, on his own legs. He went to check on Meilin, who watched the treacherous slopes they had just climbed.

The boy half-smiled at him, his face white and drawn. Probably from Bibi's hellacious ascent. Or perhaps dread of falling back into the hands of those who had captured him.

Shay had learned how to give his children big, reassuring smiles, even over his own misgivings or fears, and he gave one to Meilin. Children needed to feel safe, to feel that those in charge of their lives knew what they were doing and would take care of everything.

Meilin's smile widened, still uncertain, and his face relaxed a little.

"Our leader's name is Bibi." Shay nodded in her direction and she broke away from surveying their back trail to smile at the boy. "She's a Sheethe warrior, and a very good one."

Meilin's eyes widened and his mouth dropped open. "A Sheethe!"

A boy who's lived all his life in the middle of nowhere knows what that means, and I, living in a city full of information, did not? Shay thought. He shook his head over his own ignorance– and his ignorance of his own ignorance.

"My name is Shay Bladen. I used to be a gemsman."

Meilin gasped loudly. "Bladen! You're *Bladen*? The hero?"

The overawed look on the boy's face startled Shay. He shifted uncomfortably, then chuckled to cover the discomfort. "Well, I'm no hero, but that is my name." It was the one truth he had always known about himself.

The boy's gaze locked onto Shay's weapon. "Then that's the magic axe! The one from all the stories!"

"I'm not the same one." Shay tried to keep amusement out of his voice.

"Your name is Bladen." Meilin shrugged. "You have

127

the axe."

"Time to go," Bibi announced. "I do not see anyone yet, but they will catch up soon."

Shay boosted Meilin up in front of Bibi. "You'll have to tell me the stories sometime."

Excitement buzzed through him. Maybe those stories would offer clues to the black diamonds and the mysteries of the axe.

Still, Meilin shouldn't look at him like that, eyes full of hero worship. Now that he rode with a Sheethe and a "legendary hero," the boy seemed to have lost his fear. For that, at least, Shay was grateful.

They rode for hours, until the Eye flattened itself on the horizon. As the day dissipated into twilight, Bibi stopped long enough to distribute hard biscuits to eat as they rode.

An unsatisfying supper. Shay grumbled under his breath, subsiding when Bibi's ears twitched.

For once, Bibi passed by a dangerous path up a mountain, choosing an easier way instead. As twilight slid into dusk, Meilin fell asleep between Bibi's arms, to Silence's slow, rocking gait.

At last, she found a place huddled in rocks obscured by trees. "We can rest here tonight," she told Shay. "The overhanging branches will hide our firelight."

"Will they be able to track us?" Shay asked. "We rode some rugged trails today." He sipped at his tea next to the small campfire.

"Perhaps," said Bibi, "if they have a very good tracker. But the difficulty of working out the trail will slow them down." She kept her voice quiet because Meilin slept, wrapped in a blanket near the fire.

Shay held his mug under his chin to allow warmth to waft upward, easing evening's chill. He scowled at the pink

128

pungis cream daubed over his wounds. Bibi wore no pungis, nor did he see blood or wounds of any kind, although she'd fought harder than he had.

"No pink dots for you, Bibi? You didn't get cut even once? You must be really good with that sword."

She glared a challenge at him, her face unreadable. "What do you think?"

Shay blinked, not expecting such a chill. The silence stretched while he floundered for something to say. Why was she angry? "I think you're hiding secrets," he said at last. "But they can't be greater than what I've shared with you."

After a moment, Bibi released a long, slow breath and the stiffness dropped from her shoulders. Her gaze fell to the warm mug in her hands. "We did well because of our training. Even you, the novice, are better trained than they, if far less experienced. They did not expect that, or the woman to be the most lethal fighter, and so they did not put out the effort they would for bandits or male warriors. They will not be so casual next time.

"But there is another reason I bear no wounds. Since you have shared your secrets, I must also share mine." She glared at him, as if in warning.

Shay felt the weight of Bibi's will, of the charge she gave him. "Our secrets are already sworn, Bibi."

One corner of her lip curled up in acknowledgment. "I carry a woman warrior's stone, a deep blood-red gem to ward off blows and cuts. I barely feel their touch and my skin is rarely marred. Its power can be overcome, but not easily. It is why I bear so few scars, for all the work I have done."

"A gem? May I see it?" Shay's pulse quickened as he stretched out his palm for the stone.

Bibi reached into her pocket with some reluctance,

fumbled for a moment, and withdrew a deep-red stone the size of a pullet's egg, cut into a faceted triangular shape. Firelight sparked brilliance from deep within the stone. Without comment, she laid it in Shay's palm.

Shay examined it closely. No visible inclusions. Superb cut. "It's difficult to tell without proper equipment, but I believe this is rubellia, an exceptionally fine type of red turmali." He held it up to the firelight, fascinated by the way the light flashed as he turned it. "A beautiful stone!" He handed it back.

"Sheethe folklore ascribes protective powers to it. However, most such gems are only beautiful stones, their real protection found in the increased confidence and courage of the women who carry it–and nearly all Sheethe do carry one. Mine is different. It truly is magic, offering me real protection. I keep it in a pouch sewn inside my pocket, to avoid losing it. It was given me by my mother, a magnificent Sheethe in her own right. She whispered its secrets in my ear with her last breath."

Startled, Shay searched her face, but saw no grief or tenderness there. Of course, Bibi wouldn't display such weakness before her student. He wondered if she ever showed her heart, even in little ways, to anyone. A strange, enigmatic woman, and all the more powerful for it.

13. GOAT

Breakfast finished late and Shay sensed Bibi's irritation at the delay. But Meilin still wolfed down huge mouthfuls of skillet cakes as if he hadn't eaten for a month.

Shay arched an eyebrow at Bibi. "Boys are hollow inside. That's a lot of space to fill."

"Do not eat too much, Meilin," she chided the boy gently. "We will ride today as we did yesterday, and I would not have you lose all your breakfast and have to start over."

Meilin paused, cheeks bulging with half-chewed food, and stared at her, stricken.

Shay chuckled. "You have a stronger stomach than that, boy. But it will be a rough ride, and before we go, I'd like to hear your story. How did you come to be here? What happened?" He ignored Bibi's flared nostrils.

The boy set aside his almost empty plate, suddenly finished with breakfast. He didn't look up, but his eyes filled. He blinked them dry and straightened his shoulders, then looked back at Shay, carefully ignoring Bibi.

"I was out hunting for stones to sell, and on the way back, I saw the whole village on fire. Mother and Sissy didn't have anyone to protect them, so I ran fast down the mountain." He swallowed. "I fell twice, and it slowed me down so I couldn't get there in time.

"There were men on horses in the streets. When I got close, I hid and watched to see if I could see Mother and Sissy. The riders threw torches into buildings. They grabbed men and asked questions I couldn't hear. Then they killed them. The mean man across the street from us pointed at Mother, and they laughed and killed him, too."

Shay drew in a long, silent breath, aching for the

child's haunted eyes. Bibi left off loading the mule and joined them.

Meilin swallowed loudly. "Then they started asking women, and when they didn't answer right, they threw them down on the ground and tore their clothes and . . ." His eyes closed and a tear escaped.

"It's okay, son. We know what they did." Shay kept his voice low and calming, but his stomach churned.

"There was blood everywhere, and I could smell it from where I hid. It was awful.

"When they were done with the women, they killed them, too. I watched Mother die and didn't do a damn thing to stop them!" Self-loathing filled his voice. "And the girls. One man even grabbed Sissy like she was a grown-up. That's when I ran out to stop him, but he knocked me down and killed her.

"They stole all our stones and burned everything down and killed everyone! Everyone except me. A red-haired man told them not to. The man who . . . took me . . . beat me some more, then threw me on a horse, face down. When they left the village, they took me along."

Spinel? It had to be. He did have a soft spot for children. Still, Shay hurt for Meilin's beating. He'd been the victim of that a few times at Meilin's age, and more. Perhaps this child had suffered more than a beating, too, something he couldn't talk about, would probably never tell anyone. Fresh anger swept through him.

Meilin's voice choked. He tried to rub the tears from his cheeks, but new ones replaced them. Suddenly, he threw himself into Shay, sobbing wildly into his shirt.

Shay held him as he would have his own child, offering as much comfort as he could. That a child should be subjected to such pain was unforgivable. "They'll pay. Somehow, someday, I will make them pay for this." He

132

whispered the words, a private vow.

Bibi's eyes held fury, hard and sharp as obsis. "I will help."

The look on her face prickled Shay's scalp.

"Meilin," she said less sharply, "why did they leave you alive? Do you know? Why did they take you with them?"

The boy shrugged without moving from Shay's embrace. "They're looking for Bladen," he said, darting a glance at Shay's face, "and the red-haired man said something about a goat in a clearing, whatever that means."

"It means," said Shay, "they planned to use you to lure me in, so they could capture or kill me and take my axe."

"Never!" Meilin, spoke with all the assurance of the very young. "No one could take Bladen's axe away from him!"

If only that were true. If only he really could be the hero of Meilin's stories! "How did you escape?"

"I jumped off the horse and dived into a hole in the rocks and brambles. I heard them shouting and stomping around. When they got close, I stopped moving. When they gave up, I just kept going, until I crawled out of the rocks and there you were!"

"Do you have family anywhere else, someplace we can take you when we finish our task?" asked Bibi.

Meilin shook his head, anxious. "Can't I just stay with you two?"

"I won't abandon you, Meilin," said Shay. "Whether you're with me or a family whose children you can play with, you will be safe. I promise."

They rode fast, mostly in silence, to put as much distance as possible between them and their pursuers.

Eventually they slowed, and Meilin relaxed enough to

ask, "Where are we going?"

"To Blue Mountain. You saw it ahead of us yesterday," said Shay. "Do you know why it's blue?"

"Gems," said Meilin. "It has to be special stones of some kind."

Shay nodded. "As nearly as I can figure from this far away, the mountain's color comes from torquis, a lovely blue stone. Possibly bluestone, but torquis is likelier. Neither is faceted."

"Faceted? What's that?"

So Shay rode alongside Bibi for a while, talking to the boy about the cutting of gemstones, until their way became too steep and narrow for conversation.

Didn't Bibi know any direction but up? Especially straight up? Twice before noon they had to dismount and lead the horses–even Bibi–picking their way step-by-step over ground roughened by crystalline structures of citrine, amyth, and both smoky and ice crystal querk, which thrust up from the underlying rocks, sometimes over a foot of crystal stabbing upward. For once, Bibi seemed unconcerned with their lack of speed.

A faint jumble of sound seemed to reach up through Shay's boots. If he stopped and listened hard, he might discern individual voices, as he had with the tauz.

"At least some of our pursuers will foolishly ride too fast through this," Bibi predicted, "and injure their horses, to our advantage." Her words pulled him from his speculations.

Meilin rode with Bibi as before, but Shay wished the child rode with him. He pulled closer to Silence whenever he could to see how Meilin was doing. He's not my son, he reminded himself. But they'd both lost their families to violence, and he understood what the boy was going through.

Also like Meilin, he had been a young boy with no family and no place in the world. No child should experience that. Meilin needed an adult presence to provide stability. Few children without it survived to adulthood, and many who did became drunks or criminals. Or both. Only rarely could a lone child make something of himself, become a respectable citizen. It wouldn't be easy without adult guidance, but some managed it. Shay had, although he'd been disreputable for most of his early years.

Bibi held them to a short break at mid-day. "We need to move," she said. "I want as much distance as possible before our pursuers reorganize and give chase. If they haven't already."

"Already?" Shay's eyebrows crooked upward.

"If I commanded them, I would leave the dead and wounded with a small detachment and set out in pursuit within the hour."

Shay stretched his shoulders. "That explains why we've been riding through hell."

As they ascended, the air grew cooler and thinner. They stopped for an afternoon break on smooth ground, near a wall of rocks where they could view their back trail without being seen.

Shay stretched his legs briefly before joining Bibi by the niche overlooking the area they'd just traversed.

"Do you see them?" he asked, careful to speak well before stepping within her reach. Bibi pointed below them silently, and Shay followed her outstretched finger, surprised. He hadn't really expected visible pursuit yet.

Far below, tiny shapes moved slowly up the mountain. They paused while one rider dismounted to examine the ground and surrounding rocks. He remounted and the group turned in the direction Bibi had brought them.

"They have a very good tracker," she said. "Meilin will

135

ride behind you."

Shay nodded and went to tell him. He found the boy climbing on rocks, leaping nimbly from one to another, and smiled, his heart warm. "Ah," he said, "perhaps this is the goat in a clearing they mentioned."

Meilin dropped from the top of a rock as tall as he stood, grinning.

Shay smiled back. "You get to ride with me this time, and I see Bibi heading for her horse. Maybe as we ride you can tell me about Bladen and his magic axe, and I can start teaching you the names of the stones, as I promised."

Meilin's eyes lit up. "But you're Bladen," he said. "I can't believe you don't remember your own stories."

Shay mounted and gave Meilin a hand up. "I can't be the one in the tales. They happened long ago, before I was born."

"But the tales all say Bladen lives forever, to protect people with his magic axe."

"We ride," Bibi called, and they headed up the most difficult path she could find.

14. Bloodstone

"It appears you were right," Shay told Bibi, admiration tinting his voice. "Spinel has lost some riders to the crystal fields we came through." He peered at their back trail from between tall trees high on the mountain, squinting to count the dozen or so tiny figures far below.

"Perhaps." Bibi stood next to him, also studying their pursuers. "Or someone knows this area and has sent some of his men around us, to pinch us between two forces."

"That's a little unlikely, isn't it?"

"That manner of thought makes such a tactic effective. We must anticipate and prepare for surprises if we would prevail."

"What if the only way possible leads us to their ambush?"

Bibi snorted. "Never is only one way possible. In this instance, not knowing what lies ahead, we will backtrack the way we came and find another way forward. Their ambush, if that is what they plan, will no longer be in the right place to intercept us."

True to her word, Bibi led them back the way they'd come. Straight up meant straight down, head first. This time Meilin rode behind Bibi.

Shay tied his reins together and dropped them on Spark's neck, allowing the horse to pick his own way down. He clutched the pommel for balance, but it put his weight too far forward and Spark lurched. Fear spiking his hair, Shay leaned back and grabbed the cantle instead. The sweat of fear and summer trickled down his back underneath his shirt.

Weeks of constant fear had blunted terror's strength, but nothing felt blunted today.

Eventually, Bibi found a place to end the descent and ride around the mountain instead, taking care that their original upward tracks remained more visible than the signs of their turning off. When they reached a level area with solid footing, she increased their speed.

The only bright spot was discovering how close they'd come to Blue Mountain. Its lower flanks rose at the other end of a long, narrow valley. Shay's heart beat faster at the sight–and not from fear this time.

While Bibi climbed the nearest slopes to search for a view of their back trail, Shay took a quick look around the area for gems, Meilin at his heels.

Within minutes, he caught the brief flash of bloodstone from the corner of his eye. But Meilin had already seen it and leaped forward. Shay chuckled and helped him retrieve a thumb-sized stone, then dug out a magnificent specimen almost the size of his own hand.

He handed the larger one to Meilin to look at. "This is bloodstone, for obvious reasons."

Flecks of red sprinkled the deep-green stone like stab wounds. It appeared to be free of other inclusions, unmarred by cracks or blemishes, except those that could easily be polished out.

Meilin turned the stone this way and that in his hands, professionally impressed. "How did the blood get on it?" he asked, scratching it with his fingernail. "Why doesn't it scratch off or wash off?"

Shay couldn't stop himself from chuckling but managed to hold in the roar of laughter tickling his throat. "It's part of the rock, not real blood. The red parts are jasper. It's aptly named, isn't it?"

But when Meilin showed it to Bibi, she wouldn't touch it. "Bloodstone carries the colors of both life and death, as it bridges between the two. The blood spatter is from the violent deaths of warriors, immortalized by ascendant spirits to remind us of the glory of a warrior's death in battle, her last gift to nourish the green earth before she ascends to the blessed sphere to live and fight forever. I will not desecrate that final gift with my touch."

Disconcerted, Shay put the bloodstone away in Bray's packs, already envisioning its final shape and complementary settings.

An hour later, they dropped into the valley at the foot of Blue Mountain, and he considered throwing the beautiful bloodstone away as being an inferior stone.

Bloodstone pillars rose thickly from the floor, shaped as columns, domes, half-domes, spikes, or rough obelisks. Many grew out of jasper material, but many others did not. Sunlight flashed off the red speckles, brightened the deep bluish greens. Their size ranged from only a few inches high to perhaps forty feet tall, displayed brilliantly against the bright blue mountain and deeper blue sky. Magnificent. Amazing. Incredible. He could never have imagined bloodstone of this size and beauty.

Beside him, Bibi's bare arms pimpled. Her black face appeared smeared with ash. Shay craned his neck to look up the skirts of Blue Mountain itself. Not the most imposing or jagged mountain he had seen, its size and blue slopes nevertheless gave it a powerful presence. The blue was indeed torquis, and his fingers flexed as if already reaching for the stones.

Meilin stared at the pillars until Shay redirected his attention to the sky-blue stones that made up so much of the mountain's surface. "That," he said, "is torquis, and we should be able to pick some up soon."

"It's not shiny like the yellow stone in your pocket," said Meilin, "and neither is the bloodstone."

"These aren't crystals, but both stones make fine gems

and are easily carved."

And this time there could be no doubt. These stones had voices, as the tauz had. The sound vibrated up through his feet. Now if only they had words, too. He smiled at the idea.

They led their mounts, allowing them to pick their way through the bloodstone pillars. Unlike the tauz canyon, this surface wasn't crusted with sharp points. With care, they could step on normal, solid ground between the spikes and obelisks.

But Shay wasn't thinking of possible damage to horses' feet. One thought consumed his mind: *This is the place mentioned in Robayne's note. It really does exist. Somewhere here, there will be black diamonds, and perhaps there's still someone who knows the mysteries of my axe.* His heart pounded in his chest with excitement, and his skull buzzed lightly in anticipation. Even when he reminded himself to expect nothing, that the document might no longer mean anything.

Halfway through the valley, near a wall of Blue Mountain–a normal one, not itself blue–Shay separated from his awe enough to wonder. *If this is where the secrets of the axe can be found, how do I go about looking for them?*

Hoofbeats. Bibi's low, urgent voice called his attention from fantasy and wonder. Thrusting Meilin behind him, he spun toward the sound as Bibi did. Even he would never choose to fight here.

Their pursuers had found them, and the leader of this band of ruffians was Shay's brother-by-law, Spinel.

"Well met, *brother*!" The redhead's upper lip lifted in a sneer. "I've come for my axe."

Fury pounded through Shay, thunder in his blood. The

140

lowered, grating edge to his voice seemed to surprise the man before him. "It never has been and will never be your axe."

"My sister and her children would still be alive, if not for you! All you had to do was hand over the axe . . ."

"I tried to!"

". . . and you'd still be working in your little shop like the commoner you are, and raising your children as guttersnipes. Don't try to lay this on me! Their deaths are your fault!"

Shay's arms shook in outrage as he lifted the axe from his back and held it across his body. "Do you wish to join them this day? Step down, and I'll see you on your way."

He hoped that, behind him, Bibi was getting Meilin to safety. According to his peripheral vision, over a dozen men rode with Spinel. His heart squeezed.

As if in answer to his thoughts, Bibi spoke from behind and to his right. "Meilin is safe." She lowered her voice so that he barely heard her. "Put your back to a pillar and keep it there–preferably a pillar next to the mountain's wall. Do not allow them to draw you out. If they get behind us, we are in trouble. With so many of them and only two of us, they will get in each other's way. Watch for bows, crossbows, throwing knives, spears. Go for the vulnerable parts of the body, as I taught you. Disabling is more important than killing."

Still the teacher. On some level, Bibi's last-minute lecture amused Shay. On another, he appreciated the reminders. He moved closer to the wall, next to a stunning bloodstone pillar only two feet from it. Bibi found a similar position to one side as Spinel turned to face his men. He held up a deep blue knuckle-sized gem for all to see. "I'm offering a bonus-this priceless skystone–for the one who kills Shay Bladen. Today he must die!"

141

Shay's breath caught in his throat. Spinel? Willing to see him dead? He'd have believed it of any of these thugs, but that Cinny's brother would make such a vicious declaration?

Spinel whirled his horse and spurred him forward, toward Shay.

In one stride, his horse stepped on a short bloodstone spike and fell, screaming. Spinel tumbled off, landing on more crystals, and rolled to his feet, sword in hand. Blood scratched across his exposed flesh, one large gash between his eyebrows adding a feral ferocity.

Behind him, the riders chuckled, dismounting and letting their horses go. One smaller man in front guffawed loudly.

Spinel spun, teeth bared, and slashed his sword across the man's throat. The laughter died abruptly, as the man choked and burbled, and finally lay still. Spinel's eyes widened, jaw loose.

In the silence, a robin trilled overhead.

A man standing near the center front of the riders spoke to Shay, ignoring Spinel. "My name is Jonus. These men follow me. Your only chance to live is to hand over the axe. Bring it to me to avoid further killing."

"No." Shay's jaw firmed.

Then he saw Spinel's face, mottled and deformed by fury.

The breathy rattle of feathers brushed Shay's hair. An arrow shattered against the bloodstone just above his head, gouging out a colorful chunk. He ducked as sharp shards sprayed.

The riders ran at him. The first sword hummed through the air only inches from his face. He caught the backstroke on his haft, twisted to redirect it.

Two more closed in, swords swinging. Shay

142

sidestepped enough to slap the first downward, into the path of the second. Then he stopped thinking as battle energy infused him.

His body worked to protect him without conscious thought. The axe seemed a part of his arms.

Again and again he refused to be drawn out from his pillar, concentrating. Feet under his shoulders. Avoid being turned.

His shredded shirt soon clung to his blood and sweat.

Ducking below a sword that almost took his head, he caught the heel of his axe behind his opponent's ankle and yanked. The man fell, screaming as his blood poured onto the stones. His thrashing body laid a barricade for Shay. Building the barrier with more bodies, he ignored stinging wounds and blood dripping into his eye.

Then he saw Jonus working toward him through the men and pulled in a second wind. Pain splayed against a background of weariness. Again he dealt death, fought without thought.

Was Bibi okay? He hadn't heard her voice for a while, and panic threatened. He had no chance alone!

As if she'd heard his thought, her high, sharp ululation split the air, lending courage.

He shut out weapons' clash, horses' neighs, screams of the wounded and dying. The bodies of the fallen slowed the attack, until Jonus sent men to clear them. When Shay breathed through his nose again, sour bile boiled up from his belly, threatening to gag him. He couldn't shut out the smell of split bowels. His own body wanted to void everything. He had no time.

He turned from a dying man who had gashed his ribs viciously and found himself staring at Jonus. Strange, the man hadn't seemed this big on horseback. He stiffened his backbone.

Jonus came in hard with a two-handed sword strike. Shay caught it on his haft. Jonus's wrists twisted; his blade slid down the axe. Before it could sever his fingers, Shay released it. Jonus's blade changed direction, shot toward Shay's chest. He threw himself backwards, felt the tip sear along his breastbone as he fell. His legs reached out to Jonus's, feet placed against knee and behind ankle. Push, pull. Jonus fell away from him.

Shay scrambled for the axe, twisted onto his back and swung at a sword stabbing at his spine. The sword snapped in two under the axe's impact. The shattered end hit Shay in the head and he almost dropped the axe again. He rolled away from the attacker, tried to shove up to his feet. The world spun. His body wouldn't obey. Another downward stab with the jagged remains of the sword. Desperate, he chopped down on the swordsman's foot, yanked the axe up, and rolled as the man screamed and fell, his foot severed.

Blood dripped into his eyes as he stumbled back to his feet. He turned again just as Jonus leaped at him. His axe barely blocked a blow. Another weapon slashed across his shoulders. He felt the flesh open, the warm blood flow down his back.

Bibi's sword intercepted the next strike. Shay hadn't seen her coming. She pressed forward into the outlaw, forcing him to give ground, then spun away to handle another attacker.

Shay managed to get his back to the pillar again, bracing against it to stay on his feet.

Something hit him in the arm. He glanced down at the bone handle of a knife, imbedded just beneath his shoulder.

He sank slowly to his knees, unable to raise his arms. Blackness swirled through the redness of his vision. Then part of the mountain's wall slid aside, revealing blackness inside an open doorway. The Dark was coming to claim

144

him!

A man wearing animal skins stood in the doorway. He threw something above the horde.

Explosion. Fire. Screaming men.

Or Shay's own screams. He wanted to cover his ears, couldn't raise his arms.

The skin-clad man took the axe from his helpless fingers and slid the haft through his wide belt. He grabbed Shay under the arms and dragged him.

Shay tried to yell, to fight back, but produced only a whimper and a twitch.

Darkness. Cool air. The lone patch of brightness and color disappeared as the door closed. All sound dissipated, and all light. Shay moaned, unable to stop himself. He caved in to the darkness of pain and closed his eyes, surrendering to whatever came next. Even the Dark.

The man bent over him. "Welcome, Bladen. I'm Robayne. Sorry I'm a little late."

It wasn't supposed to be this way! Spinel pushed his back against the rough rock wall behind him, scrunching into an even smaller space. The acid stench of vomit clung to his clothes, but at least he'd gotten away from his men– Jonus's men –so they didn't see him puke up his guts. Tears ran down his face, shaming him further. He'd lost his sword, dropped it somewhere in the melee.

But he still had the new flask on his belt, and it was intact.

The smells of battle brought more bile to his throat. He swallowed. So much noise! The screaming, and cursing, and battle cries . . . and that damn woman's fierce, exultant howl. The horrors he could see from here could not be blocked out. He tried closing his eyes, but the picture narrowed to one man, and to Spinel's sword slashing across

145

his throat. To the look of surprise on the man's face, the red line growing broader below his chin. To the awful, sickening moment that would forever haunt his dreams–the moment life left the man's eyes before he even began to fall, leaving a cindered vacancy where life had burned. Spinel didn't remember the man's name, but he'd never be able to forget his face.

He'd never killed a man before.

Oh, he'd seen them die. Memories of Cinny and her children slammed into his head, and bile crept up into his throat again. He swallowed it.

Spinel curled into a tighter ball and remained still, out of the notice of the raging fighters. He hated watching the bloodbath, but closing his eyes was worse.

Then he saw the strangest thing . . .

In the side of the mountain a door opened–one he hadn't seen before. A bear surged out, snatched up the black diamond axe, and dragged someone–it had to be Shay– inside the mountain. The door disappeared.

Spinel blinked and squinted. Did that really happen?

He lifted the flask again and took a long drink of the volatile joos it contained. To his surprise, he was starting to like the stuff. If he drank enough, he would pass out and be free of this nightmare.

To the barbarians of the Snows, it might be liquid courage. To him, it was a reprieve from death.

15. Robayne

"Where am I?" Shay whispered. He cast back for his last memories. A bloodstone pillar. A battle. Shouts, screams, smells, pain. The knife in his shoulder. Falling. An expectation of death.

Silence crowded around him, permeating the darkness. Had he died? Did someone burn his body properly? Had he ridden the flames into the Light, as he should? Would he find Cinny here, with the children?

If he dwelled within the Light, it shouldn't be this dark. His skin shrank in dread.

Cool, dry air caressed his face. A faint glimmer of light pulled his attention to a low fire nearby, its pungent smoke spiraling upward to some chimney he couldn't see. He absorbed the fire's soft crackle, the faint snap as it consumed the firewood's resin, the smoky taste of the air. He heard nothing else.

He remembered the roughness of being dragged into the Dark and shuddered, trying to hold off a bone-deep fear. *If I'm dead, how can I feel pain and fear?* Given courage by the thought, he pushed away panic.

He tried to move, discovered a rank, thick-haired hide covered him in warmth. So, life hadn't finished with him yet. He was in darkness, but not the Dark.

The thin cushion beneath him rested atop a hard surface, with thicker cushions under his head. His shifting forced a groan. Pain sizzled through him, left him unsure of where he hurt. Everywhere, it felt like.

Nearby a dark, lumpy shape rose. Monsters and other wild fancies flew through his head and out again, discarded for what they were. He watched as the lump threw off a blanket and stood, drawing himself up to a full height a few inches taller than him. He'd seen this man before–the one wearing animal skins.

And smelling of them, too. Shay's nostrils flared, nose wrinkling.

"Welcome back." The man silhouetted himself as he fed the fire, then turned to Shay and squatted next to him.

Shay didn't remember the shaggy brown hair and neatly trimmed beard. His rescuer looked almost as much a bear as the skins' former owner, but his clean face and polite manner spoke better of him. "Sorry for the rough accommodations and the smelly clothes. It gets chilly in this part of the caverns, so we keep a couple of bearskins here." His hand indicated a tightly-closed chest nearby. "Can you sit up?"

He needed a strong arm for that and then sat very still until faint dizziness passed. Stiff bandages wrapped a significant portion of his body and restricted his movement.

"Would you like some tea?" Without waiting for affirmation, the man knelt by the fire and poured dark liquid into two tin mugs. "I like mine pretty strong, so if it's a little too much, let me know and I'll water it down some."

Shay watched him warily as he took the mug. The tin handle burned his hand and he set it down to cool a little. "Who are you?"

"Robayne is my name. Yours is Bladen, in case you're having trouble with it. Please allow me to fill in some gaps for you. It will ease your mind."

Robayne, the name on the parchment note. Impossible.

"Where's my axe?"

Robayne grinned, teeth flashing in the dim light. "It's by your other hand, where you can get to it easily. I would never separate Bladen from his axe. We'll talk more about that soon."

Shay reached out to place a hand on the axe, reassuring

himself of its presence. "I'm not the Bladen you're thinking of, the folk hero. I'm *Shay* Bladen." He couldn't have said why he felt stubborn, obstinate, and a little angry over this . . . *legend*. But there it was.

"The battle outside," said Robayne.

His pettiness disappeared, replaced by dread. "What of my friends?"

"Both safe. They've been taken to Echo Town for the woman's care and healing. Interesting woman. She had mostly scratches, few real cuts. Quite the warrior. I know you were busy at the time, but you should have seen her cross swords with the attackers' leader! Very impressive. Oh, and her horse and the pack mule went to Echo with them. As far as I know, the mule's packs are intact. Nothing taken." He paused to sip his tea. "Your horse is here, in our stable, waiting for you."

"The woman's name is Bibi. The boy is Meilin. What happened to the attackers?" Weariness sagged his shoulders, though he'd only been awake a few minutes. "What's in this tea?" It tasted faintly, but unmistakably, of medicine.

"The attackers left. Your disappearance, then reappearance at another entrance to the bloodstone valley, lured them away."

"*My* reappearance?"

Robayne chuckled. "I always said all Bladens look alike. For now, you need more sleep. The caverns are timeless, so you can sleep as long as you like. It's the best thing for your healing. Oh, and no, I added nothing to the tea."

Shay knew better, but said nothing as Robayne helped him back to a prone position. He felt almost as disoriented as when he first woke. *Where the hell am I? And who is this man?*

149

♦　♦　♦

Spinel eased his eyes open when the sounds of battle disappeared. His hidey-hole against the side of the mountain had kept him safe, but it couldn't protect him from seeing the residue.

The deep green bloodstones held inner sparks and splashes of red, covered by gallons of deeper, thicker red. What an apt name for this stone! Everywhere he looked he saw gore and bodies. Hacked-off limbs and hunks of bloody flesh lay strewn about the field of battle, and the stink was unbearable. The stench clogged his nostrils and filled his mouth. So he did the only thing he could do.

He threw up, retching long past the point of emptying his belly, the taste and smell of battle compounded. When he realized his bowels had voided in fear, he retched again, quivering in humiliation and self-loathing.

Clean. He needed to get clean before anyone saw him like this. His imagination supplied an image of Tarver holding his nose and laughing at him.

A clot of something red clung to his britches. He wanted to flick it off but couldn't make himself touch it. He scraped it off with a rock.

He crawled out of his hole and found his horse, but it wouldn't allow him near. Eyes rolling and ears flat, it sidled away, as if a dead man reached for the reins.

To hell with the horse. He stumbled through the bloodstones, seeking the shortest route away from the carnage.

Not until he lay soaking in a sun-warmed stream did he realize he'd seen no other living soul on that field. Nor had he looked for any of his men.

Spinel remembered the bear snatching Shay away into the mountain. He needed to find that door again, to redeem himself. The implications had possibilities, if he could only think through them.

Later. He'd worry about the bear later.

Relatively clean again, he caught his horse easily and mounted. He found the town of Echo after three days of wandering, not quite able to remember the way. Bathing in every stream or lake he encountered slowed him down, too. Despite half a dozen baths, the stink of battle still hovered.

Ah, a tavern, right on the edge of town, easily accessed. Someone was hanging a sign out front, so it must be new. The worker disappeared down the board walkway well before Spinel came close enough to read it.

The Amyth Cup, it read below a bright painting of a purple, faceted goblet. Spinel snorted in laughter. A tavern named for a gem that supposedly prevented drunkenness? A place to get drunk where you couldn't get drunk?

He pushed through the door, his nose assaulted by the smell of fresh paint. Old building, new wood for everything but the freshly whitewashed outer walls. A dozen tables or so, a thick, heavy bar, and a stairway leading up. He knew what business that implied.

A woman in flowing, colorful robes stood at one wall, painting bright-colored pictures on the wall in broad strokes. Pictures of a marketplace, apparently.

Belatedly, he noticed the charred appearance of the woman's skin, and his scrotum tightened. He swallowed. The warrior woman, here? *Painting?* No, it must be someone else. He saw no weapons, and the robes would restrict fighting. Must be the resident whore, helping the owner get the place ready to open. After all, her earnings depended on the men who came in. Come to think of it, he hadn't had a woman for a while, and she'd be different, exotic, with that odd skin color.

When she turned to see who had entered, bright obsis eyes locked onto Spinel's and he saw recognition flicker.

151

So she *was* the warrior woman. Unarmed, not dressed for fighting, and off her guard. Not much of a threat now, was she? He swaggered in, rudely running his leer up and down her body.

The woman glared, obsis becoming weapon. She seemed to swell, her chin tucking infinitesimally. She laid down her paintbrush and glided toward him. "I know you," she said. "You are not welcome here."

Oh, she was proud. But barmaids couldn't afford pride. He thought about hiring a tumble, but he wanted no part of a warrior in his bed. "I need a drink. The strongest stuff you have on hand." He swept his gaze across the counter, impressed in spite of himself with the variety of liquors there. Was that joos?

He picked up the namesake goblet pictured on the sign: Purple, faceted, beautifully carved. The reality was even finer, the amyth walls as thin and delicate as fine glass. Without his gem loupe, the goblet seemed made of clear, transparent amyth with no visible inclusions and very fine workmanship. Add in the magic, and it was, indeed, a priceless object. Assuming the magical quality was as true as she told it.

"How much for the goblet?" he asked. "I want to buy it. And a bottle of joos."

"The goblet is not for sale. It is the centerpiece of my business. I have asked you to leave. I will not ask again."

Her business? Spinel frowned. They actually allowed a woman to own a business here? It didn't belong to the man he'd seen hanging the sign?

Suddenly, he felt overwhelmed, out of his depth, with no control over what happened. He looked deep into Bibi's eyes, saw cool, deliberate insult there. Warrior or not, she was only a woman, and she had caused him a lot of trouble.

"I don't want your goblet," he told her. "I want to get

152

stinking drunk, to wash myself of the taint of you."

He hurled the priceless goblet to the floor as hard as he could, shattering it into a thousand pieces.

When Shay woke again, the cavern was softly lit. The same rank fur still covered him, but the sharp pains had dulled. How long had he slept? Wary, he opened his eyes just enough to look through his lashes.

Yes, the fire still burned, and he smelled . . . bacon? The greasy sizzle and snap made his mouth water.

"Ah, you're awake," said Robayne, his voice deep and cheerful, despite the rank bearskin.

How did he . . . oh. The prolonged inhalation of the aroma of bacon.

Shay opened his eyes all the way and sat up slowly, surprised at how little pain remained. "How long did I sleep?"

"A couple of days." Robayne shot him a grin before forking a full load of bacon onto a plate for him. "I saved a little of the bacon for you. Not much."

Two days? Impossible. But the change in how he felt made it believable. Maybe. Shay took the plate and stared at more than a dozen strips. "This qualifies as *not much*?"

"Oh, and I lied about the tea, too. It had medicine to help you sleep deeply and heal quickly. That's why I made it so strong. Although, admittedly, I do like my tea stronger than most people."

At least Robayne seemed honest about his dishonesty. The big smile and open manner led Shay to instinctive trust, which immediately made him distrustful. "You lie a lot, do you?"

"All the time."

Shay's pale smile replaced the chuckle he'd intended. "What about my friends? The battle? Did you lie about those, too?"

Robayne sobered. Looking Shay in the eye, he said, "Never. Not about something so important.

"How do you feel? Are you up to some walking?"

"Yes." Shay bit into a crisp bacon slice. His tongue tingled from the salty fat and he ate the rest almost too fast to taste it. Almost. "But I have a lot of questions to ask first."

"If your mind is working properly, you have more questions than I have spit in my mouth to answer. Let's start with a few while you eat, and we can talk more as we walk."

"Will you tell me the truth when you answer them?" Shay reached for the mug of tea Robayne brought him.

"Yes. Without reservation. That's what I'm here for. There's much you need to know, and I'll be your teacher."

"Am I a prisoner?"

"No, not at all."

"I can leave any time I like? Will you show me the door right now, and stand aside while I walk out, never to return?"

The outer tips of Robayne's eyebrows drooped, to Shay's surprise. "I can, if you insist on it. But I don't think you want to. The answers you seek are here, in these caverns–about your axe, about your past, your family . . ."

"My family? Cinny? Piper and Beryl?" That couldn't be.

Robayne smile ruefully. "No. I'm sorry, but I meant your birth family. Your parents and their parents and on back for many generations."

"You're talking about someone else. I'm not that Bladen."

Robayne scratched his beard. "We'll see. Later. Would you like more tea?"

Shay handed him the empty mug, staring at him. "Are you the same Robayne who signed that note?"

"No. My ancestor wrote it, several generations back."

Shay looked around, finally turning his attention to the lighting in the cavern. Softly glowing orbs had been set about the room, but he saw no source of the light they emitted. "What about the glowing spheres? Where do they come from? How do you make them glow?"

"They're magic. Many generations ago, our people discovered a vein of moonstone deep within the caverns. There are many stones in these caverns that may exist nowhere else on earth, and magic seems to run through its veins, as well. The moonstone from our vein is all magic. Our early people discovered that globes shaped from it could be left out in sunlight, to make them glow softly in the darkness of the caverns. We use them sparingly in the outer caverns, like this one, but we have enough moonstones to keep the deeper caverns well lit."

"The black diamonds are mined here, too?" Beneath the hide, Shay fingered his bandages. Robayne had done a good job with them.

"Yes, one of those gems with no other known source. And yes, they're magic. While you're here, I'll show you the source and tell you the secrets of the axe, and its magic."

Excitement poured through Shay. His belly and throat tightened until he could barely breathe. *Damn. Robayne's right, I have to stay. This is what I came for. Cinny would want me to learn everything I can.*

"Let's get you on your feet, so you can try out your legs a bit." Robayne reached out a hand to help Shay up.

Shay took it, glad to have Robayne's steady pull to help him. His bones and joints creaked like rusty hinges, but he made it.

His head swam from slight vertigo. He staggered a

step, but Robayne already had a steadying hand on his shoulder.

After a moment, the cavern stopped moving and Shay took a deep breath. The air tasted dry, but not stale.

He tried a few steps as Robayne hovered at his elbow, then turned to his rescuer.

"Does your knowledge include the history of the axe? Will you share it?"

"Of course. The axe is a part of these caverns, and it's a part of your personal heritage."

"No, not *my* heritage. My wife's heritage. I told you, I'm not *that* Bladen. Her father gave it to us as a wedding gift."

Robayne became thoughtful for a moment. "The axe was lost to the Blue Mountain People some time ago. It appears you know some of its history that I don't. I'd like to learn what you know and record it with the axe's lore."

"The Blue Mountain People?"

"Our people. Your people. Many of us don't live in these caverns all the time, but there are always some of us here. I do live here most of the time, because my purpose– and the purpose of my family–has always been to mentor the Bladen in the ways of the axe. This has occurred numerous times throughout our history, although it's been a long time now since the axe resided here.

"I can't tell you how pleased and proud I am to be the one serving when you arrived. This is a momentous occasion for all of us, and when we arrive in the lower caverns, you will see that they're already organizing ceremonies and festivities to welcome you home."

16. Welcome

"If you are not the true Bladen, the magic of the axe won't work for you."

Robayne and Shay ambled along the passage through the rock, stopping often to allow the gemsman to rest. Shay walked with care to avoid pulling on his wounds, grateful for a slow pace and the time to ask questions.

To his relief, Robayne now wore shirt and britches, having stored the bearskins in a sealed chest near their campfire. These were normal folks after all.

Shay snorted. "I keep telling you it's a coincidence of name. I'm a gemsman, not a warrior."

Robayne grinned. "Few of us here are warriors, except when needed. The axe will know the truth of who you are."

Smart axe. Shay didn't believe it, but he wouldn't offend his rescuer by saying so.

"Will I learn to create something the size of an axe from a single diamond?"

"I'm sure you will. Unless there's some failing within you to prevent it."

"Within me! Such as . . ."

Robayne chuckled. "Oh, like stupidity, giving up too easily, having only one arm . . ."

Shay shook his head, not in the mood for levity. Not on this topic, at least.

"What did you mean, 'work for me'? Its magic is what it is, not what it does."

"You haven't learned its full powers yet. Had you been its master, you might well have emerged from this battle uninjured."

"How so?"

"That's part of the learning, after you've been

157

confirmed by the axe."

That piqued Shay's curiosity and frustrated him, but being a guest, he let it go. "How many live here, inside the mountain?"

"We're the size of a small city. We keep to ourselves, allowing no outsiders, for reasons that will become apparent. People from Echo and other places have tried to find us, but our entrances are hidden. When the axe verifies your lineage, I'll show you all of them."

Strange man. Strange place. Again, Shay accepted the explanation without comment, despite reservations.

When his energy sagged out through his pores, he dropped onto one of many stone benches carved out of the wall at intervals, marveling at the intricate carvings along the edges that made each of them a work of art.

Robayne sat next to him. "You have family, a wife you mentioned. Do you have children? Where have you been living?"

A sharp ache cut off Shay's breath. "I have no family now." His voice came out hoarse and bristling with pain. It embarrassed him to display so openly a pain so private. He leaned forward, elbows on his knees, so Robayne couldn't see his face.

Robayne's voice gentled. "What happened?"

To answer or not? Did Robayne expect confidences in exchange for the secrets of the axe? The answer took care of itself; Shay couldn't get his breath, couldn't get his throat open to speak. He shook his head, staring at the floor, and said nothing.

After a moment of silence, Robayne caught on. "Are you ready to continue, or would you like another moment of rest?"

Shay couldn't answer, and couldn't expend the breath still trapped inside. He remained seated, staring at the floor

158

and trying to collect himself.

He'd thought he was adjusting, but the pain had been lying in wait all along. He focused on the recent battle, on the man sitting next to him, on Meilin and his gems, on the dangerous mountain trails. Slowly, he pulled away from his grief.

Breathing more easily now, he studied the soft, beautiful glow of moonstones lighting the passage in two long rows twenty feet up the walls. Now *there* was a magical wonder! With a handful of such moonstones, he could create gems to awe the wealthy and royal throughout the known world. He began to imagine the settings he would create: pendants, rings, bracelets, tiaras, even royal crowns. Moonstones surrounded by diamonds. Tiny moonstones alternating with labra, or lazh, or fire opals. The delicate findings and chains would accent their beauty without overwhelming . . .

At last, he stood up, eyes alight with plans and designs. "I'm ready to go on." The pain receded to the background–a permanent residue of anguish waiting to ambush him again.

Without comment, Robayne rose and started down the passageway with him.

"How did you know I'd arrived at the bloodstone pillars?" Shay asked. From his first reading of the note, he'd been mystified by its promise: *I will know when you arrive.*

Robayne grinned. "I knew you were coming long before your arrival. Many of us spend time in Echo and even have homes there. The day you rode in with the axe strapped across your back, rumors began.

"Unfortunately, your battle had begun by the time the sentries inside saw you and notified me. I ran all the way, but when I arrived, you were in the thick of battle, and I had to wait."

"Why? We could have used another fighter on our

side."

"I had no weapons with me. Besides, our law forbids opening an outer door where anyone not of our people might catch a glimpse of it."

"But you did open it. Eventually."

Robayne shrugged, signaling his discomfort. "You're one of us. Besides, you were close to the door, and you would have died otherwise. Our laws are very strict about hidden doors, but I did the only reasonable thing I could."

"You won't be in trouble for saving my life, will you?"

"No, not for the Bladen." Robayne's tone hinted of amusement. "Bladen and his axe are a treasure to the entire community."

"What's the usual penalty among your people for opening outer doors?"

"*Our* people. If I'd had any doubt about your identity, you wouldn't be here now. That penalty could be death, in extreme circumstances. Here's our turn."

The passageway ended just ahead of them. The only turn Shay could see was to turn about and return as they had come.

Robayne walked over to the wall on his left, slid his fingers into one of many ragged cracks in the stone, and pulled open a door Shay hadn't seen. He held it for Shay and followed him through. The door closed, and terrifyingly absolute darkness enveloped them.

"Don't worry about the darkness," said Robayne. "This is a double layer of doors, and we'll find light beyond the second one."

Shay heard Robayne move forward a step, heard fingers sliding over stone. Then a crack of light appeared and Robayne pulled the door wide.

Brightness flooded across Shay's face and he snapped his eyes shut. He opened them slowly, blinking, to a light as bright as a normal Eye-lit day.

The passage facing them looked like the one they had just left, except for a ceiling crusted with moonstone globes, each larger and brighter than the ones left behind.

The ceiling here pressed lower than in the outer passages, and for the first time, Shay felt the weight of the mountain above him. The dry, cool air raised goosebumps.

As the passages became broader, the mountain's pressure eased. Sometimes distant voices seemed to call out, but Robayne explained them as soft wind sighing through the mountain's natural vents. "That's why the air stays fresh," he said.

As they traveled deeper, the wall on their right disappeared, opening up into canyons with only a railing to separate life from death. Steeper trails led them ever downward, sometimes becoming staircases carved into the rock.

They stopped at one of several sleeping rooms hidden at wide intervals behind cracks in the wall. This one held two straw-stuffed mattresses, a fireplace, and stocked shelves of non-perishable foods: Mushrooms, several types of fungus, dried fish, and other meats Shay didn't recognize.

Robayne identified them for him. "Snake. This one grows to twenty feet long, enough to feed many people, if it can be killed before it crushes the hunters in its coils. It lives in deep pools and lakes well below the surface of the mountain. Salamander, which is sweeter and less tough. Venison, from the Bowl–a hidden canyon high on our slopes, where we keep a few crops. Great place for picnics, too. And this is dried bat. Tough and unpleasant to eat, but in a pinch, it'll keep you alive."

Shay collapsed onto a mattress, more tired than he'd realized.

"Would you like to try salamander and mushrooms for

lunch?" asked Robayne.

The voice seemed distant and ethereal. Before he could think how to open his mouth for a response, Shay slipped into sleep and dreamed of skin-clad hunters attacked by flying bats that looked like manglers.

The next day's journey, if the concept of *days* even applied, took them through more double entries located at apparent dead ends. At one of these, Robayne lifted a hand as if in greeting before opening the first door.

Shay peered at the cracks in the wall, someone's unseen scrutiny crawling across his skin. He could feel the watcher but couldn't locate him.

Then the second door slid open and Robayne stepped through ahead of him.

The watcher met them, a big, open smile on his face. "Welcome back, Robayne! It's good to see you." The, tall young man clasped Robayne's forearm.

"And you, Atich." Robayne smiled.

"And you're the Bladen," said the young man, extending his hand to Shay.

Shay took the proffered hand, opening his mouth to correct him.

"Yes, indeed." Robayne gave him no chance to speak. "Shay Bladen himself. Shay, this is Atich, your cousin, currently assigned door duty here. From here on, doors don't open at all from the outside."

Atich's open smile warmed Shay, and his peaked eyebrows looked familiar and reassuring. "The mountain is truly a fortress," Shay told him politely. At least Robayne had introduced him by his real name.

"Welcome to the Blue Mountain People," said Atich. "We've waited long for your return."

Shay laughed. "Hardly a return. I've never been here

before." He buried his small irritation at Atich's presumption.

"I regret I will not be there for the official reception," Atich told him. "I, as Robayne pointed out, have door duty and will not be home for several days yet."

The festivities Robayne had mentioned. That sounded stilted, boring, and most of all, embarrassing. He murmured something polite in response.

"And this is the famed battle-axe!" Atich stared at the weapon strapped across Shay's back. "What a beauty! I wish I could at least be there for the testing."

Formal testing. Robayne had mentioned it, but Shay had paid little attention. He groaned inside. Why couldn't they just take his word for it? He wasn't that Bladen!

Atich invited them into a sleeping room a few feet away, this one furnished with a wooden chair and additional seating in the form of stone benches carved from the mountain. Both chair and benches bore colorful cushions, and Shay sank into one gratefully. His wounds had all his attention for the moment.

"We've been walking all day," Robayne explained, choosing the plumpest cushion available, once Shay had chosen. "And days before that in the outer caverns. It seems he's made some enemies. He and the Sheethe who travels with him were beset by fighters. Shay sustained injuries, even with the battle-axe."

Atich sat on the edge of the straw mattress, eyes widening. "Even the magic of the axe wasn't enough?"

Shay must have looked a little confused, because Robayne cut in. "He's unaware of all the properties of the axe, my friend. He grew up with no knowledge of his heritage, or its tales."

"Not even the tales?" Atich grinned at Shay. "Not even about Bladen's legendary defense of the skystone people?"

163

"Skystone people?" Shay had never heard of them.

"It's an old, old tale," Robayne began.

"Let me tell it, Robayne. You'll make it as dry as the dust of the grave, where I will tell it as a story." Atich's good humor spilled over into his voice.

Robayne laughed. "Go ahead."

Shay's attention sharpened and he settled in to listen.

"Once within the land . . ." Atich grinned at the traditional opening to a children's tale. ". . .the skystone people filled a deep valley in the Crystal Mountains. They were known thus because of vast deposits of these deep blue, highly prized crystals. At one time, a single skystone might command the price of a kingdom, but after a time and a time, the deposits dwindled, due to depredations by outlaws and their own greed.

"More bandits heard the tales and came to plunder, but the people were never warriors, and their wealth had been squandered, so they couldn't hire an army of their own. Now the innocent were slaughtered by enraged bandits whose dreams of easy wealth evaporated. In desperation, the skystone people sent a messenger to Bladen, the hero of Blue Mountain, and he responded.

"The slaughter started well before he arrived, and bodies of children, women, and unarmed men made a carpet over their valley. Bladen left his horse, lest it be killed, and waded into the battle with the famed black diamond battle-axe.

"He shouted mightily to call the attention of the bandits and lifted the axe high overhead. Blue veins trickled along its haft and fire shot from the eye of the axe.

"Many fled the fight then and there, but many did not. They converged on Bladen, seeing a prize far greater than the fabulous skystones. And he fought them, swinging to one side and the other. Where the axe touched flesh, it left death, and bodies charred beyond recognition. The bandits began to fall back.

"Bladen fought all morning and all afternoon without pause. A lesser man's arms would have given out. A lesser man would have stopped for water, or food, or rest. But Bladen fought on, through the long, dark night. And when morning came, the bodies of the foe outnumbered their victims. The survivors had fled, the people saved.

"The skystone people still exist. They are few now and poor, and the skystones themselves are smaller, less brilliant stones. Though diminished, the people will never forget that one man came to their aid, fought with everything in him, and saved the skystone people. To this day, their valley displays a statue of skystone and emrel, citrine, and obsis, commemorating Bladen and his axe. It looks a lot like you, actually."

Robayne laughed. "All Bladens look pretty much alike."

Shay blinked his way back from a distant time and place. An interesting folk tale, garnished with magical fire in the axe. The real axe, though, had magic enough for him, simply by its existence. He smiled at Atich. "You tell a tale wonderfully, Atich. I was under your enchantment the whole way."

"I agree. Much better than I would have told it," Robayne said. "Atich, may I beg a favor? We have walked long, despite Shay's injuries. Would you go to the Council to tell them of our progress? Be sure they're aware that until now, Shay has known nothing of the Blue Mountain People, and little of the axe."

"I'll leave right now. Please, be at home here, Shay. Robayne will watch the door for me while you rest and eat decent food. My wife brought fresh-baked bread and soft cheese this morning, and I expect to find none left on my

165

return."

While Atich was gone, Shay and Robayne decimated his food stores, then slept. Shay awoke only minutes before Atich returned and found Robayne already on his feet.

"You didn't watch the door, did you?" Shay said, teasing.

Robayne laughed. "Ah, but I did! I've let in two parties while you slept. You didn't even stir."

Shay just shook his head.

As they said their farewells and began the final leg of their journey, Shay noticed that the one-way door had been a threshold of sorts, leading to broader passages. He had entered the inhabited area of the mountain.

The eternal stone still overwhelmed him by its strangeness and beauty.

In the first cavern they passed through, fanged ceilings and floors snarled through their teeth. Winds moaned and whispered high above them, where blackness shrouded everything and no details could be seen. Robayne called it the Dragon, and Shay could see why. The effect would have been chilling, if children hadn't been running among the spikes and pillars, screaming with laughter in a game of tag.

The second cavern contained more columns and fewer teeth. In the center a stone bubble the height of a man rose from a pool of cold, dark water. Robayne showed him the tiny, white fish swimming in the darkness. "They're blind," he explained. "They have no need of eyes in such darkness as they inhabit. These are small, but larger pools in other places hold larger fish–big enough to eat."

Robayne led him through another enclosed passage and turned off into a side corridor. It opened into yet another cavern and Shay stopped, unable to breathe beyond a whispered, "Impossible!"

An outer circle of clear querk spires enclosed black

fibrous inclusions –thin hairs of black turmali. Within the bounds of those spires rose taller spikes, of bicolor turmali, deep green meshing into cherry red. And at the center of that, a full column of blazing white bastar joined lofty ceiling and smooth floor.

Unable to help himself, Shay wandered among them all, touching, stroking, examining, hearing the faint sounds he now recognized as voices. The light of the passage's moonstones shone through querk and turmali and cast colorful, fibrous shadows against the purity of the column's base.

"Shay." Robayne's quiet voice carried easily in the open space. "We need to move on."

Still Shay looked, and touched, memorizing every detail of the unusual display. Until Robayne laughed and entered the circles to retrieve him.

"You can return here any time you like, but people are waiting for us. And we have only two more caverns to traipse through."

When they reached the next cavern, Shay just shook his head. There was so much to see in these caverns! Brilliant red and clean white streaked the walls and a fair-sized lake filled all but the broad ledges where they walked. From here Shay couldn't tell what gems he saw. Perhaps ruby? No signs of mining marred the vein, and he asked about it.

"Yes, it's ruby, but we're in the inhabited part of the mountain, now," Robayne explained. "We do no mining here. There are parts of the mountain where the mining is extensive, though. I'll show you those later, after all the ceremonies and fuss are done."

And the final cavern looked much like the Dragon, except that all the fangs lay broken on the floor, leaving stubs on the ceiling and underneath the rubble. "A

167

reminder," said Robayne. "We could have cleaned it up long ago, but we do have small quakes from time to time, and this cavern is the victim of one. It's good for us to remember the dangers, as well as the joys, of our way of life."

Shay shuddered, once again aware of the immensity of earth and stone above his head. Sunlight and blue skies beckoned as never before, and he ached to be outdoors, away from here.

Then he took a closer look at the rubble and the feeling passed. Rough gems hid here, underneath and within the rocks: blue, green, gold, and red, at least. He'd have to look much closer to determine what they might be.

But Robayne walked past without slowing.

At last, with no forewarning, they turned down a side passage which soon opened into a large, bright cavern, its domed ceiling crusted with bright moonstones.

Sound assaulted Shay's ears and he startled back a step.

Robayne's hand on his shoulder reassured him, and the sight before him registered.

People. Voices. A huge crowd, all shouting and cheering, all with his name on their lips.

"Bladen! Bladen! Bladen!"

He ran his fingers through his hair, his scalp pimpling. So many people, and all looking at him! Dazed, he allowed Robayne to guide him forward, and the people moved back, out of their way.

In the center of the room, down the endless path between people, stood a dais, bearing four men and three women. Apparently, this was the reception of which Atich had spoken.

"Lift your axe high," murmured Robayne. "They long to see it again."

168

Shay did so, and when he thrust the black diamond axe into the air, the roar redoubled. He waved it in wide arcs, found himself smiling at the people, especially the children who pushed forward between the adults or perched on their fathers' shoulders.

At last they reached the center of the room. Robayne stopped at the foot of the three steps up to the dais and gave Shay a gentle push to continue on.

He stepped onto the platform where the council stood, and the noise of the crowd dropped to silence. A strangeness overtook him, and he found himself detached from everything, hidden inside himself, waiting for what would happen next.

17. The Test

A slender man with gray hair and eyes stepped forward, hand outstretched. Shifting the axe to his other hand, Shay reached to clasp it. The man neatly stepped to one side, turning Shay with him to give the crowd a better view. Shay followed his lead clumsily. He'd never stood before a crowd. He focused on the man's face, trying to pretend the crowd didn't exist.

The man's firm voice filled the room, carrying to the farthest walls with ease. "Shay Bladen, welcome on behalf of the Blue Mountain People. It is long since the hero has graced these halls and caverns. My name is Orlait." He paused.

For Shay's response.

To speak with a thousand people awaiting every word? He pushed down the acid bubble of panic, his shoulders bearing a greater weight than all the solid rock over his head. He gripped Orlait's hand too tightly, a lifeline he dared not release.

"Focus only on Orlait," murmured a woman behind him. "You'll be fine."

Shay half-turned toward the speaker, noting dark hair streaked with gray, pale seastone eyes, and a triangular face decidedly different from most of the people here. He turned back, struggling to block out the crowd and speak man to man. "Thank you for the warm welcome, Orlait. Your home within the mountain is amazing, and I owe my life to your people. To Robayne. I am grateful for the shelter offered in dire need." Did his voice quiver? The words didn't come out right, either, but he couldn't fix it now.

The voices rose again. Cheers, whistles, and welcoming shouts bounced from the stone.

Shay wanted to hide. The wall of sound trapped him, the wide grins and dancing eyes promised expectations he couldn't possibly anticipate, let alone meet.

At last, one of the men behind Orlait held up a hand to the audience. The crowd quieted.

Behind him, the woman said, "Well done, Bladen."

Orlait turned to address the audience again.

"Shay Bladen," he told them, "is a city man and a master gemsman."

A susurrus of voices broke out and people grinned at each other.

"He grew up with no knowledge of his family's heritage, or his battle-axe, yet it came to him anyway, through his wife's family. Destiny has found him, against all odds, but he has much to learn. Robayne, of course, will be his teacher, as Robayne and Bladen have always been teacher and pupil."

How did Orlait know all that? When had Robayne had opportunity to tell him? Ah, must have been the men who came through Atich's post while Shay slept.

"First, of course, we must test this man to confirm he is truly the Bladen. The axe will know. The test is simple, so we'll put that issue behind us here and now."

Orlait turned to Shay. "It's obvious who you are," he grumbled with a smile, "so let's just get this out of the way."

"Obvious? How?" He'd never seen these people before, never heard of them! He couldn't be who they thought him.

Could he?

"Look around you," said the woman. "I'm Faltryn." She offered a handshake.

Shay clasped her hand as he would a man's, then looked at those on the dais and in the audience. Realization burst upon him. Many of the people here could only be related to each other, with the same dark hair and eyes,

171

same general size and build, and even the same thick, peaked eyebrows. Like his.

Inside him, an earthquake rumbled and cracked. He swallowed hard, shot a look at Orlait.

The older man smiled. "It's a lot to take in all at once. Let's do the public part quickly."

Shay nodded, mouth dry.

"If you would, please, bare your axe."

Mindlessly, Shay removed the hood from the axe head and handed it to Faltryn.

"The grip, too, please."

"The grip? It's attached. It doesn't come off."

"Yes, it does. Simply peel it away. It can be reattached."

Grasping the haft, Shay braced the knob against his body and peeled the covering. To his surprise, it removed easily.

"Now hand me the axe and hold out both hands, palms up."

Reluctantly, Shay obeyed. Orlait received the axe with leather-gloved hands.

With a move too quick to avoid, Orlait dipped the axe head, slicing into Shay's palm with one bit, then the other palm with the other bit.

Shay gasped in shock, although the shallow wounds barely stung. A few drops of blood welled from the cuts.

Orlait handed the axe back to him. "Now hold it as you would for battle."

Falling naturally into a basic stance, Shay wrapped both hands around the bare axe.

Lightning exploded through his palms, tingled his fingertips. He gasped aloud as the sensation spread up his arms and down every nerve. His body blazed with fire-that-wasn't-fire, burning inside, blistering his hands. Blue veins

172

of light laced up the throat and belly of the axe, crackled to the eye, shot sparks into the air. The axe quivered as if alive. He tried to drop it but couldn't unclench his grip. Flame roared through him, filling him with heat and power.

Sweet, sweet connection, as if the axe knew him. Joy burst through the joining, a fierce exultation almost sexual in its intimacy and inability to be denied.

Consumed, Shay shook with the power, with the glory, with the knowing. His soul melded into the axe, and he heard a voice inside it, a full, rich voice that split into a chorus of song. Welcoming him!

The blue power lines moved beneath the black skin, rippling and twisting in ecstasy.

Life. The axe held life. Not an inert lump of stone, but alive. The distinct, rich personality overwhelmed him with its femininity. The love of a good wife, sweet and beautiful, hot and passionate. The love of a mother for her children, ferocious in her protectiveness.

How could he have ever thought of this powerful beauty as masculine?

Hard stone bruised his knees. Hot tears streamed down his face, dripping onto his hands.

"I am Bladen," he whispered to her. "I am yours."

In his head, a strong, feminine voice sang, "I am Elegy. And I am yours. Forever." Her name was written on his heart and soul in fire, as intimate and as personal as lovemaking, never to be divulged.

Slowly, reluctantly, Shay separated his soul from the axe's. He regained self-awareness.

He lay on the dais, curled around the axe like a lover. He could not arise, not yet. For he was swollen with seed, aching with the overwhelming need for release.

He delayed opening his eyes as long as he could, not wanting to face a thousand witnesses to his arousal. Silence

173

surrounded him and stuffed his ears, except for a soft, satisfied purr that he suspected no one else could hear.

The hall had emptied. Not a single person remained. He had not heard them leave, had not been aware of them at all. He sat up and looked around, assuring himself no witnesses remained. Then, just to be safe, he crawled off the dais and made his way into the rocks far to one side. Still locked in an embrace with the axe that he could not bear to end, he found a private space there and at last found release.

18. Elegy

When Shay emerged from the rocks, he found Robayne studying something on the far wall, his back to Shay.

Shame flushed through him. How long had Robayne been there? What could he know or guess about what had just taken place?

Bad enough that Cinny knew, if she watched from within the shelter of the Light. *It's only an axe! It's not really alive!* So why did he feel as if he'd been unfaithful to the woman he loved? He wanted to be alone with his muddled thoughts. Or maybe throwing the axe away would right a world turned topsy-turvy.

Cinny's axe. From her family, not his!

He wasn't who he'd thought he was.

His hands tightened on the grip, as if to prevent the axe's forcible removal. Ridding himself of it–her–was no longer possible. Faint blue veins still rippled, still tingled his palm like the tickling of delicate fingers. Like a woman, rather than an axe. He shivered, eyes closed.

Robayne turned from the pictures drawn on the wall, which became visible to Shay for the first time. The paintings breathed ancient air, a long-gone time brought to near-life–stick figures of animal and human, hunted and hunter.

"Cover the grip," Robayne said quietly. His voice carried well to Shay in the huge, round chamber. "That will shut off the blue lightning and its tingling."

Without speaking or meeting his gaze, Shay returned to the dais and rewound the black leather clumsily around the axe's grip.

The blue lightning died away, and with it the light

song running through his head. He hadn't been aware of it until it disappeared, but then he missed it.

Elegy's voice.

He touched the haft with his bare fingers, and once again the axe's song caressed him.

A world upside down. Skewed. Confusion and humiliation twisted his heart. How could this happen to him? He knew of no man so unsuited to this destiny.

Life seemed to have run away with him, a wild stallion carrying an inexperienced rider.

"What now?" he asked, breaking the physical connection again. Weary resignation dragged at his voice.

Robayne turned and came toward him, quieter and more subdued than normal. Understanding and compassion filled his eyes, though his face didn't otherwise change.

"There's much ahead of you yet, but let's talk a little first. Then we'll go get you settled in." Robayne sat near him on the dais, turned enough to see his face.

"First, I know many of the secrets of your axe, though she won't respond to me as she does to you. Only the first-born male of each generation of your line earns the reaction you felt today."

"Then I'm the last owner," said Shay, feeling the familiar ache of loss. "My son is dead."

"There are provisions for these and other circumstances in the lore. But let's worry about that later. I'm aware your axe is female, though I do not know her name. She shares it only with Bladen. Yes, I'm aware of your emotional and physical reaction to her . . ."

Alarm prickled–the most pressing fear Shay had.

". . . but there are no witnesses and you need feel no shame. The test ends when the lightning appears, and Orlait followed tradition by dismissing the gathering as soon as he could be heard over the cheering. This affords you time to become acquainted and get used to the axe."

Cheering? Shay hadn't heard it, though he didn't doubt Robayne's word. The people would have been thrilled at the return of their mythic hero.

I'm no hero. I don't want *to be a hero.* "Find someone else," he whispered, surprised to hear his words spoken aloud. He took a deep breath. "I don't want to be a hero. I just want . . . my life back. My family. My shop."

Robayne remained quiet for a long moment. "I wish I could give them back to you, Shay. I've had my own share of loss, and I wouldn't wish it on anyone. My wife and son died in a small earthquake when he was six." He pulled from the opening of his shirt a gold chain bearing a gold medallion. A circle in the center had been enameled in green, and inside the circle sat a large ruby, with a smaller diamond snugged up beneath it. Mother and child. Shay's eyes stung.

Robayne sighed, a heavy ache in the sound. "Life only runs in one direction, just like a river. We go forward as best we can, make a new life as best we can. The Light grant that yours be a good one, even if it's not the one you would have chosen."

"I could leave," said Shay. "Walk out of the mountain, leave the axe for someone better suited, go far away and start a more docile life somewhere else."

"Could you really? Set her down and walk away? Leave all the secrets still hidden from you? Never touch her again, never feel the power flow through you? Never know your birth family? Your history?"

Shay shrugged, staring at the stone floor. The hard dais had become uncomfortable, but he couldn't find the energy to move. Nor did he want to think about Robayne's questions.

"Now is not the time to make important decisions,"

177

Robayne said. "She has taken you to the pinnacle, and confining her again in leather has dropped you to the depths. It's normal to be despondent just now. It will even out."

Shay set the axe down on the dais to gain a little distance from her, but found he couldn't bear to release his hold on her. He made himself let go. "Am I to be her slave, then? Bound to her every whim?" The feminine reference came easily to his tongue, now that he'd met her.

Robayne smiled. "No. You will control her, not the other way around. As you become better acquainted, it will become a partnership. Remember, she has lived for hundreds of years and partnered with many Bladens. It's what she wants, too, this bond between you. She is your friend. You will have access to her powers for the rest of your life, even if you pass her to a firstborn son.

"Come. Let's get you a hot bath, clean clothes, and settled into a place of your own. There will be feasting later, and you'll want to be rested."

Shay nodded slightly and stood. Somehow the axe had already returned to his hand. He followed Robayne out of the cavern.

"Oh, by the way," said Robayne as they ambled down a corridor devoid of people, "the general population doesn't know the axe has a gender. I would advise against revealing that. Except between you and me, she should be referred to as *it*."

How could Shay ever again think of the axe as an object? But he nodded. He would make it a habit. After all, he didn't want to appear insane.

Shay's new quarters weren't what he expected. Not a single, small room, as his journey with Robayne had led him to expect. Instead, he had an entire home, with a living

178

area, a bedroom, a kitchen, and a workroom, all graced with simple furniture more than fine enough for his needs. The fireplace had been laid, although not lit. In the kitchen, the cupboards and cabinets carried crockery and cookery, and drying herbs hung from racks. Its cleanliness and neat arrangement suggested that someone had prepared his home for his arrival.

To his surprise, the workroom contained the basic tools of his trade, a drawer of findings separated into small compartments, a fine gem loupe, dops with three sizes of diamond tips for carving softer gems, and a range of implements hung on the wall above the sturdy workbench, all of first quality. A scaif for polishing had its own place on the bench next to its jars of oil and diamond dust. Even a small supply of rough crystals lay clustered in one drawer; he fingered them, longing for time to examine them closely.

He thought about the tauz horse that Tarver had commissioned–the one that burned in the fire. And about the gems he'd brought from home, and the stones he'd collected along the way. If he had his saddlebags, he could add some fine specimens to this collection.

The bedroom held a wardrobe for hanging clothes and a trunk for folded items and blankets. Next to the bed stood a chest with drawers, and atop it a moonstone lantern. "That black thing next to the lantern is a hood," explained Robayne, "thick enough to hide the light so you can sleep comfortably. The glow can be adjusted by adding moonstones or by putting some of them in the drawer here."

Shay had never thought about such a lantern. What an interesting way of life!

Then he noticed the walls, where a thread of pale blue flickered in the light of glowing moonstones. His own personal vein of seastone! He ran his fingers along it, itching for a tool to extract a specimen.

179

Behind him, Robayne chuckled.

"I know what you're thinking," his mentor said. "But don't dig a hole in your wall. I'll show you larger deposits of seastone, godtears, starstone, torquis –we have a lot of torquis here; it's what makes the mountain look blue– turmali, and others. These caverns are a rich source of gem-quality stones, and many others may be found throughout the Crystal Mountains."

"This is much finer than I expected," said Shay. "Everything here is now mine?"

"Yes, although you will find it less surprising when I tell you that this suite has been Bladen's home for many years. The Bladen clan has several families, but you're *the* Bladen, the bearer of the battle-axe. You'll meet some of your kin at the feasting.

"In the meantime, your bath is coming. I normally bathe in warm springs deeper in the caverns, and you may prefer that, too, but to celebrate your arrival and to pamper your wounds and weariness, some of the men are bringing a bathtub here for you, and water to fill it. Once it's full, I promise you will be left to yourself to bathe and rest. I'll return for you in plenty of time for the feast. You'll find clean clothing in the wardrobe, and I think it should fit reasonably well."

The tub and water arrived within minutes, carried by men with varying resemblance to Robayne and each other. All had welcoming smiles and cheerful greetings. Robayne did not allow them to introduce themselves, however. "There will be plenty of time for that later," he told them. "Right now he'd forget your names anyway."

Laughing and jesting with each other, the men did their work and filed out. Then one stuck his head back in. "Remember, Bladen, Robayne is as new to his role as you are to yours, so don't give him more credence than he

180

deserves."

"Out," cried Robayne with a laugh. "At least I've been trained–unlike some others I could name." He shut the door behind them.

"Unlike me," said Shay ruefully.

"Actually, I meant him," said Robayne. "He's changed his trade three times, only half trained in each. You, on the other hand, are already a master gemsman, the most critical skill you will need. Is there anything else before I leave you to yourself?"

Shay shook his head and Robayne took his leave. "As long as your door is closed," he said, "no one will enter unless you invite them in." He disappeared.

19. Council of Elders

Dread tightened Shay's stomach as he stepped into the Great Hall with Robayne for his welcoming feast. People swarmed around him, shook his hand, pounded his shoulder, patted his arm. Smiles, welcomes, greetings crushed into him as each person in the hall sought his attention. He stubbed his toe on someone's heavy boot.

"They should have set up a receiving line," muttered Robayne in his ear. "Pure chaos is not an appropriate welcome for a hero-to-be."

In spite of himself, Shay chuckled. Then he gently fended off a young woman trying to hug him.

"Oh, yes," Robayne said, "as a hero, you will be besieged by women, and not always the young, unmarried ones."

Cinny remained his life mate. He could imagine no other in her place. Elegy's song echoed in memory, but that didn't count.

He sidestepped a woman whose eyes glowed as if he were a prize to be won.

At last, Robayne worked him through the throng to the space between long trestle tables, which restricted access to him. The crowds dropped away as they approached the council members standing near the head table. Unlike the rougher tables for the crowd, this one was a deep red wood, finely made and polished to a high gloss, with cushioned chairs to match.

Faltryn stepped forward and greeted him warmly, again with a firm handshake.

"Thank you for your kindness at the testing ceremony," he told her.

Her smile crinkled the corners of her eyes. "I

remember the first time I spoke before a large audience. I merely passed to you the advice given to me by Wildt." She tipped her head in the direction of a man so old he seemed bent in half. Still, he tottered on his own two feet with the aid of a cane. "He looks as if he could fall dead any minute," Faltryn told Shay, "but his mind is sharp as a wasp's stinger. So is his tongue."

Orlait appeared at Shay's elbow. "Don't hog Bladen's attention, Faltryn." He smiled widely, but Shay couldn't be sure he was teasing. No crinkles accented his eyes.

Robayne's fingers tightened fractionally on Shay's elbow.

Shay looked closer at Orlait, at the glint in his eye. Fraudulent friendship, perhaps? A bit of caution might be needed, at least until he could speak more with Robayne.

Wildt at last reached him, disdaining assistance. "Greetings, young man." He wheezed, his voice thin and sharp. "Do not listen to anything Orlait tells you. He's afraid you'll take over the council and oust him for poor leadership." He offered a small, soft hand with loose skin. Age spots mottled his hands and his face. "I am Wildt."

Shay took the ancient hand gently, searching the old man's face for some sign of humor or teasing. He saw none.

"Wildt," Faltryn scolded. "You should not say such things, especially to a newcomer!"

"At my age, I can say anything I want to, whenever I want to, in front of whomever I please. I'm too old to be what I'm not. Or to pretend politeness to youngsters barely old enough to speak coherently."

Faltryn gently guided Wildt away, throwing an apologetic look at Shay.

On Shay's right, Robayne radiated heightened tension.

On his left, Orlait's body had gone stiff with affront. No smile adorned mouth or eyes, only something shard-

183

sharp and bitter.

Shay wanted no part of whatever brewed here. The Council of Elders struck him as a snarl of snakes in a bucket.

Robayne seated him in the center of the head table and sat on his right. Orlait stopped his steps and glared as Robayne sat down.

"As the Eldest, I belong next to our exalted guest." Orlait's chest expanded.

Shay's mentor smiled up at him. "He's not a guest, Orlait. And I must always be at his right hand. It's been so long since we've had a new Bladen, you must have forgotten."

"Indeed." Orlait stretched a smile across his face. "Thank you for the reminder." He stepped quickly past, only to halt again, face red, as Faltryn slid into the chair on Shay's left.

Uneasy, Shay watched Orlait's jaw clench and release before he moved on to sit beyond Faltryn. Why was it so important to sit next to him? Unpleasant undercurrents swam around him in murky water he couldn't fathom.

Robayne leaned over to speak to Shay above the clatter of the crowd taking their places at the long tables. "Politics," he said. "Every group of people has them, and there's always some conflict simmering. Don't let it spoil your appetite. Part of my task will be to buffer you from such things."

Servers arrived with platters of food in quantities Shay had never imagined, as the crowd's voices blended into a controlled roar. This much food would nourish a thousand street urchins for a week! The scent of roast venison, baked fowl, and rich spices filled the air and his stomach rumbled loudly. He recognized some of the spices by scent, but many he didn't.

The rich, dark scent of klovais puzzled him, though. Why would a major ingredient of battle balm be part of a feast?

He bit into a succulent pheasant thigh smothered in a cream sauce and discovered klovais could be a wonderful addition to food. Did Bibi know of this? And then he tried a snake steak, from the giant Robayne had described to him. Pleasant spices and garnishes had tenderized the tough meat.

Wouldn't Bibi enjoy this gathering? And she would easily cow even Orlait and Wildt. Meilin would have other children to play with here and maybe find a new family. What were they doing now? Were they still in Echo, or had they moved on, giving him up for lost?

He couldn't imagine Bibi giving up on anything. So he asked Robayne.

"Yes, Bibi knows you're here. Your grandfather, Locelar, sent word to her."

"Grandfather?" Shay's heart bounced. Family! Blood family! It began to feel real at last.

Robayne grinned. "We'll talk later, when it's quieter."

A server brought Shay a small goblet of green glass, containing some beverage that fizzed gently and smelled of wine and cinnamon. "Compliments of the lady, Bladen." The server indicated the middle line of tables with his head.

A young woman with ash-pale hair sat at the near end of the table, her eyes large enough to match her bountiful breasts. She smiled at him over the rim of a matching goblet.

Lifting his, Shay tipped it slightly in her direction before bringing it to his lips.

"Unless you would share her bed tonight, take a sip only," said Robayne, "then set it down and don't touch it again. She'll understand the message. It's perfayn, a

185

powerful aphrodisiac also known as the lovers' kiss, and drinking more than a polite sip commits you to her arms tonight."

Shay shuddered at the thought. He had no desire for the woman, but stopping at a single sip took all his will. The flavor was light, sweet, and addictive. He set the goblet well away from his plate to avoid its temptation.

Robayne pointed out Shay's family as he chewed. "The far table seats mostly Bladens. The patriarch, Locelar, is that dignified man sitting in the midst of them, the one everyone defers to. In a few days, we'll have a private reception with your closest family so you can meet everyone."

His family. The thought overwhelmed Shay, leaving him light-headed. He barely remembered his parents, had never known a family until he'd married Cinny and created his own.

"There must be a hundred Bladens," Shay blurted. "Can there truly be so many?"

Robayne grinned at him. "Allow me to provide a bit of a history lesson.

"The Blue Mountain People have three major families, originating from three friends who discovered the caverns hundreds of years ago. At first they lived outside of the mountain, in a long-disappeared village. When raiders destroyed the village, they brought their families inside and devised the protections you see today. Most of the Blue Mountain People are descended from one of those first three families."

A family and a history. This would take some getting used to, but already tendrils of belonging anchored Shay's feet to the stone beneath him. Unexpectedly, his eyes filmed. He was not alone in the world after all.

"If you have finished eating," Robayne murmured, "we

186

can leave at any time."

Blinking hard, Shay noticed people beginning to move about the room, mingling with friends and family.

"Or if you prefer, we can sit quietly and allow you the opportunity to meet most of the people here tonight."

That had to be meant in jest. "I'd prefer to slip out quietly," Shay said.

"We'll do the best we can. Come." Robayne rose and Shay followed suit.

He thought no one would notice them walking back to the kitchens, but just as they reached the door, cheers erupted behind them and spread through the hall.

His first impulse was to dart through the doorway and escape, but Robayne laid a hand on his arm. "You're a public figure now. Acknowledge the cheers gracefully. They will love you the more for it."

Shay turned back. If he could face Spinel's men, he could face a crowd of people cheering and calling his name. He forced a smile and lifted a hand in acknowledgment.

The cheers redoubled, and they ducked through the door. Shay's last view of the room revealed Orlait staring after him, not cheering or even smiling, and old Wildt scowling daggers at Orlait's back. Then the uproar muted as he and Robayne left the hall behind.

Robayne chuckled. "If Orlait was planning a formal welcome speech, we've thwarted him. I hope he won't take it personally."

Shay began to suspect that Robayne enjoyed thwarting Orlait whenever possible. More politics. He made a note to stay out of it.

On their way through the vast kitchens, Robayne snagged two goblets, which he handed to Shay, and a pitcher of the wonderful spiced wine. The kitchen workers smiled and called greetings, but didn't slow their work.

187

"Robayne," called a huge voice when they had almost reached the exit. "I'll send another pitcher soon, if you'll tell me where." A very large and well-fed man waved a wooden spoon in their direction.

"My place," replied Robayne cheerfully.

The cook nodded and turned back to bellow at his workers. "More venison for the far table, gentlemen! They tire of dining solely on pheasant and salamander."

The stone hallways seemed silent as a tomb after the cacophony of the feast. Shay heard only their footsteps above the ringing in his ears. Peace at last. He took a deep, slow breath, grateful to be able to hear it.

Robayne's explanations continued without noticing. "When you hear people refer to the Center, they mean the Great Hall, the Council Hall, and the shops, businesses, and homes clustered around them. The area also includes the Cathedral of the Light. The homes in the Center are traditional dwellings of our Elders and other prominent citizens. Like you and me."

Prominent citizen. Shay sighed. He wasn't sure he wanted that designation.

Robayne's place turned out to be just around the corner from Shay's, no more than two dozen steps away. The door wasn't locked, to Shay's surprise, but the larger surprise lay within.

Thick carpets covered most of the floor. Bright tapestries smothered the walls and muffled the faint echoes off the stone. The exquisite detail and rich colors spoke of their origins in Darube, which produced the world's finest tapestries. Between them hung begemmed ornaments made from crystals that complemented the tapestry colors. A closer look at an amulet of deep blue cloudstone and pale green godtears revealed fine artistry, except for minor flaws only another accomplished gemsman would notice. And if

188

it had been him, he'd have added a little more silver here and dropped that stone just a little farther down.

"Do you like it?" Robayne's voice sounded hearty enough, but a tiny note of anxiety hinted that the answer would be important to him.

Shay looked at him and smiled. "That's fine workmanship," he answered truthfully.

Robayne's shoulders relaxed.

"Aren't these Darubian tapestries?" Shay continued. "They're beautiful. Your home feels comfortable, welcoming." Even the furniture was rich, reddish wood, polished to a high gloss–the same as the Hall's head table.

"They are, indeed," Robayne said. "We have some fine shops here in the Center you can browse. And I sometimes take a wagon train of Blue Mountain men to Sarinta and other markets to find such treasures as you see here. It allows us to experience the ways of the outer world and gives us access to things not available within our mountain.

"I predict you'll soon do some buying or trading to decorate your home in a way that brings you comfort and ease. We left it plain, to allow you to furnish it to your liking, rather than feel you must live with someone else's taste."

Shay already had ideas for his new home. Until now, he hadn't even thought about fixing it up; Cinny had always handled that part of their life. He wished he could show her Robayne's home; she would enjoy his treasures and the planning of their home's beautification. He swallowed the tightness in his throat, hoping Robayne didn't notice his sudden melancholy.

The two men settled into easy chairs facing each other across a small table, where the wine pitcher sat within easy reach. To Shay's surprise, the door remained wide open. . . to accommodate the arrival of the next pitcher, Robayne

189

told him. They sipped companionably at their wine, the silence soft and inviting.

"How does it feel?" Robayne asked. "You've fallen into something you never expected, found a home, a family, new friends, power, and magic, all in the same breath, so to speak."

"Strange," said Shay after a moment. "All the things I've wanted for so long have fallen into my lap, and more, but only because I lost the things most precious to me."

"It sounds like a tale worth hearing, if you would tell it."

Shay thought about it, fortified himself with more wine. "I will tell it. Especially since danger for everyone seems to have followed me to your doorstep." He remembered Spinel's sword slashing the throat of one of his own men—an act he'd never thought the man capable of.

"Our doorstep. This is your home, too, no matter how much or little time you choose to spend here. Your roots are here, as deeply as mine or anyone else's. Your forefather and mine were two of the three founders, after all."

Shay told his story, from the night of the fire and the loss of everything that mattered. Even in broad strokes, the telling gouged his heart. He had to stop and collect himself— and pour more wine, a barrier to the worst of the pain. He didn't remember seeing the second ceramic pitcher delivered, but there it was, sweating gently on the table.

Robayne listened, asked a question or two for clarification, but otherwise said nothing.

When he finished his tale, Shay ached all over, as if fever raged through him and over him. Robayne half carried him back to his own home-in-the-stone and put him to bed.

Just before he gave in to oblivion, Shay wondered how long the tears had been crawling down his face, for his shirt to be so wet.

20. Lost

"Does anyone ever get lost under the mountain?" Shay asked. Relieved to have Robayne's company, he walked toward Council Hall as if headed for the gallows.

"Never more than once. Eventually, someone more careful will find their bodies or bones and they'll be brought back for burial." The twinkle in Robayne's eyes hinted he might be exaggerating, but Shay couldn't be sure.

A full week after his introduction to Elegy, he'd gotten lost twice in the public areas, and he'd met several dozen of his own family in a casual reception. The community in the middle of the mountain felt familiar now but far from homey and comfortable.

How could these people worship the Light, yet live inside a mountain, shut away from its bright Eye?

"When we get to the Council Hall, I'll have to leave you; I wasn't invited to this meeting. Don't let the Elders intimidate you. They only want to know about the axe, about the years of missing history–how it became parted from your family and how it came back to you."

"I'll be glad to fill in what I can, but it won't be much. I didn't know it existed until Cinny's father gifted it to us for our wedding."

Robayne shrugged. "You can only do as you can do. But with what you can tell them, a historian may be able to trace backwards to fill in information."

They left the Great Hall and started down a passage Shay hadn't noticed before. "How did the axe come to be made? Who made it, and why? And how?"

"Questions that will be answered in due time." Robayne nodded and smiled at a young couple coming toward them. They greeted him as they passed, but they

191

looked at Shay.

Shay ground his teeth in frustration. Those secrets tantalized, always just out of reach. Even more frustrating, Robayne didn't seem to notice.

They turned a corner and Shay saw the Council Hall for the first time–a true building, growing out of the cavern floor, but standing free of the surrounding walls, with glass windows and doors and an elaborate tower at each of the four corners. Scrollwork embroidered the stone around heavy wooden doors and windows. Sixteen steps led up the wide staircase to the main entry, and Robayne mentioned a basement level, too.

"We must have at least one spectacular edifice, for those who feel they are important enough to warrant it. Sad to say, it seems our Council always has at least one such Elder." Robayne heaved an exaggerated sigh.

Shay chuckled. "Only one? You do indeed have a fine Council! Who is the current representative of the self-important?"

Robayne grinned, eyes dancing. "Can you guess?"

Shay cast his thoughts back, struggling to picture all the Elders when he only remembered a few well enough to put names to faces. "Not Faltryn, certainly. Nor Wildt, the grumpy one. I'd guess Orlait?"

Robayne's sudden clench of a hand above Shay's elbow came too late. He followed his mentor's gaze.

Orlait stood a few steps below and behind Shay, on his way into the building. By the intensity of his face, he'd heard. Orlait's burning eyes could melt stone, and Shay felt the heat all the way to the pit of his stomach.

He stuttered an apology, but the Eldest stomped past as if he didn't exist.

Robayne led him inside, pointing out a large room on their left. "We have a good library here, with texts both

192

ancient and current. The tomes detailing the axe's lore are kept elsewhere, but our other histories are here. In the base of the right tower, we store official documents, such as deeds, legal agreements, and so on. The librarian covers both areas.

"And this is the Council room itself." Robayne stopped before large doors adorned with ornately carved flowers. In the center of each carved flower nestled a red stone that Shay couldn't immediately place. "What's the red stone?"

"Bixil, a magic stone that prevents eavesdropping. You'll see more inside." Robayne pulled the door open for Shay.

It made a very solid thud when it closed, leaving him alone with the Council.

A solid line of red bixils encircled the room, on the floor next to the wall. Shay took a deep breath.

Orlait sat directly in front of him, on the far side of a circle of carved chairs, with an empty chair across from him, on Shay's side of the circle. The other elders completed the circle of chairs, and the murmur of their voices died with the closing of the door. Orlait gestured him to the empty chair. Facing him directly felt uncomfortable, but at least Shay knew how to tough it out. His childhood had provided much practice at not blinking.

"Tell us about your past," said Orlait, his voice as stiff as his body. He sat in the largest chair in the room, its posh comfort wasted on his rigid posture.

Shay winced. Waves of anger and resentment rolled off the leader of the Council of Elders.

Faltryn flashed him a smile from her chair next to Orlait. "We're looking for as much of your past as you're willing to share, particularly any clues about where your battle-axe has been, who's had it, and so on."

Grateful for the presence of an ally, Shay still wished

Robayne had been invited. They would eventually give him the information provided here, so why not include him?

"I can tell you little, since I didn't know of the axe's existence until my wedding day, eight years ago.

"My wife's family are well-to-do gem merchants, and she was the eldest child."

"Was?" interrupted Wildt.

"She and our children were murdered for the battle-axe, only a few weeks ago, by her brother and his henchmen." Just words. Only words being spoken, with no meaning. None he could allow himself to look at.

"I'm sorry for your grievous loss." Faltryn's condolences were echoed by others present.

"Spinel, her brother, has always been a drunk and a wastrel, which may be why their father presented it to my wife and me on our wedding day."

The Elders murmured at the news. "It wasn't *his* axe to bestow on anyone," grumbled Orlait, his voice strident, but not loud.

Shay responded to the comment anyway. "He told me the axe had first belonged to his grandfather, who picked it up from a battlefield where many men had died. He took it from the hand of a dead man and rifled his pockets for a handful of gems, where he also found a note referring to the axe. He kept that, too."

"What battle?"

"Which nation?"

"Who were they fighting?"

"Where was the battle?"

"Who was the fallen man?"

The questions pelted Shay like hurled pebbles. "None of that information was given me." He raised his voice to overpower the questions.

"What is your father-in-law's name?" asked Faltryn.

194

"We can send a historian to speak with him."

"He died last year, but his wife still lives and has remarried." Shay gave her name and where she could be found.

"So, the axe skipped three generations of Bladens," said Wildt. "What about your own history? That's a necessary part of this, too."

Glad to leave the discussion of his wife's family, Shay crossed an ankle over a knee and frowned in thought. "I barely remember my parents, or the plain wooden house we lived in. It burned down in a fire that killed both my parents. I must have been about six, maybe younger. I had no place to go, no family, so I grew up in the streets of Porphyr in Palernia. It was a hard, hard life."

He had been always afraid, always hungry, always dirty. He'd been teased, cursed, robbed of anything he managed to get his hands on, beaten–and worse. He'd fought when he must but had no talent for it. Better to avoid a fight, if he could.

Memories roared in, and he slammed the door on them, willing them away. He could *not* look at them now, before these people. His mouth soured; he tried to swallow the taste.

"Do you remember your parents' names?" asked Wildt. Despite his grumpy visage, he spoke more gently than Orlait. "We're not sure of your exact lineage. Many young people go out on their own; some are not heard from again."

Shay shook his head. "*Mother* and *Father* won't help you much. But my father had a scar on his cheek. A big one."

"What did the scar look like?" asked Wildt, his jaw jutting out.

"A big X." Shay drew it in the air with a finger as he

195

spoke.

Silence smothered the room for a long moment. What under the Light . . . ?

"Your father's name," pronounced Orlait at last, eyes glittering, "was Rond. He was branded a traitor and thrown out of Blue Mountain in disgrace forty years ago, barred from ever returning, his name stricken from our genealogies. Apparently, you're not one of the Blue Mountain Bladens after all."

Waves of chill and fever washed over Shay. No. He had family. For the first time in his life, he was making friends. He had a place, where maybe he could *belong*. These people had just given it to him. They couldn't turn around and take it back!

Wildt glared at Orlait. "You're saying the man who bears the battle-axe is *not* a Bladen? I submit that the fact it has bonded to him is sufficient proof that he *is* the true Bladen. Who else would the axe choose?"

"We've never tried to bond it to anyone else. For all we know, *any* of the direct descendants could claim the axe." Orlait pushed to the front of his chair.

Someone cried, "*We* don't bond the axe to anyone! *It* chooses!" And other voices broke out on one side or the other, rising in chaos and volume.

Shay felt a hand on his shoulder, and Faltryn spoke into his ear. "Please excuse us, Shay. This will be a frightful boil, with delicate issues to discuss and much political heat. You don't have to sit through it."

He nodded, accepting the dismissal. Axe in hand, he slipped out, pulling the door behind him. Slowly, he made his way down the sixteen broad steps leading to the cavern floor.

He liked taking his axe everywhere. He liked carrying her in his hand instead of harnessed to his back.

196

Shay paused in the empty passage, his stomach hollow with dread. What now? Not home. He'd only sit and brood. He could look up Robayne, but right now he didn't want to be around people, especially one who talked so much.

Would they try to take his axe from him, if they threw him out for his father's sins?

Whatever they had been. No one had thought to tell him. Or even his mother's name, if they knew it. He had the right to know. He should have insisted they answer his questions. Slapping one hand against his head, he grabbed a handful of hair and tightened his fingers until it pulled, out of pure frustration.

Bitter anger crept up his spine, intertwined with despair. To the Dark with them!

He should have known his life could never be easy, never serene and comfortable. Everything he'd hungered for had been his when he found his Cinnabar. And lost again, in too short a time. Now, just when he might have another place for himself, it was about to be riven from him, too.

In a sudden fit of despair and rage, he yanked off Elegy's hood and slammed the bit with all his strength into the Hall's steps. Stone flew, chips stinging his face and slicing his forearms.

The blow left an ugly gash in the polished stone surface, a scar that couldn't be erased. One more excuse for them to throw him out. One more story to blemish his family name. One more reason for Orlait to fear and hate him.

Shay's shoulders slumped, and all the fight slid off, leaving him weary and heartsick. A moment of jat and jagounce, ash and flame, the hated stones that seemed to punctuate his life.

He couldn't just stand here. People could appear any moment.

197

He re-covered Elegy, started walking, and turned a corner. Suddenly, he knew where he would go–the Cathedral of the Light. Two minutes later, he stopped in front of tall, wooden doors carved with the Eye of the Light ascendant over the weaker Eye of the Dark.

He calmed as he stepped inside, felt his shoulders relax when he hadn't even realized they were tight. Soft moonstones lit the entryway just inside the doors. The worship hall beyond glowed, and Shay could not look away from it.

At the far end, the Eye of the Light stretched up from the floor, a mosaic of precious gems. A sky created by skystones, seastones, torquis, and lazh arched overhead, dotted with clouds of white-splotched cloudstones and bluestones. Yellow stones created the Eye of the Light: tauz, golden beryl, citrine, and yellow turmali. Carefully placed moonstones, shielded from worshipers, lit the mosaic, striking sparks that made the Eye flicker, as if alive.

Awed as always by the beauty and workmanship, Shay walked toward it on a path of gold inlaid with emrels, godtears, and grass-green turmali. A deep peace swept him; reverence and joy swelled in his heart, allowing him to set aside his anxiety for a while. Here he found holiness, and the beauty and peace to be found in the Light after death. Cinny was there, Piper and Beryl with her. He felt their presence, surrounded by the Light. He closed his eyes. For just a moment, he wanted only to feel them, their joy in their new home.

Why couldn't he find joy for himself, in his new home? He should have died with his family.

Shay searched for the best view, then sat on the cold stone floor. He settled himself, tried to empty his muddled mind, and meditated as best he could, seeking peace and solace.

A thread of ethereal music, soft as rainsilk, trickled through his veins, helping him relax–the voices of the stones he sat on.

When he left an hour later, the outer world felt dimmer somehow, but he carried the awe in his heart still. It left him subdued and detached.

The effect only lasted until he encountered other people in the halls. Most smiled and waved, but he wasn't ready for people yet. He waved or nodded politely, then veered off for quieter places.

Maybe this would be a good time to visit some of the veins Robayne had shown him, just for someplace to go. Now that he knew how to read the marks at the corners of well-lit passages, getting lost shouldn't be a problem.

He started walking. Movement would help as much as being among the fields and veins of precious stones.

Half an hour later, the Center lay well behind him as he strode down bright corridors. He thanked whoever had assured that the ceilings remained high above him.

About to turn down the hallway to the closest mine, he caught himself. Workers would be busy there. Not for him, right now. Besides, the cool quietude closing around him eased his heart–like the cathedral, but with a different kind of beauty. Instead, he found a corridor marked for moonstone and went that way.

Long before he reached the moonstone vein, he changed his mind and turned toward a lazh deposit only recently opened, according to Robayne. His head wouldn't settle any more than his heart; restlessness afflicted both of them. He changed his mind again, heading for a vein of amyth he hadn't visited before.

The amyth area felt right, offering the solitude and beauty he craved. For a long time, he examined what he could see,

199

touching nothing. He occupied himself with evaluating the crystals, regretting he'd brought no pick, brush, or other tools. Fine, large crystals jutted seductively from their matrix, and excitement stirred a small whirlpool in his gut. Robayne had said all the amyth here was magic. He couldn't keep his hands off any longer and took his time stroking and examining crystal after crystal, looking for just the right one for a special cup for Bibi's new tavern. At last he selected a place and used the tip of Elegy's blade to chip and pry loose a large chunk. He tucked it into his elbow, lying across his forearm, for want of a better way to carry it. As it nestled against the bare flesh of wrist and hand, he began to hear its whispery voice.

Did all stones have voices? Why had he never heard them until the tauz canyons?

He remembered laying Elegy on the floor of his home for the thugs. And his inability to let go of her, causing his family's deaths. Was there a whisper of her voice even then, holding him back? Guilt and pain flooded him and he sat abruptly on the floor, dizzy, until it subsided enough to continue.

After the amyth, he found a pocket of wonderful bloodstone, but he already had a fine specimen. Could this be the same seam that left standing pillars outside the mountain? The bloodstone made him think of Bibi and her strange beliefs, and he smiled.

Not a bad smile, for a man with a life once again in shambles. How was Bibi doing? And Meilin, whom he especially missed? Shay's heart dropped again. Maybe she had room for one more helper. He might soon need a place to go.

The rumbling of his stomach caught him by surprise. Time to resurface. He sighed from the toes up. The depths of the mountain felt safe, wombed from the conflicts and foibles of men. He dreaded returning to the "real world," but it was that or go hungry. He started back to the Center, planning to return later, properly equipped for this work.

Loath to leave the treasures beneath the mountain, Shay took a lesser-used branch he hadn't traveled before. The older, narrower passage showed signs of the earth's restlessness. Rocks littered the floor, sometimes in piles he had to step over. Many of the moonstones had fallen during mountain trembles sometime in the past and some had dimmed or gone dark completely.

Shay's foot came down on a chunk of rock and his ankle twisted. He flailed for balance and fell.

For a long moment, he lay on his back, blinking to reorient himself. Nothing broken, but plenty of bruises, maybe small cuts from landing on rocks. Carefully, he rolled to his side, made a clear place for his hand to lever himself up–and a glint of light caught his eye. His attention snapped back to where he'd seen it, a magnet drawn to a lodestone.

21. Found

There. A flash of color.

The earth had split, leaving a low, narrow gap in the wall, not twenty feet from where Shay lay on the cluttered path. Within the cleft he saw color. It appeared to be a previously undiscovered vein that sparked from exposure to the light of the moonstone in the passage. *Which* color, though, changed as his head moved. Green? Blue? Red?

Carefully, Shay laid the axe down with her eye pointed directly at the cleft so he wouldn't lose sight of it. He pushed to his feet, bruises forgotten, and gathered a handful of fallen moonstones. He placed some along the edge of the corridor nearest the opening, to guide him back to the path and safety.

The colors of the spark shifted again in the light of the moonstones. Perhaps . . . He didn't finish the thought, even inside his own head, for fear it might jinx him.

Elegy in hand, he picked his way through the rubble toward the cleft. It was too low to see into while he stood upright, but he stared unblinking at where he'd seen it. Halfway there, he squatted to peer inside at the colorful gleam, adjusted his direction slightly, and walked right up to it. A faint breeze touched his ankles as he squatted again.

He crawled inside, bruising hands and knees on sharp rocks. The cleft opened up enough to stand, but no good footing existed. His feet canted different directions, but he ignored the discomfort. He laid his remaining moonstones out to light the small room, with the amyth nearby, and drew in a deep breath.

Black opal. A wide skein of it, twisting through the open spaces in the wall. Soft, shifting color of the most beautiful opals he'd ever seen. He ran his palm across the vitreous surface, wonder and awe spilling from every pore. If there had been a place, he'd have sat down and just drowned himself in color.

Shay shook himself. He couldn't stand here all day. He stumbled around, clutching Elegy. With sight and touch, he examined the vein for exactly the right place. When he found it, he cut a chunk free of the wall and set it inside his shirt, next to the skin. A low growl seemed to crawl up and down his spine.

He picked up the amyth block again.

The floor shifted under his feet, leaving him faintly dizzy.

It moved again, and rocks clattered near the entrance.

Time to go, before the whole mountain fell on him.

He started toward the entrance, but too late. With an echoing roar, the opening collapsed, half a ton of rock sealing it closed.

He ducked his head from the stinging dust, spit grit from his tongue. The shaking spread toward him, and he fell hard. He landed on the rubble with a yelp. More rocks dribbled onto him. He gripped Elegy tighter. The fall stopped.

When the dust settled, Shay took stock of his injuries. Battered and cut, he hurt like the Dark, but nothing seemed broken. He sat up, grunting at the sharp rock poking his left buttock.

The entrance had sealed. No way back. His heart wadded into a tight ball of fear.

One lone moonstone, covered in dust and half-buried in rock, still provided faint light, enough to see that the vein of black opal remained intact. And he still clenched the amyth chunk he had cut.

A vague movement of air suggested . . .

Shay battered his rising panic into submission, groaned

as he struggled to his feet. His head throbbed, and the hand that touched it came away sticky.

No one could find him here. Did anyone even remember this hole existed? If they'd ever known of it. He fought the urge to claw at the rocks, but turned instead toward the moving air, stumbled and tripped his way across the floor.

At the far end of the cleft, he found a way out of the rocky tomb. He had to turn sideways to squeeze through the opening, scraping belly and buttocks in the process.

Rocky caves, unfinished and unlit, lay on the other side. The dark dropped around him, thin and cold, as he took another step. He hadn't thought to retrieve the remaining moonstone first. *Stupid, stupid.*

Profound silence shrouded him. He feared to move in the darkness, lest he fall and break a leg in this wild place. Or worse, fall into a fissure that would swallow him whole. He stood still for a long moment, trying to decide what to do.

A puff of air touched his cheek, reminding him why he stood here, instead of next to the black opals. He turned his head, slowly, trying to discern which direction the air flowed from. If only he could see! There could be a clear path right in front of him and he wouldn't know it.

Eventually someone will find their bodies or bones . . .

He shuddered.

He couldn't get to safety without moving his feet. He couldn't move his feet without risking a fall and possible death. *So, I'm just going to stand right here for the rest of my life?*

Self-mockery wouldn't help.

He searched a long time for ideas, afraid to move. Until his feet ached. Until his legs ached. Until his eyelids sagged and he fought to keep them open. Until Elegy grew so heavy he could barely hold onto her.

Shay's eyes popped wide open. Elegy.

Axe light.

In all the hours he'd spent learning about his axe from Robayne, he'd never again bared her haft. The haft that, in contact with his hands, had sent shockwaves of power through him, veining with blue threads and lighting up the room. The power that had aroused him physically, flung him out of control where he could do nothing but hang on.

Robayne said he would learn control, learn to work with her bare grip and be the one in charge. But he hadn't gotten to that lesson yet.

What if her power knocked him to the ground? What if the fall broke his leg? What if . . .

He stopped himself. The source of light he so desperately needed was in his hands. Would he refuse to use it out of fear, and so die when he could have lived?

Not cursed likely!

Hands trembling in uncertainty more than fear, he unwound Elegy's leather grip an inch.

No glimmer of light. Disappointment tightened his throat.

Just to be sure, he unwrapped another inch. Still nothing.

Without giving himself time to think or feel, he removed the leather entirely, tucking it into his shirt with the opal. He held the haft gingerly in his fingertips, fearful of its powers, braced for the rush of energy.

Power did not explode. Instead, he felt a tingle, saw light traceries of beautiful blue work their way up the haft and engulf both bits.

Had he imagined his brief conversation with her during the test? He bent his will toward light, trying to tell the beautiful diamond what he wanted. Elegy's song whispered in his blood.

The traceries widened to ribbons, then disappeared as the entire axe glowed blue. The light flowed, opening veins of gratitude and joy inside him. Elegy brightened still further, and so did his heart.

When he turned his gaze from the glowing blue axe, he could see everything–albeit with sharp shadows. He lifted her high overhead to diminish them and looked around.

The first thing he saw drew unwilling laughter from him. He stood free of the cleft. No close-pressing walls here, but a small cavern. The trapped feeling dissipated. Even from here he saw three possible ways out.

Now he had only to cross the deep chasm running from wall to wall in front of him.

Shay found a relatively smooth rock to sit on. He released the axe with one hand to help himself onto the surface and stretched his legs flat on top of the rock.

Her light dimmed. He regarded her in wonder. Lesson learned.

Getting off his sore feet and ankles felt good. He leaned forward to take some pressure off the sore place where his rump had been poked so hard.

He'd learned more about his axe in the last few minutes than in the entire time since the testing. What else could he learn? How did he communicate his needs to her?

So he experimented, to the accompaniment of the diamond's gentle voice singing in his head. As with the tauz canyon, the closer the physical contact, the clearer her voice. He learned that the more flesh touching the haft, the more power poured forth. He could get a smaller light with one hand than with two, less still with fingertips only as she rested across his trousered legs. Of course, carrying an axe of her weight by his fingertips seemed unlikely, but if he only needed a little light . . .

The strength of his grip mattered, too. Both hands clamped tightly around the bare axe produced the screaming blue power of his first encounter with her, and he hastily eased his hands.

My energy, expressed by my hands, releases her energy. The epiphany dizzied him.

Or was the rock moving again?

This was an active and dangerous part of the mountain. He needed to get out of here.

His ankles almost gave way as he stood. He forced them to bear his weight. Shivering at the thought of another rockfall, Shay followed the chasm from one end to the other, searching for a narrow place he could jump, a shallow place he could climb through . . .

Or an ancient wooden bridge would work.

One long wooden plank, none too wide, sagged across the chasm. He pulled more light from Elegy with a slight squeeze of his grip. No rot, but the plank was dryer than he'd have liked.

Nothing for it but to try. Surely he could make it thirty feet.

He sidled out onto the plank. It bent and creaked beneath him. Despite the cavern's coolth, sweat soaked his beard before he reached the center. He feared to shift his sweaty hands on the axe, lest she slip from his grip and be lost forever.

How deep could the chasm be? Curiosity called, but fear forbade. He didn't look.

Then he laughed at himself. *I'm tired of being afraid. I'm tired of making decisions based on fear. Dying can't be worse than the torments of my childhood, of losing my parents, of losing Cinny, and my children.* He should be seeking the everlasting Light, not resisting its lure.

He let go of his fear, shoved it aside, and pictured

Cinny smiling at him from across the bridge. His feet struck out boldly, the dry plank shivering beneath them.

Elegy's voice sang through his nerves in joy and triumph, and he grinned.

Just before reaching the end, he stopped and knelt on the bridge. One hand on the wood for balance, he stretched Elegy over the chasm and looked down into the blue-lit depths. Rough walls fell into jumbled, broken-off rocks thirty, maybe forty feet below. But he thought he saw a way down–one he could also climb back up. He hesitated. Nothing below beckoned, no soft glow or sparkle or color. No reason to descend just to prove to himself he could.

He stood up and continued to the end of the bridge.

When he stepped onto solid ground, he released a long breath.

Footsore and rumble-bellied, he rested long enough to dry his sweat before going on.

Within minutes, Shay found a way out of the small cavern and onto a trail much like the one that had led him to the black opals. Littered with debris, rough-surfaced, the passage had been abandoned years ago. He used Elegy to mark the entrance to the small cavern and went on, marking each change of trail he made, just in case.

When at last he encountered a well-used and maintained corridor, relief washed through him. He closed his eyes briefly and sent up a quick prayer of thanksgiving for his survival. Then he marked the passage one last time and covered Elegy's grip again.

The direction that tilted slightly up seemed the likeliest, and he took it. In less of a hurry now, he savored the clear, even light of the moonstones, the smooth surface that wouldn't catch his toe or roll an ankle, a smoothness he had taken for granted this morning. Assuming this was the same day.

At each intersection he passed, Shay paused to examine the markings. He chose his path by where he would likeliest find people. Being in occupied halls didn't mean he knew where he was, or how to find the Center, only that help was closer.

Somewhere far down the hall, voices floated like the flutter of wings. Shay stopped. Where? Which way?

A shout, angry and harsh. Other voices answered, anger escalating. He began to run.

With the answering shout, the heavy timbre of the voice registered.

Robayne. Looking for him, no doubt.

Shay called out from the depths of his gut.

Silence filled the passages. Then, "Shay?" This shout filled the air with fear and hope. "Keep calling!"

He did.

Running footsteps echoed on stone as Shay paused in an intersection. To his left, three men raced toward him, Robayne in the lead. Shay turned in their direction, a sudden letdown draining his energy.

Robayne's grin stretched halfway around his head and he barely slowed before slamming Shay with a bear hug that nearly knocked him over. The opal matrix inside Shay's shirt bit his belly, but Robayne didn't seem aware of its presence.

His companions arrived just as Robayne released him and stepped back to arm's length. "Light! What happened to you? Why in the Dark would you just take off without telling anyone? I'd have gone with you! I thought you knew better! We've been searching for almost a full day, scared out of our minds. This is no place for beginners to wander alone."

Shay glanced at Robayne's companions. Atich, his

younger cousin, no longer on door duty. And Orlait.

Why did the Elder come? He'd been the one to question the legitimacy of Shay's ownership of the battle-axe. An unlikely man to search for him.

"Look what I found." He withdrew the black opal, knowing it would divert their attention. The opal's low growl disappeared from his spine. Without that grating, his mood lightened further.

A ravenous glaze filmed Orlait's eyes as he reached out for the opal. Shay reluctantly allowed him to take it. Here, in better light, the opal was stunning, shimmering with deep reds and vivid blues imbedded in blackness. "Where did you get this?"

Shay's jaw hardened. "It's good to see you, too, Orlait." He lifted the opal out of Orlait's hands and tucked it back into his shirt, where the opal's voice resumed. He shouldn't have been so quick to show off his treasure. "Atich, thank you for joining the party." He clasped the young man's forearm.

Atich grinned, clearly pleased to see him again. His warmth and sincerity thawed the deep cold inside Shay. Robayne's friendship grew out of his duty, but Atich's was freely given, a type of friendship Shay hadn't been offered for a very long time. If ever.

"You're a mess," Robayne told him happily. "You're so gray with dust, at first I thought you were a ghost. Except for all the cuts, of course. Maybe more like the walking dead."

"I'm starving," said Shay. "Do you have any food with you?"

"Here," offered Atich. "I have some hard-biscuit, until we get you back to some real food." He produced three biscuits every bit as hard as their name, which Shay had to soak in his mouth before he could chew. Fortunately,

Robayne had a waterskin, which Shay half emptied even before starting on the biscuit.

"And the axe?" asked Orlait. "Did it survive undamaged?"

"The axe is as it always is, Orlait." Shay stared at him. "Tell me, why are you here?"

Orlait's stretched lips didn't curve up. "To help find you, of course. And to assure that the axe, a symbol and icon of the Blue Mountain People, did not disappear from its rightful place among us."

An insult far more vile than Shay's jest had been. His jaw ached with anger. "And to think, I almost considered apologizing again," he murmured, turning his back on the Elder. "Robayne, point me toward home, if you would, please."

The worry in Robayne's eyes lightened. "Are you sure you don't want to wait for a litter? You're not moving too well."

Shay forced a chuckle. "I've walked a hundred miles through these caverns. What's another ten or so?"

Atich laughed loudly. "More like two, Cousin. Allow me to take your arm and some of your weight to help you up the trail. I'd be honored to help the wounded hero return home."

The banter helped. For now, he could ignore Orlait and his own possible expulsion from Blue Mountain. "Then let's go." He laid a hand on Atich's teasingly offered arm.

"Just a minute," said Orlait.

Robayne's sudden wariness prompted Shay to glance back at the Eldest.

"I need to examine the axe, assure that it's undamaged and unblemished."

22. Anger

Shay threw back his head and laughed. "That's my job, Orlait, and my axe. I've already told you it's fine."

Orlait puffed himself up. "As a representative of the Council of Elders . . ."

Shay snorted, turned his back on Orlait again, and made a low-voiced comment to Atich about Orlait's ancestry. Then he turned back, held Elegy as if for battle, and extended his arms toward Orlait. "Satisfied?"

Orlait reached for the axe.

"Don't touch it," Shay shouted, drawing her back. His voice quieted. "Only look."

Orlait's gaze flitted along the battle-axe, pausing several times, and his fingers twitched. He licked his lips. Then he lifted his chin. "It looks fine, if dusty and ill-cared-for."

Anger surged through Shay, and he pictured the axe descending on Orlait's head. Shock shivered through him at the vehemence of his reaction but couldn't stop his words. "If you ever try to touch my axe again, I'll use it on you!"

Robayne set a calm hand on Shay's arm, but Shay twitched out from under it.

Orlait spun back, face contorted with fury. "*My* axe, Bladen! It should have been mine! And if you think you can keep it . . ." He clamped his mouth over his teeth, ice filming his eyes.

Rage shook Shay, burst from his mouth. "If you want to take her from me, try now or try never. You will find she wants no part of you."

Robayne's fingers bit into his arm and yanked him back.

Consumed by fire, Shay barely knew he had stepped

toward Orlait, axe raised. Horror fought fury but couldn't break through.

Orlait backed up, eyes widening in fear. "You go too far, Bladen! I will see you banished as your father was, and for greater cause. It seems he bred true, after all."

Atich had Shay's other arm now, and they dragged him away from Orlait, Atich mouthing conciliatory nothings.

It made Shay even angrier. He struggled to break free.

"Shay, stop now, or I'll punch you out myself," Robayne growled in his ear.

"And I'll help, Cousin," said Atich through gritted teeth. "The damage you're causing may be irreparable."

Shay sputtered. "But he . . ."

"Stop," commanded Robayne. "Now!"

"We're trying to protect you, Cousin. Allow us to do this for you."

Shay forced himself to slow his breath. He forced his facial muscles to relax, letting go of as much fury as he could. They were right. He'd lost control. He sought it desperately, trying to figure out how he got here. *I'm never like this!*

Atich released his arm and went to speak quietly with Orlait.

Robayne turned Shay and started down the passage with him, still gripping his arm, less tightly now. "Come on. Let's go find you some real food. Hard-biscuit hardly counts."

They walked. Hard. The exercise helped use up the excess energy that had boiled out of Shay. He set the incident away from him as best he could, refusing to acknowledge it. Dwelling on it would give the anger more power and encourage its grip on him. He heard Atich and Orlait behind them, but didn't dare look around.

Nausea gripped his stomach; it had nothing to do with

213

food. What had gotten into him?

The hunger, the exhaustion, his own physical let-down caught up with him, turning his legs to willow withes. All the anger had dissipated over the last mile of marching, mostly uphill.

Without speaking, Robayne guided him to a place to sit.

Robayne always knew what he needed. Any space in his heart not consumed with guilt and shame now filled with gratitude. He collapsed onto the bench, buried his face in his hands.

"None of that, now," Robayne murmured. "Be strong. Don't ever let Orlait see you weak or remorseful. He'll take full advantage."

Shay sat up straight as Atich and Orlait sat down across the passage, still talking, although the tone seemed friendlier now. Watching them, Shay felt another wave of gratitude, this time for his cousin. So this is how it felt to have family–family he was born into, not married into. As much as he liked Cinny's parents, he couldn't imagine them taking his side in an argument. Shay sighed heavily.

After a while, Atich rose and came over, gaze on the battle-axe. "It's beautiful," he breathed, eyes shining. "I haven't had a chance to take a good look yet. May I touch it?"

Shay smiled. "Of course."

Cautiously, Atich stroked his fingers down the axe like jackrabs ready to bolt. He touched an ever-sharp bit, careful not to slice a finger.

"Here," said Shay, "you can hold it." He held out the axe to his cousin. Strange word, cousin. Strange to have a cousin.

Eyes wide with wonder, Atich took the axe and hefted it. "It's heavy. I hadn't thought about the weight of the diamond."

Even with Atich, Shay found himself hovering protectively over the axe and soon took her back.

As they resumed walking, Shay thought about Orlait's reaction to him. Why did the man hate him so? He could see nothing he had done to earn the man's enmity, except that one minor insult. A joke, for the Light's sake! Common banter meant nothing. Where he grew up, much more insulting and obscene teasing was laughed off all the time, like a minor test of manly toughness. This one was far too petty for the hate oozing out of Orlait's pores with every breath.

At some point, Atich and Orlait dropped back, immersed in a discussion about some pending action before the Council. Shay took the opportunity to ask Robayne, "Why did Orlait come with you? He hates me!"

"He wants to be seen as concerned about you. And he fears the loss of the axe again."

Shay snorted. "He acts like it's his axe! He even said so." He stopped talking abruptly, following a thready thought. "Does he have Bladen blood? Enough to give him a legitimate claim to the axe?"

"Yes to the first question, several generations back. At that time, Bladen had firstborn twin sons. A huge dispute arose over which was the true Bladen, resolved finally by the axe after much Council wrangling. Had she chosen differently, Orlait might be the true bearer of the axe today."

"So anyone who bears the axe is his enemy."

Robayne shrugged. "Unfortunately, because it's not Orlait's fault, it must be someone else's."

Shay shuddered. "Is it just him, or is it an anger that reaches back all those years?"

"Orlait learned his bitterness at his father's knee. It

215

seems to be his family's curse."

Shay considered for a moment. "With that kind of animosity, I'd bet few of her bearers have lived in Blue Mountain."

"Most have, or have lived in Echo, to be near family. No one else understands what it means to bear the axe. It's sometimes a heavy burden and sometimes the lightest of joys. It helps to have someone who understands."

"Like you do. Do you bear any Bladen blood?"

Robayne smiled. "A drop or two, from far, far back in my lineage. And I think you have a similar amount of Robayne blood in you. It's not enough to matter, for either of us.

"I see you've learned about your battle-axe during your sojourn. We need to discuss what you've learned, and I'll fill in any gaps."

Shay nodded. "Good. I want to learn all the ways in which she can be used."

"You're more than ready to learn everything I can teach you."

Shay remained quiet, gnawing on a question for several minutes before asking, "Does she ever affect the bearer's mood, or his feelings?"

Robayne twisted to look Shay in the eye without slowing. "'There's nothing in the lore to indicate that. Why?"

"Because I've experienced strange feelings today, very unlike me, and I've wondered if she's responsible."

"You can tell me specifics later, but I'd guess whatever happened wasn't her doing."

Atich spoke from directly behind Shay. "You two are way too serious for the occasion. We just found Bladen when he was lost in Blue Mountain! No one survives being that lost!"

The grin in his voice brought a chuckle from Shay. "Robayne told me that when a man gets lost, his bones are only recovered by chance. And I was well and truly in the dark!"

"Do you need a break, Shay?" Atich asked. "We've been walking for a while, and your feet are getting worse, judging by the odd way you're limping."

Shay liked Atich more every minute. The teasing felt friendly, and his considerate manner felt especially good, with Shay's feet and ankles so sore right now. "I could use a few minutes just to sit."

With exaggerated care, Atich took his elbow, guided him to a nearby more-or-less flat rock, and seated him as if he were an old, old man. He soon found himself laughing at his cousin's antics. The laughter felt good.

The banter continued until they arrived in the Center.

Atich stayed with him until Orlait turned off with scant farewells. A few minutes later, Atich invited Shay to visit him soon and took a much warmer leave of them.

Robayne didn't leave his side. "We need to talk, but first you need food and a good bath. Once again, I must have a tub and bath water brought to you." He heaved an exaggerated sigh. "You are so pampered!"

Shay tried for an answering grin, but with the tension gone, he couldn't dredge one up. "Food first, so I have the energy to get into the tub."

They stopped in the Great Hall for plain but plentiful food and carried it away. Shay wanted out of the public eye.

People didn't look at him the same way today. In some eyes he saw doubt, in others suspicion. A few encouraging smiles, a handful of turned-away faces. Lots of sympathy, some shaken heads, and from one older man, a bald look of disgust.

What did they know that he didn't?

217

He wanted to ask Robayne but didn't dare. Not here. Not for such bad news as this appeared to be. His throat closed so tight he could barely speak. The Council had repudiated him, as they had his father. He would be forced to leave forever, forced to give up his axe.

No. Not that. Orlait couldn't have resisted telling him as they returned to the Center. Besides, the Elders could never take her, not with him wielding her as a weapon. Then he shuddered and released that anger, too.

"Atich will have already set your bath in motion." Robayne's voice broke through the churning in Shay's head. "My place, this time. By the time we've eaten, your bath will be ready. We'll talk as you bathe, and after. I know you haven't slept for a day and a half or more, but it must wait a little longer. I'm sorry."

The crushing weight on Shay's shoulders pressed heavier. "It's bad news, isn't it?"

"Not here, my friend."

"Yes. Here. Now!" Anger built a fire so hot it burned inside. Violence geysered up Shay's spine so hard he shook.

"Shay! What's wrong?"

Robayne's alarm did nothing to curb the flow. Shay ground his teeth, trying not to hurl his full plate into Robayne's face.

As fast as it had come, the insanity drained out. *What's happening to me?*

Robayne studied him carefully. "This is the 'strange feeling' you mentioned."

Shay nodded, still trying to come to terms with it. "Am I going insane?"

"No." Robayne was adamant. "This feels like magic, like something from outside you triggers it. Not your axe, though. Let's get you to your bath and worry about the rest later. I'll be watching for it now."

The door of Robayne's home stood wide open. Inside, Atich already supervised bath preparations. He threw Shay a friendly smile and a wink.

Shay ate, preoccupied with worry, while Robayne bantered with the water carriers.

"Hai! Shay!" Standing next to him, Atich spoke loudly enough for all to hear. "You look like droopy donkey ears! Perk up! We're all family here. Except that Robayne fellow, of course, but we like him anyway."

Shay glanced up in surprise. "*All* family?"

"Yep," said one man close to his age. "All Bladens. Family means something here, Shay."

"Family is everything," said someone behind him.

Another added, "Blood is blood. We all share the same blood."

"And that unites us," Atich said softly. "We have our squabbles like any family, but in truth, at the core, family matters above all."

Shay looked around. No one moved. No one else spoke, as if they waited for him.

"I . . ." Shay cleared his throat, swallowed, cleared his throat again. "I've never had a family before." *Except Cinny and the children*. "Please forgive me if I don't know how to be part of one. And thank you for being here, for the support you've offered by your presence. I'm . . . overwhelmed." He tried to touch the gaze of every man in the room, difficult with his eyes watering. He blinked them dry, embarrassed.

Movement resumed, and smiles, and each of them paused to welcome him to the family. When everyone had gone, one taking the dirty plates from Shay and Robayne, Atich stopped in front of Shay. "May I borrow your axe, Cousin? I'll be on guard before the door, to assure you're not interrupted. And to make clear our intent."

Shay's skin crawled. Worse than he thought. With only slight hesitation, he handed Elegy to Atich and watched him step outside with her, pulling the door firmly closed.

Robayne got up and locked it. "Hop into the tub, Shay. I'll break out the ale."

23. Break

Shay set aside the chunks of black opal and purple amyth before he stripped and eased into the steaming water.

"No wonder you're exhausted," Robayne said, chuckling. "Look at all the extra weight you've been carrying."

Shay ignored him, closed his eyes, and slid under the surface. Ah, the heat felt good. He stayed under as long as he could, allowing it to loosen and relax him. Emerging at last, he wiped the water from his face with his hands.

The chill of the ale contrasted sharply with the hot water, but it only made the cool slide down his throat more satisfying. He handed the empty glass back to Robayne.

"You don't have to get drunk all at once," Robayne teased.

"Just preparing myself for bad news. I saw the way people looked at me, and Orlait certainly hinted at dire tidings. Tell me."

Robayne sobered, ran a hand through his hair. Twice. He emptied his own glass and refilled both of them. "Nothing is resolved yet. The Elders are still bickering over whether you have a right to the axe. Orlait's faction says you do not. That your father's banishment included his descendants, forever, so that you can't be a part of this community. They claim the axe is community property and Bladen is only her caretaker, not her owner. They claim the Council of Elders can overrule the public test when necessary for the good of the community.

"Oh, and to make matters worse, someone started a rumor that you absconded with the axe, with the intent to ensure no one else could have it. Some people even believe it. We took the long way home today to lose Orlait and

Atich, so those who believe in tall tales wouldn't assume you'd been taken into custody."

Shay ground his teeth. That explained the varied looks he'd received. "She's confirmed me as the rightful owner! I thought that was the whole purpose of the test. Besides, she was gifted to me eight years ago. I own her legally. And unless I've missed something, the magic won't work for anyone but me."

"True. And that's a powerful argument. But legally, we're in uncharted waters now. No Bladen had ever been banished before your father. Some argue your father's disgrace changes everything. Others say she's stolen property, so cannot lawfully be given or sold."

"Stolen! She changed hands as the spoils of war, which go to the victor. Now she's returned to her original and rightful place." Shay's hands clenched the sides of the tub, fingernails digging into the wood.

"Those are both points argued by the other faction. Both sides are scrambling for historical texts and documents to support their views and have visited me, as the keeper of the axe's lore, to seek support."

"What did you tell them?" Surely Robayne wouldn't betray him, but he asked anyway.

"The truth. There is no precedent for trying to remove the axe from Bladen. She will not respond to another Bladen, and there is no legal basis to think the axe belongs to anyone except *the* Bladen. That's why blood is a necessary component of the test. Anyone else who undergoes the test would be incinerated on the spot."

Shay froze, his second glass halfway to his lips. "You never told me."

"You'd have never agreed to the test."

"You owed me that information first! I could have been killed!"

222

"We needed Bladen and his axe. If you'd died, you wouldn't have cared anymore. If you lived–as I knew you would–you'd be one of the most powerful people in the community. You look like a Bladen and you have the axe. I had no doubt."

The chill texturing Shay's skin had nothing to do with cool air and hot water. Where was Robayne's first loyalty? To the bearer of the axe, or to the Blue Mountain People? Was there any truth at all to their friendship? To cover his reaction, Shay grumbled liberally before tossing down his ale. "My father. Rond Bladen. I've never even had a name for him before. I still don't know my mother's name. What happened? Why were they banished?"

"'Palia, your mother, wasn't banished. Only Rond. She chose to accompany him.

"As for what he did . . ." Robayne hesitated. "He betrayed us all by bringing an outsider into Blue Mountain."

"What? That's it?" Water sloshed over the tub's rim as Shay sat up. "People come in all the time. Many spouses are from outside, and they live here."

"Not a new addition to the community, but a visitor. He wanted to show our cathedral to an outsider, so he brought him into the very heart of the Center, revealing the entire cavern city. That he'd sworn his friend to secrecy first meant nothing to the Council. Or to me, for that matter. He put all of us–our way of life–at risk. Few men could hold such a secret for any length of time, and none here would trust him to. Rond took too much risk, far too casually. The doorkeeper who allowed them in was removed permanently from door duty, as not being reliable and trustworthy himself."

"Surely others have betrayed our existence over so many generations."

"You have to remember our history." Robayne began to pace about the room, as if he could no longer sit still. "Our people were nearly destroyed for the wealth here. That's why we have so many safeguards–doors, locks, sentries. That's why we remove temptation from outsiders by not allowing them to see how casually we live with the richest gem deposits in the world. That's why only one other, in all this time, has brought a visitor into Blue Mountain. He and his guest were executed on the spot."

Robayne sat down, but a moment later he stood again, as if pacing helped him think. "Your father, Rond, was Bladen, firstborn of the firstborn, even with the axe long since missing, and his wife's pregnancy moved people's hearts. Instead of execution, the Council only banished him, not just from Blue Mountain, but from the Crystal Mountains. They threatened execution if he ever returned to this range, to ensure he couldn't gather a following and make trouble for our people."

And so he had been born in distant Porphyr. Shay shuddered, colder than ever, and sank deeper into the water for warmth. But the water had cooled as they talked. Heart aching and mind numbed by what he'd learned, Shay finished washing, climbed out of the tub, and dressed in clean clothes. His own. Apparently, Atich had visited Shay's home first.

He scrubbed a towel through his hair and sighed. "The axe is a non-issue; anyone can own her, but no one else can trigger her magic. Without me, the people would lose the benefit of her greatest powers. Permanently."

Robayne hesitated, and when he spoke, his voice gentled. "They're going to lose that anyway, unless you remarry and produce a male heir."

Because my son was murdered. Fresh grief pierced Shay's heart, as if it had happened yesterday. He worked to control his voice. "I'm going to get some sleep," he announced. "And then I'm going to go visit my friends in Echo. If Bibi has room for me, I'll stay there a while, until some of the furor dies down."

Robayne's eyes widened and his bottom lip dropped. "That will confirm for many people that you've taken the axe and run."

"It's my axe. I can take it where I please. And you can tell them where I went, if you like." Shay set the gem materials into one boot and clutched it against his chest. "How does anyone live a peaceful life here, when the Council constantly bickers and fights?"

"Here. Take this." Robayne held out the half-full pitcher of ale.

"I want an answer," Shay shouted, face twisting painfully. Horrified, he stammered an apology. Robayne waved it off. "The answer is the same as it would be anywhere. Life isn't always peaceful; that's the way of it. We just put the bad times behind us and cling to the good ones."

Mortified, Shay took the pitcher, nodded at Robayne, and walked out, hoping his boiling thoughts would settle enough for him to get the long sleep he so desperately needed.

Late the next morning, still groggy from sleep, Shay set the opal on the workbench in his home. The gem tugged at him like a living thing, its faint, guttural song deep in his bones demanding creation. Despite his urgent desire to get out of the caverns, he couldn't resist.

Something simple, something quick. A belt, with three large black opal cabochons. No, not cabochons. Cut the opals into smaller chunks, polish them lightly, entwine them in leather openwork. He didn't even need to shape

225

them fully. The leather belt could tie, to speed his work. It wouldn't be pretty, but it would get him on the road sooner. He could shape the opals later and give them a finer, more protective setting. He cringed at the thought of leather rubbing against the stones–the gentle abrasion of the belt as he moved would dull the soft opals. At least the leather lattice would protect them somewhat from chipping or other damage.

He set to work.

Time disappeared, as it always did when he handled fine gems, the opal's energy transferring to him through his hands. The quiet knock on his door didn't register for a moment, but slowly the sound drew him from that place deep inside himself where creation took place.

About to call out an invitation to enter, he hesitated. He didn't want to face any of the Elders at the moment, although he couldn't think why any of them would visit.

"Shay?" called a low voice.

Robayne.

"Come," called Shay, suddenly annoyed at the interruption of his work. His sense of urgency increased, infused with a mild anger. He needed to finish the belt and be on his way!

A moment later, Robayne appeared in the doorway of his workshop, a full plate of food in each hand. "I wasn't sure if you'd be awake yet. Or still here, instead of on your way to Echo." He held out a plate.

The aroma of hot cakes fried in bacon grease and topped with warm fruit made Shay's mouth water. He'd forgotten about food, although he could remember his stomach snarling as he worked. When he lost himself in the gems like that, nothing else existed, not even the discomforts of his own body.

He had a hard time releasing the opals, but he wiped

his hands and face and accepted the plate. "Thank you. I've been up a while, getting ready to go."

Robayne laughed. "Gem fever. I recognize the signs."

As they ate, Robayne talked. "I mostly stopped by to warn you. You may want to leave the opals until later and start for Echo at once. The Elders want to meet with you again today, a difficult and unhappy experience you'll want to avoid, if you can."

"Won't that just make it worse later?"

"For them, not for you. If they haven't told you about it, they can't expect you to be here, now can they?"

Shay heaved an exasperated sigh. "Will they send someone to Echo to get me?"

"I wouldn't put it beyond them."

"Tell them to save themselves a trip. I won't be meeting them there at all, unless Orlait abandons his attempt to steal my axe and apologizes publicly. He's stirred up a rat's nest, and I want no part of it." Something in Shay hardened. No more putting up with this idiocy. *He* held the axe, and the power it represented. Time to take advantage of that, if he could. He would *not* live under Orlait's thumb. Any man worthy of the name controlled his own life.

Robayne's eyes widened. Then he chuckled. "That'll give them something to think about!

"Take your time, enjoy your visit, come back when you're ready. If you wait long enough, maybe something else will turn their attention from you and allow them to forget this issue entirely. The whole community is stirred up, and the Elders know that's not healthy. Some just want to put it behind them and get back to normal."

Shay searched Robayne's face for a moment. "How do you always know so much of the Council's business?"

Robayne grinned. "Wildt is my father's uncle."

"*Wildt* is related to you?" Shay's mouth hung open.

227

"Feisty old fellow, isn't he? Here, let me have your plate. Enjoy your visit. I'll see you when you get back." Robayne left.

For a long moment, Shay sat thinking. But the call of black opals hummed in his veins and he returned to them, a lover returning to his seductive mistress.

24. Black Opals

To Shay's surprise, Spark seemed pleased to see him, neighing loudly when he entered the stable.

No horse should be such a bright red. It wasn't natural. Nevertheless, he liked the easy, comfortable nature of the beast–and the surefootedness that had kept him alive on all those terrifying trails.

He saddled up and rode out, his new belt of black opals tied about his waist and Elegy strapped to his back. His saddlebags carried the large amyth chunk for Bibi.

Bright sunshine, an enthusiastic horse, and a breeze in his face lifted Shay's spirits. He hadn't realized how much he missed the outdoors. His visits to the Bowl, the outdoor playground and picnic area, had been all too brief.

By comparison, the cavern community seemed dark and cramped, despite the thousands of moonstones.

The trip went fast. In no time he reached the tauz canyons, awed by the sun-struck beauty of the jagged crystals. Had the stones really sung here? He'd been the only one to hear . . .

He slowed Spark, listening, then stopped, and dismounted. Leading the horse, he heard nothing for several steps. Then he felt–heard?–the gradual buildup of sound through his feet. A groan, deep-rooted in the earth, rose in pitch and volume as he reached the thickest part of the fields. When higher, discordant tones added to the hum, then higher ones still, uneasiness crept up his spine. He could feel the enmity of the tauz, and it brought back fearful memories of the struggle to free Bibi from the grandfather pillar. The sound clawing at his bones became strident, angry, and he soon remounted, knowing the song would increase in volume and hatred until he became helpless with it, as he had before. Even Spark seemed anxious to put this place behind them.

Echo lay only a few miles from the tauz and soon came into view, a pretty little town nestled into a beautiful valley. He looked forward to seeing his friends again and quickened his pace. True friends, the kind he could count on. Like Bibi.

The Amyth Cup sat on the edge of town, the first building encountered by visitors coming up the mountain. Shay recognized Bibi's bold style of painting on the sign, a simple but lovely purple goblet above the name of the tavern.

Behind this building Shay found a stable where he left Spark with an aged stabler.

It had been a long time since he'd so looked forward to seeing someone. Anticipation lightened his steps as he rounded the corner of the tavern.

"Bladen!" Meilin ran toward him down the wooden walkway, arms wide. "Bladen! Where were you? You disappeared! Where were you?"

Laughing, Shay squatted, arms held open, and Meilin ran into them, almost knocking him over. Just like Beryl used to. As he hugged the child, the familiar greeting swept a knife of grief through him. But Meilin was here now, and he hugged him tighter.

Then he stood, as Bibi appeared in the doorway. As she had in The Dainty Slipper, she wore a loose, colorful robe, her black hair pulled up under a colorful turban. Her smile was smaller, professional, her chin held as high as ever.

The warmth in her eyes, though, displayed a rare concession to friendship. "Meilin saw you ride in and ran to greet you, but you were nowhere in sight. It is a good thing you reappeared, or he would be hunting the town for you."

"It's good to see you, my friends," said Shay from his heart. "I'm sorry I couldn't come sooner, but there is much to tell."

"Come in, Shay. While you are here, my home is your home." Bibi turned and led the way inside.

Shay followed, Meilin dancing alongside him and describing the halfpony Bibi had acquired for him. "His name is Chase, and he's a colored horse, white with big blobs of red color, brown-red like a real horse, not red-red like Spark."

Chuckling, Shay tried to look around the tavern while giving Meilin his full attention. Like her last tavern, this one felt easy and inviting, many of the tables gathered close to the fireplace where a small, comfortable blaze danced. Ale casks clustered in one corner near the counter. Neatly lined-up bottles stood on shelves behind the long bar, where a red-haired man wiped dust from them.

Strange. Why would she hire help, with Meilin available?

The worker turned.

Spinel.

A trickle of cold chilled the base of Shay's skull. Their gazes met and anger filled his pores. This man had killed his own sister, his own niece and nephew, for a chance to steal the battle-axe.

Spinel's gaze met his, flicked away, came back. Filled with bitterness and humiliation, the gray eyes slipped off again. He turned his shoulder and reached for another bottle to wipe.

Behind Shay, Bibi spoke, her voice sharp as flint. "He smashed my amyth cup, a beautiful, delicate object, and magic as well. A priceless gemwork. Spinel serves me until the cost of the goblet is repaid."

"For life, then." Even the sight of Cinny's brother hurt

231

Shay's stomach.

Bibi smiled, an icicle of amusement, and raised her voice. "Spinel, you will obey Shay Bladen as you would me."

A strange gladness leaped in Shay's belly. What he couldn't do with that boon! Spinel would yet pay for what he'd done.

The sudden stiffening of Spinel's shoulders showed he heard. Slowly, he turned, eyes smoking with hate. He glared at Shay as he replied to Bibi. "Obey a man who got my sister killed? I think not."

Rage exploded through Shay. "You killed your sister, Spinel! And her children. *My* children! *My* wife!" At his sides, his fists tightened so fiercely his entire body quivered. "All for a damned gemwork!" Something buried deep in him cringed at the insult to Elegy, while his fingers itched for the axe strapped to his back. He couldn't allow himself that luxury now.

Spinel curled his lip. "Cinny was *my* family first." Bitterness snarled his voice.

"She loved you every day of your life," Shay shouted. "And you broke into her home with murderers at your heels!"

"Whatever you think, I loved her, and I loved her *children*!" Without warning, Spinel snatched the closest liquor bottle and hurled it at Shay. The impact of bottle to brow dropped him straight down. He rolled back and forth, holding his forehead. When he could breathe, he grabbed the bottle off the floor by its neck. He launched to his feet. Toward Spinel.

Crazed with pain and soul-spun fury, he attacked. Two steps, and he dived across the counter. He landed belly down atop it, snatching the front of Spinel's shirt. He yanked his enemy forward, smashed the bottom edge of the bottle into his face. He pulled himself across and hit Spinel again. And again.

The fear in Spinel's eyes only made him angrier, more intense.

Spinel groped for a bottle of his own.

Shay pounded the grasping fingers, rewarded by Spinel's screams. The world glazed red.

He'd kill this Dark-damned monster! He didn't deserve to live! He struck a vicious blow across Spinel's head.

Spinel dropped, his weight dragging Shay with him.

Shay didn't release his grip, only struck the limp form again. And again.

The roaring in his ears obliterated all other sound. "Die," he screamed in Spinel's face. "Die, you child-murdering bastard!"

"Shay! No," Bibi's voice commanded, but he paid no heed.

Something snagged his collar, caught the bottle before it hit Spinel. "Stop! You will not kill him!"

"Let go!" Shay twisted on the floor atop Spinel, wrenched the bottle from a charcoal grip, and swung it at his brother-enemy.

He got in one more strike before Bibi levered the bottle from his hand.

Shay gasped, groped for another weapon.

Something pricked his cheek. He froze.

A sword? Here?

A sword. Bibi's. Held in a steady hand. Her obsis eyes were a deluge of cold water. The red haze dissipated.

A little more pressure from the sword. A slight sting as the flesh on his cheek parted.

Shay surrendered, relaxing his body in complete submission.

For a long moment, he lay still, the anger drained all at

once.

Bibi's sword withdrew slowly. "Come out from the bar. Sit." The sword choreographed his movements to a nearby table. Then the sword point dropped and her strong hand shoved him into a chair so hard a chair leg broke under the impact.

Shay landed amid the crashing splinters and scrambled to his feet.

Bibi shoved him into another chair, her jaw tight with determination. "Sit. And do not move!" She stood in front of him, steel in her face and her voice. "Spinel still lives, if you care."

"Shay?" A tiny, timid voice.

Shay turned his head. Meilin, emrel eyes wide in a white face. Oh, Light! The child had seen the whole thing. Sickened and shamed, Shay hung his head.

"Meilin." Bibi spoke in a low, controlled voice, as if nothing out of the ordinary had happened. "I need you to go find Ansel, the apothecary."

Meilin ran for the door, almost tangling his feet in his haste.

Bibi turned on Shay. "In front of the boy! Have you no sense? Would you have wanted your children to see that?"

"No, Senesa," he whispered, head still down.

"That child worships you. He thinks you are a hero. And you have just shown him how a hero handles anger."

Shay roused his anger again, briefly. "Spinel deserves death!"

"So do we all. Would you destroy my property? Without even asking? Spinel belongs to me! Do not touch him again."

"Yes, Senesa." Shay forced the words through clenched teeth.

Bibi glared at him a moment longer. "Now. What will

234

you do about Meilin?"

"I'll talk to him." Shay's voice came out as a rough half-whisper. As the last of the hate and fury dripped away, weariness and self-loathing moved in.

"What happened, Shay? I know you hate him, and with good cause. But I have never seen you so out of control."

Shay leaned forward and put his face in his hands. "It's been happening a lot lately, and I don't know why. And it's getting worse." He described tersely the previous anger incidents, wanting to have it done before Meilin's return.

Bibi's eyes narrowed in thought. "This is unnatural for you, Shay. I wonder if magic might be involved."

He'd heard that twice now, and suddenly he knew. He untied the belt bearing three fabulous black opals, startled at the reluctance dragging at his fingers. Gingerly, he laid the belt on the table next to him.

The opals. Why did he delay his journey here to half-polish them? Why would he forego cutting them? And why secure them in a leather lattice belt that could rub them dull? None of that made sense to someone who loved the gems of the earth, who made his living with them.

The fits of anger had begun after harvesting, when he carried the matrix inside his shirt.

Maybe he hadn't discovered a new vein of black opals. Maybe it had been closed deliberately, and only reopened by the movement of the earth. How long since anyone else had been there? Neither Robayne, nor Atich, nor Orlait had said anything when he showed them the matrix, so it must have been long ago.

No, not true. Orlait had asked where they came from, but Shay had ignored him, already under the opals' influence. The Elder must have known about their magic.

Before he could think about it, he snatched up the belt again, holding it at arm's length like a poisonous snake. He reached the fire in three strides and threw it in. The heat would dry out and destroy the opals and burn up the leather. And good riddance. He watched them burn, part of him shrieking in protest. They were so beautiful!

These, he wanted no part of. He had no desire to take them back home to be reworked.

He hated Spinel, but he hated worse what he'd become under the opals' influence.

Meilin returned with Ansel, a robust man of middle years, bald as a moonstone, with neither beard nor eyebrows. The lack of hair made his skystone eyes startling. He greeted Bibi heartily, but his gaze went straight to Spinel, and his body followed.

Bibi helped Ansel move Spinel's unconscious body to the top of a long table and they spoke quietly as the apothecary examined his patient.

Now was the time to talk to Meilin. Shay had to mend what he'd broken as soon as possible. He walked over to where the boy watched anxiously and set a hand on his shoulder.

It hurt when the boy flinched.

"Meilin, I need to talk to you." He felt the sudden fear in Meilin's face like tongs closing on his heart.

Bibi looked over her shoulder, catching Shay's glance. Black eyes held a warning, or concern, or both. "It is all right, Meilin. He is himself again."

Shay led the boy outdoors, where Meilin could run if he felt the need. It's what Shay would have wanted, in the boy's place. They sat on the edge of the board walkway.

Shay noticed the gap between him and the boy, not the usual shoulder-to-shoulder, companionable closeness he'd enjoyed on the trail.

"I'm sorry you saw all that. And I want to explain, so you can put it into perspective."

236

Oh, it hurt to see Meilin hunch into himself, as if he expected to be struck. It hurt worse to know he had created this fear.

"I know you're a little scared of me after what you saw, but you don't need to be. I would never hurt you. You've . . . become like a son to me, and I loved my son very much." Shay took a deep breath, released it slowly. "Spinel was my wife's brother. He's also the one responsible for her death, and the deaths of my son and my daughter."

"I like Spinel." Meilin defended him with a quivering lip and anxious eyes. "He's nice to me and tells me stories."

Shay swallowed down the urge to refute Meilin's opinion. "He wants my battle-axe and has chased me all the way from the city of Porphyr, in Palernia. He is my enemy."

Meilin's stillness indicated, perhaps, that he listened.

Encouraged, Shay continued. "You've seen me in battle before, but this was different. This time I was angry. Men should never allow their anger to control them, and I have rarely in my life given in to it. But it's been happening a lot lately, and I didn't understand why until today. The black opals in my belt hold an unusual magic, a magic that made me angry out of all proportion for even the smallest cause."

Meilin looked at him, eyes wide. "The opals made you do it?"

Dangerous ground, here. Shay sought the words. "No, the opals could make me angry, but they couldn't control what I did with that anger. Even if they could, it wouldn't matter. A man is responsible for his own actions. Always. No matter what other influence is brought to bear."

"But the opals . . ."

"If I'd known they were affecting me, my actions might have been different. I'd like to think so, anyway. But *if onlys* don't excuse what I did today. A man controls his anger; he doesn't allow it to control him. What I did, I am responsible for. Sometimes taking responsibility is hard. We look for excuses for our behavior, but no excuse is adequate.

"I was wrong today, and I don't like that you saw it. I'm sorry for that, and for what I did. I don't want to lose your good opinion of me."

"I didn't like seeing it, either." Meilin looked down. "I thought you'd kill him."

"And I probably would have, if Bibi hadn't stopped me. Thank the Light she did!"

"Will . . ." Meilin hesitated. "Will they make you hurt . . . someone who's your friend? Not just your enemy?"

"I've destroyed the opals, Meilin. They'll never again influence me to hurt anyone. *Especially* a friend."

"Destroyed? But they were beautiful!"

Shay's jaw set. "No beauty is worth that. I threw the belt into the fire.

"Opals are very soft, and they have a lot of water in them. We call them 'aqueous' for the water content. Heat will dry them out and they'll crack and be destroyed."

"Ay-kwee-us," Meilin repeated, struggling a little with pronunciation.

Shay grinned at the boy, pleased. A likely apprentice down the road. If . . . when he set up a shop of his own.

Longing filled him again. He released it with a heavy sigh.

25. The Amyth Cup

"When are you going to get a new amyth cup, Bibi?" called a grizzled man with dirt beneath his nails. He was halfway through his third ale–at least. "My wife beats me when I come home drunk!" The crowd roared with laughter. He grinned, pleased with the attention.

"As soon as I find the right piece of amyth," she called back. "Not all amyth is magic, no matter what you've heard. And Metchal–finding one with enough magic to keep *you* sober could be difficult!"

The regulars roared with laughter. Their victim grinned proudly.

Smiling at the exchange, Shay relaxed into the comfortable atmosphere of Bibi's new tavern. The mostly local clientele knew each other, and the energy of their friendships enlivened the place. Bibi deftly filled orders and sent Spinel into the crowd with food and drink. The evening regulars, ready for ale and stronger liquors after a long day, would be more boisterous. If the inevitable scuffle broke out, though, those nearby broke it up–or Bibi would, which the regulars already knew to avoid.

Meilin wanted to help, too, but Bibi only allowed him to serve those sitting around the edges of the room, where his small size wouldn't get him run over. Shay made it a point to sit where Meilin could serve him, careful to keep a close eye on the boy. He noticed the regulars did the same. A young child did not really belong in a tavern, even Bibi's.

Once again, Spinel cleaned and polished. A ragged red cut still marred the scalp above his ear and spectacular bruises clouded much of his face. Shay did not apologize for creating them, and often watched him from a corner seat across the room from the bar. Anger still bit the back of his neck–a normal anger, not tinged by the opals' madness.

And Spinel watched back, hate in his eyes. And sometimes–fear?

Despite his general discomfort with crowds, Shay felt good here. The people's friendliness and easy acceptance, without expectations, drew him and he fell naturally into conversation with local men, to his surprise.

During a lull in the custom, Bibi brought Shay another ale and sat down with her own. "You seem to like it here," she said.

"Your tavern is well-run and comfortable, your customers hard-working and friendly. Who wouldn't like it?"

She smiled at him, a rare crinkling at the corners of her eyes displaying true friendship. Bibi didn't share herself easily, and it warmed Shay all the way through. "You may stay as long as you like. There will always be room for you here."

Settled Bibi was very different from traveling Bibi. Shay liked this side of her. "Thank you. Blue Mountain is fascinating, but they have some strange customs, and I seem to be caught up in their politics."

Bibi quirked an eyebrow, signaled Spinel for more ale. Oh, how he hated having to wait on Shay! He couldn't even bring himself to look at the man he'd wronged! The gemsman gloated privately, careful not to let Bibi see it.

When Spinel had gone, Shay told Bibi what had happened in Blue Mountain, leaving out only Elegy's name and skimping on her full powers.

"I would like to see that place someday," she said, "if they open it up to visitors."

"I would enjoy showing it to you, but I don't think they ever will. I've never seen people so distrusting of outsiders."

"You are the axe bearer," she reminded him. "You

share her power. Thus your word carries much weight, if you choose to use it."

But how did he do that? The Blue Mountain People certainly didn't seem to give his opinions any special weight, and some opposed him outright, based on something that happened forty years ago.

He changed the subject. "I brought you a gift."

Bibi's eyebrows lifted.

He smiled, enjoying the moment. "I heard the name of your new tavern. Not knowing you already had a magic cup, I harvested a block of magic amyth to create one for you."

Bibi's eyes lit up. "You have it here?"

"It's in my room upstairs. I'll sketch some designs to show you, too. And if I can find the space and tools, I'll work on it while I'm here."

Bibi stared at him, seeming not to breathe. "A gift? Shay, such a goblet is priceless!"

Shay swelled with pride, with the euphoria of offering a gift so highly prized by the recipient. "So is your friendship, Bibi."

"Can you set two additional stones into the designs?" Bibi asked, eyes alight.

"Such as?"

"I have two magic sunstones, which will nullify any poison in the cup. I acquired them too late for the first cup but would have them in the new one if possible."

Shay regarded her in wonder. Knowing his affinity for stones, she'd carried them all that way without ever mentioning them. "Of course."

She seemed to read his mind. "A little mystery is good for the soul." Her eyes sparkled.

He chuckled.

The next day, Shay allowed Meilin to drag him

enthusiastically on a tour of Echo. As they walked, Shay studied the few empty buildings against the needs of a gemsman's shop. *Have I decided to live here, then?*

He began to pay more attention to the town itself, to evaluate it as a place to live and work, but the unfinished business at Blue Mountain gnawed his belly. He needed resolution there, first.

The day after that, Robayne walked into The Amyth Cup, looking for him.

Momentary pleasure washed through Shay, chased by apprehension. More bad news?

The Cup hosted few customers in early afternoon, so they had no trouble finding a quiet table to talk. Across the room, Bibi worked with Meilin, teaching him his numbers, a task Shay sometimes shared.

Interesting, the way Spinel's head snapped around to stare at Robayne, as if he'd seen him before. But if they knew each other, neither gave any other sign.

"What news, Robayne?" asked Shay, his tone casual.

From the corner of his eye, he saw Spinel's ears prick up. Of course. He'd read the note that came with the axe and would recognize the name. "Speak softly," he murmured. "We have an eavesdropper."

Robayne lowered his voice to near inaudibility. "The uproar is dying down, finally, after Orlait's loudly expressed opinion that you stole the axe and ran."

"*Stole? Stole something I own*?" Shay whispered. He cut a glance at Spinel, wishing for more crowd to cover the conversation. His brother-by-law's ears almost stretched with the effort to hear.

Robayne smiled. "That sparked some pretty harsh accusations and debates, until your esteemed grandfather, Locelar, spoke with the Council of Elders in a closed meeting. No one knows what he said, but afterward,

Locelar stalked the halls with a stony face and flashing eyes, exuding all the power and ire of the current head of a Founder Family. The Council held an emergency session the next day–another closed meeting, this one without Locelar. Again no one knows what was said, but Orlait has been very subdued. And Uncle Wildt looks very satisfied, in my opinion. With no one speaking publicly, the place has settled down."

Shay couldn't catch his breath for a moment. "My grandfather stood up for me to the Council?" What did he know about family? He'd spent his life longing for one, never dreaming it already existed. No one had ever stood up for him before, except Cinny, and he'd only met Locelar twice, on more formal occasions.

The newness and brightness of family nearly overwhelmed him.

Robayne grimaced. "Yes, but there are larger issues here, too. Matters concerning your battle-axe are important to all Bladens, especially the issue of whether she is Bladen property or community property. If she's community property, the Council has more rights to her than Bladen, even if only a Bladen can wield her. Locelar can't allow that. It would be a loss of Family power."

Robayne paused to raise his empty mug high. When Bibi saw it and nodded, he set it down and continued. "And that's the other issue–maintaining the family's influence. The leadership and vision of three men created the community, and their leadership has always been there, even if very quietly. It would be a disservice to all the Founder Families to lose the *only* advantage of being the founders. And the community would be poorer without their leadership. So yes, Locelar stood up for you, and for the axe, and for all Bladens, and for the Founder Families and the community."

243

"I didn't realize the Families took such an active role in leadership." No wonder Shay hated politics. Much too complicated for a simple man like him. He felt a touch of disappointment that his grandfather's support hadn't been more personal, but he couldn't fault Robayne's reasoning.

"They don't, generally. So when they do take a stand, it has much greater impact. Locelar himself doesn't like the limelight, but he did what was necessary."

Shay didn't speak as Meilin proudly marched over with a heavy pitcher and refilled their mugs. If the boy took more time than necessary, he only took care not to spill; he wasn't avoiding his lesson with Bibi. Shay tried not to show his amusement.

To Robayne he said, "So, everything's back to normal and I should return?"

Robayne grinned. "Think of yourself as a loose end that needs to be secured. The Council would like to meet with you again, and this time I suspect it will be a much pleasanter meeting. As you requested, I gave them your message, almost word for word. They're coming here."

Closure. Putting a formal end to the disharmony. Shay longed to put the uncertainty and discomfort behind him. Going back to Blue Mountain, though, raised its own issues.

He liked living under the Eye of the Light again, and he dreaded living in the caverns. The closed-in feeling no longer bothered him, and searching for gem materials tugged at him without pause, but he much preferred real sky and natural light. At Blue Mountain, he could only find that in the Bowl, where no one could be allowed to live, for security reasons.

"You will need to return eventually, to learn the secrets of how the axe was made. Blue Mountain has a carefully hidden workshop for that purpose, and it's the last of the major secrets you need to learn."

Yearning nearly overpowered him. He could almost taste the desire for those mysteries.

"Teach me here. I can arrange a private and secure place for the lessons."

"I can't." Robayne's voice dropped to a whisper and he leaned in toward Shay. "Part of the sealed area includes the vein of magic black diamond. You need to know where it is, how to get to it. It has to be there."

Shay thought about it, about what he really wanted. Respect, damn it. Those people–meaning Orlait–weren't his superiors, though they acted like it. He knew gems as well as any of them, was as much a man as any of them. And only he could handle Elegy. He was *entitled* to what Robayne offered.

"Fine. I will return to finish my training. After Orlait's apology."

Bibi's high, ululating war cry jolted Shay out of sleep near dawn.

He pulled on britches and ran for the door, barefoot and bare chested.

Abruptly awakened by the cry, guests poured into the hall, including Meilin, whom Shay sent back into his room.

Bibi emerged from a room not her own. Sword in hand, she joined Shay. "That little bastard is gone! Your wife's brother has not yet completed what he owes me." Her eyes glittered dangerously.

She glanced around at the milling customers and raised her voice. "It is all right, gentlemen! There is no danger here. Please return to your beds and sleep well; this is a family matter and you need not be concerned."

Grumbling and questioning, the guests nevertheless did as she asked.

245

"I will refund part of the night's stay to each customer," Bibi told Shay, "when the day's normal beginning wakes them. With my apology for the inconvenience."

"Why were you yelling, if he was already gone?" Shay stepped past Bibi into Spinel's room. He knew Bibi kept the shutters locked from the outside and that, being Sheethe, she slept lightly. But Spinel, over time, had dug out the hinges of one shutter, keeping the damage covered by the single tall chest in the room.

"I saw him running and wanted him to have nightmares." She spoke from behind him as he crossed to examine the window. "The top hinge was undisturbed when I locked him in last night. In his haste to destroy it in one night, he popped it loose when he got close. That is what woke me."

Shay looked out the window and down. A blanket hung from the windowsill; it would have gotten Spinel close enough to the ground to land without breaking a leg.

"Will you go after him?" He hated having to look at Spinel's face every day, but he *was* Cinny's brother. "Will you kill him for defying you?"

Bibi didn't speak for a moment. "Would you like me to? He has done you great wrong."

He wanted to say yes, but he felt Cinny's disapproval and horror. She had loved her brother, and so had their children. "No. Good riddance, from my perspective."

Bibi nodded, then a wide grin stretched across her face below hard eyes. "How far will he run, do you think?"

Shay smiled back. "As far as he can. With luck, he'll spend the rest of his life looking over his shoulder."

"The battle cry will do that to the weak of heart and soul. It will amuse me, in my old age, to think of him still running."

246

26. Apology

The first riders to arrive from Blue Mountain were Atich and Locelar. The patrician looked too ordinary for the influence he wielded, Shay decided–hair bereft of color, dark eyes, the thick, peaked eyebrows of a Bladen still unbleached, and an erect posture more common to men Atich's age. He might be old, but he certainly wasn't bent.

"Why is everyone wearing a sword?" Shay murmured to Robayne as Locelar dismounted.

His mentor grinned. "We have a long habit of not trusting the outside world."

Atich attended Locelar as he dismounted slowly. His first graceless steps loosened up until he walked like a much younger man. He smiled with an unexpected hint of shyness.

Shay held out his hand and Locelar took it. He hesitated, then pulled Shay into a rough embrace. "It's good to see you, Grandson."

Emotions swirled through Shay. His previous interactions with Locelar had been brief and formal, nothing at all like this. Why the sudden offering of affection? Why now? And yet . . . his own grandfather acknowledged him and apparently wanted to close the gap of formality between them. Shay wanted to reciprocate, but should he trust so easily?

"We're the vanguard," Atich explained. "The Council comes behind us."

The entire Council? Did that mean Orlait would apologize? Or had they come to make more trouble? Shay found himself grateful for his grandfather's presence.

Locelar snorted. "He means Orlait and his cronies are too self-important to be risked, and the Bladens offered protection to get them to come."

"Welcome, Localar," said Shay. "I'm glad you're here. And welcome, Cousin." He nodded at Atich.

"I would be pleased if you called me Grandfather," said Localar, his voice rough. Tears stood in his eyes, and he didn't blink them back.

Shay swallowed, unsure of his voice. "Thank you, Grandfather." Perhaps it was a true offering of family closeness after all.

"May I speak with you in private?" the old man asked.

Shay nodded. "My room is this way."

As they walked through the common room, he introduced Localar to Bibi, who agreed to arrange a meeting place for a dozen people. To Shay's regret, Meilin had gone out to play somewhere.

For just the two of them, though, his room would do. He offered Localar the only chair and sat on the bed facing him.

Localar leaned back, arms crossed over his chest. Then he uncrossed them and left his hands in his lap.

Shay broke the ice. "Thank you for standing up for me before the Elders, Loc–Grandfather. I know you stood up for the family and the community as well, but . . . no one's ever stood up for me before, except Cinny. My wife." He couldn't speak of her death out loud right now.

"I should have stood up for your father long ago, Shay. If I had, your life would have been very different."

"Why didn't you?" Shay blurted. He looked down at his hands, embarrassed, but he wouldn't take back the question. He forced himself to look Localar in the eye. "He was your firstborn son, and you let them throw him out." He hadn't realized the anger he hoarded for this one act–or lack of one.

"This is why I asked to speak to you privately, so we

could clear the air and not leave such hurts unspoken between us. I want to explain . . . to tell you what happened, although no explanation could ever be adequate. And then I want to hear what you can tell me of my son."

Shay chose to share first. "Not much. I remember my mother better, but even her face is . . . unclear. Of my father, I remember a big smile, and strong arms, but not much else. I was very young when they died. I knew my own name, but I couldn't remember theirs. To me, they were Father and Mother. I remember their voices, but not distinctly."

Tears slid down the old man's cheeks. "That's all?"

A lifetime of buried anger and resentment boiled up. "Where were you when I ran through the streets, frightened of both the inferno behind me and the world outside my parents' home? Where were you when my belly cramped with hunger, and I slept in coal bins and manure piles and shitty alleys? When the children my age teased me and called me names? When the older boys beat me out of boredom, and for the feeling of power it brought? When I learned to do the same in my turn? When I learned to steal? And to beg? When men grabbed . . . "" He broke off, breathing heavily, just short of sobs.

Almost, he'd said too much. Unwilling to look his grandfather in the eye, lest Locelar see a horrible truth hidden there, Shay leaped to his feet and crossed to the room's lone window.

He heard a strangled noise and turned back to his horrified grandfather.

Pounding down the past as best he could, Shay took control of himself enough to speak.

"I cried myself to sleep every night, wanting my parents, wanting their protection, a safe place to sleep, food on a table. Scraps found in alleys and bread stolen as

249

opportunity allowed, did little for a growing boy."

"My son." Locelar's voice broke. He cleared his throat. "I was raised on the requirement for dignity and duty to the community, on the idea that the community's welfare was my responsibility. I stood by, followed protocol, protected the community instead of my own flesh and blood. And I've paid for it every day since he left. As I deserved to."

"I heard he brought a visitor into Blue Mountain. That they used to execute anyone who committed such an offense."

Locelar nodded. "Rond didn't believe in excluding visitors. We could have visitors in the Center without revealing all the tunnels and the mines and riches. He thought it would be better for the community, too, make us more normal and more accepted by the rest of the world. He even wanted the community to move from the mountain's belly to its slopes. Healthier for the children, he said. Privately, I agreed with him, at least on that score, though I never said so out loud. Until now. I was raised to believe our riches would tempt outsiders beyond their capacity to resist. They would send spies to visit us, attack our community, destroy our people and our way of life. It was so deeply ingrained I couldn't overcome it, and in the end remained silent when I should have spoken.

"I betrayed my son, his wife, their son—you—and my own heart and soul. Not until I lived with the grievous loss of my son did I realize what I had done, and the realization nearly killed me. All my sleep held nightmares, and I couldn't bear to be around the Council that banished him. And so, when the issue of the Bladen battle-axe came before the Council, I determined that this time I would not be silent."

Shay's gut wrenched. He wanted to shout at Locelar. To accuse him of betraying his own blood, his own family.

But the old man had just admitted it. Shay longed to hit someone, break something. To rage. To release the fear and shame and anger of a lifetime. To demand whether destroying their lives and his had been worth it. To somehow force the old man to . . . what? What could he say or do to Locelar worse than the pain he'd inflicted on himself?

He swallowed old grief and new tears, struggling to come to terms with his own life and his own blood.

A quiet knock on the door interrupted his thoughts. Bibi's voice carried through the wood. "The Council has arrived. I have shown them to the meeting room you requested."

Shay listened to the fading of her quiet footsteps.

Locelar remained silent until she'd gone. "I'm sorry, Grandson. I can never express my anger at my own closed-minded stupidity. I would give anything to take it back, to remove the hurt and fear of your early years."

Shay swallowed, his throat tight. An incompatible mix of emotions snarled through him–anger, pain, sorrow, bitterness, love, gratitude–and he couldn't reconcile them. Not yet, at least. His intertwined fingers wrenched at each other between white knuckles.

He needed his grandfather, his family. That gaping hole in his life had always been the absence of family. He couldn't turn away from the gift being offered–not without being as shortsighted as Locelar had been all those years ago.

"Grandfather, if my life had not been as it was, I would never have met Cinnabar, the most wonderful woman in the world. We would not have borne two bright, beautiful children. Having them in my life, even so briefly, was worth everything that happened later.

"Besides, that life has led to the recovery of the

251

Bladens' battle-axe, which could never have happened if I'd been raised here, safe and happy." Tears tracked down his cheeks. He made no attempt to stop them.

"Then the Light's will has been done, using our pain to mold the world as It chooses."

Shay entered the private meeting room at his grandfather's side. They claimed adjacent chairs cushioned in blue and black. Trust Bibi to assure equal status for everyone in the circular seating pattern.

"Would anyone care for something from the bar?" After a moment of silence, Bibi said, "Should you need anything, I will be downstairs." She left the room, closing the door behind her.

Locelar remained standing behind his chair, strength and authority carried in his shoulders. All eyes turned to him. He waited on their attention before speaking. No sign of his recent tears remained. His strong, clear voice filled the room, thought he didn't raise his voice. "Before we begin, I would like to say a few words, to explain recent events to my grandson.

"In particular, Shay, you should know that, in your absence, the Elders met in closed council to discuss, at Orlait's behest, whether the battle-axe should rightfully be community property instead of belonging to an individual."

Shay nodded. That much he knew–and now the Council knew he did.

"In the early days of our community, greedy, unscrupulous men came–not to mine or work the land, but to take the fruits of hard labor from honest folk. Some of them went well beyond mere theft. They burned homes, farms, and towns, killing and raping as they went.

"Then one of the early Bladens, Nathair, discovered and claimed a vein of black diamond such as never seen elsewhere in the world, and it was magic. It took a lifetime to uncover its secrets, but in his old age he created the battle-axe you carry. His grandson, Kever, became the first to wield it against the greedy and corrupt, in defense of all the homes and communities of the Crystal Mountains, as best he could.

"After him, his son–and the firstborn Bladen son of every generation since–has wielded the axe in protection of the people. Down through all the years, Bladen and his axe have gained the status of legend. For his sake, the people in the area tolerate all the Blue Mountain People, though we are a strange and mysterious people to them. The legend has come to define us to the outside world, bringing status and a certain amount of awe."

Shay had picked up bits and pieces of the story, but not with this much detail.

"My father, Vyskyr, took the battle-axe with him when he went off to war shortly after my birth. The Robayne of that day sent a note with him, promising to teach him the mysteries of its creation when he returned from the war. He never did. Men went to look for him, and for the axe, but neither was ever found. I grew up on stories of the axe, but never saw it until you brought it home, Shay. The Council would like to assure that the priceless battle-axe is never again lost to the community. And *that* is why Orlait convened the Elders, in an attempt to steal the axe from its rightful owner. That and sheer hubris."

From the corner of his eye, Shay saw Orlait's stubborn jaw and reddening face. Nothing good could come of Locelar's trampling of his dignity. But then, nothing bad could come of putting the old man in his place, either. He braced for more trouble.

Faltryn spoke up from her place in the circle. "Several Elders agreed with him, Shay. We lost much status as a people during the hundred years or more the axe was lost. But many of us opposed the action, as well. We believed that the value of the axe to the community didn't make a change in ownership the right thing to do. It was quite a discussion."

"Just short of a brawl when I arrived," said Locelar. "But I explained to them that no such transfer of ownership would take place. That no Elder who backed such insanity would ever again have the support of the Bladen family, for anything. And that Orlait, as the ringleader of the rebellion, must cease and desist lest the heads of the Founder Families unite to cast him out of Blue Mountain forever. And then I said a few words about his treatment of the man who would one day become the head of the Bladen family. A poor choice of enemy, indeed."

Stunned, Shay stared at Locelar. The head of a Founder Family? Him?

Did that mean he'd have to live inside the mountain?

"And now," said Locelar, "I believe the Elders have said they wanted to speak to you." He sat at last in his cushioned chair. "Beginning with Orlait, as you requested, Grandson."

Everyone's attention riveted on Orlait, who looked off into space and mumbled something unintelligible.

Silence fell and expanded. Faint voices from the common room beaded the air softly.

That was the apology? Shay's anger burned. He strode for the door.

Voices cried out and hands reached toward him as if to stop his progress.

Locelar didn't move, didn't speak.

Halfway to the door, Shay turned. "If you can't do better than that, this meeting is over." Spinning back toward the door, he left, ignoring the outcry behind him.

Amid the noise, he thought he heard his grandfather's soft chuckle.

He smiled inside as he started down the hall. Locelar seemed to enjoy that at least.

"Wait!"

Recognizing the voice, Shay reluctantly stopped and turned toward Orlait. No one else had followed him out.

"I do owe you an apology, Shay. My intent was only to do what was best for the community, never to hurt you in any way. I–"

"Save it, Orlait." Shay's voice dropped like ice daggers breaking off of trees. "You think you've manipulated a private apology instead of a public one. You can do this twice, or we can go back inside now and you can do it only once. In front of everyone."

The Elder hesitated, looking everywhere but at Shay.

"And I'm not interested in explanations where you try to mitigate your actions, as if you're misunderstood instead of wrong."

Orlait met his gaze this time, as if measuring Shay's resolve. At last he nodded, slowly. "It will be done."

Shay followed him back inside, surprised to see some perturbed faces, and some outright angry. Faltryn and Wildt glared at Orlait, but Shay noticed he wouldn't meet their eyes.

Then, before them all, Orlait apologized. "Shay Bladen, I am truly sorry for my recent actions toward you. I have earned your just anger for advocating actions by the Council that would deprive you of the black diamond battle-axe. That I had the community's best interests at heart is no excuse; I lost sight of what was right. I should, instead, have welcomed you with open arms, for your arrival and bonding with the axe have restored to us what we longed for. Once again we have the axe among us, in the hands of the man to whom it rightfully belongs. You will have no more animosity from me, on my honor."

In the ensuing silence, Locelar turned to Shay. "Grandson, will you accept this apology so we may have peace again?"

"I will. Peace among us is all I want–the peace of close-knit family, not just a veneer of peace overlying troubled hearts. Thank you, Orlait, for your openness and honesty with me." He took his seat again, as did Orlait. "I believe the Council wanted to meet with me?"

After a moment of silence, Wildt glanced around at the other Elders, his lower lip stuck out as usual. "I believe everything has now been resolved."

Faltryn added, "And on behalf of the Council of Elders, Shay, I apologize for what we've put you through. We are fortunate your grandfather took the time to visit us. He spoke very strongly on your behalf. We're usually much more level-headed, and you will come to see that, over time. Thank you for listening, and for your tolerance."

Shay nodded. "I have already set it aside, as if it hadn't happened." Not entirely true. Time would have to erase the scars in his relationship with the Council, but he could at least move forward now.

And he could return to the caverns to explore–and at last to learn the final secrets of the axe, the secrets that had drawn him so far, through so much travail.

27. Amyth

"I do not mean to push, Shay, but now that the Elders have left, will you soon have time to create my goblet?" Bibi hefted the block of amyth with both hands, eyes shining. "This is such a deep, rich purple!"

Shay smiled, pleased. "I have three designs for you to look at."

While Bibi studied the designs Shay brought her, he and Locelar visited the local gemsman's shop. The aged, withered owner had few finished pieces for sale, all of fine journeyman quality, but no masterwork. What a shame to waste such fine gems on anything less.

Shay rented the shop from the old man, who wanted to visit his daughter in Sarinta. At his age, he might never return, so Shay paid him generously for a year's use. The old man left the next day, and the shop was Shay's.

He stepped inside and closed his eyes. He inhaled, slow and deep. Dust, old wood, oils, metals, the gem dust created by cutting and grinding . . . like home. Or it would be, once he'd cleaned it up. Bibi and Robayne pitched in with cleaning, while Locelar sharpened and oiled tools, replacing handles on two of them. The brushes needed replacement, but these would do for now. He found the scaif and single dop in good condition, and the jars of oil and diamond dust would do for now.

At last Shay could begin his work. The shop became his retreat, the place he sought when a wild mix of pain, joy, longing, and peace became overwhelming.

Here he lost himself in shaping Bibi's amyth goblet. As always, the work soothed and excited and healed him. The deep hunger for beauty and creation eased his heart as he worked, as if to make up for a life of loss and destruction.

Locelar dropped by often, as if he couldn't get enough of his grandson, and they talked about gems and the working of gems. His grandfather's knowledge proved deep and true, as he imparted insights into the nature of amyth, sunstone, and other stones. In return, Shay showed Locelar some newer techniques unknown to the older man.

Locelar soon became an authority figure, someone he trusted to know everything, to be everything, like a small child trusting a parent. A deep contentment settled over him, unlike anything he had ever experienced. Except with Cinny and the children.

Immersed in his work and his grandfather's paternal love, Shay decided the axe's secrets could wait just a little longer. Some things were more important than even the priceless weapon.

He found no flaws in the deep, bright purple of the amyth block, no inclusions at all–a breathtaking gem, wasted as a tavern gimmick. Cinny would have been scandalized, but the cup would belong to Bibi, and he did not begrudge her choice of its use. He cut it as if working on the king's crown gems. The intricate design Bibi had selected filled his mind; he had only to make the cup match that image.

With Locelar watching, Shay shaped the gem into a two-handled drinking cup both sturdy and magnificent. On each side, as a centerpiece, he set one of the magic sunstone cabochons Bibi had provided.

"A masterpiece," Locelar declared. "Some of the finest work I've ever seen. I couldn't be prouder had you been under my own tutelage all these years."

"Perhaps we should try it out?" Shay said, half serious. Joy and pride sang in his veins.

"Or let Bibi do so." Locelar's smile, to Shay's eyes, matched the beauty of the cup.

258

They walked back to The Amyth Cup companionably and found Robayne immersed in ale and tales with some of the local men. He rose when he saw them, as Bibi emerged from the kitchen. Her eyes lit up when she saw what Shay carried.

Shay held it out as she came forward, and Robayne started his way, too. "For all the times you've saved my life, for everything you've taught me, for being my friend, only my best work will do."

Meilin appeared, too, and Shay basked in the admiration. Even the handful of mid-afternoon customers gathered to see.

"Shay, this is amazing," said Bibi, her smile broad beneath sparkling eyes. "I knew you to be a master gemsman, but this is finer than anything I have ever seen!" Her strong fingers caressed it as she twisted and turned the cup, held it to the sunlight streaming through her glass window to watch the amyth ignite. "But I cannot accept this! It is worth a king's ransom!"

"It's already paid for, Bibi. It's worth much less than you've already given me."

"We thought," added Locelar, "you might like to try it out."

"I rarely drink, myself, but for this special occasion, I have just the right liquor. Robayne, would you please bring me the silver flask under the counter, at the back?"

When he retrieved it, she held up the flask for all to see. "This," she said, "is Malice, said to be the most beautiful liquor in the world. Three swallows is enough to make you drunk. If the cup can prevent drunkenness with Malice, it is proof against anything."

She poured the shining silver liquor, thick and glossy, into the cup and drank half a dozen swallows in one breath.

The small crowd cheered her on.

"I hearda that stuff," said Metchal, her most regular customer. "They say it burns bad goin' down."

"It does, indeed," said Bibi with a smile. "I have heard it called liquid fire."

"Don't look like it burned much to me," called another customer.

Bibi peered at him from under her brow. "I am Sheethe. You will never know whether I am in pain."

"Are you drunk?" asked a farmer.

Bibi lifted her chin. "Of course not. Everyone knows that drinking from magic amyth prevents drunkenness."

"Here, let me try it." Metchal reached for the cup.

Bibi moved it out of his reach with a haughty smile. "You cannot afford it, Metchal. The use of the cup is expensive, and the Malice more so. Beatris would beat you if you wasted a year's wages on one drink."

The group broke into good-natured jeering and ribbing, while Metchal bowed to his audience, glorying in the attention.

Shay and Locelar both tasted the Malice before the day ended, in private. Liquid fire burned Shay's insides from one end to the other, but he remained as sober as a three-year-old.

The warmth spreading inside him wasn't all Malice, though. He looked around at the people–at the friends, and the family. The loss of Cinny and the children would always hurt, but the acceptance and warmth of these people made life worth living again.

Shay, Locelar, and Robayne took their time riding back toward Blue Mountain, chatting amiably and enjoying the summer heat of the Eye of the Light.

Yet, as they rode through the tauz canyons, memory flooded back. Shay's contentment turned to unease, and he stopped to study the area. The crystal beds glittered and the bright summer sun struck flashes of gold from the pillars, leaving golden shadows on the ground. But he saw nothing to explain the animosity of the stones during his last encounter with them.

"Is there history connected with this area?" he asked his companions. He couldn't fathom the cruelty of the crystals. All the lore he knew of the stones of the earth showed them to be benevolent, adding physical and spiritual wealth to the world; these defied the lore.

"There are some old, odd stories," said Robayne. "But they don't make much sense."

Locelar smiled, as he did often these days. "Supposedly, long before the Blue Mountain community, an ancient farming people lived in the canyons alongside their gods. But the gods, over time, became insane, thrusting tauz daggers up from the canyon floor, covering rich soil with glittering crystal. At last the people and their gods fought a battle. The people, with great strength and cunning, defeated the gods and, unable to kill the immortals, managed to imprison them within these pillars and obelisks, possible only because tauz receives and absorbs the metaphysical properties of the world around it.

"Some say the immortals will remain there for all time."

"An interesting children's story," said Robayne.

Shay nodded. "That explains much. Have you stood here on foot and felt them?"

Locelar ignored Robayne. "Once, as a young man, I ran among the pillars. My feet burned and I . . . heard them singing. Their songs were not pleasant ones."

"I've often wondered what it would be like to hear the voices of the stones," said Robayne. "You have a rare and beautiful gift."

"Beware touching these stones," Shay said. "They'll try to eat you."

Robayne threw back his head and laughed, but Locelar frowned in thought.

Shay pointed out the bones visible within the golden crystals. "That big pillar, over there? I had to break it with the axe to free Bibi's arm. It had sunk in halfway to the elbow."

That sobered Robayne. He squatted to look closely at the grandfather pillar's plunder. He wanted a chunk to work into a bracelet later, he said. After appropriate cleansing rituals. Eyes glinting, he used his belt knife to chip off a chunk

A sudden roar of pain and anger assaulted Shay's ears and he clamped his hands over them. It didn't help. Nearby, Locelar doubled over in pain, ears also covered.

The tauz. Shay grabbed Locelar's arm and ran for the horses, before the voices could overwhelm him.

Locelar stumbled and went to his knees atop the crystal. Sharp shards stabbed upward into his legs, and Shay snatched him back up to his feet. "Robayne! Help him!"

Already he felt the pricking of angry crystal at the soles of his boots.

Robayne rode over. "What's the matter with him?"

"Help me get him mounted! It's the tauz! No, don't get off your horse!"

Leaning from the saddle, Robayne closed a hand around Locelar's upper arm and pulled. With Shay helping from the ground, dancing from foot to foot, they got him aboard his horse, who shifted nervously.

Robayne's horse neighed, and Spark joined him.

Still dancing from foot to foot, Shay managed to calm the red horse enough to get himself into the saddle with only a few small pricks in the leather of his boots.

All three put heels to their horses, Robayne leading the way. Shay and his grandfather wrapped their arms about their heads, but the sound wasn't muffled. The screaming came through their skin, not their ears.

They slowed once free of it but they didn't stop. Shay's entire body trembled in reaction to the scraping voice of the tauz, fear sweat coating his face. Locelar didn't look much better. The sensations paled gradually, but the fear took longer to abate.

When they finally reached the bloodstone pillars, Shay stopped among them on an impulse. He hadn't been here since the battle, though these lay just outside his door, so to speak. Was there a song here, as well? He dismounted, closed his eyes, and listened.

Locelar's quiet voice carried confidence and knowledge. "Take off your boots. Barefoot works best for bloodstone."

Shay hastened to comply.

"Now just stand still. It will be soft, and it may take a few minutes."

"More singing stones?" said Robayne. "Not for me. I don't mean to be rude, but I'll ride on. I have preparations to make for Shay's training."

"Go on, then, my friend. We'll talk later." Shay's eyes remained closed.

Hoofbeats died away.

Shay opened himself to the stones as best he could, a process he had no words to explain. Stillness wrapped him like a baby's blanket, full of warmth and comfort. Somewhere nearby, a meadowlark sang its arpeggio. Sunlight warmed his eyelids. Leather creaked as Spark shifted nearby. Shay drew air into his mouth, tasting the soft freshness of the light breeze. He relaxed, slowed his mental pace, and waited.

It was worth the wait.

He became aware of . . . something . . . beneath his feet, tingling them. A vibration so faint as to be barely there, climbing up his legs with ponderous weight, working its way higher, as if the red-dropped green stone reached for his heart.

He held his breath to hear better. The tone was multi-layered, deep bass chords drifting up from the depths of the earth in complex arrangements. A lullaby, perhaps, a slow movement of sound that rippled gently through his heart, warmed his fingertips. Peace. Eternity. The basic components of life, carried in tones audible to few, the meaning buried in the listener's soul. Not so much beautiful as . . . elemental.

Without opening his eyes, Shay reached out to a bloodstone pillar next to him and placed a hand on it.

The wide vibration intensified, the voice of the stone infusing his blood, drawing him into the music, where he could live forever, floating . . .

"Shay."

He opened his eyes when his grandfather touched him.

Locelar's face was wet, but calm serenity looked out of his brown eyes. His feet, too, were bare.

Shay blinked and took a deep breath, as if returning from another land to this one. The sharper coolness of the breeze on his cheeks identified his own tears.

"What was that?" he whispered, surprising himself with the question.

"I believe the magic of the bloodstones is in the song. I've always thought of them as comforters, as absorbers of the spirit's ills. But most people think bloodstones have no magic."

Shay nodded, slowly.

"A word of caution, if you'll hear it, Grandson."

"Of course, Grandfather. I value your advice in all things." *Whether I follow it or not.*

"I would not speak to others of singing stone. Some outside of Blue Mountain merely smile, secure in the conviction stones don't sing, and you lose their trust by speaking of it. Others cannot hear the song themselves, and so carry envy in their hearts. Sometimes envy can fester into something worse and cause trouble between men."

Shay searched Locelar's eyes. "You don't mean Robayne."

"Not Robayne. He's a good man. I speak of no individual, make no judgments. I only counsel caution."

Shay nodded and reached for his boots, and they soon rode on toward home. Still, something niggled at him.

"Grandfather, I worked with stones for many years in Porphyr. But I never heard singing until the tauz canyons, and some black opals, and now the bloodstone valley. Why?"

Locelar shrugged. "Have you ever held a single gem in your hands, closed your eyes, and listened?"

"No. It never occurred to me." Except for Elegy, a giant gem. But her voice was personal.

"If you listen carefully, even individual stones have voices and may tell a skilled gemsman how best to cut them. But their voices are tiny, and it takes a long time to hear them."

28. Sanctuary

The ride to Porphyr seemed both longer and shorter than usual to Spinel. Longer because he rode alone, responsible for finding his own way and managing his own survival. And for the amount of time he must spend inside his own head, with so little to distract him.

Shorter because of the dread curdling his gut. Tarver, the friend who may not be one after all, would expect a report. He'd want to hear about the battle, a story Spinel didn't want to tell. He'd want to be told of Shay's death– only Shay wasn't dead. He'd want the axe. Only Spinel didn't have it, nor did any of his men.

He doled out to himself, as stingily as he could, a skin of ale and three sealed jars of joos stolen from Bibi. Fortunately, he'd picked up some fine stones in the Crystal Mountains, so if he ran out he could buy more.

His biggest problem was Jonus. If only he'd died in the battle! But Spinel could never be so lucky. From his safe hideaway, he'd watched as bright boomers had exploded above the horde. A moment later, Shay appeared high on the side of the mountain, brandishing the axe and roaring a battle cry, even though Spinel had seen him dragged unconscious into the mountain. The warrior woman had slipped away, and he hadn't seen the boy since the battle began.

He had to assume Jonus still lived, and that he had long since returned to Porphyr and reported to Tarver. What had he said? How black a brush had he used to paint Spinel's part in their attempt? Everyone blamed him for everything; Jonus would be no different.

He spent most of his ride telling his story to himself, smoothing out the rough edges and trying to think of what he could offer his friend to distract him from that failure. And to deflect the anger toward Jonus.

He was still working on it when he left his horse with Tarver's stableman, took a deep breath, and went inside to do what he must.

Tarver stared at him silently when he walked into the exquisite sitting room.

Spinel had a sudden, violent urge to piss.

Worse, Jonus smirked at him from the chair Spinel normally sat in.

Silence weighted the room. Fear twisted a knot in Spinel's throat so tight he couldn't speak, not even the jovial greeting he'd practiced on the road.

At last Tarver spoke, his thin lips barely moving. "You had a battle at Blue Mountain. Tell me everything."

Spinel forced a smile, took a moment to remember his latest version, and nodded. "I remembered that the document mentioned bloodstone pillars. We found them and ambushed Shay there. He was traveling with a Sheethe warrior and a child we took from a village in the foothills, to lure Shay and slow him down, because the boy looks much like my nephew, whom Shay got killed." He took a deep breath. Was that even coherent? He tried to hide his shaking hands by crossing his arms.

Tarver sat down in his gold-threaded chair and gestured Spinel to the third-best chair.

He was allowed to sit–a good sign. Spinel licked dry lips as he sat and crossed his legs, arms folded comfortably across his abdomen.

Jonus started to speak, but Tarver's raised hand cut him off. "Go on," he said to Spinel.

A better sign would be an offer of something to drink, but Spinel didn't want to risk Tarver's anger by asking. "The Sheethe was a fierce fighter, and when Shay was hard-

267

pressed, she always stepped in to defend him. He fought with the magic battle-axe. Last time I saw him do that, he could barely lift it. This time he looked comfortable with it."

Jonus shrugged. "'He didn't look all that dangerous to me."

Tarver's head turned slowly toward Jonus. "I've heard your report. With embellishments. Now you will be silent while I hear Spinel's."

Spinel gloated as Jonus's face paled. Until Tarver's tawny eyes returned to him.

"Go on." Tarver watched without blinking.

"I made the first kill myself." That would impress Tarver, and indeed an eyebrow twitched. "Unfortunately, I couldn't get close to Shay in the melee. Since Jonus was closer, I figured he'd get the job done. He didn't." He took a moment, as if thinking, to savor his neat jab at Jonus. "Then someone knocked my sword from my hand and I nearly died looking for it.

"Suddenly boomers exploded overhead, the horses panicked, and everyone ducked for cover."

Tarver's nostrils expanded. "Where were the Sheethe and the boy?"

"The Sheethe kept trying to defend Shay, although with the axe he didn't need much help. The last I saw before the boomers went off, she and Jonus were dueling. I never saw the boy after the battle began." Spinel stopped and licked dry lips, swallowed in a dry throat. Surely Tarver would allow a drink now.

"Go on."

Spinel dared to lick his lips again. "When the boomers went off, I thought another force had joined the battle. Without a sword, I had to scramble to stay alive. Shay had somehow escaped the fight and taunted us from the side of

268

the mountain."

Tarver glared at him, again holding Jonus's words back with his hand, although the bandit leaned forward on the edge of his chair.

For a moment, Spinel shrank from Jonus's eagerness to refute his story. But the truth was close enough to cover him. He made himself relax, wait in silence while Tarver mulled it over.

"Anything else?"

Here came the trickiest part. Spinel leaned forward earnestly, clasping his hands around his knees. "Shay disappeared and we didn't see him again. By then the woman had slipped away, too. It took me several days to find my way to a nearby town after Jonus and the others left. And when I got there, she was working in a tavern. Since I was weaponless, she captured and enslaved me. I only managed to escape a few days ago and rode straight here, almost without stopping." He waited for Tarver's reaction.

Elbows on armrests, Tarver stared at the wall above Spinel's head, fingers steepled in front of him. Without looking at him, he asked, "Why didn't you find another weapon when you– lost–yours? Surely the dead no longer needed theirs."

Spinel's mouth dropped open and his breath caught painfully in his chest. "Uh . . . I tried twice and got kicked by fighters. And then came the boomers and I forgot about it."

"The woman was Sheethe? Are you sure? How do you know?"

He shrugged. "I just assumed. I've never heard of any other women who can fight."

"Why didn't you chase Shay when he appeared after the boomers went off?"

269

Spinel licked his lips. Again. "He disappeared too fast!"

Without looking, Tarver said, "Jonus, will you please excuse us? I would like to speak with our friend without you hanging on every word. Come back this evening for instructions."

Reluctance clear in every movement, Jonus rose and left, eyes glittering at Spinel every step of the way.

Tarver said nothing until the outer door closed behind Jonus.

"Come with me." He rose, his height filling the room, and walked away.

Spinel followed, wishing he'd never come here. He could have ridden on, found another city, where he'd never see Tarver again. Why didn't he think of that earlier?

A long, shadowed passage he'd never seen before increased his nervousness. Following Tarver down the steep, unlit stairs at the end of it was worse. At least he could see a light around the corner, in the room at the bottom.

Stone blocks formed the walls. A single rope surrounded what looked like a sizeable pit in one corner. The old wooden floor had little give, and in this light it appeared to be badly stained. With what, he couldn't tell.

Tarver led him to the pit, probably eight feet deep with walls of packed dirt.

"What's this?"

Tarver's lip curled. "My practice pit. Usually dogs, sometimes a big cat, or a bear. I carry scars, but I always win. And unlike you, I never run." He turned toward Spinel. "Climb down. The rope ladder is over by that wall."

Spinel backed up, shaking his head. If he went down there, Tarver would pull up the rope and leave him. He knew it in the pit of his stomach.

"Come on, my friend. It's a game! I'll be right behind you."

Excuse! He needed an excuse! "It's too confined for me. I'll watch from up here."

Too late he saw the change in Tarver's jaw. The man snatched his arm and flung him over the enclosing rope. For an interminable moment Spinel flew. He hit the floor inside the pit. His chin smacked the ground hard and he bit his tongue. He gasped, inhaling dirt with the scent of dust and blood. He gagged at the thought, managing not to throw up.

Tarver landed beside him, bending his knees to absorb the impact. A big hand snatched Spinel to his feet by the nape of the neck. "You've become good at lying, my friend. Very inventive. But Jonus has already reported, so I know exactly where your 'truth' went astray. I thought you knew better than to lie to me, but apparently I must school you in that lesson."

A stomach blow punctuated the statement, dropped Spinel to his knees. He retched.

Tarver lifted him and hit him again. "Defend yourself, Spinel! Show me you're not a complete coward!" And again.

And again, until Spinel had no more breath for sobbing.

He would die at Tarver's hands. He knew that now. He'd have been better off staying with Bibi.

He retched again, emptily this time, at the sight of his own blood slinging through the air when Tarver hit his face. The world narrowed and blackened. There had to be a way out of this! Some way to stop Tarver from beating him to death.

"Wait," he cried. And then his left arm broke and he screamed. Tarver was still laughing when Spinel caught his breath again. The tears pouring down his face became a minor matter.

"Wait! Wait! There's something I haven't told you yet!"

Tarver stopped his fist, still grinning down at Spinel's struggles. "Oh, there were a number of things you didn't tell me. That's what you're paying for now."

"This is important!" And he began babbling before Tarver could hit him again. "Gems. Blue Mountain is full of them."

Tarver stayed his hand. "Keep talking."

"Rumor says Blue Mountain has some of the richest gem deposits in the world, many of them magic. People live inside the mountain, but there aren't any doors. Everyone knows that. But I saw one!" Spinel paused to breathe. Tarver was listening! He might still have a chance. "I saw a door open when the boomers went off. Someone dragged Shay inside and the door closed again. I can show you where it is!"

Tarver sneered. "Jonus could show me, too. I don't need you for that."

"No! He didn't see! They were already chasing the false Shay!"

"Where were you?"

"In hiding. I had no weapon, remember? So I found a safe place nearby to watch and get my second wind. I saw the door! I know where it is!"

Slowly, Tarver lowered his fist. "Show me."

Shay ate a leisurely breakfast in the Great Hall with Locelar, Atich and his wife, and their three children, lending a hand with the youngest when needed. The children were noisy, boisterous, and seemed each to be in three places at once. Shay smiled indulgently and pulled one up on his lap to tickle her tummy. The child shrieked joyously. The horrified looks on her parents' faces reminded Shay how he'd felt at his own children's childish shrieks in public. Abruptly, he set the child back on her feet as grief sloshed over him.

Memory hurt less these days, but some pain would always be there. It had become part of him, and as long as he didn't stir it up–by playing with children, for instance–he wasn't as baldly aware of it.

He could almost bear to watch Atich and his wife together now. The look in the eyes, the constant knowledge of where the other was, the casual help and support they gave each other in little ways.

Shay blinked rapidly. That was a little harder to handle.

At last he excused himself to meet Robayne, taking plates back to the kitchen for everyone.

He still marveled at his new family, still met more Bladens almost daily. After a youth with no family at all, he'd become part of a very large one, as open and welcoming as if he'd always been there. Their easy acceptance thawed some of the ice around his heart.

Elegy lay in her harness across his back this morning and he took comfort from her presence. Robayne said she had a part to play in today's work, too.

Even so, the anticipation both scared and exhilarated him. His palms dampened.

At last. At last, at last. He would learn the secrets that had drawn him here when he had nowhere to go, no place of his own in the entire world, no one to *be* without his wife and children to define him. Robayne had promised those mysteries generations before they'd ever met.

How was Elegy created? How could he make more like her? He hadn't even seen the black diamond material yet, didn't know where to look for it. If the material was here, the secrets known, why hadn't his predecessors created other such weapons?

Then he shuddered. A world with armies equipped with weapons like Elegy? Death and destruction would be far too easy, and too common. The violence he'd seen in his childhood would be the greater for such weapons. Families would be destroyed. Too many would die.

He just wanted to create beautiful things of black diamond–perhaps a single special gem? Or even a set of fine plates that could never be scratched? Unless he also made eating utensils of the diamond . . .

Robayne awaited him near a corridor deep inside the mountain, in a grotto filled with deep green emrel, blue seastone, rose-red bixil, and golden beryl–all beryls, his son's namesake. The grotto was a beautiful place, easily found but far enough from the Center to be private.

Memory lay too close to the surface today.

"Welcome, Bladen." Robayne said, his voice solemn, almost sepulchral, his face smooth and cool. The grotto was lit at floor level by a sparse array of moonstones, darkening his face with shadow and mystery while flicking colored light from the crystals.

This had the feel of ritual, but Shay didn't know his part in it, which set him on edge. "Good morning, Robayne."

"This will be the first of many long, hard days for both of us. We won't return to the Center for at least a week, subsisting on food stores I set in for this purpose, as well as mushrooms, fungus, snakes, cavern fish–and maybe a bat or two, if necessary." He made a face. "I hope it doesn't come to that."

Shay hesitated, caught off-guard. "I didn't plan on being gone so long, didn't bring even one change of clothes or anything else."

274

Robayne smiled, finally. "Then we'll stink together. It's part of the tradition, to avoid drawing attention by our heavy packs or our constant comings and goings. Others may notice our absence, but not until too late to follow."

Shay shrugged. "Okay, then, as long as you stink, too."

Robayne laughed. "Then come with me to a secret place, locked away from the world. It's a place known only to the firstborn sons of Robayne and the bearers of the axe. Sanctuary is part of the mystery; we take great care to assure no one even knows what part of Blue Mountain hides it. What you will see there, and what you will learn, mustn't be spoken of. In this generation, only you and I know of it."

"What about your father? And Locelar?"

Robayne began walking and Shay fell into step. "My father knows, and he taught me. These days, though, his mind wanders most of the time. Locelar does not know, as he's never been the bearer of the axe. You'll be the only living Bladen who holds the secrets.

"And that's all I'll say until we're behind locked doors."

Speaking casually of mundane things, the men traveled deeper into the caverns, down lit and half-lit corridors, until Shay's feet began to ache.

Robayne stopped. He turned to a large column of undressed stone that seemed a part of the wall. He reached into shadow and a moment later something clicked. He had Shay feel for and find the release.

Then, with a shove of his shoulder, Robayne slid the stone to one side and gestured Shay through the opening, into the lit corridor beyond, and shoved it closed again. "I came through a few days ago and replaced several moonstones to be sure we'd have good light."

"There's no lock on the door?" asked Shay.

"Not this one," Robayne said. "The remaining three are

locked, and the final door opens only for me, unless your Bladen blood provides you access. If not, I'll pass my access to you. It's Bladen's Sanctuary, not Robayne's."

"You don't know whether I have access already?"

Robayne shrugged. "I'd guess you do, but I have no way to verify it without you here."

The bottom dropped out of Shay's stomach. Scary day, indeed. He swallowed his dread–or tried to–and followed his mentor through three nigh-invisible doors set into the cavern walls. The same key fit every lock–a top quality granata of the deepest red, hanging on a thick, rolled-leather cord around Robayne's neck. Robayne set it into a perfect-fit hole and the door opened.

Then came the final door.

"Place your right palm flat on this smooth place." Robayne indicated it with his hand.

Shay flattened his palm against the cool, flat black surface and held it there. The door slid back, and his heartbeat quickened.

"*This* is Sanctuary," said Robayne, his voice reverent.

Shay saw first the black, curved walls and ceiling, covered with eight-sided crystals thrusting outward from matrix. His breath caught–and so did his imagination, as he envisioned the magnificent gemworks he could create with these. Especially combined with the beryls from the grotto.

"Everything in the Sanctuary belongs to the bearer of the battle-axe, with the Robaynes as custodians," said Robayne, his voice quieter, more awed than Shay had ever heard it. "This is only the anteroom."

He gestured toward a door Shay hadn't noticed.

Shay approached it slowly, savoring the diamonds, the pricking of light deep within, sparked by the moonstones.

Then he stepped into darkness.

The glow of moonstones allowed him to see the

darkness–the thick vein of solid black that seemed to fill the room, as if he stood inside a gigantic black diamond.

Robayne murmured, "This is where your axe was mined. You can see where the vein has been worked. It had to be a long, tedious process to cut her from the vein. It wasn't a process of freeing a diamond from the wall, but of cutting a piece from the single diamond that forms the wall. No one knows how large this diamond is, but the part that became your axe is only a tiny bit of the whole.

"They say the diamond screamed when she was removed, and after that no one could bear the thought of cutting here again."

Shay touched the wounded area with his fingers, feeling the sharp, smooth edges.

The huge, partially-revealed diamond flickered faintly with blue lightning.

He stilled his fingers within the wound and closed his eyes.

She cried, her wail smashing into him with the force of thunder. All the stone song he'd ever heard seemed weak, timid, quiet by comparison. His heart clenched in the shared agony of the gem as its song roared through him. His chin dropped to his chest as if borne down by a great weight. The floor quivered beneath his knees–he'd fallen?–and he tightened his grip on Elegy.

Let her loose. Free her.

Without thinking, he pulled off Elegy's hood and unwound the leather from her grip, leaving her naked and glorious, surging with blue veins. He stood again and set her inside the gap from where she'd been cut free. A perfect fit.

It felt like a reunion, a daughter with her parent. Warmth and glow spread through Shay. He swallowed, knowing what he should do but fearing it. What if he lost

277

Elegy forever? Squeezing his eyes tight, he forced himself to let go, to leave her inside the gap, to relinquish his claim on her.

Removing his fingers was one of the hardest things he'd ever done.

29. Mother Lode

Tarver pulled on close-fitting black britches and shirt. A knife went up each sleeve, another into each boot, and the largest into the special sheath hanging down his spine. The garrotte coiled neatly into a pocket.

He loaded poisons, potions, and powders into small bags secreted about his body, with a small set of lock picks and a few boomers. The expensive-as-hell boomers were a product of Malnisia, across the continent and the land bridge. The blue ones produced a flash when thrown, the yellow gave a sharp bang, the green ones did both, and the explosion of the larger red ones could take a man's hand off—or even kill him if used right.

Tarver always used them right. Salivating, he swallowed, remembering the tearing of flesh and shattering of blood that accompanied those deaths.

The pincers and pullers and penis ring would ride in his saddlebags, just in case he had an opportunity to use them. His scrotum tightened in anticipation. He paused and closed his eyes, imagining the delights of applying that ring to Spinel later. Oh, the pain! The blood! The screams until his victim grew hoarse, the fear exploding from him, stroking Tarver's skin like a lover, filling his nose and mouth with its scent.

The little pigshit would play his part first. Tarver could indulge himself later.

A corner of Tarver's lip twitched upward in amusement. Interesting how a description of Spinel always included the word "little."

He'd pick up Jonus and his gang on the way, leave them somewhere he could call them from easily. The Crystal Mountains teemed with riches, and he might as well use the bandit to help collect some of them while there. He shook his head in annoyance. He'd had to set it up for Spinel to select Jonus and his gang to pursue Shay Bladen; the little fuck-up's choice of men in a tavern would be wretched, at best. Even with Jonus he hadn't accomplished his mission.

Tarver added his executioner's hood, and his eyeless victim's hood to the saddlebags and started for the door.

The little drunkard waited, his face a mass of cuts and bruises, his arm in a sling. He grabbed the back of Spinel's shirt as if dragging a dog by its collar, allowing himself a fantasy of pincers and screams, until Spinel's body became as red as his hair. It gave him an erection.

He forced his thoughts back to the mundane. "Imbecile! If you'd done what you should have, I wouldn't have to go for the battle-axe myself. If we fail this time, I'll take it out of your worthless hide." Bit by bit.

He shoved Spinel. "Pick up Jonus and his men and meet me at those abandoned horse pens a few miles north of the city. I'll expect the lot of you no more than an hour after I arrive there. And I'm leaving now."

Spinel stumbled, caught himself, and nearly ran toward the likeliest tavern.

Tarver snarled to himself. When all was accomplished, Spinel would die–as slowly and painfully as Tarver knew how. With his skill, his pleasure could be drawn out for weeks.

As if at a distance, Shay heard Robayne's voice. "What are you doing?"

The words registered after a long moment. He lifted his fingers out of the crevice now cradling the axe. "It's a womb. All this diamond in the walls and ceiling is her mother." Shay gestured at the black mother lode.

Robayne's eyes widened. "Interesting analogy," he said carefully. "Not literally true, of course, but that's an interesting way to look at it."

"No, my friend. It *is* literally true." Shay hesitated, reminded himself that Robayne couldn't hear the stones.

His attention returned to the wall of black diamond. Filled with excitement and wonder, he reached out with trembling hands, placed his palms against the surface near Elegy, and leaned into the wall. He set his forehead against it and closed his eyes in anticipation.

Robayne disappeared from his mind. So did everything else but the diamond.

The diamond sang a multilayered song. Its deep, resonant bass released the tightness he habitually carried in jaw, neck, and shoulders. Rich baritones soothed the ache behind his eyes, and the next layers washed peace through him, as if removing debris from a streambed. Full tones supported wispy ones, softness and thunder rolled together. Higher tones shivered his flesh, cooling and lightening him, releasing him from burden and worry. Almost beyond hearing, the very highest tones surged through him with lightness and joy and renewal. Somewhere in the enormous chords and arpeggios he recognized Elegy's voice.

Laughter exploded from his throat, clashing with the diamond's song.

When was the last time he'd laughed like this? Forehead still pressed against the smoothness, he tried to remember. When he closed up his shop the last time and the children came bursting through the door and into his arms . . . for the last time. Regardless of the darkness that followed, it had been a joyous moment, a time to hold close in his heart, not at arm's length. Sorrow could not be resisted. Its pain could only be held at bay by joy, not by resistance.

281

Was that his thought? Or was it gifted to him by the mother lode?

"Bladen!"

A heavy hand spun him away from the wall, out of physical contact. Surprised, Shay looked up into frightened gray eyes in an ashen face.

"Robayne? What's wrong?"

Robayne stared, focused intently on Shay's eyes, as if to discern truth. "Are you all right?" he asked at last.

Until you pulled me away from the most amazing . . . Shay couldn't even think of the word he wanted. "Why did you do that?" he asked, trying to reorient. He blinked rapidly, a man suddenly awakened by bright light.

"I've been talking and talking, and you've been ignoring me. When I called your name, you didn't even hear." Robayne's grip on his shoulder didn't ease.

"Let go of me." He had to get back to the music. Only the music mattered.

"We still have work to do, Shay." Robayne slowly released his shoulder. "We still have to figure out the magic of the black diamond."

"Figure out? You're supposed to teach it to me." The memory of ethereal music in his head quieted, jarring him back into the here and now.

"I'll teach what I can, but I have only a few hints and oblique references. We'll use those and the chronicles written through the years to discover them, but the deepest secrets aren't written down anywhere. They were lost during the axe's long absence."

"Do you mean you *can't* teach me? You *lied*? None of your promises meant anything?" Betrayed. Bamboozled. Misled. The one true friend he thought he'd found was no different than the bullies of his childhood. Maybe there was no such thing as a true friend. He was still a child after all,

282

blindly trusting. Every "friend" he'd ever had had let him down, sent him alone and lonely into the future. Robayne was no better than any of them.

"I couldn't tell you the truth, under orders from the Council."

"Orlait again!"

"Yes, and all the other Elders as well. Only for a while, they said. Only until you accepted your rightful place in Blue Mountain. Only on our return from Echo was I given permission for today's introduction." Robayne held out empty hands, palms up. "I'm sorry, Shay. It wasn't my choice. And I'll do everything I can to recover the lost secrets."

Shay ran a hand through his hair, then again. He walked in a short circle, trying to collect himself. Still agitated, he faced Robayne, hands on hips.

The secrets of the axe lost. Irrevocably. No one would ever know them now.

Except him. Shay realized in awe that he already knew them. The secrets—all of the secrets—lived in his head, his hands, his heart. He knew what to do and how to do it. The truth had been hidden in the song of the stones. He no longer needed Robayne.

Anger drained out and a chill heated the back of his neck as he discerned Robayne's true role and the difficulties it posed. Robayne's part was custodial, to give him access, keep the Sanctuary clean and in good repair. None of the tools here mattered. And Robayne didn't know. No lore master of the battle-axe had ever known, because no Robayne could hear the singing of stones.

Robayne didn't know the mysteries. Maybe he wasn't meant to know. Shay floundered, drowning in deep waters.

He couldn't bring himself to tell his mentor. It would devastate him. The man had saved his life, had stood by him in the trouble with Orlait, had sought him when he became lost in the depths of Blue Mountain.

Telling Robayne such bitter truths would be cruel. But he had to know, to understand, and who else could tell him?

What if he reacted with disbelief, with anger, perhaps even violence? No, Robayne wasn't a violent man. But he'd be the one writing the chronicles, and the written word had power. Would he take out his disappointment on Shay, when writing for future generations?

Shay took a deep breath and steeled himself, but the words he spoke weren't the ones he'd intended. "Is Robayne supposed to know the secrets?"

"I've never heard that. But with so much lost in the years of despair, during the axe's absence, it's impossible to know what's been done in the past."

"Or have the deepest of them always been hidden from everyone but Bladen? Am I to learn the final secrets alone, so they cannot be recorded?"

Shock widened Robayne's eyes, which searched Shay's face, perhaps for deception. "Why wouldn't Robayne know the secrets? They wouldn't have to be recorded, but to deny me the right to know, to attend the climax of our adventure, seems unnecessary, even cruel." His eyes narrowed. "Do you not trust me? After all we've been through?"

"It's not a matter of trust. Some secrets are too dangerous to be known by more than one person. Yet these same secrets are just too good *not* to share with one person you trust–a wife, for instance. And then she'd face the same dilemma, and on it would go."

Robayne sagged–shoulders, chin, face, hips–like a child learning that Daddy wasn't coming home today. "Blue Mountain has kept a lot of secrets for a lot of years."

"If this secret got out, Blue Mountain would become the target for three-quarters of the world's thieves–for the black diamond's gifts, as well as the wealth buried in these caverns," Shay argued. "The community would be under constant siege, its quiet way of life destroyed."

"I've kept many secrets for many years," Robayne shouted. Anger sharpened his tone; hurt increased its volume. His hands shook.

Guilt wrenched at Shay. He turned toward the trunk containing the lore of the battle-axe. "Perhaps the records tell us how this has been handled in the past. They're in here?" His stomach knotted. *Coward*, he told himself, *you're only putting off the inevitable*.

With visible effort, Robayne calmed, looking sick. "You need to read everything in the histories anyway. You can get started on that, and I'll throw some dinner together. We'll worry about secrets when you finish your reading." His chin jutted out briefly, as if he fought some battle with himself.

Fixing dinner. A servant's task. Shay winced.

"Start with the oldest records first," Robayne called over his shoulder as he headed for the kitchen. "That large tome at the bottom of the chest. They're arranged in chronological order, with the most recent on top, where it can be easily reached and added to."

With a sigh, Shay knelt on the hard floor next to the iron-bound wooden chest with the elaborate scrollwork that signaled a master carver. The cool, dry air of the caverns had kept the wood free of rot, but even so, part of the whorled wood looked almost new.

To his surprise, the chest wasn't locked. But then, it didn't need to be, with Sanctuary itself so well protected. When he lifted the lid, a thick camphor smell rolled out. Another protection, this one from insects.

Besides, if the wood rotted or insects appeared, Robayne would arrange for a new chest, fresh camphor.

285

Shay sighed again. Why did things have be so complicated?

He lifted out a large tome bound in tooled leather. The elaborate decorations depicted a battle scene, with a lone man standing atop a knoll, battle-axe lifted over his head and descending on one of the attacking horde below him. Dyes had been meticulously worked into the leather, to create a blue sky behind the hero, a green knoll under his feet, and red blood flowing freely from the fallen. A work of art in itself, a labor of love, the masterpiece of a skilled leather worker.

The tomes that followed were equally magnificent, with tooled leather, beautiful dyes, and sometimes gems set into the borders, or into the scenes themselves. Each unique and priceless. Shay lingered over them, admiring. He wished for his loupe, but his instincts said each golden beryl, deep blue skystone, or clear white diamond was flawless. Only the best would be good enough for these treasures.

As he removed them, Shay stacked the heavy tomes carefully in reverse order for easy replacement in the chest as he finished it. He'd be blind before he could finish them all! This would take a while.

Shay's knees popped and he groaned as he pushed up to his feet. *I'm a little too old to take on the role of hero. Elegy needs someone younger, more agile.*

Like his son, who would never know the axe existed.

The realization hit like a belly blow. Again. He would never share with Beryl the art of cutting fine gems, of setting them, of creating something beautiful. He would never again guide tiny hands along the smooth, glossy surfaces of unset stones, never teach him Elegy's secrets, never show him how to hold the axe, or introduce him to Bibi to learn its use.

Shay doubled over in physical pain, clenching his

teeth. Grief usurped his body, as fresh and new as if Beryl had been murdered yesterday.

Minutes passed as Shay struggled for control. In the background, Robayne's fine tenor rang in an ancient drinking song, accompanied by the clattering of pots and pans. Shay groaned, managed to push away his thoughts of what could never be, and straightened. Sweat drenched him from head to toe and the cool air chilled him.

At last, his breathing slowed and he began to feel more normal.

He'd thought he was adjusting to the loss of his family.

He picked up the original, most magnificent volume and sat in one of the stuffed chairs next to the chest. This should be interesting enough to distract him, at least at first. He set the book on his crossed knee and opened it, hoping for an answer to his dilemma.

"I have to get out of here."

Three straight days of reading had fuzzed Shay's brain. The weight of information stuffed into his head, the lack of movement, and no chance to be alone with his vein of black diamond itched at him. Tedious information. Every new axe bearer, every new Robayne, with the date. Every battle. Every celebration. Every time the axe left Blue Mountain. Every return. Every legality, change of status, Council interaction around the axe. Each Bladen decision that involved the axe. The stories of battles and lives saved and towns liberated or protected interested him more, although the telling remained as dry and bare as the rest. The loss of the axe and the search efforts were chronicled in a scholarly style. Shay took a number of unintended naps as he read. Worse, some of the writing was an archaic version of the language in almost illegible handwriting, and deciphering the letters took time.

Besides, Robayne irritated him at every corner. Any time he took a moment to commune with the mother lode, Robayne found an excuse to separate him from her.

The walls sometimes seemed to close in, he had no room to move, and Robayne was *right there*. All the time!

Robayne set aside his own volume and stretched. "A hot bath would feel really good right now. I can't even stand my own smell, let alone yours." He grinned, but the humor barely touched his eyes. "I wish we had a way to get more fresh air in here. That would help."

They had propped open the Sanctuary door and the next one farther out for more air circulation, but although fresh air vented in, it didn't flow well.

"The air is fine, except for our smell." Shay didn't even

attempt humor. "I feel like a prisoner. I'm going for a walk." He set aside the chronicles where he'd just read about the disappearance of the battle-axe. Robayne had already updated the records about its reappearance, but Shay hadn't reached that part yet.

Robayne stood. "I'll go with you."

Shay attempted a smile this time. "No offense, but I've been solitary most of my life. And right now I'm missing that solitude. I'll be back in an hour, more or less."

"No offense," said Robayne, "but I can't let you go alone. Do you remember reading about that? During this time, until you've read everything and we've figured out the secrets, I'm to be with you."

Shay clamped his teeth over the words, *Don't you trust me?* He had no right to speak those words to Robayne. Even if the man did get on his nerves. His confinement here abraded his soul. He'd spent more time in dark caverns than was good for him. He longed for time outdoors, in the Light; he'd settle for some time out in the caverns.

But he couldn't manage to keep his teeth together. "I already know the secrets, Robayne. *All* of them. There's nothing more to figure out. Now can I go for a walk? Alone?" He froze in shock. He hadn't meant to say that out loud. His stomach knotted at the look of betrayal on Robayne's face.

"What do you mean?" Robayne's voice came out in a croaked whisper. "What are you talking about?"

Shay wanted to chew off his tongue. Why couldn't he keep his mouth shut? Not just the words themselves, but the irritation, the spite . . . Robayne hadn't earned that.

"Shay!" Robayne's voice cut, as sharp as Elegy's blade. "What the hell are you playing at?" His black brows met at the bridge of his nose, mouth curled to the bottom of his chin.

289

Shay couldn't look him in the eye. The room closed in, suffocating, and he spun on his heel, headed for the door. "Come on, Robayne. I really do need to get out of here." Talking would be easier side by side as they walked.

When he stepped out of Sanctuary's door, Robayne's heavy footsteps followed him fast, and a moment later, Robayne grabbed his arm hard enough to bruise.

Shay jerked loose and kept going.

Robayne's next grab yanked back, spinning him. "Explain yourself. Now!"

"Let go of me. I won't tell you again." He tried for tough and menacing, but he'd scolded his children with more force.

Robayne tightened his grip and opened his mouth.

Shay flinched. Ancient memories bubbled up, of bigger boys grabbing, and of beatings and worse. They flooded in, and Shay couldn't block them. Sudden cold sweat drenched him and fear spiked–a needless, heedless fear he still couldn't control, after all these years.

He bounced clenched knuckles off the back of his mentor's hand and the fist sprang open, clutched in pain to Robayne's chest.

Shaking all over, Shay walked on, trying to get his ragged breathing under control before he panicked completely and ran. As he had in childhood.

No footsteps followed.

He turned without stopping. "Come on, Robayne." He turned back at the same pace.

Footsteps ran to catch up with him.

By the time he realized Robayne wasn't slowing, it was too late. Robayne's hands struck his shoulder blades and slammed him into a wall. Blood sprayed from his nose and the black diamond crystals in the matrix muttered angrily.

The mutter escalated to a rumble that shook Shay's

insides. Still in contact with the wall, he gasped. The mother lode knew his blood, as Elegy did.

Her anger escalated, her song no longer multi-layered and harmonious. Deep bass, shrieking and discordant soprano, all scratchy levels in between, all opposing each other, on the verge of rage. Shay's arms pimpled in fear and his scalp felt suddenly too tight for his skull.

She wasn't angry with him, but with Robayne. "Don't touch the wall, Robayne. Not now."

But Robayne had finished. He stood in front of Shay, the lines of his body and angles of his face drawn in bewilderment and anger. "You can't say something like that, then just turn and walk away." His voice cracked.

"I told you, I need to walk. This place is too confined, stifling. You want to talk, fine. But I need to be moving."

"We can't leave the area." Robayne's eyes bore flecks of anger, glints of fury.

"We have to get away from the mother lode. She picks up on what I'm feeling, and right now she's in a rage." Shay started down the hall, agitation lengthening his strides.

"Picks up your feelings?" Disbelief showed in Robayne's voice and jutting jaw. But he fell into step.

"When I'm in contact with her."

"When she explains everything to you. And you keep it secret."

The corridors turned and twisted, but Shay didn't slow. Movement felt good, after days of inactivity, and the breeze of his passage blew the cobwebs from his mind. He finally began to lose the day's tension.

With his mind clearing, he reviewed the events of the morning. And winced. He'd been too focused on the diamond, had lost sight of the importance of the first man ever to value him as a friend. With the clarity of hindsight, he saw more than he wanted to. His steps slowed. How to

291

fix the mess he'd made?

And at last he stopped, gestured Robayne to a more-or-less comfortable rock, and sat across from him.

"You're right," he said. "I have information you don't, and I didn't handle it well. I trust you to write none of this in the chronicles, and to speak of it to no one–not even to your own son, during his training. Will you hear me?"

Robayne's face remained angry and tight. "How can I promise, without knowing what I must keep hidden?"

"How can I tell you the secrets until I have your promise to keep them secret?"

"Why would you keep that information from me? Without secrets between us?"

Shay didn't know how to answer him. The answer seemed too complex. "Does it matter?"

Robayne stared at him for long seconds. All the anger and tension disappeared from his shoulders. "You know I will never reveal any secret unless it's necessary to protect the Blue Mountain People. You should not have to ask for my promise."

"I also have made a promise–several, actually–that may cause anger if I reveal these secrets to you."

"Whose anger?"

Shay looked into his eyes without responding.

Robayne opened his mouth and Shay braced for his objection. But instead he closed his mouth and shook his head. "The mother lode." He took a deep breath and released it slowly. "I will accept your words as best I can, without argument or skepticism."

"Thank you." Shay nodded. "You already know my axe is female, her name known only to Bladen. And you remember when I said all the black diamond surrounding us is a womb? The mother of the axe?"

Robayne frowned. "I remember. It seemed the fancy of

a man excited by Sanctuary's treasure. Are you telling me the diamond 'sang' this to you?"

Shay hesitated. "The knowledge appeared suddenly in my head, but I believe it came from the mother lode. I knew it immediately for truth. That hole in the wall is the place from which the axe was . . . taken. It is her birthplace, where she was separated from her mother. She needs to return there from time to time for renewal, if only briefly. The power of the black diamond axe dimmed over the long separation from the mother lode, but now she is once again at full strength." Whatever that might mean. He closed his eyes, remembering the feel of Elegy as he removed her from the wall niche–and shuddered. But for their bond, he would fear her more than anything else in the world.

"You know all this from being told by the vein of diamond." Robayne's face struggled with neutrality. "Well, that explains some of the notes in the chronicles."

"Unless you've experienced it, how could you accept my words without skepticism?" Shay rose and paced. There was so much . . . so much. He ran a hand through his hair. "How do I ask you to believe the unbelievable?" He scratched at his beard, winced at the dirty feel of it. "How do I make it believable to you?"

He stopped, lost in thought. "The singing of the stones is felt, as much as heard. Different stones have different voices. A significant amount of stone may be necessary for us to hear it, for I'd never heard their songs before first entering the tauz canyons. The voices are . . . layered, at least for the black diamond, with low tones, mid-tones, and high tones. I think . . . some tones are too high or low for men to be aware of, but . . ." His words trailed off, and the agitation of his pacing increased. "I think these are the tones that conveyed this first information to me, when I lay E . . . the axe into her cradle for renewal." This would be so

293

much easier if Robayne could also hear the voices of stones.

Robayne ran a hand through his hair, leaving a tuft upright above his forehead. "*These* are the secrets of the black diamond? Did you ask questions? *Can* you ask questions? Shay, I really am trying to accept and believe, but . . ."

Shay heard the frustration in his voice. "I know. It's hard to believe even after experiencing it. It breaks the natural laws of the universe. Like any other magic. And the most important secrets must still be told."

Robayne stood. "I understand why you pace. It's too much to take in. How could I describe colors to a man blind from birth?" He hesitated. "I need more space. Come on."

They strode through the remaining doors, which Robayne made Shay open and close, unlock and lock as they walked out into the caverns of Blue Mountain.

For a while they just walked, working their way deeper into corridors unlikely to be visited by others. By habit, Shay checked the markings at each intersection so he could find his way back. The exercise cleared his head, freshened his lungs if not his odor.

"Can we talk here safely?" he asked.

Robayne halted, lifted a hand to stay Shay's pace as well. They listened. Voices in these caverns carried substantial distances, but they heard nothing.

Silence pressed in on Shay's ears, as if wrapping them in cotton. He gathered his thoughts as best he could. When he spoke again, his voice remained quiet, assuring they couldn't be heard.

"The most important secrets, my friend, are the most astounding. The diamond shared them with me clearly and directly, as I stood with my head and hands pressed against the wall. I know how the axe was made. And I know how to create new things from the mother lode."

"Jonus! Count off six men to ride for Echo and put someone else in charge," ordered Tarver. "Tell him to watch for a signal fire, then destroy the town and everyone in it. Make sure he keeps someone in The Amyth Cup at all times. Bladen has friends there.

"You'll ride with the rest of us to Blue Mountain. When we reach the green and red rocks, Spinel will show me where Bladen entered the mountain. I'll find a way in, then you'll help me get to Bladen to retrieve the battle-axe. If he gets past us, he'll likely head for Echo and his friends.

"Let's ride!"

Tarver slammed sharp spurs into his horse, yanking back on the harsh bit. The horse reared with a pained cry, but Tarver kept his seat easily. He spurred again, released the bit, and the horse bolted forward.

Just because he could, the assassin slammed spurs into the horse again and again.

The sideways looks from the men he rode with told him his point was made.

31. Preparation

Sanctuary felt good to Shay after his walk. Already it had become more than a secret place. Here he found peace, and the solitude that softened his soul. Robayne's presence did not disturb his peace.

Shay gathered his thoughts, calmer than he had been for days. "The tools you've so carefully provided and tended for Bladen all these years aren't necessary," he began.

Robayne's lower lip dropped. "What do you mean?"

"They're for show, which I thought meant Robayne wasn't supposed to know everything. Why else the pretense?"

His mentor frowned. "They *are* necessary, to shape whatever diamond you choose to work on."

"What's necessary is communion with the mother lode through the singing of the stone. The mother lode will birth it for me as I picture it for her."

Robayne sat with elbows on his knees, hands clasped above the floor, deep worry creasing his face. He took a breath as if to speak, exhaled again, and shook his head. "How? I don't understand."

"That's pretty much all I understand, too. I know I'll need a very clear picture of what I want, but beyond that will be a mystery until I try it."

"So you talk to a wall of black diamond and it talks back. Sings back. It tells you secrets and it gets angry. The Robayne has guarded the mysteries hidden here generations, and in a few minutes, you know more about them than any Robayne."

Shay didn't answer, allowing him to work through it.

"Does my life, then, have no purpose? Why are the

Robaynes even a part of this? If you're right, I've spent my life preparing for something I'm connected to only by tradition!"

Shay spoke to the pain in Robayne's voice. "You don't know that, and neither do I. There's a reason your family has always been involved, and not just as lore masters. We'll figure it out while I work on the first design."

Silence again. Robayne appeared to be locked in an internal struggle that Shay couldn't help him with. It was a lot to absorb, especially for someone who couldn't hear the voices of stones. Quietly, Shay stood and walked away, half expecting to be called back.

He spent his time cleaning and reordering the kitchen, raking the ashes from the fireplace, and laying the wood for a new fire. This part of Blue Mountain was *Bladen's* Sanctuary, and he rearranged shelves and supplies to suit himself, knowing Robayne wouldn't mind and would maintain its new organization.

He swept floors, aired blankets, and made beds, accepting the servant role for himself. So wrong about everything, he was at once chagrined at thinking it and relieved he'd never used that word aloud. All the while, he kept his ears pricked for Robayne's voice, for any sound he made.

Once Robayne appeared in the kitchen doorway, frowning in deep thought. He seemed to have a question he couldn't verbalize and soon left again without speaking.

A little while later, Shay took him a plate of meats and fruits, then sat nearby with his own plate, careful not to speak until Robayne was ready.

Robayne took his plate absently and set it on his knees. He still stared into space, and Shay wondered what moral or philosophical concept he fought. Change came hard for some people, and Robayne had been raised with many

297

generations of tradition behind him. At least he was giving it serious thought.

Had other Robaynes encountered this same moment of truth, or was this Robayne the first to learn the greatest secrets? The lore didn't mention it, so he couldn't know.

Robayne reached for a piece of fruit, then stared at it for a long moment. "Have you tried it yet?" He didn't mean the food.

"No, I haven't. I've been digesting the information, as you have."

"I want to watch when you do." Robayne bit into the fruit and juice ran down his chin.

Shay salivated and reached for his own peach. He wiped juice from his chin as the flesh crunched and dripped. Perfect. Especially for someone who hadn't eaten a peach in a very long time. "I think I'll need you there anyway, to draw me back if necessary."

Robayne thought a moment. "How do I do that?"

"I don't know."

That little twit! Put him in charge of setting up a simple campsite, and his incompetence fell to new depths! Tarver spat near his polished boots.

Spinel's crude attempt had been set up half a mile from the green and red pillars–with no organization. If Jonus hadn't stopped him, he'd have set up the latrines next to food storage!

His time would end soon.

Tarver didn't allow himself to plan that death right now. Too distracting, when he had work to do.

"Spinel," he snarled through clenched teeth. He could no longer force himself to pretend friendship. Disgust closed his throat when he even thought about it.

The fear in Spinel's eyes as he ran up made him feel

better. There'd be much more, later.

"Come with me." He spun on his heel and strode away.

Spinel trotted to keep up. "But I haven't finished setting up camp. Where are we going?"

"Jonus will take care of that." And had done most of the work so far. "This is more important."

They turned past a tall column of rock, out of sight of the gang, and Tarver stopped. He faced Spinel. "Take me to the fancy pillars. To the place where you hid after you lost your sword." Not that he believed the sword lost. Discarded, perhaps, to make the story convincing.

"Uh . . ." Spinel snapped his head in several directions, eyes wide.

As if they were already among the bloody rocks. Tarver would have rolled his eyes if their friendship had been real. Instead, he stared at Spinel. When he had the smaller man's attention, he slowly widened his eyes under a ledge of thick brows and tucked his chin just the slightest bit.

Spinel almost pissed his pants.

"Now."

Spinel's face paled. "Uh . . . we have to get to the bloodstone field before I can find it."

Tarver inhaled slowly and deeply, leaning forward an inch.

"Uh. This way." Spinel started off, almost running.

Were his britches darker now? The coward was too easily intimidated to be much fun. Dolt. Idiot. Tarver's longer legs kept up without effort.

The blood-flecked stones appeared first along the ground in rounded beds, but soon the sharp crystals and columns appeared, as Spinel had described. That Spinel knew the names of stones and used words Tarver didn't recognize didn't impress him. After all, the little turd came from an old family of wealthy gem merchants who had named all their children after stones of varying value.

He had his access to polite society and wealth. He didn't need Spinel anymore, except to help him get the axe. He'd never even seen it for himself, but the little pisspants had described it as magic. Tarver could picture it in his mind clearly, the largest and most valuable diamond known to man. And deadly. He grinned to himself.

"Here." The younger man's voice brought him up short.

Spinel crouched behind a natural wall of stone, looking out across the site of the battle he'd run from. The little bitch.

"Get down," Spinel insisted. "They may be watching!"

Taking his time, Tarver sank to his heels. "This is where you hid?"

"No. It's across the field, over there. But there are people inside the mountain, like the one who dragged Shay inside. His rescuer had to have a view of the area, to know Shay needed help. That means they may have other hidden sentries, watching us now."

The little mongrel actually made sense. Tarver searched the face of Blue Mountain, looking for where sentries could hide, seeing a short handful of places. But there were other, shadowed places he couldn't see into.

He paid special attention to the place where Spinel had hidden, studying the area around it. "Come." He'd return to this spot later–several times, over several days, if necessary–to see if those shadows might clear as the sun moved. He wouldn't need Spinel for that, thank the gods. An expression, not a belief. A man controlled his own life. There were no gods.

Without looking to see if Spinel followed, he backtracked and took another way to the hiding place, one

300

where they didn't have to cross the open field of pillars.

They soon found Spinel's hiding place close to the mountain, next to the wall he'd seen from across the field. Tarver sent the little prick back to camp while he stayed, watching for hours without a twitch. The little shitass had pointed out where the doorway had opened for Shay, but even so, the edges of the thing couldn't be seen from here.

Patience is the greatest virtue of man, he reflected. Lack of patience had killed many an assassin. The armed warrior sneaking up on you could be eliminated, if one had but the courage to wait . . . wait . . . wait . . . and then strike, swiftly and surely. Fear galvanized lesser men to leap into action too soon. True courage was impossible without patience.

That evening, Tarver returned to camp to eat and sleep, and the next day he took food and water with him. An indulgence, but he might as well be comfortable. At noon shade became scarce, but the sweat dripping off his chin didn't matter. He thought he saw someone on the side of the mountain once, and as the second day darkened, a rider trotted toward the mountain, maybe a quarter mile from him. Tarver couldn't see where he went, but he didn't come back the other way.

Interesting. Blue Mountain appeared to be his destination. He could have ridden elsewhere once he was out of sight, but still . . .

When full dark obscured vision, Tarver waited another hour, then left his hiding place to scout the exterior of the mountain.

He began with the invisible door Bladen had been dragged through—a wall, blank and impenetrable. Even with his hand on it, Tarver found no seams or cracks. That damn Spinel! Couldn't he get anything right? But he found them after all as he ran his fingertips lightly over the wall. The seams were so tight, it took him the better part of an hour to trace the entire doorway. And he never did find a way to open it, although he tried everything he could think of.

The mountain itself was a fairly easy climb, at least on this side. He explored its surface for hours, but when dawn came he still hadn't reached the other side.

Lack of sleep meant little to him. He'd gone days without sleep before, to set up a kill properly. His body responded more reluctantly; he just had to use a little more care. But in his exhaustion, in the darkness before the sun's first glow, he stepped down crookedly. His ankle buckled and he fell.

He slid, abrading elbows and trousers, tearing fingernails as he tried to grab onto something. He snarled at the rocks and the mountain just before he found himself in the air, touching nothing.

He landed on his back, head down, and slid again.

Interesting, how an exhausted body found energy in a crisis. Furious with the mountain, he flung his legs to one side, out of the precipitous path. He tumbled twice over immovable rocks before crashing into a larger one. He stopped falling, started feeling the bruises and scrapes. He lay still, mentally checking for pain that meant damage. Nothing broken, so it didn't matter. He ignored the pain, refusing to limp or make other concession to injury, as if it didn't exist.

Pain, like exhaustion, was an obstacle to be gotten through, like any other.

He rolled over and sat up, huddled against the mountain, and listened to the sound of tumbling rock die away. He sat for hours as the sun rose and beat down upon his head. Long enough that any listeners would no longer be interested, plus two hours. Long enough for exposed skin to redden with sunburn and sweat to create mud trails down his face.

Finally, he glanced out from behind the rock. With a little wiggling and a lot of care, he worked his way lower, to an outcropping that would shelter him from anyone below and provide some small protection from the sun. A narrow opening gave a good view down the mountain.

Just after midday, his patience was rewarded. In a shadowed area below him, one of those that had so frustrated his first surveillance, he caught a glimpse of movement.

His eyes swam with fatigue, his lids drooped heavily under the sun's beating. He blinked harder, jaw set, brows rumpled in concentration.

A light appeared where the movement had been, dim but still visible.

More movement, and the light disappeared gradually, from left to right. A few moments later, he saw two men appear farther down the slope, working their way to the bloodstone pillars, where they joined another man holding three horses. Their companion must have arrived as he watched the doorway.

Grunting in satisfaction, Tarver allowed himself an hour's sleep. And then, as daylight faded, he backtracked the horses and found the hidden stable in a cave tucked back among several shoulders of rock. He hid there until nightfall; none of the cave's natural walls and niches had been developed, carved out, or whatever they did to change natural formations, so he easily found concealment. Talk and laughter drifted from the stable.

At last the voices died and people departed. An old, grizzled man he'd glimpsed earlier picked up all the shining, magical moonstones and placed them in a chest–to avoid discovery of the cave at night, when their light might be seen, of course. The man left with a final pat to one of the horses, carrying a single moonstone with him like a torch. Tarver noted where he disappeared from view. A faint light appeared momentarily, a door opening and closing.

Tarver marked the placement of the wooden chest and made a mental note to pick it up at the end of their raid, when he had the battle-axe and anything else of value he wanted.

Silence smothered the stable. He heard only the occasional movement and snort of a horse, perhaps the squeak of a few bats. Water dripped somewhere in the darkness.

He allowed himself no sleep here, in case someone rode in late at night–or out, for that matter. He waited in stillness, moving no muscle but his eyelids, for two hours. He didn't even think of it as patience anymore, only necessity.

Then, in the silent way only an experienced assassin could move, he left his hiding place and opened the chest. He caught his breath. The stones were exquisite, mostly white but with a few blue ones, as well. And very bright, when all in one place. He selected one and closed the chest quickly, hiding the light of the smooth, cool stone in his fist.

He waited, listening, but the open chest had attracted no attention. Not that he expected any, but caution came second only to patience in an assassin's toolbox. After a few minutes, he opened his hand. The single moonstone would be sufficient to find his way.

The old man's path was smooth, the door easy to find and open. They'd made some changes to the natural formations after all, making it easy to follow.

From there the path rose, twisting through narrow corridors for several hundred yards before a few scattered moonstones began to provide light.

He pressed against the rough stone wall and eased forward. A quarter mile. And another hundred yards.

Then he reached an intersection where the stable path met a broad, smooth corridor stretching in either direction.

No guards. One door, easily found and opened. Such arrogance, to think no one would find this entrance!

The Blue Mountain People apparently trusted to the well-hidden stable to protect them from discovery. In three days, he'd found no other way in. All other doors opened only from the inside.

Cautiously, he returned to the stable and slipped out into the dark night. He pocketed the moonstone, one of the loveliest he'd ever seen.

This time, as he drifted like poisonous vapor through the darkness, he indulged in planning Spinel's death, bit by bit, using the simplest weapons he'd brought. And after that, he'd play with the nastier ones on Bladen, drag it out even longer. He licked his lips.

Back at camp, he rolled into a blanket and slept soundly for the first time in days.

32. Birth

The more Shay thought about it, the more uneasy he became. He would be alone in a kind of darkness he didn't know how to think about, let alone describe, except to know it wasn't the Dark. He hoped.

Although he knew more details than he'd given Robayne, the mother lode hadn't been very specific about the creation process. His brooding on the rest near suffocated him. Sometimes he imagined soaring heights of joy and wonder. Then he would sleep, and dream. The dreams drew him back to the mother lode, where the multi-leveled songs would slip and crash and the creation would be misshapen and ugly–or worse, the music would rise in discordance and volume until he collapsed, lost in insanity. He awoke sweating and near panic.

Finishing the chronicles took priority and he read feverishly, searching for hidden instructions and reassurances. He found none.

Then he paced, worrying about what he didn't know and thinking about his first attempt. He didn't need another axe, but his first creation need not be a weapon or implement at all. Freed of all constraints, he began to plan in earnest, making countless sketches in charcoal–on the table, the cabinets, anywhere the charcoal would show. He even went into the locked corridors outside Sanctuary to draw on the rough walls there.

He spent many hours scrubbing and sanding charcoal off of everything to get a new palette, until Robayne wordlessly took over for him.

Every day he made time to lean against the black diamond walls, feeling the vibrations and the voices of the mother lode. Hard to tell, but he thought she approved of the design he carried in his head. The picture she gave him back wasn't quite right, but he'd be clearer, more certain when he gave her the final "drawing."

He held Elegy naked in his hand as he paced, not wanting the leather between them now. Sometimes he wondered if a particular idea came from her, instead of his own mind.

Robayne watched him, worry and excitement warring across his face. He studied the designs Shay drew, an admiring look in his eyes. "Shouldn't you start with something simpler?" he asked. "Then work your way up to the complex?"

Shay laughed. "This *is* simple, for me. It's what I know best, have the most experience with." Another thought hit, and he grinned. If he used this angle instead of the one he'd been planning . . . And he became lost in his work again.

Time meant nothing now. He knew when Robayne left Sanctuary for supplies, but barely noticed when he returned clean and new-shaven–and wrinkle-nosed at Shay's continued stench.

"Are you always like this when you create new designs?" asked Robayne.

"Except for the smell, the disheveled hair, the outgrown beard, and the wild eyes."

Robayne laughed. "It's been interesting to watch, at least. Your design must be unique–I've never seen a diamond both faceted and carved. I didn't even know it was possible!"

"It's not, except here, in this manner. The battle-axe herself is all carved, no facets. That's why I want to try this design first. If it doesn't work, I'll try something else."

Until at last he felt ready. Fear balanced the quickened heartbeat of anticipation. He turned to see Robayne watching him. Taking a deep breath, he blew it out and

307

said, "Now."

"Where do you want me?"

Shay shrugged. "Anywhere in the room should be fine. Just watch me, and do whatever seems appropriate. I have little idea what to expect, or how long this will take." He focused on the wall ahead of him, wondering if it mattered where *he* stood.

Probably not. He selected a place near Elegy's cradle and leaned head and hands against the wall, as usual. Slowly, the voice of the black diamond filled him, from the rumbling bass to the light, airy music almost out of hearing. He settled in, to let the song fill him so completely rays of light must be pouring from his body. As he sank deeper into harmony with the black diamond, he lost awareness of the physical world. There was only the diamond. Only the song.

And the picture in his mind. How to do this? The full picture formed slowly, inside him–not just a picture in his head, but a feeling–beauty, joy, light, and song.

Shay had never thought of himself as a singer, but song poured from him now, a full, vibrant sharing of self, similar to the ecstasy of loving Cinnabar, gentle and exciting and sensual. All the song that was in him flowed directly into the diamond–not a body's voice, but a soul's voice. He emptied all of him into the wall, all the detail of what he sought, the shapes he'd designed, the cut, the flow of light, the black fire that only this particular black diamond could give him. He offered up the way the design made him feel, the emotions he wanted his work to evoke in others. His soul's voice blended with the diamond's and filled him.

He became one with the mother lode's harmonies. Electricity shocked through him as her magic and power poured across his nerve endings in a rush like thunder and lightning and glory. He tasted the electricity, smelled the full, over-sweet scent of power. Every hair of his body stood on end, electrified. An explosion jolted him repeatedly, emptied him, arched his back and feet . . .

Shay became self-aware again, lying on his back on the hard floor, sated and empty.

That discordant noise wasn't inside him, wasn't Elegy's sweet fingers of sound releasing his seed.

Robayne's voice. Harsh. Loud. Frightened.

He blinked his way back to Sanctuary, wincing at the world's cold gray textures.

"Shay! Shay! Are you all right?"

Robayne's hands clenched his shoulders. Shaking him. His voice hurt Shay's ears–shouting, blended with panic.

He lifted a hand from the floor and the shouting slowed, dropped in volume.

"Thank the Light! You're alive! Let me help you sit up." Robayne spoke so fast his words jumbled together.

Shay moved his hand. "Not . . . ready. Yet. Let me be. A moment."

Gradually, the mundane world re-formed around him, dull and colorless. And silent in a way that made his ears ring. His faint dizziness passed, and at last he looked directly at Robayne.

The panic drained from Robayne's eyes.

Shay discovered his fingertips remained in light contact with the wall. He listened as the soft, gentle song of the mother lode quieted. He released the touch, then ached to reach out again, to remain always in contact with ecstasy at his fingertips.

Then he rolled onto his side, away from Robayne. Oh, Light! Robayne had witnessed his orgasm!

"Leave me alone, Robayne. Just for a few minutes. I'm all right." In his embarrassment he couldn't even look at his mentor.

Robayne rose. "I'll bring you water to wash with, and then I'll be in the kitchen if you need me."

Shay closed his eyes as Robayne's footsteps receded. He felt drained, empty of energy, of thought, of emotion. By the time Robayne returned with wash water, he slept where he lay.

33. Afterbirth

Shay woke in bed, disoriented. Alone in the room, he sat up through the creaking of stiff joints and aching muscles and looked down at his naked body.

Robayne had washed him with soap and water head to toe. Must have become too disgusted with the smell. A hot wave of embarrassment gushed through him at the very personal tending, then subsided to gratitude. He felt his newly trimmed beard and the no-longer-wild cap of his hair. Shorter than he was used to, but it would grow.

With a quick glance at the doorway, he eased himself out of bed, surprised at the achy lassitude of muscles and mind both. Clean clothes lay neatly folded on a chair. He dressed and went looking for Robayne. His friend–the word still felt strange in Shay's mind–puttered in the kitchen.

His drawn face bespoke hours of worry, but he turned, anxiety clearing, at the sound of Shay's bare feet shuffling on the stone floor. "There's the sleepyhead! How do you feel?"

Shay managed an exhausted smile and dropped onto a chair at the table. "Tired and sore. How long was I out?"

Robayne's smile faltered. "A full day. I was about to run for a healer."

"You can't bring a healer here!"

"I guess I could have dragged you out by your heels . . ." They were bantering words, but Robayne's tone held no such lightness.

Shay didn't speak for a moment, to give his words more weight. "Thank you, Robayne. No man could ask for a better friend than you have been to me." He put his heart into his words and face. It felt strange.

"Or a more frightened one. You didn't hear me yelling,

wouldn't leave the wall. I had to physically knock you away from it, and then you collapsed. That's where the bruises came from.

"The walls of the entire room! Could you believe it?"

"The walls?"

"You didn't see it?"

Shay shook his head.

"Lightning. The kind of blue power lines I've seen from your axe, but larger, brighter, flickering throughout the entire vein . . . the mother lode, you call it."

"Her. Like the axe."

Robayne nodded. "It's the most fearsome, awesome sight I've ever seen. I thought we both would die."

"I don't remember seeing much, but the songs . . . " Shay's voice trailed off as he remembered. He shook his head to clear it. "How did it come out?"

"What? Come out?" Robayne's face cleared. "Ah. The gem. I don't know. I forgot to look for it."

"You forgot?" Shay put more energy into the question than anything else since waking.

Robayne cocked a brow at him. "I had other things on my mind."

"Well, we'd better go see, then, hadn't we?" Shay pushed up to his feet, took one step toward the door, and staggered.

"Easy there!" Robayne lunged toward him, but Shay had already caught himself on the edge of the table. Robayne took his arm firmly.

"Now I feel like an invalid," grumbled Shay. "Let's see if the result is worth it." But he knew it was. The experience–joy so sharp it hurt, life, blending, harmony, ecstasy–was worth far more than any object born of it. He pitied Robayne, that he could never experience it.

The workshop looked no different than before, quiet

and still, awaiting the Bladen. Shay's gaze went immediately to the cradle where Elegy had been born, then slid to one side. A new cradle, much smaller, shadowed the sleek black mother lode.

He caught his breath. In only a moment he would know. Excitement brimmed and spilled until his hands shook with it. If he could have run, he would have.

He forced himself to stop, face Robayne eye to eye. No matter the outcome of his experiment, this was more important. "You should know," he started. He hesitated, swallowed. "How very important it is for you to know everything. With the sanity and clarity of hindsight, I can see that the Robayne must *not* be able to hear the singing of stones. You could not fulfill your role otherwise, for the song would have drawn you into itself as it did me, and who would rescue us both? I did not realize, and I'm sorry for my idiocy before."

"Thank you. In hindsight, I see as you do. This is something you need me for, but it's nothing that can be written down. This part must always remain a mystery learned the hard way, especially for the Robayne.

"Come, let's see what you've made."

The diamond Shay found in its cradle was larger than his fist, blackness stroked with deep sparks of color that set him afire with awe. He could barely breathe as he lifted the diamond from its cradle. He held it up between himself and Robayne, so they could both examine it.

The angles cut into the diamond were perfect–a faceted diamond core for an eight-point star, each point three inches long and as sharp as a dagger. And she included a handle that Shay had not envisioned. Without intending it, he had created a mace. When he gripped her firmly, tiny blue veins laced the points and edges of the gem and traced the length of the handle.

Perfect, and more than perfect. He would check it with the workshop's loupe, but the mother lode would not have produced any but a flawless diamond.

He set his palm against the diamond wall next to the cradle to convey his delight to the mother lode, and to ask about the handle.

As usual, he heard a voice but no words, yet the sense of the song seeped into him. *She is part of the same diamond, Bladen. Her magic is Elegy's magic. She contains much power, will not shatter or break. Be aware: No diamond birthed here is an object of beauty only. As all of my children–as I am–she is a weapon by nature and cannot be other than she is.*

Find her name.

He wrapped both hands about the handle and closed his eyes.

Nothing.

He waited. Shifted his grip. Waited more.

At last, frustrated and longing for a response, he leaned against the mother lode.

Your tiny ears cannot yet hear one so small. Her name is Eternity.

"Eternity," Shay repeated softly.

"What?" asked Robayne from behind his shoulder.

"The diamond's name. Eternity." Seeing the question in Robayne's eyes, he elaborated. "She's a weapon, just like her older sister. Apparently that's the nature of the mother lode. On our return to the Center, we'll have to get a leather grip made for her handle."

"A beautiful name for a beautiful stone. May I?" Robayne held out his hand almost reverently. He touched Eternity with a fingertip, as if she were fragile. Or holy. He turned her this way and that, examining her. "This is fine, fine work, Shay."

Shay smiled like a proud father. "The design is mine, but the cut can only be credited to the mother lode. It's perfect."

Robayne nodded in agreement.

"Without the magic of the mother lode, Eternity couldn't exist," said Shay. "I may gift her to the cathedral, to glorify the Light.

"Not to some special woman?"

Shay shook his head. "No. No woman for me ever but Cinny, I'm afraid. Or at least for a very long time."

He touched one of the new diamond's sharp spikes. "Eternity doesn't really need the magic, you know," he said. "Her beauty is magic enough for any gem."

Robayne chuckled. "Yes, it is."

And they left it at that.

Robayne wrote slowly as he updated the lore of the black diamond while Shay watched. "On this day the power of the black diamond battle-axe was renewed." And again, "Shay Bladen created a single black diamond. Flawless stone, star mace with 8 points, 9300 carats, cut." As cryptic as any of his predecessors.

With one final note. "The Bladen hears the voices of the stones. Robayne does not." That part of the puzzle he would write down, but only that.

Shay, reading over his shoulder, nodded with approval. "That should do it."

"I think we need a community gathering on our return," said Robayne.

"Why?"

"To introduce Eternity. Her existence cannot be kept secret for long, so we might as well show her off early."

Shay nodded. "They need to recognize her as Elegy's little sister."

315

Robayne jumped as if he'd been poked. "*Elegy*? Are you mad? That's not for me to know, only Bladen!"

"Not to be written down, of course, but you know everything else. Why not her name? I trust you, Robayne. Her name is safe with you."

Robayne stared at him, eyes wide, and spoke in a choked voice. "You honor me, Bladen. I will not betray your trust."

"I know." Strange, that goosebumps covered Robayne's arms, but also amusing.

His face open in wonder and astonishment, Robayne murmured, "You have given me a gift beyond price." He swallowed. "Elegy. A beautiful and deadly name, like the diamond that bears it."

Working together over the next two days, the friends tidied up Sanctuary and set everything to rights. Shay even sanded away the last of his charcoal sketches from the furniture.

At the last, just before they left, Shay handed Eternity to Robayne to carry on their journey back to the Center.

Robayne whispered her name as Shay handed her to him, his face still filled with awe.

Shay smiled. "*Now* can we go home?"

He spent a few moments leaning against the black diamond wall, listening to the voice of the mother lode, careful not to get lost in the song before pulling back. His farewell to the mother lode, and a promise to return soon.

They left without speaking, sealing the Sanctuary door, and the door after that, and the one after that.

Shay's mind began to make the transition back to the world of men even as they began walking down the corridor, without speaking.

They made a peaceful transition from Sanctuary back to the outer passages. Shay walked with deep reverence for the most amazing few days he could remember, almost as sweet as making love with Cinnabar the first time, or watching the birth of his children. A friendship cleared and cemented, a fabulous new gem, a Sanctuary when he needed one, the voice of the mother lode . . . He found himself enumerating the wonders of his time in Sanctuary, then added the wonders of Cinny and the children, of a street urchin having his own prosperous business, of watching his family rising to the Light in flames . . . Sometimes the most awe-filled moments also brimmed with pain. He accepted that because he couldn't change it.

Robayne must be having similar thoughts, since he wasn't talking, either. Nor could he keep his eyes off Eternity. A small, besotted smile played with the corners of his lips.

Their footsteps echoed palely in the narrower corridors, disappeared when the space around them opened up. The vast silence reminded Shay of the infinity of the Light, which filled him with reverence and awe.

But it was the quiet around them that allowed him to hear something much farther away, a blended roar punctuated with sharper sounds.

34. Carnage

"Do you hear that?" Shay asked.

"What is it?"

They stopped and listened. Shay held his breath to hear better.

"Is that metal?" Robayne said.

An explosion went off in Shay's stomach, his mouth suddenly dry, but he was already reaching over his shoulder to release Elegy from her harness, his feet throwing him forward.

The noise of battle roared louder as they raced through twisting corridors of rock.

Screams mingled with the collision of weaponry, and a child's wail, and the solid thunk of something striking flesh.

How could anyone bring battle this far into the mountain?

Shay tried to close his ears. Echoes multiplied the screams to a deafening crescendo.

Then he turned a final corner. A severed arm lay across his path, still clutching a short shovel edged in blood. He managed not to step on it.

His vision hazed, the black and orange of jat and jagounce dirtying the scene before him.

The ear-splitting sound of battle dropped to background noise. His hair stood on end and fear dried his mouth. He forced himself to see the scene before him.

Was *everyone* here? *All* the Blue Mountain People? He hadn't seen so many in one place since the day he'd bonded with Elegy. No one could escape, not even women and children, for the press of human beings.

Without slowing, he strained to identify the attackers. That one, the tall one over there, looked vaguely familiar, but he couldn't place him. The man's face held no anger, no cruelty. He simply killed whoever stood in front of him—man, woman, or child.

Another stranger lifted a sword overhead and brought it down hard. Shay ducked, although he was nowhere near, tried to avert his eyes, but too late. He caught a glimpse of the Elder, Faltryn, thrusting a child behind her, just before the sword split her head in twain, splattering brains and blood everywhere.

Shay tasted a gush of bile, but had no time to throw up. With a wild roar, he lifted Elegy high and shook it at the murderer. Some part of him watched what he did in horror.

The man turned in his direction.

Shay roared again and charged toward the man, almost knocking people over in his haste.

"It's Bladen," someone yelled.

"Bladen and his axe," cried another voice.

"Bladen!" More voices raised in concert.

"Bladen! Bladen! Bladen!"

Shay was no hero, but the people rallied at the sight of the battle-axe, and roars and cheers greeted the sudden blazing forth of her blue energy. Above the noise of the crowd, Elegy's song rose, exultant and fierce. He absorbed it, his energy and courage rising.

He turned from Robayne, intent on Faltryn's murderer.

He took the man's head clean from his shoulders, leaving a cauterized and steaming stump before the dead man fell.

The power made it so easy, as Elegy responded to his intent. He needed little muscle, only a small effort to reach a target with Elegy's head. Her magic did the rest, drenching everyone around him in blood and bone and tissue.

"The children," he cried. "Get the women and children

to safety!"

A voice in his ear. "I'll take them to Sanctuary. Tell the men their families are safe and be sure no one follows us."

And then Robayne raced among the people, sorting the vulnerable and grabbing others to assist him.

Shay had no time to watch. His arms swung faster. All the attackers–how many *were* there?–seemed bent on reaching him. He cut them down one by one, always the taste of scorched blood in his mouth.

He stepped over an old man who lay on the floor, moaning from a long, red gash across his chest and an eyeball on his cheek, hanging by a thread. Wildt. Robayne's uncle.

Shay couldn't stop to help him. Only he could do what needed to be done. A matter of survival for his people.

He swung again, jabbed the axe behind him hard. A line of fire traced down his back, its length interrupted when Elegy's knob made contact. Bless Bibi for her insistence on using every surface of a weapon. He used the axe's rebound to swing the knob upward into a man's head. The enemy's hair caught fire from the blue flash of contact, and Shay turned away as Elegy's voice trumpeted triumph.

He heard his name, over and over, as people screamed for help. He rarely reached them in time, but he tried. Helplessness beat at him when he couldn't.

The stench of burning flesh choked him. Men died on contact as Elegy's blade cut flesh and her lightning incinerated muscle and bone as easily as paper. Blue light flickered on the walls and on people's faces. Her song rose gloriously, infusing Shay with something near ecstasy. It frightened him even as it renewed him.

A flash of red hair caught Shay's eye and his head snapped around to follow the movement. Spinel! Of course he'd be connected to this! And of course he was running away.

Shay made no effort to pursue him.

But now he recognized the tall man: Spinel's friend, Tarver, the one who commissioned the tauz horse that burned in Cinny's funeral fire. He snatched a small girl away from a thrusting knife with one hand. Fury burst through him, and his other hand sliced Elegy's blade through the man's wrist.

He turned away before the hand landed on the floor.

Atich was there to grab the little girl, his face ashen. "I've got her, Shay."

"Robayne is taking women and children into the caverns, to a safe place. Go with him, keep them all safe." Shay blocked a weapon whose movement he caught from the corner of his eye, barely in time. He tipped Elegy's head enough to cut the man's shoulder and blue magic fired death into him.

"You need someone to help you here!"

"Go, Atich! I'm fine!" He saw a child face down on the floor, lifeless. Men trampled her body, and one tripped over her and fell on her yarn doll a few feet away.

Grief nearly overwhelmed Shay. His fury forced it away. He watched Atich fight his way toward the girl, then forgot about him as a knife blade slashed his cheek.

He felt no pain and the blood wasn't in his way. He killed the knifeman.

"Get it, you shitheads!" The bellow carried over the crowd. Shay turned to see who.

Tarver. Shay stopped to watch the man's cold, efficient deaths. No anger, no feeling at all, just slice-stab-cut thrust. As if the ones who died weren't even people. The smooth, quick techniques bespoke long habit as Tarver began clearing a path toward Shay.

"Fucking idiot," Tarver roared at someone. "I don't

321

care about him! Get me that damned axe!"

Shay thrust the axe head at the man Tarver had addressed, seeing him in time only because of Tarver's attention.

This had to end–and soon. Too many people were dying.

He needed to separate the attackers from the people. They weren't the target, only an impediment to reaching Tarver's real goal–Elegy.

Well, let them come. He would gladly give her to them–edge first. But not over the bodies of friends and family. Again he fought grief, filling the sudden void with his anger.

He bounded to the top of a tall rock near the wall and thrust Elegy high overhead. Then he roared, filling the sound with a fury that expanded his veins, his grief over the little girl's body, the horror of the first severed arm, his fear of once again–Light, not again!–losing the foundations of his life. His parents. Cinny and their children. And now his new-found family? No! He clenched his fist tighter on Elegy's haft, sending an explosion of blue veins shooting toward the distant roof and drawing every eye.

"You want the battle-axe?" he roared. "Come and get it!"

Then he leaped to the floor and ran, careful to keep Elegy high enough to be seen easily.

"We're with you, Shay," cried a voice at his elbow.

Locelar! And with his grandfather came other Bladens, falling into step alongside.

"No," Shay said. "Go back! I don't need help!" And he turned away and ran on, into the corridors and away from the Center.

To his astonishment, his family obeyed. They slowed and turned back toward the conflict.

He saw that Tarver and his men ignored the Bladen clan, except for one coward who slashed at a cousin in passing. The coward died at Locelar's hands. Someone else helped the injured man to his feet.

The black opals. If Shay could find them again . . .He raced down a corridor away from the Center, checking behind to be sure Tarver followed. The man's head rose above the pack of men between them. He seemed not to hurry, but he kept up.

Shay took the first turn possible, then a few more, but he wasn't a fast runner. He needed more twists in the passages.

The citrine corridor. The rubies far down that way. Past the agates and jaspers.

Footsteps closed in behind him, as expected. He may be no warrior, but he *was* a desperate man trying to help his people.

He'd thought never to belong anywhere again. Now he had Bibi and Meilin, safe in Echo. He had blood kin, and all the Blue Mountain People.

Light, please help me not to let them down. Not now!

The footsteps came too close. Fingertips brushed his collar.

He spun, stumbled from excess momentum. Elegy slashed across the man's face; Shay had misguessed his height. An explosion like a small clap of thunder matched the blue lightning and the man's face disappeared. His fall slowed pursuit momentarily as the others avoided him.

The delay didn't help much, as Shay struggled not to vomit. The memory of a charred hole where a face had been would not clear from his vision. Worse than the manglers.

The clearly marked intersections faded behind him and Shay began taking more turns, adding twists, doubling back through neighboring passages.

The footsteps behind him faltered as the moonstones became more widely spaced.

"Go, you assholes," shouted Tarver from the back of the pack. "You think you'll get a better chance? Move your sorry asses! Now!"

"Not me, Tarver."

The new voice startled Shay. He ducked into an alcove next to another unmarked intersection and dropped low, shielding Elegy's light as he worked to calm himself.

Everyone had paused, but Tarver glared at them. "Go! I'll catch up!"

Uncertainly, the thugs started off again, running within inches of Shay as they continued down the dim corridor.

He didn't dare move until the last two had gone past. Trying to quiet his pounding heart, he listened.

"What shit is this, Jonus? Are you a weak pussy like that asshole Spinel? He was the first coward to run, but I didn't expect you to be next."

"Think about it, Tarver," said the man called Jonus. "We've already passed a lifetime's riches and more! No one in his right mind wants to go up against that axe, when we can be filthy rich without the risks."

"You idiot. I want the *axe*! The rest doesn't matter."

"It does to me. I'm out, Tarver. I want to be rich and alive."

"You little cocksucker! Go forward now, or die by my hand, right here!"

Shay had to look. And then he couldn't look away.

Tarver slammed his left hand into Jonus's testicles, gripped hard, and twisted. Jonus's weapon clattered to the stone floor.

His victim screamed and punched at Tarver's face with both fists.

Tarver didn't flinch, as if he didn't feel the assault. He

324

wrenched his wrist around, gripping harder. He leaned in closer to Jonus and smiled.

Shay swallowed hard, his own groin aching in sympathy.

With his right hand Tarver began to break bones, one at a time, beginning with fingers.

Jonus tried to knee him, but too much of his weight was off the floor, and he had no leverage. He screamed, pausing only to breathe. "Stop! Stop! Okay, I'm in! I'm in!"

Tarver laughed, his voice thick with lust. "Too late to change your mind, Jonus. You chose." Wrapping a hand about the man's throat, he flung him to the floor, then knelt atop him, methodically breaking bone after bone. The loud snap of the larger bones echoed in the stone passage. "You're lucky, you know, Jonus. If I wasn't in such a hurry, I'd skin you alive, starting with your prick. Just imagine having all that skin peeled off, a bit at a time! And your testicles would be next. But I don't have time to play."

Light, no! Shay swallowed his gorge, barely. How could he sit here, safely hidden, and let this happen? He gripped Elegy's haft a little tighter, preparing to leap into the passage to draw Tarver off his victim. But Jonus had killed Shay's people, too. He waited.

Tarver stripped Jonus's clothes from him, tossed them in a heap, drew long, bloody lines down his screaming victim's chest and groin, and stood. "I wonder how long it will take the vermin to find you–rats, spiders, scorpions, and who knows what all hides here? It will be a long, slow death, and you won't even be able to scream." He suddenly dropped to one knee, driving a fist into Jonus's throat with the weight of his body behind it.

The sound of wheezing and gurgling turned Shay's stomach.

Tarver turned to glare down the passage, seeming to

stare directly at Shay's hiding place. "You're next, Bladen. Oh, yes, I know you're close. My men are chasing a wild goose. But you won't die like this. I have plans for you.

"Your art is gems. Mine is death. For you, I've brought special tools that will make you long to die Jonus's death. And I'm coming for you now."

35. Hero

Shay heard Elegy singing softly, joyous in anticipation of victorious battle. How she loved a good fight! He closed his eyes and tightened his grip in dread.

A real hero would have stood up slowly, chest expanding and eyes fierce. He would have stood tall, challenged Tarver man to man, and beaten him in fair combat. Fair except for the magic of the battle-axe.

Shay was no hero. He fled.

He bolted out of his alcove like a jackrab, ducked around the nearest corner, and found an unfinished passage twisting away into darkness.

Tarver's laughter chased after him, accompanied by the staccato of running feet.

Desperately, he ducked down a wider branch–and collided with warm flesh.

The collision threw him from his feet, along with the thug he'd run into.

"I've got him, Tarver," yelled the man, whose overgrown mustache intercepted spittle with every word.

Shay smashed Elegy's butt into the top of the man's foot. Even through the thick boot he heard and felt bones breaking just before the scream covered the sound.

"Shut up, you idiot," hissed someone amidst other mutters.

Shay rolled to his feet and ran for the corner he'd just turned. Barely avoiding a hand that clutched at him, he fled on down the corridor. Tarver's footsteps closed in, but he didn't look back to see. The men poured out of the side tunnel, taking up the chase once again.

Narrow. He needed narrow, to limit how many attackers could come at him. Where were the black opals from here, dammit!

Again he changed passages, opting now for twisty and black. Elegy's power provided the only light, and he kept it dim. The thugs had settled down to quiet pursuit, harangued from behind by Tarver.

He spun, swinging Elegy and himself all the way around. He barely felt the catch in human flesh that left a man screaming and Tarver cursing.

The pursuers dropped back a pace and Shay pulled in a huge lungful of air. How far before his trembling legs gave out?

His gasping breaths covered the sounds of pursuit. He stumbled, killed another pursuer who got too close, ran on.

There. The passage he sought. His abrupt spin into it almost jerked him off balance.

The path was barely a path, the footing rocky and uneven. Just as he remembered. He slowed to pick his way more carefully. If he tripped and fell here, they would catch him.

He shoved away the terror of Jonus's execution, but it wouldn't stay gone. Only now *he* was Tarver's target.

He stumbled again, too caught up in imagination, and skinned palms and knees as he caught himself and lurched forward.

But he'd seen a familiar configuration of rocks. The den of angry opals. Frantically, he tripped his way to the low opening he remembered.

Gone. Filled with rock. He'd forgotten the shivers of the earth that collapsed the opening.

His great and glorious plan to use the opal cleft dissipated like hot fog.

Behind him, cursing peppered the air when someone fell, blocking the narrow corridor.

Shay didn't know what lay ahead in this passage, past

the cleft, or even whether it would dead-end, trapping him at Tarver's mercy. That, or go now to face Tarver and hope for a quick death.

Or . . .

Squeezing his eyes shut to protect them, he wrapped his hands more tightly about Elegy's haft. He swung with all his might at the buried cleft. Power crackled in his hands, even before the bit struck. Shattered stone gashed his head and hands, stung through his clothes.

Nearer than he'd hoped, voices cried out as shards struck his pursuers.

"Get him!" Tarver's voice rose in thunder, his menace flinging his men forward.

They feared Tarver more than a magic battle-axe?

He suddenly understood something Bibi had told him. The axe didn't cause pain and death. The man wielding it did. The menace wasn't Tarver's weapons but Tarver himself.

Shay squinted, adjusted to angle more shards toward his attackers, then swung again. And again. Faster, harder. His arms turned to wood. Elegy's blue fire painted dancing shadows on the walls of the passage. The lightning surged. Rock fell, flew, disappeared.

The blue lightning held the pursuers back, until one man screamed and kept screaming. Another's scream cut off.

"Move, you sons of bitch whores!"

The steel edge in Tarver's voice drove them forward.

The last of the rock fell, lying blue-black in the pulsing throb of Elegy's light. The way was open.

"Gotcha, you prick!" A hand closed on Shay's shoulder.

Shay butted Elegy into him, twisted her in his grip as he spun, and cut the man in two, careful not to look at his handiwork. The fallen body blocked the pursuers' rush.

He leaped through the opening into the cleft and stumbled his way along the rough, debris-strewn floor. He clambered through the fallen rock that slowed his flight.

Newly-loosened stone dropped from the ceiling. One bounced off his skull. His knees struck the floor and his head spun. He forced himself up and onward.

Slipping and tripping, Shay damped Elegy's light, leaving only a trickle in front of him.

Lost in blackness. Forever. No way out. Fear squelched up from his feet; his breath came in short, shallow pants. Not enough air. Light-headed. The opals muttered angrily.

Had to get out. Had to get out. Had to get out.

He found the narrow exit he'd used the last time. As before, he turned sideways to squeeze through, leaving skin and threads on the rocks.

Curses and yells followed him through the narrow confines that blocked Elegy's light from them.

Pressure lifted from Shay's spirit when he left the cleft of opals. A few deep breaths restored some calm.

The fearsome chasm he'd conquered once lay in front of him, stretching the width of the cavern where he now stood. He found again the ancient wooden bridge, one plank wide and thirty sagging feet long.

This time, he trusted the bridge better. This time, he trusted himself better.

He charged onto the bridge at full speed, ignoring the abyss below him.

As he stepped off the far end and turned, he saw a tiny glimmer of light approaching the bridge. Tarver held a single moonstone.

Shay watched over a dozen men inch onto the plank, until the first ones neared his end. Then he gasped in a huge breath and shattered the ancient wooden supports. The men dropped into darkness, their screams cut off abruptly.

As for the others? Let Blue Mountain kill them. Let their bones feed the denizens of the deep places.

Shay turned and walked away, Elegy held loosely in the hand dangling at his side, her light dim and content.

His arms and legs shook violently during the trek back toward the Center, but he dared not sit to rest. Exhaustion lay on his shoulders like a cloak of granite, every step a struggle to stay on his feet. If he sat, he wouldn't get up soon.

He hurt. Especially the long, painful slice down his back. Especially where his sweat stung it. And his head, gashed and pounded by knife and rock. Elegy, already the heaviest of axes, felt twice her normal weight.

As he walked, pictures trickled through memory, soon building to a flood. A severed arm. Faltryn's awful death. An exploding face. He distracted himself by wondering whether Robayne had gotten the women and children to safety, and by worrying about his family, the ones he'd ordered to stay with the battle. But that led back to memory of blood and viscera, of scattered teeth lying on the floor, some still attached to part of a jaw, of . . .Shay threw up. Hard and fast, unable to catch his breath without inhaling vomit. Frantic, he coughed, spewed more, coughed again. He dropped to his knees, head hanging, the wet smell sickening enough to start yet another round.

The tears began long before his stomach emptied. He gulped in huge sobs that shook his whole body, left him unable to catch his breath. Worse, he had no water to rinse his mouth.

When at last the sobs abated, chills flushed through him. Cold sweat laved his face and the back of his neck.

He forced himself slowly to his feet, Elegy gripped

lightly in both hands.

Her song began softly, a mother's caress he'd never heard from her before. He planted his feet and closed his eyes to listen. The music trickled down from the crown of his head to his shoulders and he wiped his face with a sleeve, as if he removed faint cobwebs. The notes buzzed through arms and fingertips, floated down his back, flooded his legs, teased his toes. And in the song he heard reassurance, pride in his work, strength to bear him up when his own strength failed him. Again her words floated, "I am Elegy. And I am yours, forever."

Renewed, he opened his eyes, took a deep breath, and moved forward. The People waited, and they still had need of him.

36. Battle's Aftermath

Three sullen thugs sat on the floor amid the carnage in the Center, their legs stretched in front of them and hands bound so tightly that even from here they appeared red and swollen. Orlait stood over them with a sword, blood congealing from numerous wounds, mostly minor.

The Blue Mountain People barely looked up when Shay appeared. Some of the men carried away bodies. The eyes of the most horribly injured would haunt him forever; they recognized death–and longed for it.

Shay couldn't bear to look at the moaning men, but his gaze slid off the women completely. Many of them had fought, too, using whatever came to hand as a weapon. One dead woman still held a round pot by its wire bail and had apparently done some damage with it, judging by the blood smeared over the bottom. Near her lay a small shape he avoided, although from the corner of his eye he saw a small arm stretched toward the mother who'd died trying to protect her. Or him. Shay couldn't look any closer.

The all-too-familiar smells of a battlefield tried to suffocate him–iron blood, urine, feces, burning flesh, sweat, fear, despair. After all the fighting he'd done since leaving Porphyr, the smells shouldn't affect him so terribly, but they did.

Moans and cries supplied the dirge of the dying, and someone screamed as the surgeon sawed at an arm while four men held him down. Shay forced himself not to look away. Hadn't he severed limbs himself–and done other, more hideous butcheries? He should be willing to face what he had done. Belly clenching, he started across the field of the fallen.

He swallowed bile, wishing for a steadier stomach, and

approached the screaming man and the sawbones who peered through sweat at the gash. A bandage wrapped the arm tightly above the awful wound.

The longer the amputation procedure lasted, the longer this man's scream would tear at Shay. The more blood the man would lose. The greater chance he would die. With Elegy, Shay had the means to speed the process, both the cutting and the sealing. He could save the man much pain and release the sawbones to tend others sooner. Morally, he had an obligation to help this man.

If he could bring himself to do it, not in the heat of battle, but in the iron-cold aftermath.

Tarver had invaded because of him, after all. That made him responsible for this mess. As he'd been responsible for Cinny's death, and the children's, by surrendering the axe too late.

If he hesitated, he'd never be able to do this. "I'll do it. Move over."

The sawbones looked up in startlement. His gaze flicked to the battle-axe. "It has to be a clean cut, no shattering or splintering of bone. Can you do that?"

"Yes."

The sawbones snapped an order to the small man assisting him. "Bring that red-hot poker now. We'll only have a few moments to cauterize the stump."

"No," said Shay. "I can do that, too, in the same blow." *Oh, Light! What am I doing? Am I saving a life, or destroying one?*

The men looked at each other and at the sawbones, who simply nodded at one of them.

"Keep that arm stretched just like you've been doing." He moved to the victim's shoulders, out of the way.

Shay forced himself to look at the arm, where blood flowed out in a steady stream. If I don't do this, he reminded himself, this man will bleed to death. He positioned himself above the wound, set his stance, and closed his eyes briefly. He opened them and tightened his grip on Elegy, tapping into her blood hunger. With everything in him, he focused on what he wanted to do, felt a small change in Elegy's power.

He focused on the target and swung.

Blue fire crackled in the air as Elegy's bit descended. He felt the strike land, felt the proper follow-through in his wrists, smelled burning blood.

The victim's screams broke off abruptly as he passed out. The attendants yelled and flung themselves away from the axe.

Shay staggered a step as he turned his back, afraid to look at what he'd done. Then he retched emptily, unable to stop. Hands closed on his arms. "Don't touch the axe," he rasped as he retched again.

The men led him away, sat him down, brought him something to drink. A woman brought a cool, wet rag to bathe his face, then gave him small sips of water as the retching slowed.

"I have to see," he choked, fighting the hands on his shoulders. "Is he all right? Oh, Light, I didn't kill him, did I?"

"No," one of the men said. "You didn't kill him. You saved him."

"Bladen," said a quiet, authoritative voice.

He looked up into the haunted, exhausted eyes of the sawbones.

"As you promised, a fine, sharp cut, cauterized in the same blow. He'd already lost much blood, but I think we have some hope of saving him now. Come, there are others."

Horror flashed through Shay. Others?

He allowed the men to help him to his feet. "I have to see first."

It wasn't what he feared. No more blood leaked; the wound was well sealed, and the severed limb had already been taken away, much to his relief. "How many more?"

"Three I'm aware of, although none so severe. Come."

Spirit numbed, Shay did what he had to do to help the People. Swinging the axe at a human being was much harder when his victim lay quiescent instead of trying to kill him. It's necessary, he said to himself, over and over. If I'd just given Spinel the axe, none of this would have happened. Just like with my family. This is my fault.

When he finally finished the bloody business, Shay staggered away from the mess and looked around. The three bound men still sat in the middle of the floor, guarded by a blood-smeared, exhausted Orlait.

The Elder looked up and their eyes met. He spoke to someone nearby, then left the three prisoners in his care and came toward Shay, sword in hand.

Orlait still wore the authority of his position, but he wore it more quietly today. Twice he stopped for a word with one or another of the People, apparently expressing concern or encouragement. Shay had not seen this side of Orlait before.

He wanted to greet Orlait as he approached, to at least acknowledge him, but his throat closed in horror and sorrow. He couldn't speak. Old angers at Orlait threatened, but the pain in the older man's face quieted them. Startled, he saw tear tracks in the dust of Orlait's face. Before him stood the man chosen to be an Elder of the people, and finally he understood the choice. A man who cared, who was willing to make the difficult decisions, whatever the personal cost.

Orlait sighed heavily, glancing around the Center. "A hero at last, eh, Bladen? Arrived in the nip of time to draw off the attackers and save the day." His voice sounded only tired, with no trace of sarcasm or enmity.

"What happened, Orlait? How did they get in?"

The older man's eyes filled with grief. "Through the stables–the only access available to a stranger. We thought no one could find it and became complacent. Once, four guards remained on duty there at all times. But over time, the number of guards dwindled to one. Last night the guard was your mother's brother, Guth. We just found him a few minutes ago. They slit his throat. I'm sorry."

Guth. One of the men who had carried water for his bath after he was lost in the mountain. Shay didn't know him well, but a man who had grown up with no family treasured every relative he had. How many others had he lost here?

How many others of the community had lost family?

If Tarver had been in front of him now, Shay would have gladly destroyed him.

Elegy flared briefly in his hands and Orlait took a step back. He forced himself to relax his grip. Pain and exhaustion made it easier than he'd expected. "Thank you."

"How badly are you hurt? Do you need a healer now, or can you bide for a bit?"

Shay shrugged, and the slice down his back tore again. His physical hurts blended with the emotional ones until he couldn't separate them. He had no idea what needed to be treated right away.

"Robayne got most of the women and children away safely," he said. "They're in hiding until I go get them–after we've done what we can here, so they won't have to see this."

Orlait nodded an acknowledgment. "What about the

337

ones you led away from the Center?"

"I left them at the black opal vein. Someday someone will find their bones."

"A good ending for them. One or two may find their way back, but it's not likely."

Shay suddenly remembered Jonus. "There's a man in the tunnels, left alive–but barely. His own leader tortured him and left him to die."

"I'll send someone to look for him when I can spare someone. But I will not spend our resources on our attackers. He and any others of their wounded will be taken outside of Blue Mountain and left on a mountainside somewhere to fend for themselves. Their own actions brought them here to cause harm; their own actions must save them now."

Justice, and more mercy than Tarver had shown the People. Shay approved.

Orlait cleared his throat. "We lost Faltryn and Wildt from the Council. Two others hang by the merest of threads and may never walk again, even if they survive." His eyes hardened. "And we may lose one more before all is done."

"Another near death?" One more grief, piled atop so many. How could anyone bear it?

"Not yet." Orlait shook his head, closed his mouth hard.

Shay nodded and turned to move on, thinking Orlait would say no more.

"Bladen."

He stopped, turned back.

"We'd have lost more if you hadn't been here. Thank you for saving so many."

I didn't save anyone! My presence here brought death! "Please, don't thank me," he whispered through a too-narrow throat.

338

"You do know you're now one of the leaders of our people? Whether you choose it or not? We'll need to replace the Council members lost today. Your name is at the top of our list."

"Me!"

"You're no longer a newcomer, Bladen. Whatever our differences in the past, you've earned a leadership role in our community. As you are likely to become a new Elder, I will tell you what may be shared with no one yet.

"The Council of Elders do not simply rule. I don't know how much detail Robayne has explained to you, but we are also tasked to protect the People. Our charter requires that we do not lead from behind, but from the front. One of our number did not do so this day. He hid. How many died because he did not do his duty?" Orlait stopped and caught what might have been a sob before it escaped, then took a moment to compose himself.

"Alas, he is my own nephew. If a death sentence is pronounced, mine must be the hand to strike him down, as I'm the Eldest."

Shay felt the horror, though he'd thought his sensibilities long since numbed. "I'm sorry, Orlait. I hope that burden doesn't come to you."

The Elder, looking years older, turned and shuffled away, the tip of his sword sagging almost to the floor.

What a strange conversation! For Orlait to tell him all these things, after their prior disagreements, set the whole world akilter. Who'd have thought they could put aside old animosities so easily?

No, not easily at all. Not if it required death and destruction for pettiness to disappear.

Shay's head hurt. Too much had been stuffed into it, exacerbating the blows it had taken.

The cook appeared, accompanied by helpers. Shay

watched him slather something from his kitchen onto some of the smaller wounds, while his assistants took water, broth, and fruit to everyone who wanted them.

He thought about the aching muscles many of these good people would suffer, from overusing them in ways they'd never used them before. He caught up with the cook.

"Do you know how to make battle balm?" he asked. "For sore, over-used muscles?"

The cook tilted his head. "I'm not familiar with it, but it sounds like something a lot of the folks would be glad to have."

"There's no hurry; they probably won't even notice for a couple of hours, but when you have a little time, look me up and I'll show you how to make it."

"What's in it?"

Shay listed the ingredients.

The cook tilted his head, thinking. "Klovais? Well, well. Yes, I have everything. I'll let you know when I have a little time to learn." He turned back to his helpers.

The slice down Shay's back ached and throbbed, demanding his attention. Maybe he should look for a healer for himself.

But they were busy, and their patients looked much worse off than he. Instead, he asked someone to coordinate clean-up–at least enough to allow the return of the women and children.

And then, telling no one where he went, he quietly left the Center to bring them home.

37. WRONG

Something felt wrong–something not related to mourning, or loss, or the wails and tears of the people.

Deep down, Shay bore a terrible certainty that Tarver yet lived.

Two days after the battle, he gave in to the uneasy feeling and sent three of the people's best fighters to search the endless tunnels and lightless places of the mountain, looking for lost survivors and collecting bodies. Then he and Atich headed for the cleft of black opals, hoping to find Tarver's body.

Shay carried Elegy, and Atich bore Eternity, handling her with fingertips only at first. Like Elegy, the black diamond mace would invoke her full powers only for Shay, but even without her lightning, she was a formidable weapon.

What if Tarver had survived and still lurked in these deep caverns? Shay had to wonder if two men with magic weapons would be enough against Tarver, if he still lived.

Fear trickled down Shay's spine with his sudden sweat. Atich seemed less affected, but then, Atich hadn't listened to Jonus's torture. And he hadn't heard Tarver's boast: *I've brought special toys that will make you long to die like Jonus.* The threat repeated endlessly through his head, to the background refrain of Jonus's raw screams, like the scratch of diamonds across the soft face of lazh or amber.

Elegy flared, her blue light spurting from Shay's intensified grip on her haft. He forced himself to ease his fingers. The reminder of the extraordinary weapon helped, though. Her magical powers made up for his lack of skills and courage.

For a moment, Shay heard what felt like a purr from

341

his axe.

"How many men did Tarver bring with him into the mountain?" Atich asked quietly.

Shay shook his head. "I think over a dozen followed me from the Center."

Atich's pale face held a blush of blue, reflected from Elegy's light. "You know, we could spend years down here looking for them and still have nothing to show for it. Maybe we should go home and let the mountain do its job."

"Don't feel you have to play nursemaid, Cousin, much as I prefer to have your company. Tarver's a wily bastard, smart, tough, and capable of anything. If anyone can survive being lost down here, he would be the one. But I have to be sure, if I ever want a good night's sleep again."

"Even if we don't find him, he's most likely dead."

"It's this . . . hunch I've had ever since the attack. That something's wrong. Tarver's survival is about the worst wrongness I can think of, so I have to look. Just in case. Finding his body would set my mind at ease."

Atich heaved an exaggerated sigh. "Well, I'm not leaving you alone down here. Which way to the opals?"

"I'm tracing the roundabout way I led them, so it may take longer, but I can get us there."

After that, conversation lagged. The pressure of darkness seemed to stuff the senses and muffle noise. Even their quiet footsteps sounded unnatural, intrusive. He boosted Elegy's light, pushing back the shadows a little farther. If Tarver leaped from the darkness, at least he'd see him in time to react. He hoped.

Something skittered behind him and he spun, Elegy at the ready. A faint splash jerked his attention to a pale salamander sliding into a pool of water at the base of two small stalagmites. He swallowed, sucked moisture from his cheeks into a suddenly dry mouth.

342

Atich's thready chuckle in the darkness betold nerves no steadier.

Shay struggled to identify the front of the cleft where black opals lay, wondering if he was in the right passage. Then he found it, gaping wide behind the rubble left from chopping his way in with Tarver at his heels.

Behind him, Atich rubbed his thumb constantly over the black leather grip added this morning to Eternity.

Shay's heart pounded so loud he expected Atich to complain about the noise. For the thirtieth time, he reminded himself that Tarver was most likely dead. Still, he didn't extend Elegy ahead of him to light the way better, as if the fearsome killer might suddenly leap from the shadows to grab her.

He gripped Elegy tighter with both hands and stopped walking. His eyes closed, his thumbs caressed the smooth, cool haft. He listened. Hearing nothing, he gripped more firmly, with stronger intent.

Gradually, as he released more power, he began to hear her voice. The song took on energy, running an arpeggio of brightness through his veins. For this time, in this place, he truly felt one with the diamond.

Even when Atich poked him in the ribs he neither startled nor lost focus on the song. Even when he slowly opened his eyes.

"Shay? What's wrong?" Atich's hushed voice echoed from the walls.

"Not a thing," he said softly.

"Then can you move? I can't stand up straight, and I can't get past you to a flatter area."

Another time Shay would have smiled. Instead, he moved ahead without looking at the poor footing, still in communion with his battle-axe.

They found a body, one of Tarver's men. Shay

343

wrinkled his nose against the smell.

Could Tarver even now be close enough to hear him? Perhaps he lay in wait somewhere ahead.

He lifted Elegy higher and invoked a brighter light. No light could reveal what lay deep in shadow, but he felt better anyway.

They stepped around the corpse, headed for the back way out. Another body blocked the exit and they moved it, gagging and dry retching at the smell, and at the hard ice of the skin.

Out into the cavern, they faced the long chasm stretching to either side. Shay gasped for a breath of clean air, Atich doing the same next to him.

"Help!" A breathy voice seemed to rise from the depths of the chasm.

Shay paused in mid-breath to listen.

"Help me!" The voice dropped to a whisper that echoed off the chasm walls.

Tarver? Shay couldn't imagine Tarver ever asking for help, from anyone. A trap? Someone pretending to be hurt, to lure in Shay and his axe?

Shay saw the same questions in Atich's eyes.

Could more than one still live, deep in the chasm?

"I have to go look," Shay whispered, startled at the volume of his voice bouncing from the rock walls.

"I'm right behind you," whispered Atich.

Together, they crept to the very edge of the drop-off and knelt. Shay slowly extended Elegy over the chasm, released more light. Blueness flared, reflected back from the walls of the chasm. Far below, perhaps forty feet, lay a moaning man. Nothing moved but his head.

"Tarver?" Atich asked on a wisp of breath.

Shay shrugged. "I'd have to climb down to see. It may be possible to climb, but the way down I saw is on the far

344

wall, and I cut down the bridge to leave Tarver stranded."

"Have you looked for another way?"

Shay shook his head. "Don't look at the axe. I'm going to need a lot of light."

Atich nodded, still peering into the depths.

"Yell if you need me." Shay walked away, examining the walls as he went. With a sudden burst of power, he could almost hear, Elegy erupted into blazing blue that reached clear across the chasm and the cavern beyond, lighting the entire space as bright as daylight.

Shay winced and stopped moving until his eyes adjusted. A quick look around revealed no one scurrying for cover. The axe's power shone steadily, with no flickering to distract the eye. He moved along the edge of the chasm, searching for a way down. Every few steps he glanced back at Atich, clearly visible in the eerie brightness.

A full hour later, he found a place he thought looked accessible. He whistled and beckoned to Atich.

"Finally! I'm tired of listening to the moaning and groaning," Atich tried to joke. Squinting in the brightness, he examined the descent. "I'll go. You stand guard with the axe."

"It's mine to do, Cousin. I appreciate the offer, but I still have to do this."

"No offense, Shay, but I'm almost twenty years younger and stronger. Let me break trail." Atich's teeth flashed pale blue in the axe light as he grinned.

Shay sighed, giving up, and stepped out of the way.

Atich pronounced the climb easier than expected and called up frequently to keep Shay updated. Even so, waiting was hard.

He hated this feeling of helplessness and uselessness, especially without a clear view of most of Atich's climb, given the rocky contours of the chasm walls and its twists and turns.

Then he heard a thump, followed by sliding rock. It lasted only a moment before Atich called up to him. "I'm down and starting toward the enemy."

A gush of relief touched Shay. Atich *did* remember this man was an enemy, not a victim to be rescued.

The moaning stopped.

Shay waited, holding his breath. Nothing, for long minutes. No report from Atich at all. Then the faint murmur of his cousin's voice.

At last the murmuring stopped. Silence, and more silence. Then Atich's voice again, directly below Shay.

"I'm coming up."

The first Shay saw of Atich was his eyes, bleak, haunted, miserable. The younger man pulled himself onto the lip of the chasm and just sat, not speaking, looking at nothing.

"Atich?"

"Eight men dead. If I count the pieces right. One left alive, to give you a message."

Shay's stomach tightened. He should have gone. Atich shouldn't have had to see that. "Message?"

Atich nodded. "Tarver's alive, and he's headed for your friends in Echo. Surrender the axe, or all of them will die."

38. Crystal Death

"Tarver killed all the other survivors," said Atich, eyes bleak, "and left this one barely alive, so he could give you a message."

Shay couldn't bring himself to ask the question that pressed against his heart. *Did you leave him there to complete his slow death? Or did you hasten his exit from this life?*

Which is the correct moral choice, if a man must choose between them—between murder and cruelty? Even inaction is a choice, with consequences to the soul.

Atich turned away from Shay, chin dropping to his chest. "I killed him," he whispered in a voice thrust roughly through a too-small throat.

Shay inhaled a slow, painful breath. Which choice would he have made in Atich's place? He nodded and clasped Atich's shoulder briefly.

To turn the mood, he asked, "Did Tarver take anyone with him when he left? Do others still live?"

"I didn't think to ask." And at last Atich turned, lifted his head, and looked Shay in the eye. "What next?"

With a shrug, Shay said, "I don't know. I wish we knew for sure, but it sounds as if he rides for Echo."

"What does your gut tell you?"

Shay thought a moment. "I want you to warn the people, tell them to remain alert and armed. Ask Orlait to organize guards and patrols for the tunnels. Keep the people calm, but don't let them become complacent. Be watchful as you travel home, and stay safe."

"And you?"

Shay clenched his jaw so hard a muscle jumped by his ear. "I'm going after Tarver. This has to end now."

Atich nodded. "May the Light be with you." He left to return to his family.

Shay watched him for a moment, before taking the back ways to the stable to avoid contact with others. Bloodstains marked the straw and worn wood there, but some effort at cleanup had already been made.

Spark was still skittish and seemed glad to leave. Shay wanted to run instead of picking his way through the bloodstone, but no matter when he left, no matter how fast he went, or which path he took, he could be too late.

Clear of the bloodstone at last, he surged into a gallop, urgency biting at his heels like bozyflies. Once again the little horse's willingness, speed, and agility surprised him. A great horse, except for the bright coat. Maybe a drop of Curzon blood somewhere in his lineage? They were said to come in astonishing and unnatural colors.

He pushed as fast as he dared through the rough terrain, for once grateful that Bibi had provided so much experience on challenging trails. At last, far ahead of him he thought he glimpsed a puff of dust rising above the rocks. More riders, perhaps. He slowed. Tarver?

Shay cursed. Nothing said Tarver wouldn't be watching his back trail, or that he hadn't seen Spark's dust hanging in the air. How could he be so stupid?

As he entered the tauz canyons he slowed Spark to a walk and allowed him to pick his own way. Sunlight sparked on pale cream, smooth yellow-orange, deep rich gold–a garden of beautiful crystals. But Shay no longer saw the beauty. He didn't want to dismount, to expose himself to the hatred of the pillars and the rough sharpness of the footing. Why hadn't people found a way to reach Echo without going through the tauz?

A sizzling, snapping sound ripped across his ears just as Spark's feet went out from under him. He shucked out of the stirrups as the horse crashed down, screaming, ropes encircling his front feet.

He landed on a dagger of tauz crystal, cried out as it punched into his left shoulder. The crystals awoke.

Voracious voices of starving stone, howls of icy rage, and thirst . . . His own saliva filled his mouth, tasting of fear, a primal reaction to the hatred and hunger of the stones. As if they remembered him breaking the grandfather pillar. He could feel their pull on his flesh, reaching to consume him.

He had no breath to cry out. His fingers were already caught inside tauz and he couldn't break free.

Above him he heard deep laughter. "I waited for you, Bladen. It took you longer than I thought to find my dying friend."

The pain, the burn, the odd feel of the tauz dagger drawing in his blood like fine wine sparked terror. From the corner of his eye he watched the dagger turn reddish from his blood, the thirsty crystals intent on drinking him dry. Faint howls of hunger and triumph screeched across his senses.

Beside him, Spark thrashed, hooves flailing near Shay's head. Dark pinpricks showed where tauz had nicked his hide. The horse surged to his feet, a hoof landing only inches from Shay's face.

No escape this time. I'm going to die.

"Whoa! Easy, fella!"

Hoofbeats stopped. They had his horse.

The tauz dagger held him fast. The sucking sensation in his shoulder increased, and the dagger exploded through the front of his shoulder, impaling him from back to front as the dagger grew, bloated on his blood.

Shay screamed as the world turned red, then gray. Pain, terror, and dread dropped over him, smothering and hot.

Elegy lay beneath his trapped shoulder. Shay reached for her, scrabbling at her harness, twisting it to bring her within reach. His shoulder tore with every small movement.

Tauz burned the back of his head, dripped flame into his body. He could feel smaller points of stone pushing into his head, his shoulders, his buttocks . . .

He panicked, thrashing. His head pulled free, but his fingers and shoulder remained trapped. He couldn't reach Elegy with his free hand. He had to, to live. But he couldn't.

Desperation flooded him with energy. Focus on Elegy. Ignore all else. Shay twisted himself toward her haft. Her smooth coolness soothed his palm as his shoulder tore. He closed his hand, swung her up toward Tarver.

The assassin stepped casually out of reach of the ineffectual blow. Bright, glassy eyes filled with lust, Tarver laughed at Shay's painful efforts. The diamond bit clunked back down, shattering and enraging tiny crystals.

The laughter infuriated Shay and increased his helplessness. Tarver had only to wait.

But he held Elegy in his hand, at last. He smashed her into the tauz he could reach, forehand and back, frenzied by fear.

The tauz beneath rose up in battle voice, singing discordant songs in his bones. He felt the piercings in arms and legs, anywhere he touched crystal. Screaming in fear and anger, he smashed as much crystal as he could reach with the axe, while Tarver stood out of range and watched, the corner of his mouth twitched up in amusement.

The roar of anger nearly deafened him. The crystals seemed to rise up, hovering, trying to enfold him.

Why couldn't he release more power from Elegy? Why didn't more crystals give way?

Intent. He needed to stop this wild flailing, focus on

what he wanted from the axe.

Tarver laughed louder, reaching for Elegy.

Just as the gloved hand started to close around her, Shay slipped her bit sideways out of reach, struck the glove with her knob.

Tarver jerked his hand back with a curse.

Shay slammed the knob down right next to his imprisoned fingers, smashing and smashing. He shifted his grip to her throat for direct control of her head.

Then he chopped. The next strike came dangerously close to fingers he couldn't see for the blood rolling into his eyes.

The tauz voice changed.

Squeals of rage, of hatred, of pain, screeching like rusty nails pulled from tight wood–the assault audible only to him stirred his brain and scrambled it.

On the edge of insanity, Shay caught his breath as his fingers pulled free of the crystal, bloody, but whole.

He gritted his teeth to hold in a scream as he forced himself to his feet and the golden dagger ripped free of his flesh.

His boots gave him a barrier. The voices muted suddenly–not gone, but with less access to him. He spun toward Tarver–and ran into a gloved fist.

Blood sprayed from his nose as he dropped back onto the bed of tauz. He rolled, giving no crystal a chance to pierce and trap.

Back up to his feet. Elegy in hand. The thick soles of his boots muffled golden voices.

That strange thing in Tarver's hand–a wire? Circular, with two short handles, one in each hand. What on earth? A garrotte, perhaps?

Sickened, Shay couldn't look away from the deadly loop.

Tarver, watching him, laughed, backed up by nervous chuckles from the two men with him. "Lovely, isn't it, Bladen?" Tarver's voice dropped into a croon, eyes bright and glistening. "It works well on hands, feet, throat . . . You should see what it does to a fully engorged penis. One of my favorite toys."

Shay took an awkward grip on Elegy's haft. She was too heavy for one hand, but his left arm refused to help. He tried for a proper stance, but the tauz made poor footing. Dizziness swept through him.

With no hope of winning here, outnumbered and battered, he prepared to run.

The tauz he stood on prickled, seeking a way through boots to flesh. Tarver's men stood between him and his horse.

He had to get away from the crystals. Tarver couldn't hear the tauz voices, but Shay could. They would drive him insane, drink his blood, absorb his flesh–and he couldn't fight the stones and the men at the same time.

He needed a distraction.

What the hell? His enemies didn't know what the dazzling crystals could do. He could use that, should have thought of it earlier.

He turned and walked away from Tarver, deeper into the crystal canyons.

"Leave the axe, Bladen. It's mine now, and you know it. Lay it on the ground and keep moving, and I'll allow you to live."

Shay stopped and turned briefly. "No. It's mine. You want her? Come get her." He kept walking. *Now why the hell did I say that? I don't want to fight him. Not here. Not without Bibi to help me.*

Behind him, he heard running footsteps. Too light for Tarver.

He whirled, dropped Elegy on the ground near his foot. The man reached for him. He caught the arm and used it to throw the attacker at a pillar.

The thug put out a hand to catch himself, then screamed as it sank into the golden crystal.

Let the tauz have his blood.

Shay ducked under the second man's arm and bodily slammed him head-first into the remains of the grandfather pillar that had trapped Bibi.

The screams had already started when he turned away and picked up his axe. He looked for Spark, who whinnied in fear and pain from the pricking tauz crystals.

Shay darted toward him.

Tarver moved to cut him off.

He spun, swinging wildly at Tarver to slow him down. Three seconds, with Elegy's help, and the ropes fell from the horse's legs. He tucked Elegy between his injured arm and his body, pulled himself up clumsily with one arm. He clucked Spark into motion even before he landed across leather, belly down, and hung on for dear life.

Tarver grabbed the reins of another horse. and threw himself into the saddle, legs flailing as he spurred it after Spark.

But Shay had a head start and a fast horse. Tarver cursed viciously as he gave up the chase. Shay sent a quick prayer of thanksgiving to the Light at last.

The pillars would gorge on flesh and blood today. Human flesh. Men he had deliberately fed to the crystals. He cringed.

And then, with no emergency to distract him, the burning, blazing pain of his injuries made themselves known.

39. Refuge

Tarver laughed. "Idiot!" What could be funnier than someone standing stupidly with his hand stuck in tauz, mouth open and eyes wide, dancing on tiptoe?

"You let him take you by surprise," he yelled at the victim. "How could you *not* stop a man hurt so bad he could barely stand?" Irritation and amusement mingled.

Irritation won. "Ah, hell! You want to wait a couple days for me to get back? Or shall I release you now?" He snapped his wire loop like a belt. "It'll be quick, and you'll be free. You can manage with only one hand, right? Choose, Cawby!"

Tarver cut his eyes toward the second man. Lost cause, that one. He'd hit the pillar head first, and most of his upper body had disappeared inside the giant crystal as he watched, fascinated.

Who would have thought tauz could eat people?

He turned away, shaking his head in disgust. He'd have to find a few more men before heading to Echo, maybe a dozen. The warrior woman would be there, as well as Bladen; it could be a hard fight.

The axe would be his so soon he could almost taste it!

"I choose! I choose! You can't leave me here!"

He'd almost forgotten Cawby. Pitiful man. It would serve him right to be left alone until someone else came along. But no, he'd offered him a choice.

What difference did it make how he died?

He strode over to the man hanging helplessly from the pillar. He separated the loop ends so he could pass the loop around Cawby's wrist, rejoined the ends, and with a quick jerk of the wrists snapped the loop closed.

Cawby screamed and fell, blood spurting from the

stump. The hand itself disappeared into the tauz. Amazing.

Tarver watched for a moment, fascinated, then started for his horse.

"Stop the bleeding! Stop the bleeding! Before I die," Cawby screeched in hysteria.

The assassin glanced back to where Cawby sat on the ground, desperately trying to hold his wrist closed while blood sprayed across his face, his shirt, the ground–where it disappeared instantly into the crystal beds.

"I only promised to free you from the crystal, not to save your life. You're on your own for that." Tarver mounted, Cawby's screams and curses licking deliciously at his belly, and below–the seat of his sweetest appetites. He strained his ears to hear over the hoofbeats as long as he could, as the cries became weaker and more desperate.

At least he'd salvaged something from this debacle. He smiled, upper lip curling, and spurred his horse.

Shay rode hard, teeth gritted against pain and light-headedness. Tarver would soon find a way to break the pillars and free his men, but the necessity would make him furious. Shay had only one chance—to reach Echo before the thugs caught up with him.

Spark swerved slightly beneath him. The motion kept him in the saddle when dizziness would have dropped him from it. Fear flashed through him. If he'd fallen, maybe caught a foot in the stirrup . . . He hung onto the pommel as hard as he could, but blood slicked his fingers. A whimper crawled up out of his throat and he swallowed it again.

He didn't have to stop at Echo. He could be in Sarinta in three days. Bibi would surely make short work of Tarver and the men he had left. The assassin wasn't as fearsome face to face, being most dangerous behind his victim's back. Bibi was Sheethe, for the Light's sake! She probably had more knowledge and skill in her little finger than Tarver had in his whole body. And she had the rubellia.

He did *not* want to face Tarver. His meager skills would not be enough, and his injuries left him in no condition for a fight. The man made his stomach crawl and cramp. Fear would interfere with his abilities; he'd never survive this time. Just the thought of Tarver's casual cruelty almost loosened his bowels. Waves of cold rolled up and down his body and he caught himself breathing in short, hard gasps, on the verge of panic.

What have I told you about your imagination, Shay? He closed his eyes and took several deep, slow breaths before opening them again.

Right and wrong mattered. Honor and integrity mattered. Friends mattered even more, being in shorter supply. Would Bibi flee rather than risk herself to a madman? Would Locelar? Or Atich or Robayne?

Shay laughed, one short, explosive sound. He had more friends than he realized, more people he could count on than he'd ever dreamed.

Taking a deep, slow breath, he sent Spark flying toward Echo, clutching the pommel to keep his seat.

He'd never been so glad to enter the mountain caldron where Echo nestled. Even Spark increased his speed, until Shay, doubled over the pommel, pulled up in front of Bibi's tavern.

One of Bibi's regulars saw him first and reached him well before Meilin. Strong hands caught Shay as he started to tilt. Grateful, Shay let go, sliding from the saddle.

"Meilin! Tell Bibi Bladen's injured, then go get Ansel!" The man's voice snapped like a whip and Meilin scurried to do his bidding.

At least for the moment, Shay didn't have to do anything, say anything, be responsible for anything. Or anyone.

The man eased him to the ground, murmuring reassurances Shay paid no attention to.

Bibi's voice rang out in the background. "Spinel! Take care of the horse!"

Spinel here? Again? He heard footsteps, then Spark's hooves tapping the dusty street as someone led him away. *My axe!* But he couldn't get the words out.

"Get him indoors," Bibi commanded. She turned in a different direction. "Metchal! Push some tables together for us."

No one could disobey the command in her voice, not even a customer. Shay turned his head toward The Amyth Cup, where early evening customers crowded out the doors to see. Their faces seemed to be swimming in a pool of water. The world darkened, as if the Eye had gone behind a cloud, then darkened again.

He had to warn them, if his tongue would just work. No, no! Not yet! He resisted the Dark with all his might, but it swallowed him up . . . and when he opened his eyes, everything had changed.

"Where am I?" Even as the words whispered from his throat, he reoriented, working outward from himself. Bed. Room. Indoors. People. Bibi. Ansel. The Amyth Cup. He'd made it.

Pain. *That* hadn't gone away. He closed his teeth over a groan. Sharp, ugly pain in his back and shoulder.

Memory stung and he tried to sit up. Strong hands pushed him back into soft pillows. "I have to . . ."

"Easy, Shay. Rest a while yet. There will be time later to tell us what happened." Ansel's voice carried a soothing, professional tone.

"No." He forced his voice stronger. "Warning. Bibi?"

"Let him speak, Ansel. He will rest no more until he

357

tells us." The warm, chocolate voice rich as cream brought comfort. Bibi was here. Everything would be all right.

He tried again to sit up, and this time Ansel's strong arm behind his shoulders helped lift him into position. Someone stuffed pillows and folded blankets under his shoulders and head.

"Ansel, if you would be kind, please let Meilin know that Bladen will be fine."

"Of course, Bibi. You know the use of these salves and medicines, but please send word if you need me. Shay, speak briefly, then rest. The body will heal itself if allowed to do so." The hairless man gazed at Shay earnestly from skystone eyes before departing.

As soon as the door closed, Bibi asked, "What warning, Shay?"

Something was missing. His gaze began to search the bed, the walls, the corners of the room. "My axe!"

"It is here, next to the bed. What warning?"

Shay relaxed again, though he would rather hold Elegy in his hand. "Tarver. He and a band of thugs attacked the Blue Mountain People. Many died, but he escaped with two of his men. He left me a message. He's coming here! He'll kill all of my friends if I don't give him the axe."

"You will not do that," Bibi said. "Tell me the rest."

He did, in detail. It took a while.

Damn that bitch! Spinel scrubbed a plate so hard it shattered in his hands. Twice damned! She'd add the cost of the plate to his debt, a ploy to keep him enslaved forever. He slammed the largest remaining piece against the edge of the basin. Shards flew about the kitchen.

Now he'd have to clean up the mess, which would involve emptying the basin of both water and ceramic shards, reheating water, and being careful with the

358

remaining crockery. Unless he wanted to slice himself up washing dishes.

He crossed his arms atop the basin and laid his head on them, just for a moment. And damn her again. Enforced sobriety didn't suit him at all. Nausea, sweating, a body that wouldn't stop trembling–he'd never been so miserable. He'd been accidentally sober before and he didn't like it much. He drank for a reason! He just couldn't remember what it was right now.

After the fight in Blue Mountain, he'd gone for the strongest drink he could find. He knew Tarver had a mean streak, but to see him murder a child as if she meant nothing . . . His stomach curdled. That scene played over and over every waking moment. Not the children! Not the innocent! He'd had to get out of there, but he hadn't meant to bring that horror with him.

The betrayal on the little girl's face. . . . . . adults were supposed to take care of children, to play with them and protect them and soothe their fears.

Funny, how sometimes Tarver seemed to wear Father's face.

Sometimes only Cinny had stood between him and Father's wrath. Father would never hurt her, his favorite. And Spinel had done some stupid things, even hurtful things, when goaded, but he had never harmed a living being deliberately. As Father had so often told him, he needed to toughen up, to be a man.

Oh, how he missed his sister!

Spinel's tears dropped into the cooling water beneath his crossed arms. It hurt! Getting sober was hell! He had headaches all the time, and his body trembled enough that his balance seemed just out of reach. His hands shook visibly, forcing him to take extra care with eating and cooking utensils.

359

Worst of all, he remembered all his idiocy.

What had he been thinking, to tell Tarver about the magic axe? Now the man was obsessed. And why would he ever have gone with Tarver's thugs to Cinny's home in the middle of the night, just because Tarver said so? Other than being scared to his toes of him. The picture that lurked always in the back of his head was Cinny's throat opening, her head falling back, the gush of blood.

Spinel scrabbled through the cupboards, desperate for something to drink.

And the children! Who could do that to little ones? He'd played with those children, taught them, enjoyed their delight at little things–Piper's first word, Beryl struggling to say the names of stones. Children always accepted, never judged, the only pure things in the world.

Sweat oozed out of every pore. He found no drink in the kitchen. Shaking, he carried the basin outside to clean and refill from the kettle kept simmering in the kitchen fireplace.

Then there was Meilin, a good boy who loved to talk to him–under Bibi's watchful eye–about gems and the toad in the tomato patch and other little boy things. Who asked Spinel *first* to help him dig a small stone from his pony's shoe. A constant thorn in his side, with his questions and boisterousness and playful tricks. And easier to be around than the adults.

By the time Bibi came into the kitchen, no sign of a broken dish could be seen. He'd heard her soft steps in time to be working hard when she entered.

He thought every day about running again. But except for forbidding alcohol–in a tavern!–and working him too hard, Bibi treated him fairly. The Amyth Cup seemed a safe place for him, and he hadn't found many of those. For now, at least, he'd stay.

Besides, Tarver couldn't find him here. He'd throw up if Tarver ever looked at him again.

Tarver. Murderer of children. Spinel shuddered.

"Spinel! Guess what!" Meilin's voice dragged Spinel from the muck of his misery. The boy burst into the kitchen, shining with excitement and joy.

How could so much goodness be tucked into such a small package? Spinel felt his lips curve up into a smile, despite himself. "What?" It was the response children expected, and he always gave it.

"Bladen's back! They had to carry him inside, and I ran to get Ansel, but he's already gone, and there's blood all over him!"

Children loved being the first to bring news. Spinel had to chuckle, even while his stomach turned over. "It's a good thing you were there, then. You run like the wind! What happened to him?"

"I don't know, but he said something about a warning. Bibi's with him now."

Opportunity presented itself. With Bibi occupied, he could sneak a quick drink from the well-supplied bar.

And set back the whole process of sobering up. He'd spend even more time being miserable. Even if Bibi never found out.

He spoke without giving himself time to think about it. "Want to go for a walk, Meilin? I saw a snake down by the riverbank this morning. And you can tell me every detail about Shay's arrival." Not that he wanted to hear about it. He wanted nothing to do with Shay.

But he did enjoy spending time with Meilin. And he needed the distraction.

"Come on! Maybe it's still there!" Meilin reversed direction.

Diverting a child was so easy. Even Meilin, the most

adult child Spinel had ever met. He left his apron in a heap by the sink and followed him out the door.

40. The Finish

Whatever the medications Ansel had left for him, Shay wanted no more of them. They made the room tilt if he moved his head too quickly. In the quiet of the darkened room, he sat up, holding in a groan. If the salves and potions under the bandages dulled the pain in his shoulder, back, and fingers, he couldn't tell it. He hadn't even been able to sleep.

Tarver was coming. He knew it. Why wasn't he here yet?

The delay presented a different type of battle, one Shay had little training to handle. The murderer had chosen fear as his weapon, and he seemed as skilled with this one as with so many others. In his absence, fear kept Shay awake, every small sound translated into a stealthy footfall or the soft slithering of sword from sheath.

He couldn't stand it. The darkness hid him, the room confined him. He had to see for himself to calm his nerves. Moving slowly, hands trembling with weakness, he eased off the side of the bed, bare feet noiseless against the cool floor. Prudently, he kept one hand on bed or wall as he pulled on trousers and shoved his feet into his boots, his movements slow and careful. The wobble in his legs shouldn't have surprised him, given how much the room moved even when he lay still. He picked up Elegy.

Stepping into the hall, he pulled the door behind him slowly enough to produce only a tiny click as it caught.

The door across from his opened a crack, revealing Bibi's obsis eyes above a sword held vertically before her.

He should have known she would be guarding him.

"Bibi?" said a sleepy male voice behind her.

Her eyes disappeared as she spoke over her shoulder.

"It is nothing. Go back to sleep."

One corner of Shay's lips quirked up in amusement.

A similar quirk in Bibi's answered. "He is too pretty to pass up," she murmured, glancing back. She stepped into the hall and closed the door. "Why are you out of bed?"

"I can't sleep. I thought Tarver would have been here hours ago."

"May I bring you warm milk?"

Shay shook his head. "No, thank you." He started for the stairs, one hand on the wall.

Bibi went with him, offering unspoken support if he needed it, without touching him.

From the front walkway, the town appeared silent and dark. Shay heard crickets and the tiny frogs from the lake behind the town, nothing else. A candle flickered in someone's window near the center of town, if he could rely on his vision. Questionable, that.

Beside him, Bibi tensed. "Stay here!" She leaped from the board walkway, her voice a ferocious shout loud enough to wake the town. "Fire! Fire! All out to fight the fire!"

Other townspeople joined her as she ran.

Then the male guests upstairs clattered down, some still tying their britches, most shirtless. Last out to help came Spinel. He hesitated when he saw Shay, then paused.

"Meilin's behind me," he said. "Don't let him run after us. He could be hurt." He ran on.

Meilin burst out the door then, already at full speed. Shay lunged, managed to stop him as his shoulder tore open again and his knees buckled.

"Shay!" Instantly Meilin reached for him, eyes wide. "I'm so sorry! Are you okay?"

The boy tried to catch him! Shay found his balance. "Stay with me. Bibi's orders."

"But . . ." Meilin stared down the street, toward the

screams, the popping of wood, the frantic efforts of the townspeople to fight the fire.

"Bibi's orders," Shay repeated. "She wants both of us here, where we'll be safe and she won't be distracted."

Almost dancing in excitement and agitation, Meilin obeyed. "I understand," he said. "You're safe with me, Bladen."

Shay held his smile inside. Had the boy really grown so much, in so little time? He leaned back against the tavern wall for balance. How much would Beryl have changed by now? Would Piper have lost the freckles that distinguished her from Cinnabar? Would Cinny have found her first silver hair by now?

His eyes blurred, filled by pain and exhaustion—and the deep well of grief that underlay his life.

Down the street, the sounds changed. A new, metallic sound, slender and bright, underlay the roar of flames. The screams intensified, became panicked.

Swords. Tarver had arrived. Even through blurred vision, Shay glimpsed the silhouette of blades against the flames, the flickering of their rise and fall.

Without thinking he launched himself toward the battle. "Stay here, Meilin!" He lifted Elegy from his side to clasp her with both hands as he ran, ignoring the pain in his cut-up fingers.

But his shoulder stabbed pain through his upper body, even through the sudden thrust of battle energy. He stumbled and nearly fell. The weight of the axe was too much for his wounded side. He dropped his left hand from the haft.

He forced his grip tighter on the eight-pound axe, to be sure he didn't drop her.

The attackers had been watching for him. He knew it by the way their heads turned to one man, who lifted an arm

365

high and brought it down.

They left off their slaughter and converged on Shay.

He changed course, set his back to the wall of a small pottery shop, and faced them.

A man on the left feinted in and Shay took one step toward him, Elegy poised in his hand. The swordsman's stroke knocked Elegy out of the way, pulling Shay off balance. He threw himself to one side to avoid the blow.

He landed in the dirt of the street, choked on a small cloud of it. He rolled sideways and back up.

He'd already left the wall. Bibi would have his hide for that–if he still had one after this. Six men surrounded him, two laughing, and the others grim-faced and focused.

Using both hands, he muscled through broad, clumsy strokes of the axe, his shoulder tearing with every strike. He couldn't control Elegy's heavy head, even with his hold choked high on the haft.

Swords slashed down at him. One cut across the muscle of his calf, another nicked his hairline as he rolled again.

Too close. Shay invoked Elegy's power and dropped her cheek onto the attacker's foot. The blow had no momentum. Her shoulder struck, not her bit, but blue veins crackled audibly on contact. The man screamed and fell as the magic severed half his foot.

The screaming didn't stop as Shay climbed back to his feet, dragging Elegy with him. He swung at another sword.

Agony shot downward from shoulder to ankle, but he had no time for it. He spoke to Elegy with his hands and his intent.

She answered, blue veins of magic rippling her length, leaving light echoes on his hands. He touched her to the nearest attacker and the man died, a horrible charred wound in his chest.

Then he stopped thinking entirely. Elegy swung again and again, dealing pain and death. He focused on seeing what came at him, let the rest go. A distant awareness of pain provided a background to the full-throated roar of flames, the splashing of water, the cries, and flurry of movement all around him.

He had no choice.

A woman screamed almost in his ear and he whirled. A middle-aged widow held her new-dead husband on his feet, fell with him as his body crumpled to the dirt.

Beyond her, a man with a pitchfork forced someone backwards until he fell into the fire. He rolled up and ran, screaming and wrapped in flame. No one moved to help him.

Once he caught a glimpse of Spinel, carrying buckets of water. Someone took the buckets from him, threw the water on the fire and handed them back, reached for full buckets from the next man.

A sharp whistle cut the air. Attackers melted away until only one remained, backing away as Shay pressed the attack. Fear rolled in the man's eyes. He stumbled with every step, desperation drenching his face in sweat.

If he stopped pressing, the man would turn and run. Shay knew it, read it in his body's language. He should stop, let him go. But he wasn't in a forgiving mood.

He forced his shoulder to hold, ignored the igniting damage there, and chased the man around the corner of the potter's shop.

The man spun toward him and ducked low. Shay braced to be struck in the knees. But his attacker twisted to the side, rolled once, and ran. Shay started to go after him.

"Are you sure you want to do that?"

Shock laced down Shay's spine at the low grating of Tarver's voice. He spun toward it, Elegy shielding his body.

Tarver glowed in the flickering flames now a block behind them. The shadows gave his face an ugly twist.

He held a large, steel knife pressed lightly against Meilin's throat.

Meilin's eyes squeezed tight, tears leaking from beneath child-length eyelashes. He trembled visibly, even in the darkness.

Shay attended to his peripheral vision. Flickers of light from the town revealed he stood in a flat area strewn with blocks and shavings of wood. Iron hoops leaned against the building and the rich, moist odor of new-sawn oak tickled his nose. Behind the cooper's shop, then. That black square shutting off faint stars must be the toolshed. Who knew what tools and barrel parts lay scattered across the ground to catch an unwary foot?

Then his full attention returned to Tarver, and anger roared up in him like the blazing town. He saw again his children's throats opening, felt his hair rising in horror. The memory twisted his stomach.

But Shay was no longer the same man. This time would be different.

This time had to be different.

"Let the child go, Tarver. He's not part of this." He poured every jot of fury, of diamond-hard determination into the words. This time his voice didn't squeak at the end.

Tarver's laugh frosted Shay's heart. "He is now. I'll trade him for the axe, Bladen. Do we have a deal? Or would you rather fight me for him?"

"The axe? What will you do? Hang it on a wall and admire it? It's too heavy to be that useful in battle."

"I've seen the magic, Bladen! Which do you want more–the axe or the boy?"

"The magic won't work for you, Tarver. Only for me."

Was that movement behind Tarver? Must be his

imagination.

Tarver's laugh wrenched the air. "You'll have to teach me how to use the magic, of course. The boy will remain mine until then. And my, isn't he going to be fun to play with tonight! Of course, tomorrow there will be less of him to trade."

Meilin whimpered.

There it was again, that hint of movement. An ally, perhaps? Or another of Tarver's men?

Shay shut down his imagination. He'd seen too much of Tarver's handiwork already. "It's the bloodline, Tarver. I'm the only one who can invoke the magic."

"Liar!" Tarver's elbow jerked with the knife's slice.

Horror slashed through Shay.

Tarver's elbow flew up, hard, and the blade scraped down the front of Meilin's chest, instead of across his throat.

Spinel! Here?

The drunk staggered back, tipsy. "Oops! Sorry, old friend. I was coming up to help and lost my balance for a second." He swayed on his feet. "Here, let me . . ."

Tarver's knife swung in a backhand arc, the thick blade imbedding deep in Spinel's skull.

Cinny's brother dropped without a sound as Shay moved.

Tarver released the knife. His hands slammed into Meilin's head with pressure just short of crushing. Meilin screamed.

Shay froze in mid-step.

"If you want the child to live, lay the axe on the ground and back away." Tarver increased the pressure on Meilin's skull until the child whimpered with every breath.

Frantic, Shay squatted and laid Elegy down, never taking his gaze from Tarver. Not Meilin. He couldn't lose this child, too.

"Stay strong, Meilin," he said. "I'm still here." He backed away, one step, then another.

Big hands pressing against Meilin's skull, Tarver stepped forward as Shay stepped back. When he reached Elegy, he squatted slowly, pulling Meilin with him.

"Run along, little boy. I'll catch up with you later and we'll play without interference." He shoved Meilin hard toward Shay, snatched up the axe, and backed away fast.

Meilin's impact knocked Shay off balance. Pain knifed through his shoulder. He caught the sobbing child and gave him a quick hug. "Stay right here, Meilin, and stay strong. We're almost done."

He released the boy and walked toward his enemy, the source of all his grief and anger and despair, the destroyer of his perfect life.

"Tarver, wait. The magic . . ."

Tarver stopped. "Tell me."

"It's in the grip, in the way you hold her." He took two steps toward his enemy.

"No closer! Tell me from there."

"What are you worried about? You have a magic battle-axe. I have no weapon at all. You're a skilled murderer. I'm a shopkeeper." Shay spread his hands wide, took two more steps, slow and as unthreatening as he could make them.

"I'm also no fool, Bladen. Stop there. Tell me."

Shay stopped. Ten feet away, not far enough to keep him safe and not close enough to put Tarver at risk. His heart hammered his ribs so hard he thought one of them might break. "Okay, just take a normal grip and we'll start there."

Wary and suspicious, eyes narrowed, Tarver gripped the axe with both hands. "And . . .?"

"Hands closer. No, no. The bottom hand has to completely engulf the knob." Shay limped forward a few cautious steps, stretching out his hands. In the flickering light, his enemy's long, powerful fingers looked like claws.

Tarver glanced at his hands, adjusted the left one.

"Almost. Here. May I . . .?"

Tarver's quick glance gave tacit permission and Shay took one last, lopsided step, closed his right hand over Tarver's. Keeping his gaze riveted on Tarver's hands, he reached his left for Elegy's bare haft.

Now! He threw his desire into the axe with the entire force of his being.

Her song rose in his head, powerful and thrilling, making his bones ache. Electricity sizzled through him. Every hair on his body stood on end as he felt the rise toward orgasm. Blue veins along her length thickened until she was solid blue, knob to eye.

He heard Tarver's gasp of surprise and pleasure . . .

. . . and released Elegy's power.

The explosion knocked him from his feet. His head snapped back against hard ground. Dazed, he struggled to sit up. He still held Tarver's hand against Elegy's knob, but the rest of him wasn't there.

Shay hastily released the charred hand and let it fall away. Scrambling to his feet, he searched for Tarver. He had to be sure.

He stumbled twice against something on the ground before looking down. In the blue light of the still-glowing axe, he saw a blackened leg.

Elegy's exultant song soared in triumph, reaching toward the climactic moment, taking him with her. His body trembled with need, with desire. But first . . .

He found Tarver's lower body, then his upper body. He wanted to throw up but had no chance. Joined with Elegy, his body's reactions soared out of his control. Without looking back to where Meilin waited, Shay stumbled into the darkness, felt the rising orgasm, and hid behind a shed just in time.

His body exploded, joy and rapture, lust and excitement pounding through him. The ecstasy of power, of victory, the sweetness of Elegy's song. His orgasm seemed to last forever, until finally he rolled over Elegy's light, holding her like a lover beneath his body. At last he began to come down. Her light faded with him, until darkness wrapped him and his beloved Elegy into a soft, warm cocoon. He slept.

41. Transition

Shay swam up out of layers of undulating darkness. *Where am I?* But his tongue seemed as immobile as the rest of his body. He couldn't get oriented.

"Be calm," said an elegant, chocolate voice. "There is no hurry. The danger is past, and you may take your time. All is well."

Bibi, his anchor. He clung to her voice. Darkness faded. Somewhere above he saw light.

"Will he be okay?" Meilin, anxious and worried.

"He will be fine, with time and care."

"Go on to bed now and allow us to tend him." Robayne's voice.

A door opened and closed before Bibi spoke again.

"His wounds are severe. I have sent Atich to Sarinta with gold to buy what help may be available. He may be able to procure a magical item to bring Shay back to wholeness."

Atich had come to Echo?

"He will bear scars, however, little ones that few will notice, with a large one down his back from a sword slice. The stab wound through his shoulder will be the worst, most likely puckered and tight. Magic will be needed for that shoulder to heal well."

Silence. Shay felt cool air as she pulled back the blanket covering him.

Robayne chuckled. "He's never going to be pretty again."

Bibi snorted. "With magical assistance, perhaps. But to a real woman, one who appreciates a man from the inside out, he has the look of courage, of a hero born, of the manliest of men."

"Ah, well." Robayne breathed out from the toes up. "He may have been born for battle, but I wasn't. I've had enough battle for a lifetime, myself."

Robayne said something else, but Shay lost his grip on the paler darkness and slid softly down the billowing folds of sleep once again.

Pain greeted Shay when the sound of his own moans woke him.

"Hush, warrior. The enemy will hear you. The name of your enemy is Death. Hide from him, taunt him by living."

Bibi's voice again. How long had he been elsewhere? He wanted to ask, but could form no coherent words, even in the privacy of his mind.

Dim light filtered into the room. He found thoughts, if not words. Bibi was wrong. The Dark was already giving way to the Light.

"All will be well."

Soothing, rich chocolate. He'd tasted chocolate once, but he couldn't remember where. At a gathering of gem merchants of some kind?

He listened to Bibi as he always did, closed his mouth to hold the moans inside–or at least to muffle them.

A light breeze touched him as she lifted the blanket. It had to be Bibi. No one else was here, right?

Hard, calloused hands probed his shoulder, half turned him and poked at the searing pain of his back. Strength held him on his side as a cool, gelatinous something was applied generously to the long slice down his back and the tauz entry point.

Shay clenched his teeth to hold in screams. It almost worked, until she laid him on his back again and applied the substance to the front of the stab wound. Then sound poured out of him in uncontrollable waves.

374

He lay shuddering, chills drenching his bare skin, and finally drifted back into the pillows of sleep to the refrain, "All will be well, my hero. All will be well."

"Light! Look at this mess! How did you keep him alive?" Atich's voice.

Shay opened his eyes, but they fluttered, unable to make out the faces above him, and dropped again. But he knew the voices.

"He is very strong, and his will to live is most admirable."

Was that Bibi? Her voice had degenerated to gravel and scratches and slurred words.

"What did you bring us?" she asked.

"This."

"A vial? And so small. What does it contain?"

Shay flicked his eyes open again, this time seeing faces that wavered like rising flames. He blinked twice, reaching for the world again.

"The distilled essence of mouse breath. Mix two drops in a cup of water and pour it over the wounds to destroy the infection. Repeat every two hours, as long as the essence lasts. He has more, if I can afford it. I should have taken more gold and gems."

"Mouse breath?"

"Apparently it's a tiny flower that grows in the tall grass."

"Is it magic? Or a natural part of the flower?"

Atich's usually mild voice turned impatient. "Does it matter? Apply the damned stuff before those sourced wounds kill him."

Even in pain and half-conscious, Shay recognized the chill in Bibi's silence. He heard the uncomfortable shuffle of Atich's feet.

375

"Get some rest." Bibi's words dripped icicles. "Return when you can stand without falling over. I will care for him."

This time Atich sounded contrite. "Have you slept at all since I left, Bibi? I can watch a while."

"I am Sheethe, and your assumption of my weakness offends me. Go!"

Shay wanted to say something to Atich, but he couldn't think what, not even after his cousin's footsteps faded and the door closed.

He would speak to Bibi instead. But his eyelids fell and he slid away again.

Mouse breath had to be magic, Shay decided. After days hovering over the inescapable darkness, he awoke to light and air, eyes focused properly and his mind clear. He could just make out the room's occupants through his eyelashes.

Bibi, on the other hand, looked like a wild animal–disheveled, her ferocious eyes dangerous. She smelled, too, and not in the pleasant, feminine way of a woman in her prime.

"You need to rest, Bibi," said Robayne. His tone said this discussion had been going on for a while already. He stood just inside the door, whether to avoid the potent odors of bodies and illness, or Bibi's wrath.

Shay drifted, thinking, she's being stubborn. A stubborn Bibi will never move.

Her rich voice had disintegrated to dull and hoarse, her charred complexion paled to dark brown. Only the stubborn set of her jaw and the warrior's flame in her eyes hadn't changed.

The door at Robayne's back opened and he moved aside to let Ansel enter.

"Ansel, can you get her to go get some rest? Convince her we're not incompetent to care for Shay in her absence?"

"I don't care if she rests or not, but she reeks. Bibi, you need a bath. Shay will be fine with us for a little while." Ansel's voice sounded almost jovial, compared to Shay's friends.

She glared, but after a moment rose to her feet and placed a cool, dry hand on Shay's brow. "Are you with us, Shay? Have you returned to us at last, or are you pretending again?" Her smile didn't quite reach her lips, let alone her eyes.

"I'm here." His voice rasped like used sandpaper. "All is well, Bibi. It's your turn to rest. I'll still be here." He'd meant more than the words spoken, but weariness obscured his intent.

Her stumping walk and bent posture bespoke too much sitting, too little activity. Robayne made the mistake of taking her elbow to help her toward the door. He should have known better, no matter her exhaustion. Shay's chuckle was only in his mind.

Robayne grinned as the door closed behind Bibi and Ansel. "I don't envy you that one, Shay! She's a she-bear in early spring. For all her competence, though, I notice I'm the one who gets to clean you up. Again."

When she had gone, a brigade of family brought steaming water buckets. Atich, Locelar, and assorted cousins and uncles.

Maybe that hadn't been Bibi he smelled, only himself. Robayne had to assist him from the bed into the water, then help scrub him when his own hands shook from weakness. Then the tub was refilled and he washed again, his movements slow, half-crippled and clumsy. While he bathed, Robayne remade his bed with clean sheets.

All the bucket bearers stayed to visit while he washed,

to his consternation, but they told him much of the aftermath of the battle. He heard the names of the dead in Echo and those who succumbed in Blue Mountain after his departure. Raw heart exposed, he wept for the losses.

"The People *and* the town have survived," Locelar told him. "Some of us have offered to help the townsmen rebuild from the fire. Some of them have offered to help us rebuild, too. Of course, the Council is wrangling about whether to allow that, and Orlait is at the center of the resistance to change."

Shay said, "Tell Orlait to let them in. They are good people, and no one can afford to refuse friendship with the good folk of this earth."

Robayne chuckled, but Locelar laughed aloud. "Clearly, you're aware the hero will be denied nothing he asks."

"It won't last long. I'll have to make demands quickly, before anyone realizes I brought the threat I saved them from."

An uncle on his mother's side spoke up. "Are you sure it's wise to open the doors to Blue Mountain after all these years? We have much to lose to the greedy and untrustworthy, after all. I'd hate to see another attack like that one."

"Echo has its own wealth, Uncle. But never have its people denied us access to its crops and goods, as if afraid we'd strip them of all they own, given the chance."

"But gems seem to bring out a special greed in men– gems and precious metals. Nothing else inspires such a desire to *own*."

"Would we strip their fields if we were starving? No. We'd barter or purchase. Why do you think them less honest and less honorable than we are?"

Voices piled up quickly, and Shay ducked under the

water to rinse soap from his hair.

". . . for another time," Locelar was saying as he emerged. "For now, let it be."

"How long have I been . . . ill?" Shay asked, changing the subject. Already weariness weighted his shoulders and he wanted to rest.

"Forever," said Robayne. "Never knew a Bladen so lazy." The grin looked more relieved than friendly.

"All of Echo's funerals have been held, then?" Shay felt his gut tighten in dread. He had to know about Cinny's brother, but he couldn't bring himself to ask directly. That little bastard had gotten Cinny killed, and both children. Still, the last moments of his truncated life were so clear in Shay's memory . . . if he could trust it.

"Yes," said Locelar. "Tarver and his men are buried in a mass grave covered by heaps of rock, well out of town."

Including Spinel?

One of the cousins spoke up, awe in his voice. "We're not sure we got all of Tarver. I can't even imagine what could do that to a man! Bits and pieces everywhere!"

"Where's my axe?" Shay swiveled his head in a frantic search. How had he not remembered her before now?

"Easy, Shay," said Robayne. "No one has touched it–or wanted to."

"Where?"

Robayne walked to the foot of the bed and retrieved Elegy from the space between bed and wall, gripping her carefully by her leather.

Shay's breath blew out in a rush. "Did you clean her up? Is she all right?"

"Yes, and yes. I'm going to put it back now, and you can tell me if you want it again."

"Anyway," Locelar said, as if continuing the cousin's conversation, "there is a mass grave. With a sign posted, carved into sturdy oak."

"'Here lie evil men,'" intoned the cousin, "'foolish enough to defy Bladen and his axe.'"

Already people's memories were adjusting to the long-standing folk tale of Bladen. Shay realized nothing he said would change that, so he let it go. "I think I'm clean enough for a nap."

"Bibi won't be gone long," said Robayne, "and we're better off being gone on her return."

Shay asked for Meilin when he woke again. He didn't ask about Bibi, whose chair remained empty. She would return when rested and clean, a fact he didn't question.

By the time the door opened for the boy, Shay sat propped against pillows. He felt surprisingly good, the pain distanced to a faint murmur.

The anxiety in the small face wrenched Shay's heart. He smiled at Meilin, as big and reassuring a smile as he could dredge up.

Meilin broke into a radiant smile of his own, anxiety gone, and hurled himself across the room into Shay's arms.

The thud of small boy into wounds ignited them momentarily, but Shay enfolded the boy in his arms and didn't let go.

Meilin's sobs drenched bandages and sheets, but some of the wetting had to be Shay's own tears. He clung to the boy, unsure if he offered comfort or took it.

"You're okay?" he whispered when he could push the words through a rough throat.

The blond head nodded against his chest.

"Are you sure? Let me see."

Meilin sat up. "Are *you* okay?"

Shay nodded, touching gentle fingers to Meilin's chest. "I'll heal fine. Did he cut you? Were you hurt?" *Because if you were, I'll dig up the sonofabitch and desecrate what's left of his corpse in every way I can think of.*

Meilin sat up and lifted his shirt. A long, dull red scrape across his chest had almost healed, and Shay saw once again–in memory–Tarver's elbow being knocked upward, the knife sliding sideways across Meilin's chest instead of slicing across his throat.

The intensity of his rage and his relief warred within him, resolved by more tears he couldn't control, although he managed to avoid sobbing. Not a very manly example for his son.

And then the flood did come. He clutched Meilin to him, letting everything loose.

Meilin, the son of his heart. He was Piper's age, but Shay suddenly knew that Meilin and Beryl would have been best friends, had they ever met.

When at last they wore themselves out, Meilin sat up, wiping his eyes with his hand and his nose with his shirttail.

"You didn't like Spinel," he said, staring into Shay's eyes, "but he saved my life."

"His actions led to the murder of my wife and children. That's something I can never forgive." Shay took a deep breath. *Tarver's knife hand jerked sharply, his elbow flew up, and the look on Spinel's face . . .*

"I liked him," said Meilin with a child's conviction. "Especially when Bibi made him stop drinking. He was always nice to me."

Shay swallowed hard, tentatively touching old memories. "He got along better with children than adults, I think. My children loved him, too. I'd forgotten."

Tarver's arm slicing, Spinel's lurch suddenly a solid step, the look in his eye, the deliberation . . .

Shay fought it. Spinel, selfless? And sober at the same time? He wasn't sure he'd ever seen Cinny's brother sober before this.

But his eyes . . . *Tarver's elbow knocked skyward, the sober intensity of Spinel's eyes.*

With an effort, he accepted. Spinel the drunk, Spinel the hero. He'd saved Meilin's life, and his eyes said he knew he would die of it.

Shay swallowed again, took a long, slow breath and released it. "Yes, Meilin, you're right. Spinel saved your life. He died a hero." The habit of hate gave way slowly, the words slower to emerge than they should have been.

Tears slid down Meilin's cheeks again. "They buried him with all the bad men."

The answer Shay had been needing. He closed his eyes. "That wasn't right," he said. The thought hurt, of Cinny's brother being treated like that, no matter how despised.

"I told them he wasn't a bad man! But they did it anyway. We have to move him, Shay! He's not one of them!"

Shay stroked Meilin's yellow curls. "It's too late to do that, son. It's not possible. But he didn't deserve that." Even though he *had* been one of them.

"You have to do something!"

Oh, the faith of children. Shay wished his own could match it. "I will, Meilin. I'll set a monument on the grave site, I promise, to tell all who see it that a hero is also buried there." Cinny would like that, too.

When Robayne retrieved Meilin, telling him Shay needed to rest, Bibi came with him. She settled into the chair as if she'd never moved.

"You look better," Shay observed. Now, this was the clean, rested, vibrant Bibi he knew.

"And you, as well. The mouse breath is a wonder, is it

382

not?" Her face bore its usual serenity, her body its normal coiled energy.

"*Is* it magic? The mouse breath?"

Bibi laughed, a real laugh this time. "I do not believe so. Magic does not inhabit living things, after all."

"But in medicine form it wasn't living anymore, right?" This was where the nature of magic became confusing to Shay.

Bibi shrugged. "That I cannot tell you. But I do not care, as long as it works.

"What will you do now, Shay? You are rid of your enemies. You have learned the mysteries of the battle-axe. You have made a place for yourself in the hearts of the Blue Mountain People. It is time to think what you want next for your life."

"I . . . haven't thought that far ahead. Everything's happened so fast."

Bibi left her chair for the edge of the bed. "I need to check your bandages." She began unwrapping linens, her fingers strong, cool, and calloused.

Shay closed his eyes under her soothing touch.

"You have things to think about, Shay." Her tone dropped a few notes, a more intimate voice than he'd ever heard her use, as she smoothed her fingers over his bare chest.

Her touch excited and frightened him. He stiffened slightly.

"Oh, come, Shay. A handsome man with the marks of a warrior should not fear to be with a woman. Especially one who appreciates him properly." Her fingers began to knead the tight muscles in his neck and shoulder.

He caught her wrist, trying not to show his panic. "Bibi, I can't. . . . it's too soon for me . . ." *Cinny will be watching*.

383

"Perhaps you haven't considered fully your duties as Bladen of the black diamond battle-axe. To whom will the axe come when you are gone? You will need a son of your blood . . ."

"I can't, Bibi. Not yet." He'd always known she was casual about her choice of men, but he hadn't expected it to include him.

She finished changing his bandages and moved back to her chair. "Do you remember the man whose shop you rented while he went to visit his daughter? He will not return and wishes to sell it. That is also a part of the future you must consider."

So much to think about, things he'd thought to put off until later–a "later" he hadn't expected to have. Shay sighed.

42. After

Old grief lay quiet most of the time now, a familiar ache rather than a searing sharpness. The emptiness inside him was filling slowly, as Shay allowed more people into it.

He stood behind the counter next to his nine-year-old son, below the black diamond battle-axe displayed high on the wall, near a spiked mace of the same material. Nearby sat the figurine of a tauz horse with skystone eyes and rainsilk mane, tail, and feathers. It glittered enticingly in the bright sunlight warming the new glass window.

Before Shay and Meilin lay an array of polished and faceted stones.

"Tell me the name of each stone," Shay said, "and its luster."

Meilin gazed at the stones in wonder and touched the first. "Agate, waxy."

Shay nodded. "That's right."

"Emrel, vitreous. That's an easy one." His fingers moved from stone to stone. "Ruby, vitreous. Cinnabar, adamantine. That was your wife's name."

"Yes, it was. Go on."

"Beryl, vitreous. Your son's stone."

"And the next?"

"Which one is Piper? I don't know that stone." Meilin frowned, studying the stones.

Shay chuckled. "My daughter is the only one with a normal name, like me."

Meilin moved his finger to tauz, malkait, sunstone, seastone, lazh, torquis, godtears, and turmali, naming each and its luster perfectly. He turned to Shay, eyes shining.

"Well done, my son!" Shay laughed, clapping Meilin gently on the shoulder.

The door to the shop opened and Bibi glided in. Shay's gaze met hers, then dropped immediately to the huge swell of her belly beneath her flowing robes.

"If you two can drag yourselves away for a few minutes," she said, "my chief cook is about to serve a new recipe." She smiled the radiant smile of a woman with child, her hand resting protectively on her belly. These days, she carried three knives–that Shay had found–secreted on her person. Her sword remained hidden behind the bar of The Amyth Cup.

"We're coming! Meilin, would you please return the stones to their places?"

He did, then skipped over to join Shay and Bibi. "Is it a girl or a boy?" he asked, eying Bibi's bulge. "What will you name it?"

She laughed. "We will not know for sure until the birth. If it is a girl, I will be leaving to join my Sheethe sisters, so that she may be raised Sheethe. I think I will name her Rinnah, after my mother. If it is a boy, he will belong to Shay. Either way, the child will bear the blood of mighty warriors–from both parents."

Meilin looked up at Shay. "If it's a boy, what will you name him?"

Shay traded a quick glance with Bibi. They had talked about this at some length.

"I think," he said slowly, "I'll name him Spinel."

The End

Martha Gilstrap's life is filled with stories: the ones she reads, the ones she writes, and the ones she lives. Her family's oral tradition claims descent from the legendary Leif Erickson, a tale of which she is inordinately proud, although her mother always wondered why she'd claim "that old pirate."

She's ridden motorcycles, earned a black belt in RyuTe® Karate, owned her own dojo, trained on the grounds of an Okinawan castle destroyed in WWII, and edited and published an international karate newsletter. She's taught Latin to grade-school children, worn a bite sleeve for a Rottweiler "attack," got thrown by a horse — twice — within five minutes, and spent New Year's Eve on the Puerta del Sol in Madrid.

She lives with a rescue dog driven 1000 miles to her in one day by lovely people to give the pup a home. Her biggest adventure, however, was bearing and raising a bright, beautiful daughter, now grown.

The other thing you need to know about me is that martial arts has been an important part of my life for many years, even though I no longer train actively. My instructor is Taika Seiyu Oyata, the founder of Ryu-Te Karate®, and his lessons are physical, mental, spiritual, and moral lessons. For years I was responsible for his international newsletter, and for several years I also had my own dojo. I earned a 5th-degree black belt and membership in the elite Oyata Shin Shu Ho Ryu organization within Ryu-Te®. The rank isn't that important–what I learned is what matters–but it shows a solid background for writing fight scenes in my stories.